YOUR BLOOD, MY BONES

YOUR BLOOD, MY BONES

KELLY ANDREW

SCHOLASTIC PRESS/NEW YORK

Library of Congress Cataloging-in-Publication Data available

ISBN 978-1-338-88507-1

10 9 8 7 6 5 4 3   24 25 26 27 28

Printed in Italy   183

First edition, April 2024

Book design by Maeve Norton

FOR ANYONE WHO HAS EVER LEFT A PART
OF THEMSELVES BEHIND.

PART ONE

THE HOMECOMING

I had liefer to die with honour than to
live with shame;
and if it were possible for me to die a
hundred times,
I had liefer to die so oft than yield me to thee.
Le Morte d'Arthur, Thomas Malory

1

WYATT

She meant to burn it down. The house, with its pitched gables and chipped paint, leaded windows glazed in yellow glass. The roof was leaved in curling gray shingles, the undersides fringed in moss, and there was something undeniably morose about it—the way it sagged, the way the wrought iron parapets of the widow's watch had gone red with rust.

She stood at the edge of the flagstone walk, hemmed in by a meadow of fat purple coneflowers, and gripped a red jerrican in her left hand. In her right, she clutched a thin paperboard matchbook. She thought about dousing the porch in gasoline. She thought about enjoying one last sit on the weathered swing.

And then she thought about setting it aflame.

About the way it would feel to watch her ghosts go up in smoke.

Memory was a fickle thing. She'd remembered her father's house as white. Instead, she'd been surprised to find the wraparound porch done in a splintering evergreen trim, the broad-paneled siding a dull infection-colored yellow. The last time she'd seen it, it had been through the rearview window of her mother's rusted Ford. Her backpack sat on the seat beside her, stuffed full of books. Her Maine coon cat, Slightly, was clutched in her arms and she'd been openly weeping. On the porch, her father grew smaller and smaller.

"*She'll find her way back*," he'd bellowed.

And she had.

Her father's death had come as a surprise. It wasn't that they'd been close—they hadn't. He sent her letters on Christmas, which she dutifully ignored. He sent her gifts on her birthday, which she passed off to her cousin. She didn't write back. She didn't return his calls. It still felt like a rug had been pulled out from underneath her the day she received the news of his passing.

"*He didn't want you to know he was ill,*" Joseph Campbell said, framed in the open door of her aunt's apartment, his coat wet from the April rain. The last time she'd seen her father's right-hand man, he'd been restraining his son James, his hands tacky with blood and his face contorted into rage. Now those same hands spun and spun a flat herringbone cap. He looked startlingly contrite. "*He wanted you to remember him the way he was.*"

"*Estranged?*" Wyatt's grip on the door had begun to hurt.

"*Robust,*" Joseph corrected, his mouth twitching into a frown. "*Strong. Dedicated. A proper steward of Willow Heath.*"

A steward. It was a funny word to describe Wyatt's father. She'd had plenty of words to define him, back when she still lived at the farm. A steward wasn't one of them. He'd been a botanist, locked in his greenhouse with his eclectic collection of plant life—a naturalist, his attic full of taxidermized quadrupeds and antler sheds, a curio cabinet he kept locked tight as a drum.

A ghost, too swallowed up in his passions to take notice of the child floundering in his care. His letters and his gifts had come too late. Postmarked with regrets she didn't care to receive. Sealed with apologies she didn't have the space to break open.

"As you know," Joseph told her, oblivious to the way her thoughts spun out like a top, *"your father was my oldest and dearest friend. He appointed me executor of his estate just after receiving his diagnosis. It was his dying wish that the Westlock family farm should go to you. The last living Westlock."*

Standing on the front walk, Wyatt could just see the mist rising off the meadows in curls of gray. Beyond that, the first shingled rooftop of a clapboard cottage poked its dormered head over the rise. If she closed her eyes, she could still picture the fields beyond—the half-dozen outbuildings baked into the creases of Willow Heath's sixty-five considerable acres. Once livestock shelters and poultry coops, the buildings had long since been remodeled into modest lodgings for her father's revolving door of summertime callers.

And now they were hers.

She wondered if they'd burn, too. Hot and bright, like kindling.

"They come for the summit," her mother told her, when she'd grown old enough to dig into her father's mysterious circle of guests. *"Try and stay out of their way, if you can help it. They'll be gone by summer's end."*

At seven years old, Wyatt had no idea what made up a summit. She only knew what it meant to her. It meant roomfuls of strangers who went quiet whenever she entered. It meant the stink of incense cling-ing to everything she owned. It meant lanterns in the field after dark, the Gregorian cadence of chanting in the dawn.

But more than anything, it meant Peter and James.

For nearly as long as Wyatt could remember, her summers at Willow Heath had included the two of them. Each autumn she was shipped off to boarding school, kicking and screaming in her plaid skirts and her Mary Janes. Each spring she returned and found James and Peter there waiting, bored out of their skulls and stalking cottontails behind the rusted silo. Where to Wyatt, Willow Heath was home, to James and Peter, it was a sort of bucolic prison—an eight-week sentence they were forced to carry out while their guardians convened in secret alongside Wyatt's father.

Gangling and barefoot and a little bit feral, Peter had been the sort of boy who always looked hungry. He'd had a stare like ice, a shock of white hair that stuck up every which way. Where Wyatt was an open book—eager to spill her innermost thoughts to whoever or whatever was willing to listen—Peter had been infuriatingly tight-lipped. As such, Wyatt had never quite managed to puzzle out who he belonged to. Their first few summers together, she'd peppered him with an endless barrage of questions—*Are you here with your dad? An uncle? Where do you go to school? Did you take the train? Which cottage are you staying in?*—until he became so fed up with her interrogation, he began avoiding her altogether. After that, she'd stopped asking. She let him remain a mystery, so long as he was her mystery to keep.

James Campbell, older than the two of them by a year, had been every bit Peter's opposite. Cunning, where Peter was guileless. Chatty, where Peter was withdrawn. Charming, where Peter was wild. He wore his dark hair cropped short, preferring to dress according to the stringent codes of his stuffy English boarding school, even when no one required it of him.

A budding renegade and a reckless thief, James arrived each summer with yet another expulsion under his belt, his suitcase stuffed full of stolen things—an old Polaroid camera, a silver butane lighter, an exported pack of cigars he'd pilfered from his headmaster's office. The three of them would tuck away their treasure in the barn's termite-eaten loft and cuff the legs of their pants, spending the rest of their day catching frogs in the reeded shallows of the millpond.

They hadn't been friends. Not in the usual sense of the word, and certainly not at the start. Wyatt had often thought that if the three of them had gone to the same school, they likely would have gone out of their way to avoid crossing paths. She'd have her circle, and they'd have theirs, and that would be that.

But at Willow Heath, all they'd had was one another.

That wasn't to say they'd gotten along. Far from it. Their days back then were filled with petty squabbles and ceaseless bickering, their elaborate war games often coming to very real blows. James—the schemer of the group—had kept the trio plenty busy, doling out daily expeditions with all the confidence of a prince. Eager to avoid the droves of adults, they'd stuff their pockets full of breakfast biscuits and hike out to the farthest reaches of the farm, spending their mornings climbing into trees to look for birds' nests, their afternoons collecting snakeskin sheds from the stony northern ridge. They'd dreamed together. They'd fought together. And eventually—reluctantly—they'd grown together.

The rattle caw of a crow dragged Wyatt back into the present and the task at hand. Match. Accelerant. Flame. Her childhood in smoke. She didn't want to think about Peter and James. Not standing in the shadow of her father's house with a drumful of gasoline and a vendetta. Not with the memory of her final night at the farm burned into her brain like a brand.

All these years later, and she could still picture it so clearly: Peter

7

on his knees, his eyes shining red and unrepentant in the eclipse-dark. James, spitting blood, the collar of his shirt clutched in his father's fist. She couldn't help but wonder what she'd find, if she were to hike out to the old wooden chapel where she'd seen them last. Would there be remnants of their final, brutal moments together? Or had it all been scrubbed away?

Once, the chilly chantry had been their hideaway. Their sanctuary and their home base. It sat out on the northernmost acreage, tucked away in a grove of dying pine. Its western face was bordered in a grave-yard of crumbling headstones, its steeple crusted blue with lichen, and they'd loved it because it was theirs—a sole pocket of solace in their fathers' busy, secret world. Oftentimes, when the days wore on and the heat became insufferable, they'd stow away in the shadowed ambula-tory and hold court. Wyatt would climb onto the empty altar and claim it as her throne, spending the endless afternoons doling out cru-sades to her dutiful knights.

And there they were again, persistent as hornets—Peter and James, the memory of them sharp as a sting. She hadn't spoken to either of them in five long years. Not since her father dragged her from the chapel, the echo of his disdain pinging off the trees: *This has gone quite far enough.*

As hard as she'd worked to forget that night, she still remembered the way James had bellowed after them, railing against his father's restraints. She remembered Peter's silence, the feel of his stare prick-ling the back of her neck. And beneath it—buried deeper still—she remembered the funny pulsing in her veins. The sliding and slipping of something dark and formidable in her belly.

Her mother had packed Wyatt's bags the very next morning. She'd been loaded into the car like luggage and shipped to her aunt's apartment in Salem. Neither Peter nor James had come to say goodbye.

For months, she'd waited. For a call. For a text. For an encoded letter.

But all she'd gotten was silence.

All Willow Heath had ever brought her was a bellyful of grief—a headful of questions without answers. The sooner she could burn this place to the ground, the better.

And yet, when she crossed over the threshold and into the house, it wasn't with a lit match. Instead, she was drawn toward the white doorframe where her mother had tracked her yearly growth in neat pencil notations. Peter's were knifed in like an afterthought, towering over her more and more as the summers trickled past. Every now and again, there was James, his Catholic name penned in a private-school longhand.

The feel in her chest was that of stitches ripped clean. There, beneath her bones, was a wound she thought she'd healed. Raw and weeping as the day she'd received it. She breathed in deep. It put a prickle in the back of her throat. When she blinked, her lashes came away wet.

She'd learned, in the past year, that no good could come of tears. And so, she didn't let them fall. Readjusting the canister, she continued on. This wasn't a walk down memory lane—it was a mission. A final crusade. She moved through the house room by room, kicking up dust as she went.

By the time she reached her old bedroom, there was a saltwater sting in her throat that wouldn't abate. She stood in the silence and breathed in the mothball camphor of her childhood room. Flooded with lace and taffeta and frumpy, faded florals, the entire space was a colorful, cluttered mess. The window seat was stuffed with animals, the bedspread hand-quilted from scraps of her baby clothes, and it would have looked exactly as she'd remembered it if it hadn't been good and thoroughly ransacked.

It took her a beat to understand what she was seeing. Someone had shattered the mirror on her vanity, and broken glass glimmered like diamonds on the rug. The dresser drawers sat askew, and her jewelry box had been upended, hinges split and wind-up ballerina contorted on her spring. Several bits of old costume jewelry sat strewn about the room in a wild scattering of beads.

She might have felt violated, had she left anything of value behind. But she hadn't. She'd scraped up every last piece of herself and gone. Whatever the intruder had been looking for, they were welcome to it. Stepping inside, she plucked the jewelry box off the floor and set it atop the pillaged dresser. The ballerina listed hopelessly to the left.

An eddy of wind swirled through the room, and Wyatt glanced up to find the window ajar, the old willow outside her bedroom dripping with yellow springtime catkins. The sight of it brought forth another unwanted memory—deep summer, an eleven-year-old James scaling the branches under cover of dark.

"My father's downstairs with the rest of them," he'd said, climbing into bed beside her. *"What do you think they're doing?"*

"Sacrificing a lamb, probably," Wyatt returned. *"Eating small children."*

They'd loved to wonder—to theorize about what their fathers did, cloaked and secretive and chanting in the meadows.

"I think it has to do with Peter," James said, rolling on his side to face

her. His eyes had been the color of deep midnight, starlit and secretive, and he always talked like he knew more than he was letting on.

"I heard them whispering about him yesterday."

"That's stupid," Wyatt said. *"Nobody is interested in Peter but us."*

The boy in question had appeared not long after, crawling in through the window as a pale dawn bled into the horizon. Wyatt lifted her quilt, half-asleep and shivering as a cool crest of nighttime air slipped beneath the covers.

"You would tell me, right?" she'd asked as they lay nose to nose in the dark. *"If someone was hurting you?"*

But Peter hadn't answered. He'd already drifted asleep.

When she pulled her bedroom door shut, the click of it reverberated through the empty house like a gunshot. Her stomach sat in a tight coil, her nerves knotting along her veins. She hadn't invited it—this unearthing of things she'd meant to leave buried. She hadn't come back to visit with her ghosts—she'd come to set them alight.

As she made her way back downstairs, she paused.

She'd heard it. She was sure of it. One moment the house had been silent as a tomb, and the next she'd heard her name, drifting up from the cellar. Across the hall, the door to the stairs sat open. She moved toward it with caution, gas canister in hand, her heart skipping every other beat.

"Hello," she called. "Is someone there?"

When no one answered, she went down. The cellar was long and low, the poured concrete spiderwebbed in cracks. A chill clung to the air, and the feel of it pebbled her skin.

The very first thing she noticed were the roots. It looked as though the white willow outside her bedroom had launched an assault of its own, wooded extremities wending through wide cracks in the foundation. Smaller feeders crept along the wall in a thinning network of veins. They looked as though they'd been pruned into shape the way an arborist trained ivy through a pergola. Only, instead of wooden lattice, the ropy tubers had been carefully braided through a pair of fat iron chains someone had bolted to the ceiling.

And there, suspended in the shackles, was the second thing she noticed:

Peter. Not a boy anymore, the way she remembered him, but grown.

He hung slack in the chains, his arms bracketed overhead, his lean frame pale as marble. The white mess of his hair curtained his brow, and he was bare save for a pair of trousers and a round pendant strung on a thick leather cord.

A sharp spate of horror twisted up and through her. Her vendetta momentarily forgotten, the canister slammed to the ground at her feet. Peter's chin drew up at the sound, and she was met with a stare the color of liquid silver. A stare she'd done everything she could to leave behind.

He didn't look afraid to be there, gaunt and starving and half-swallowed in roots. He didn't look relieved to see her. Instead, his dark brows tented. The corners of his bloodless mouth turned down in an imperious frown.

"You finally came home," he said, and he sounded impatient. "It's about time."

2

PEDYR

No one remembered Pedyr Criafol's name.

His anonymity was an accident. He'd spent so long saying so little—tucking his secrets into his cheek like sugar candies—that when he finally went looking for them, they were gone. By that time, there'd been no one alive who remembered who he'd been before he came to Willow Heath.

It was an unfortunate side effect of immortality.

It wasn't that Pedyr couldn't die. He was, as a whole, extremely good at dying. It was only that he couldn't seem to stay dead. It didn't matter how he went—if it was quick and painless or slow and excruciating. Each time it happened, he was struck down and buried deep, his body fed to the lifeless grove out back. The following dawn would find him cradled in the shallow roots of a towering pine. Not a little boy anymore, begging and pleading, but pink and keening as a newborn.

And no one knew why.

"Death-defying," said the Westlocks, when he'd first stumbled into their care. *"A medical marvel! An oddity! A paradigm!"* Men of science and thaumaturgy alike gathered in droves to poke at him with lancets and knives. They slathered his cells on strips of glass and studied him beneath a microscope. They dissected him like a frog.

They killed him in increasingly imaginative ways, until he learned to bear it all without so much as a whimper. He didn't carry much with him from life to life, but at least he always managed to remember how to die with decorum. It was inborn, he supposed—the way domesticated dogs still buried bones in winter, or the way crows remembered faces across generations.

He had, lying dormant within him, a primal instinct that made him extremely adept at suffering in silence.

And he'd suffered Wyatt Westlock for thirteen long summers.

He couldn't remember meeting her, only that she'd always been there this particular lifetime—loud and volatile and prone to fits that left him covering his ears, running for the hills fast enough to set the deer in flight.

He couldn't remember meeting James Campbell, either, only that he always accompanied his father to Willow Heath in the summer and he always, *always* brought pocketsful of candies. Toffees and Maltesers, paper bags stuffed with jelly babies and bars of half-melted chocolates. They'd sit out in the twilit meadow, a jar of fireflies winking gold between them, and eat until their teeth were furred and their stomachs hurt.

"Don't save any for Wyatt," James would say. *"She's been a brat all day."*

By then, Pedyr had lived so long that he'd already begun to forget the taste of death. Wyatt Westlock's father had come back from the city with a college degree and a pregnant wife and a contemporary outlook on ritual sacrifice. His very first decree as steward of Willow Heath was to call an end to the centuries-long practice.

"It's barbaric," Pedyr once heard him tell Wyatt's mother. He'd been

14

stuffed in the kitchen cupboards, watching them have their morning coffee. In his fist, the biscuit he'd pilfered from the pantry had begun to crumble. *"Irremissible, the way things have been done around here. I've spent my entire life watching these foolish old men harvest that boy year after year. And for what?"*

"Necessity makes monsters out of men," came the mother's careful reply. *"You know better than anyone what's waiting out there in the forest."*

"There must be a better way," said the father. *"He's just a child."*

"For now." A spoon clinked against the lip of a mug. *"But he'll grow, if you let him. I only wonder what a boy like that will grow into, after so many lifetimes of torment."*

Though the killings had stopped by then, the excruciating pain of the ceremony remained. One midnight a summer, Pedyr still drew every eye in Willow Heath. Watched by the Westlock patriarch's handpicked inner circle, he became Pedyr the deathless: a living icon and a modern miracle. He'd lie bleeding on his altar, his flesh closing up around a knife wound, and watch as grown men fell to their knees. He'd swallow lungfuls of incense, his belly full of fire, and promise himself that one day he'd seize his chance and wriggle free.

Because, like any captive, he had an escape plan.

And Wyatt Westlock was the key.

She looked different than he remembered. When she'd left, she'd been willowy and restless, her face kissed in freckles—crawling out of her skin, the way Pedyr crawled out of his. Now, framed by the root-riven concrete, she stood perfectly still. Her hazel eyes were wide and bright, her hair unbound in a loose strawberry spill, and she looked both intensely familiar and entirely new.

"Peter? Holy *shit.*"

And then, there she was in front of him—her touch like lit cinders on his throat. Clumsy fingers fumbled against his carotid, feeling for the thready pulse flickering beneath his skin.

"Peter," she said again, more forcefully this time than before. "Peter, can you hear me?"

She ducked into his line of sight and he was met with her piercing stare—a stare he'd spent thirteen turbulent years trying his level best not to commit to memory.

Because the thing of it was, Pedyr had never wanted Wyatt Westlock for a friend.

He wanted her dead.

"God." She was babbling now, panic sapping the color from her cheeks. "Are you okay? Don't answer that—of course you're not okay. That was a stupid question, forget I asked. Should I call the police? A-an ambulance?"

She fished her phone out of the pocket of her pants, her feet scuffing concrete as she fell to pacing. Back and forth, forth and back, rambling as she went.

"Come *on.* I have no service. Are you *kidding me?*" She drew to a stop and peered round the dark, her gaze cutting intermittently to his. "Where are the keys? There's got to be keys. They'd have to be close by, right?"

At this proximity he could see her pulse hammering in the triangle of her throat. Westlock blood, unspilled. His way out of this endless, deathless loop, at last. It was all he'd thought about for nearly eighteen long years.

"Shit." She speared her fingers through her hair. "James's dad told me the house has been empty since my dad went into hospice. Why would he say that? Did he not know you were here? He told me he did a final walk-through; didn't you call out for help?" She fell to a stop, going gimlet-eyed in the gloom. "Did he *put you down here?*"

He glowered down at her, grinding his molars hard enough to hurt. She was asking all the wrong questions, worrying about all the wrong things. They didn't have time for an inquisition. Not with the days trickling by like water, the house dying around them.

In life, her father had been Willow Heath's sole greenskeeper. A last stronghold against the wild forest, the farm's perennial gardens were all that kept the stygian dark of the wood at bay. Each day since her father's passing, the grounds had withered a little bit more. Left untended, the entirety of Willow Heath would soon be swallowed up in the hostile creep of weeds. The wards would fall, and an endless night would descend, bringing with it an army of creatures from the deep.

Pedyr didn't want to be here when that happened, chained like a hound in the cellar. Not when he'd finally found a way out. To survive, he needed a Westlock warden to tend the gardens. To escape, he needed a Westlock heart to feed to the starveling dark. Here she was in front of him, both the prodigal daughter and the sacrificial lamb, and he wasn't about to do or say anything that might make her run.

Not this time.

"I don't understand how you're even alive," she said, still pacing. The smell of gasoline was making him dizzy and she was babbling a mile a minute, with no concern at all for the way the sound of her voice made him want to succumb to a seething fit. "Strung up like this, I mean. What the hell was happening here?"

"Please." His throat was raw from lack of use. "Don't shout."

His head was a click-wheel spin of unasked-for memories—the crunch of gravel as she pulled out of the driveway for the very last time. The barn in flames, the dirt under his nails. The seven guildsmen strung up in white, their arms spread in thin dark crucifixes. The ceaseless susurrus of the forest, wending along his bones. Stitching itself into the space between his ears.

Coward. You let her slip through your fingers, and now we both starve.

"I can't find a key anywhere," Wyatt said, desperation crawling into her voice. "There has to be one somewhere, right?"

The irony bled through him, bitter and metallic. She was the only key in the room. "The bindings are organic," he ground out. "You'll have to let me out yourself."

Her gaze snapped to his. "And how am I supposed to do that?"

"Blood tilling. Hematic farming?" Frustration rose into his stomach when her expression stayed blank. "It's only the core tenet of the Westlock legacy, *your* legacy—what have you been doing these past five years?"

"Going to *public school*," she shot back, though he didn't miss the downward twitch in her scowl, the way her fingers snarled together. Five years away, and her tells hadn't changed. She wasn't being entirely truthful. "I've been writing papers on Jane Austen and learning about isosceles triangles. Like a normal person."

"But you're not a normal person." The words scraped out of him in a rasp. "Your father was the most sought-after environmental alchemist in New England."

Another twitch. Her fingers were so tightly intertwined that her

18

knuckles had gone white. "Maybe you've forgotten, but my dad barely gave me the time of day when I was here. We weren't exactly spending quality father-daughter time together."

"But you paid attention," he reasoned, his throat screaming for water. "You suspected. You were always convinced there was something strange going on around the farm."

"Yeah. I thought my dad was a hobby homesteader who was super into live-action role-play." Her gaze flicked to the tangled web of roots looped through his chains. "Clearly, I was wrong. Unless this is all part of some extremely involved campaign."

He tried again, his wrists aching. "Your mother is a witch."

"Wiccan," she corrected, still eyeballing the roots. "And yes, she's very passionate about astrology. I'm not sure how your rising moon sign is going to get you out of there. Look, I really think we should call someone. The fire department, maybe? They have saws."

"Don't bother," he said tiredly. "I wasn't left here for them."

"But you *were* left here for someone? Who?"

You, he thought, but didn't say. He had far too much pride to admit it aloud. "This isn't difficult magic," he said instead. "I can walk you through it. The locking mechanism requires Westlock blood to disengage it."

Wyatt blinked. "You want me to bleed on you."

"Not me. On the roots."

The ensuing silence was as profound as if they'd both stepped underwater. "Sorry to disappoint," Wyatt said, after a beat, "but I'm not your girl."

Except she was. There was no one else but her. His childhood confidant. His reluctant warden. His final sacrifice. Though she didn't

19

yet know it, Wyatt Westlock was the only thing standing between him and the mouth of hell.

If she wouldn't help him, they were both as good as dead.

As if she'd read his mind, she doubled down. "I don't know what you think I'm doing here, but I didn't come back to take up where my dad left off. I came to raze this place to the ground."

Burn it—the way he'd set fire to the barn the day she'd left. He still remembered the kiss of lit cinders on his skin. The gray columns of smoke darkening the sky. A pyre, missing its witch.

His witch stood in front of him now, Westlock blood beating in her veins, and no idea how to harness it. He could teach her. He could show her how to mix the compounds, how to bleed, how to nurture the wards along the forest's edge. He could bide his time, the way he'd done when they were children—biting his tongue, doing as she bid, waiting for his chance to strike.

And then.

And *then*.

"You really don't know," he hedged. "No one ever told you what went on here?"

Wariness shuttered her gaze. "This might surprise you to hear, but I didn't give a single thought to this place after I left."

He thought of the way she'd looked through the cellar windows that final morning—openly weeping, the sky spitting rain as her mother loaded the luggage into the car. Nearby, Wyatt's father stood stoic and silent beneath the tearful hailstorm of his daughter's demands: *Where did you take Peter? What will you do with him? No, I won't. I won't go without saying goodbye.*

"In Romania," he said, louder than he'd meant to, "people used to sew blackthorn into their clothing to ward off vampires." He felt like he was speaking around a mouthful of shattered glass. He didn't want to think about her leaving. About James racing down the graveled walk after her, his pajamas halfway on and his left eye swollen shut. He didn't want to remember the last day he'd ever seen them. "Branches of buckthorn were set in doorways to keep the dead from entering. Holly was hung in windows to ward off evil."

"O-*kay*." That walled-off look hadn't left Wyatt's eyes. "And you're telling me this, why?"

"Because nature has always been used as a ward against the dark. This high up in the mountains, the air is thin enough to slip through in places. It forms a door, of sorts. A gap between this world and the next." He shifted as best he could, chains chattering like teeth. Silver spills of dust fell into the light between them. "Didn't you ever wonder why your father used to forbid us from going out to the old chapel by the woods? Why it always felt cold in the grove, even in the thick of summer? Your father's family has spent centuries cultivating the grounds of Willow Heath. Without an acting steward, there's nothing to prevent unwanted things from crossing over."

Another twist of her fingers. Her knuckles popped. "What kinds of things?"

A beast, he thought. *And a boy stupid enough to bargain with it.*

Aloud, he said, "Monsters."

"Monsters," she echoed, and he could tell she didn't believe him.

Outside the house, the wind picked up. It rattled the branches of the willow, dragged yellow catkins across the roof. Beneath the earthen rustle, he heard the beast's insidious whisper, and he was no

21

longer sure—after five long years of listening—if it came from inside his head or out of it.

Here she is, it said. *Home with us at last.*

The leather cord around his throat felt like a noose, slowly tightening.

"If nothing is done," he said, "Willow Heath will wither and die. When it does, the dark between worlds will devour us both."

3

WYATT

There was no cell service at the house. The only phone was a corded monstrosity by the refrigerator, yellow and ancient and knocked partway off its wall jack. When Wyatt lifted it to her ear, she was met only with the dull tone of disconnect. She stood at the butcher-block island, sunlight streaming through the shutters, and held her cell in the air like she was at a stadium concert. She waved it through the dusky light of the parlor. She tromped through the meadow out front, her arm growing sore, the grass tickling her shins. Nothing. Nothing. Nothing.

She'd meant to call her mother. To ask her what she should do.

Theodora Beckett had never liked Peter. For as long as Wyatt could remember, her mother had been guarded around him—wary in a way she wasn't with James. A practiced menace, James would steal from the coop, rile up the chickens, and smile while he did it, and Wyatt's mother still snuck him extra slices of frozen watermelon whenever he passed through the kitchen. Peter, on the other hand, was quiet and polite. He didn't make ripples. He didn't go looking for trouble.

But when he came inside, Wyatt's mother chased him out.

Wyatt wondered what her mom would say if she knew Peter had been chained in the cellar all this time—shackled like a dog and left

23

for dead. She wondered, too, what sort of advice her mom would give her if she knew Peter had asked Wyatt to bleed for him.

It wasn't an entirely odd request. Once, when Wyatt had still been small and prone to tantrums, she'd wept for so long and so loudly that when she finally quieted, little white hedgehog mushrooms had sprouted in the grass around her feet. When her mother saw, she pulled the mushrooms up one by flattened one. She threw them in the compost and forbade Wyatt from mentioning the incident to her father.

"But I did that," Wyatt insisted, pawing at her tears. *"I grew them with my teardrops."*

"What a silly thing to say." Her mother's eyes darted nervously around the garden. *"You have quite the imagination, turtle. It's been a wet summer, that's all it is."*

But it wasn't. Phenol-sweet and slightly fevered, Wyatt had always been able to feel it inside her—a strangeness, hard and swollen as a blister. Sometimes, late at night, she'd lie awake and wonder if whatever nameless thing pulsed through her veins would one day split her open and leak out all on its own.

"Power like that isn't something you trip and fall into, dove," her mother would tell her as she brushed and braided her hair before bed. *"You have to nurture it, like any other beating thing."*

For a time, Wyatt thought maybe that was true—thought if she ignored the searing ache in her blood, eventually it would go away.

It didn't, of course. It did what blisters did.

It popped. It happened on a January night, on the beer-slick floor of a dirty room, in a house full of thumping music. Water pooled beneath her bloodred hands as, directly over her, a broad, angry frame swam in and out of focus.

"Wyatt, you bitch. What the hell did you do to me?"

Shaking herself free of the uninvited memory, Wyatt marched down the long dirt walk, gripping her phone just a touch too tight. The single half bar on the screen stared dimly up at her. She wouldn't be making any calls from Willow Heath. Not to her mother, and not to anyone.

The realization made her feel itchy. Trapped. She didn't like being back here, or the way it made her feel. She didn't like the way Peter had looked at her, down in the cellar—the slate gray of his stare as cold and unreadable as it had been that final night in the chapel.

She was met with the sudden urge to run—far and fast, without looking back. It was three hours to her aunt's cramped apartment in Salem, where she'd lived with her mother ever since leaving Willow Heath. If she left now, she'd be home well before dark. She could call the police from the road. Let *them* drive out to the farm and deal with Peter. Let them figure out what to do with him.

She'd never have to think of Willow Heath again.

On a whim, she glanced back at her father's house. In her hurry to find service, she'd left the front door open. Shadows spilled like ink from the empty foyer. She thought of Peter strung up alone in the crumbling cellar, his cheeks gaunt and his ribs poking through.

She couldn't do it. It didn't matter what had happened between them, or how deeply she'd resented him these past five years. Those were childish grudges, and this—whatever *this* was—was real. She couldn't leave him there alone.

She'd drive up the road a little ways—just far enough to find service—and call her mother for help. She'd left for Maine without telling anyone her plans, though she had no doubt her mom suspected where she'd gone. Theodora Beckett always had an uncanny way of knowing exactly what sort of trouble Wyatt had gotten herself into.

Still, Wyatt wasn't certain how she'd manage to explain her current predicament.

Peter in chains. Monsters in the woods. It sounded insane.

Wyatt didn't doubt that monsters were real. She knew they were. She knew, too, that they didn't lurk in forests, the way Peter seemed to think. They didn't have fangs and fur, sharp teeth and crooked talons. They looked like a girl with summertime freckles and strawberry hair. Beer-slick hands and a tear-tracked face.

Peter had no idea what he was asking Wyatt to do. If she tapped into the thing that pulsed inside her veins, she wouldn't be muzzling a monster.

She'd be unleashing one.

Heart lodged in her throat, she picked her way past the millpond matted in flat green lily pads and headed toward her truck—a red monstrosity she'd borrowed from her cousin for the drive north. The wide bed, once black, had long since rusted to a flaking orange. The handle on the passenger side was almost completely ripped away.

"*She drives,*" Mackenzie had assured her, handing over the keys. "*Just as long as you don't go over thirty miles an hour. Or try to use the air-conditioning. Or play the radio too loud. Definitely don't play the radio too loud. Bertha startles very easily.*"

The instant she pried open the door, Slightly let out a vicious hiss from her cat carrier.

"I'm sorry," she said, climbing inside. "I know I promised you mice, but we can't stay."

She'd read online that old cats tended to slink away and find somewhere solitary to die. Slightly was older than old. She'd spent the first half of her life gleefully stalking the grounds of Willow Heath, hunting mice and basking in the sun.

In Salem, Slightly spent her days holed up in Aunt Violet's too-small apartment, watching the world through a too-small window. The last time Wyatt had taken her to the vet, the tech told her that the geriatric cat was quickly nearing the end of her life.

Wyatt had brought her home to set her free.

"Peter's here," she told the cat, and was met with another disconsolate mew. "He needs our help."

She punctuated her words with the turn of the key in the ignition. The engine let out a single heroic chuff and immediately died. She tried again, to the same effect.

"Shit," she said. Then again, because she felt the situation merited it, *"Shit."*

Five months ago, she would have met this moment with tears. She would have sat with her forehead against the steering wheel and cried until there was nothing left inside her but air. But that Wyatt was buried. This Wyatt knew better. She'd seen what happened when she wept without end. Swallowing a measured breath, she forced herself to feel only a ready apathy. A calculated numb.

She climbed out of the truck and headed to the front, popping open the hood. Beneath, the engine bed was gray with soot and packed with pine, as though something had been living in it. *Don't get mad,* went the mantra in her head. *Don't get mad.* She took another breath. She set the hood gingerly back into place and gave the bumper a single, half-hearted kick. The unlit headlights stared dolefully back at her.

"Okay." Her voice came out gritted with a false optimism. "Looks like we're walking."

She withdrew Slightly's carrier and set off through the field, heading for the gate along the property line. The morning was warm and bright, but there was a lingering bite in the mountain air that hurried her along. At least, if she was quick about it, she might find service a few miles down the road. The instant she had a viable bar, she'd call her mother.

She made it within a hundred yards of the road before her plans were once again waylaid. She heard it first—the crack of a twig. The scrape of a hoof. It was followed by the angry *maa* of a barnyard animal. She didn't manage to get out of the way before a hard head pummeled her directly in the rear. She stumbled forward, barely managing to hold tight to Slightly's carrier as she caught her footing. Jostled, the cat let out a furious yowl.

"Hey!" Wyatt whipped around to come face-to-face with a piebald pygmy goat, its horns shorn to stubs. Already, the creature was readying itself for another assault, side-slanted pupils eyeing her in contempt. She darted out of the way, narrowly avoiding being taken out at the knees.

"Are you *serious?*"

The answering bleat told her the goat was every bit serious.

"Okay, *okay.*" Wyatt sidestepped a second time as it reared up onto its hind legs. "I'm leaving. I'm gone. The meadow is yours."

But when she stepped forward, the goat ran at her again. Head down. Hooves kicking up dirt. It took her several more breathless evasions to realize that it wasn't the meadow the goat was driving her away from. It was the property line.

And when she looked up, she saw why.

Seven hooded men had gathered behind the rusted bull gate, each one of them clad in robes of black. They didn't speak. They didn't advance. They only waited, staring, with preternatural stillness. Mercifully, the goat stopped moving the instant Wyatt did. It hovered at her side like a wiry bicorn sentinel.

"Hello," Wyatt called.

The voice that drifted back to her was strange, the accent implacable. "Wyatt Westlock III, I presume? We heard a rumor the deed to the house had changed hands."

"That's right." She held tight to Slightly's carrier. "Who are you?"

Beneath the hood of the man closest to the gate, a shadowed smile formed. "We were friends of your father."

Wariness crept into her skin. "I don't recognize you."

"With all due respect, you have been away for some time." The stranger inclined his head, scrutinizing her from beneath the shadow of his cloak. "It's safe to say you don't know very much about your father and the company he kept."

At Wyatt's side, the goat let out a throaty bleat. The trees rustled overhead, wind bowing the branches. Peter's warning came to her, unbidden: *Without an acting steward, there's nothing to prevent unwanted things from crossing over.*

Feeling ridiculous, she cupped a hand to her mouth and called, "If my dad liked you so much, then why aren't you over here instead of bellowing at me from the other side of the gate? It's not locked."

29

She braced herself for movement—half expecting the man to call her bluff and tug the metal gate wide. Instead, his smile changed, its edges sharpening into something distinctly unfriendly. Glancing down at his feet, he surveyed the fragrant tangles of buttonbush twined along the loose-wire fencing.

"You think yourself clever," he said, "but there is a very thin line between courage and foolishness. We've come here today as a kindness to you."

They hadn't moved. Not an inch.

Monsters, she thought, and felt immediately ridiculous.

"There is a young man being held in the basement," continued the stranger. "His presence in your father's home presents an immediate threat to you."

Something in his voice raised the hair along the back of her neck. "What kind of a threat?"

Her question was met with quiet. Off in the woods, several crows took flight, dragging their shadows over the meadow in broad swaths of dark.

"The boy is highly volatile," the man called over to her. "We wouldn't want you to get hurt. We can tell you what it is you need to do, to guarantee your safety."

Something about the way the strangers clustered together, their eyes hidden, left her cold. There was an undercurrent of malice in their posture—a malevolence she couldn't quite name—and she wished they'd go away. They were blocking the road. If she couldn't get off the property, she couldn't call her mother. And if she couldn't call her mother, there would be no answers, and there would be no help. Peter would remain trapped at Willow Heath. And so would she.

There was no way in hell she was setting foot in the woods with these men lurking.

"I don't know if I should take your advice," she said, when they continued to stare without speaking. "I don't think my goat likes you very much."

As if in agreement, the creature at her side unleashed an angry bleat.

The man let out a laugh that was thin and cold. "Go ahead and brush us off. The wards on this land grow weaker by the day, and you are no seasoned witch. You cannot hold the line all on your own. The boy is marked by the beast, and the beast will come to collect what he is owed."

The menacing way he said it—the *beast*—sent a shiver down her spine. She dug in her heels and opted not to answer, holding on to the cat carrier like a shield. One by one, the men at the gate began to disperse, fading like shadows beneath the thick canopy of trees. Only the first man remained, his smile a bone-chilling gash upon the lower half of his face.

"Consider this a mercy," he said. "The boy will do whatever it takes to survive. If you're as clever as you seem to think, you will offer him up to the beast yourself. Quickly, before the blood moon rises."

When he'd gone, Wyatt turned her back to the gate, doing what she could to ignore the riddle of his parting words. Nonsense words, from a nonsense person. Who in their right mind wore a riding cape to trek through the woods in northern Maine? Someone unhinged, that was who.

Not a monster at all, but a man.

Even so, it didn't seem like the best idea to wander alone in the woods knowing they might be waiting. She'd let a few hours pass—give them time to clear out—and then she'd try again.

Smothering the lit kindling of her irritation, she trekked back up the walk—past the useless truck and the lily pad pond and the covey of grouse in the meadow—and right back into the house. For several seconds, she stood on the threshold and considered slamming the front door hard enough to rattle its glass. As she mulled it over, the door drifted slowly closed on its own, hinges squealing, and the decision was made for her.

In the kitchen, she set the cat carrier on the island and opened the door. Slightly tumbled out in a mat of fur, streaking out of sight without a backward glance. She watched her go, mulling over her next steps. She knew she ought to go back downstairs and talk to Peter—that to avoid him was only delaying the inevitable—but she didn't think she could bring herself to look him in the eye. Every time she did, she was slammed with unwanted memories—the rosy hush of the grove and the feel of Peter's heart hammering into the palm of her hand. James's blood-soaked grimace gone silver beneath the sweep of a flashlight, the slice of his voice through darkness: *"Get out of here, Wyatt. Don't let them see you."*

She'd spent five long years hating Peter for his radio silence. Resenting him for abandoning her when she'd needed him most. Cursing him for carrying on with his life and forgetting about her. And all this time, his lack of contact hadn't been by choice.

It didn't make sense. Polar opposites in nearly every way, Peter and James had always fought. Their petty disagreements had a tendency to escalate into violence in the blink of an eye. They moved on just as quickly, making their peace over frozen bags of peas and matching shiners.

That final night at Willow Heath had been no different.

And yet, even as she thought it, she knew it was wrong.

That night had changed everything.

She wondered how long it had been since Peter had eaten. How long could a person survive like that, strung in the dark without any food or water? Uneasy at the thought, she ducked into the pantry in search of something edible. The shelves were largely bare, and she was forced to scrimp together what little was leftover. She was halfway through filling a basket with stale oat bars when the phone began to ring.

It let out a single jangling shiver, the handset rattling in its hook. She set the basket on the counter and frowned up at the yellow wall mount, half-convinced she'd imagined it. Another ring sounded, its echo rattling all through the house. Snapping out of her stupor, she scrambled across the kitchen and lifted the receiver tentatively to her ear.

"Hello?"

Feedback fizzled along the wire and—for the second time that day—Wyatt Westlock found herself talking to a ghost.

"Wyatt?"

James Campbell's voice had hardened over the last five years. The unsteady crack of boyhood was gone, and in its place was a clean Lancaster elocution that left her more than a little bit startled. It was achingly familiar. It was entirely strange. "Shit," he said. "You weren't supposed to answer."

Wyatt frowned down at the receiver. "Don't sound so excited to hear from me."

"I've just got off the phone with my father," he said, sounding harried. "He told me he sent you to Willow Heath, but I was hoping you might have ignored him. Wyatt, I heard about your dad. I'm so sorry. I should have been there for the funeral."

"It's okay." The words came out muffled. She imagined herself hollow as a tree, her insides scraped away. *Don't cry, don't cry.* It was ridiculous to even feel like she could. She hadn't spoken a word to her father in nearly a year.

"Well, look," James said, "I'm going to make up for it, yeah? I'm headed to Heathrow as we speak. I've got a flight booked to JFK." The connection sputtered, sizzling, and his voice was momentarily swallowed up in static.

"Hello-o?" Wyatt pulled the phone from her ear, listening to the indecipherable crackle of James's voice through the speaker. "James? Are you still there?"

"Yes," he said. "I'm here. Wyatt, listen to me. This is important. Peter is still at Willow Heath."

"Oh." Wyatt spun the coil between her fingers, unease splintering through her. "Yeah, I know. He's here in the house."

A curse followed, its edges fuzzed. The sad yellow phone managed to eke out a single broken "Get—" before the connection flagged and died.

"Hello?" Wyatt let the coil spring out of her grasp. "Jamie?"

Static, again. For a second, Wyatt thought maybe the call had dropped. But then there was James, his voice spilling through the receiver as clear as day. "You need to get out of there, Wyatt. Now. Today. Or he'll kill you."

It felt like the echo of a game they used to play, noses burnt and

34

fingers pruning, knee-deep in the millpond. James, the daring rogue, his broadsword whittled from the arm of a sapling oak. Wyatt, the captured queen, moored upon the rocky outcrop of a stone.

And Peter, the shark. Circling her in the shallows.

But that was then. A freeze-frame memory. They weren't children anymore—they were too old for games. And there was nothing in James's tone to suggest he might be playing one. The hooded stranger's voice looped through her head: *"The boy will do whatever it takes to survive."*

She glanced toward the far side of the kitchen, where the open cellar door was just barely visible in the outer hall. Where Peter hung in the shadows, the familiar lines of him carved away, until he'd become something starving and strange. She stared and she stared and she coaxed herself not to feel anything at all.

Don't cry. Don't cry.

Bringing the speaker close to her lips, she whispered, "How do you know?"

"Because," James said, "he's tried before."

4

PEDYR

Inside Pedyr Criafol, there was a knot, impossibly tangled. Day after day, he worked the stitches loose. Sometimes his threads came undone in colors. Sometimes he remembered pictures—a house on a hill, a tree engorged with rot, a lifeless body, an ax protruding from its chest. He unraveled spools of string from past lives and forgotten selves, tangling himself in the unremitting snare of memory, until he could no longer tell what was real and what was in his head.

He knew this: He was five years old the first time he saw the beast. It was the earliest memory he had from this lifetime. He remembered the color gray, an April rain that fell for days on end. He'd been tracking a salamander along the bank of a vernal pool, his socks soaked through and his knees dark with mud. He hadn't realized he'd wandered too far from the house until the light changed. At first, he'd thought maybe night had fallen, but then he'd looked up to find the wood looming heavily before him.

The forest of Willow Heath had always seemed ominous, but that particular day, the shadows between the trees leered down at him with a palpable menace. It took him several blinks to realize that it wasn't a shadow he was seeing at all, but a creature. Taller than a man. Narrower than a root. Fingers long and double-jointed. Pedyr's first instinct was to run. Far and fast—back toward the farm, and the yellowy warmth of the Westlock kitchen.

But then the creature spoke.

"Pedyr Criafol," it whispered, and suddenly Pedyr remembered that that was his name. That he *had* a name, the little lost boy of Willow Heath. Pale and quiet as a ghost. Underfoot in a house stuffed full of strangers, never quite sure which of them he belonged to. If he belonged to anyone at all, or if he'd just appeared one day, small and angry and rooting through the kitchen cabinets.

Moreover, he remembered dying. Over and over, one brittle gasp after another. Standing there in the shadow of the forest, dwarfed by the storming sky and that terrible, towering beast, he felt the first icy fingers of fear grip his little throat.

"How do you know who I am?" he'd asked, and the quaver of his voice was snuffed out at once beneath the patter of rain against the leaves.

Framed by the trees, the beast inclined its head. *"You and I came here through the sky together. Do you remember?"*

He'd shaken his head. He couldn't remember anything but Willow Heath.

"Too many years have passed us by," said the beast. *"It is time for me to return home. You as well. Your mother is waiting."*

And then—just then—Pedyr remembered that he'd had a mother. He remembered quiet—the *click, hum* of a loom, the distant burble of a stream. The feeling of being rocked to sleep. A mother, the way Wyatt had a mother. Someone to clean up his scrapes and kiss his head and sing him songs. In that moment, and with the trees standing over him like sentinels, she seemed very, very far from here.

37

Mantled in dark, the beast watched him sideways, its elongated skull clicking on a swivel.

"Would you like that? To see your mother? To go back home? You must be terribly tired of dying. I can tell you what you need to do to live. It's very easy."

He woke to the sound of a phone ringing.

Just a dream, he told himself. Remnants of a different Pedyr, from an earlier life, tailing him into the waking world. There was only one phone in the house, and it hadn't worked in years.

Now Pedyr strained against his chains, desperate to hear hints of Wyatt moving upstairs. That last fateful night before she left for good, he'd planned to go through with it—to drive a blade through her belly and let her bleed, the way her family had done to him for years. To carry her out into the grove and let the beast lap up her final heartbeats. A last bloody offering in exchange for his freedom.

But when the time had come to make his move, he'd faltered.

Somewhere overhead, a kettle screamed. A pair of shoes hit the hardwood in twin clumps. The farmhouse groaned beneath Wyatt's movements, old bones resettling on their haunches. She'd gone upstairs hours ago—likely to call her mother—and she hadn't come back since. Not to set him loose. Not to question him. Not to stare.

The minutes slipped past, the afternoon fading from gold to red to violet, moonlight spilling in through the windows in thin silver frets. Eventually—impossibly—Pedyr slept, his arms strained to breaking and his head full of dreams.

She was there when he woke again. He felt her presence like a bruise, as though she'd been beaten into his bones.

38

"Peter," she said, not for the first time. "Wake *up*."

He took his time about it, one eye squeezed tight, lifting his head from where it had lolled against his chest. Directly beneath him stood Wyatt, swallowed up in a white, mothy sweater and clutching a leather-bound journal like a shield. The pages fanned open, revealing margins stuffed with flattened sprigs of clover. There was something guarded in the muted hazel of her eyes—something cautious in the way she hovered on her toes, like a doe on the cusp of flight.

He knew instantly: Something had changed.

When she'd first discovered him strung up in the dark, she'd been frantic, desperate for a way to cut him loose. Now she studied him sideways, as though he were a wolf she'd encountered in the woods. As though one wrong move might make him lunge.

"I couldn't get in touch with my mom," she said, in a voice flat enough to be dead. When he only looked on in silence, she sighed. "I've been going through my dad's things for the past several hours. Looking for answers."

"Did you find any?"

"I don't know," she said. "You tell me."

She flipped to a new page, still peering warily up at him. Dried lobelia fell to their feet in powder-blue crumbles. *"'This winter is the coldest on record,'"* she read, and in her voice, he heard her father's words. *"'The icicles hang like fangs, nearly touching the snowdrifts. At night, the temperature drops well below freezing. Twice now, the boy has asked if he might come inside. It is Theodora, this time, who turned him away. She doesn't trust him. She doesn't want him close to Wyatt. And yet, I know it eats at her. On Christmas Eve, I caught her filling a fourth stocking with some of my childhood things she'd uncovered in the attic.'"*

39

Her voice caught, her eyes flitting across the remainder of the passage. He didn't need her to read it to him; he remembered that winter perfectly well. He'd woken in the tiny dormered rectory where he slept, his muscles stiff after another night shivering in his cot. He'd stumbled out into the chapel to find ferns of ice on the windows, a single stocking atop his altar. It was a silent sort of sacrament—a grudging offering of little green army men and plastic yo-yos, sweets wrapped in foil.

Every year after that, the tradition continued—he'd wake each Christmas to a stocking overflowing with knickknacks, a guilty conscience stuffed inside a knitted sock. He'd spend the remainder of his lonely morning standing at the frozen bank of the millpond, his feet stuffed into boots two sizes too big. He'd let his gifts sink one by one beneath the ice. He hadn't wanted baseball cards and Hot Wheels and knotted yellow yo-yos.

He'd wanted a mother he remembered. A home that was warm.

"*'Theodora's sister phones day and night,'*" continued Wyatt, and the crinkle of a turning page chafed through him. "*'She claims she has witnessed the worst in dreams—that something in the forest is speaking to the boy. That soon it will leave its home in the shadows and come for us all. Joseph Campbell and the others have called for a return to the old ways. They say only a total offering will appease the eldritch dark, but I'm not so sure. One thing is resolutely clear: The boy will continue to grow, if I let him. One day, his confusion will harden into anger, and he will seek retribution for what has been done to him. It is in my power to end it—to muzzle the mouth of hell and subdue the boy in one bloody stroke. But what will become of me, if I take the life of a child? If I start the cycle anew?'*"

"Stop," said Pedyr, and she did. She closed the journal as though it might shatter beneath her thumb, its edges cutting her to the quick. She didn't look up at him as she traced the branded pelican along its leather cover.

"It's funny," she said, in a voice so small he was forced to strain his ears to hear her. "I always sort of thought that Billy Deacon was your father. Isn't that ridiculous?"

Her eyes lifted to his, and he found that some of her wariness had melted away. In its place was something soft and imploring. He knew what it was she wanted—an explanation for the pages and pages of similar entries she'd likely thumbed through upstairs. She wanted answers. She wanted confessions. She wanted to unspool his secrets skein by skein, pick them apart until he was good and thoroughly frayed.

He wouldn't give her an inch.

"He had those blue eyes, just like yours." Her voice wobbled through the cellar's muddled hush. "He showed up every year for the summit, and we'd spend the summer avoiding him like the plague. Whenever he caught you by the house, he'd box your ears so hard, they'd be pink the rest of the day." Her thumbnail dug into the embossed stigmata etched into the pelican's feathered chest. "I used to think it must be terrible, having a father like that. That maybe it wasn't so awful to be ignored."

He hadn't realized he'd been biting the inside of his cheek until he tasted blood. He swallowed it down, his ears ringing.

"I never questioned it," Wyatt added, when he only stared. "I never questioned anything."

"My father is dead." The admission came out in a rasp.

41

"And your mother?"

Her question was expected—a natural follow-up—and yet he recoiled from it all the same. He wouldn't talk to Wyatt Westlock about his mother. He wouldn't admit to her that he could only conjure her in shades and in silhouettes, like the hum of a half-forgotten lullaby.

He wouldn't tell her he couldn't even remember her name.

"You don't want to talk about it." She studied him through the slanted sweeps of moonlight, reading him far too easily. "I get it. You don't have to. Let's talk about James instead. He and I had an extremely interesting conversation today."

Pedyr's blood turned to ice in his veins. He *knew it*—it was the phone's ceaseless jangle that woke him the first time. The phone that didn't work. The line that didn't connect. All thoughts of the journal and his mother and Billy Deacon's swinging fist slipped away, his world tipping on its axis. Oblivious to the way he suddenly struggled to breathe, Wyatt drew nearer.

"He had a lot to say."

"Sound like James," Pedyr admitted, though it came out strained.

Her gaze dropped to the pendant around his neck and lingered there. "Don't you want to know what he told me?"

"No."

He wanted to writhe away from her stare, to fold his fingers around the little blue button pendant and tuck it out of sight. He wanted to never hear the name James Campbell again.

"I didn't believe him at first," Wyatt went on. "James has always been an excellent liar. I thought maybe this was all part of one of his elaborate pranks. But then I remembered my dad used to keep these journals. That's why I went looking. If James was lying to me, I knew I'd find proof in there."

"Let me guess." His voice came out graveled. "Your father's diaries left you with more questions than answers."

"Only one. If I let you out of these bindings, will you kill me?"

Her question zippered up his spine. Left him reeling. He should have been angry—that after so many years carefully guarding his biggest secret, the knot had been tugged loose by something other than him. Instead, all he felt was relief. A palpable slackening, deep inside his chest.

He could tell her everything now that the truth was out—how he'd died so many times that death threaded through him like sinew. How the feel of falling to dust had become blunted as an old blade, but the thought of Wyatt under his thumb had been anything but. It was a sharp and punishing daydream, a knife between his ribs.

He *wanted* to tell her everything, but his instinct was misguided. She wasn't his confidant; she was his sacrifice. And so, he did what he'd always done—he held his tongue.

His silence was as good a confirmation as anything. Directly beneath him, Wyatt drew in breath, sharp and shallow, as though she'd been impaled. "What about my last night at Willow Heath? Did you plan to kill me then?"

That final incident and all that happened afterward still kept him awake at night. He remembered their final hours together in full-bodied flinches—the otherworldly hush of the grove, the three of them lying side by side on a bed of pine.

The knife in his boot. His heart in his throat.

Wyatt's fingers threading hesitantly through his under cover of dark.

43

All those years with the beast whispering in his head—all that time hungering for his chance at freedom—and that night all he could think about was how perfect Wyatt's hand felt in his. How much he liked the way James watched them both through his keen obsidian stare.

Stupid, childish whims. They'd cost him everything.

Coward, jeered the beast in the wood, once Wyatt was gone. *Coward*, came its taunt on the wind, its rumble in the thunder. *You let her get away, and now you will never see your mother again.*

"You had a knife with you that night," Wyatt said, when Pedyr took too long to reply. "I remember."

His mouth had gone dry as cotton. He blinked, and there was James, the memory as clear as yesterday: *"You absolute wanker. They'll gut you if they find it on you."*

"Was it meant for me?" Wyatt asked, oblivious to the way he grappled with his ghosts.

She was standing unbearably close, her proximity dizzying. His fingers twitched in their chains as James's voice crowded his thoughts: *"What were you planning to do with it, huh?"*

He didn't like to think about how quickly everything had turned— didn't like to remember the crack of James's nose beneath his fist, the way the flowers popped into pale midnight blooms at Wyatt's cry. All impulse and no thought, he'd lost James and Wyatt in the same bloodied stroke. He was older now. Friendless and starving. He'd spent years hardening the bits of him that were weak, letting his heart ossify into bone. He wouldn't make the same mistakes twice.

Beneath him, the first wick of hurt lit in Wyatt's gaze. "There was a blood moon the night before I left. You were the one who insisted we go out to the chapel to watch the eclipse. You were *adamant* about it, which—now that I think about it—should have been the first red flag, because you were never adamant about anything."

Another beat of quiet passed. She peered up at him, waiting for him to speak, her unblinking scrutiny slicing clean through his mettle. He fixed his gaze on a point just over her head and ground his jaw, resolving to keep quiet if it killed him. He wouldn't confess and risk frightening her off.

Not this close to the end.

"James says there's going to be another eclipse two and a half weeks from now," she said, undeterred by his silence. "He says that whatever is out there in the forest demands a blood moon and an offering." She pulled the journal open, thumbing aside a broken bit of clover as she skimmed through the blocks of her father's sloppy shorthand. "My dad wrote the same exact thing in his journal. Where was it? I just read—here. *They say only a total offering will appease the eldritch dark.'*" She snapped the journal shut, and the sound made him flinch. "Is that what this is? Are you planning to use me as some sort of ritual sacrifice?"

Her voice hitched on the last word, as though she couldn't quite bring herself to say it aloud. *Sacrifice.* In all the years of his captivity, Pedyr had worked to train his body into a preternatural numbness. With her here, he felt everything—the hollow gnaw of his stomach and the needle-ache in his arms, the slow atrophy of muscle tissue and the erratic beat of his heart. He was certain she could hear it hammering in the quiet.

"If the phone rings again," he said, "don't pick up."

Frustration colored her cheeks in twin splotches of pink. "I don't

45

understand. Earlier, you told me you wanted us to work together. You told me Willow Heath needed a witch to maintain its wards. I can't do that for you if I'm dead."

"No," he admitted. "You can't."

"So, then what? What do you get out of killing me?"

What did it matter if he told her? If she wouldn't even *try* to practice Westlock magic—if she wouldn't work with him to set him free—they'd both rot before the end. The farm was dying. The beast was waiting. They were already as good as dead.

"I get to go home," he said, the truth fraying from him like thread pushed through a too-small needle. Wyatt reared back as though she'd been slapped. Dust flurried after her in pale silver fractals.

"Home," she echoed.

The pinprick of anger in his stomach was muscle memory. It was the righteous fury of a little boy on the bank of the millpond, drowning army men beneath the ice. "Did you really think Willow Heath was my home?"

"But it was." Something raw crept into her voice. "It was all of our home."

"Says the girl who showed up after five years with a can of gasoline and a match."

"Don't," she spat. "Don't pretend like you have any idea what drives me."

He could have told her she was dead wrong—that he'd studied her for so long, for so many years, that he knew her like a sailor knew the sea. That he felt the shifts in her moods the way a lightkeeper's knees ached before a storm.

Instead, he gritted his teeth and said, "Likewise."

Like the silvering of a leaf before the rain, he saw the glimmer of decision in her eyes a heartbeat before she made her move. Reaching for him, she closed her fingers around his button pendant and gave it a single violent tug. The shoelace bit into the nape of his neck, leather snapping against skin hard enough to draw a wince between his teeth.

He should have seen it coming. Of course she'd recognize it. For years, he'd kept the little plastic button tucked away. In his pocket. In his boot. In the crack-riven crook of his altar—a tiny blue trophy he carried like a lucky coin. Now there was nowhere to hide it. The leather cord hung slack in her fist, damnable and obvious. Over the rush of blood between his ears, he heard the pretty sotto of her voice.

"This is mine."

It hadn't been posed as a question, and so he didn't answer.

"God." She unfolded her fingers and stared down at the little blue button in the palm of her hand. He'd drilled it through the middle, leaving it sleek and flat as a metal washer. When she spoke again, her question came out quiet. "Was any of it real?"

The question sank into his blood. *Was any of it real?*

He thought of the stars wheeling overhead and her hand in his. The hard beat of her pulse against his fingertips and the way he'd thought maybe another lifetime on the wrong side of the sky wouldn't be so unbearable with Wyatt and James at his side.

He thought about what his hesitation had cost him, in the end.

"No," he said, and meant it. "You believed what I wanted you to believe."

Her hazel eyes flicked to his, and he saw the faintest shimmer of tears gathering in her lower lids. Outside, the wind picked up. It drove winged sycamore seeds into the glass in a frenzied *plink-plonk-plink*.

"At least she's not an ugly crier," James said once as they'd watched her streak through the gathered trees, her palms red with abrasions where she'd fallen into the dirt. *"She explodes into tears at least ten times a day. I'll bet she practices in the mirror."*

She didn't explode into tears now.

She only fisted her hand over the button and took a slow, steadying breath.

She only said, "In that case, you can go ahead and rot."

5

WYATT

Wyatt's mother once told her that growing up was like shedding snakeskin. Each time you did, you came out just a little bit changed—patterned and pigmented in new and different ways. She'd carried that thought with her through the years, imagining herself shedding bits and pieces each time she blew out another set of birthday candles.

By the time she graduated from high school, she'd left most things behind. Willow Heath, and all its memories. The braces she'd worn freshman year. The little starry night-lights she'd slept with until her sixteenth birthday. Detritus from her youth, discarded like litter as she grew too old to care for it.

But not Cubby. Cubby stayed. He came with her to softball camp. To sleepovers. To her college's prospective student weekend, tucked in the little side pouch of her duffel bag, his overlarge head folded against the pilled velveteen of his belly.

He was an ugly bear, old and shabby, stitches crawling across his stomach in the place where he'd once hemorrhaged stuffing. He took the brunt of her abuse back then, dragging along behind Wyatt as she traipsed over hills and under glades, snagging his soft velvet on glossy buckthorn and sticky cockleburs. Bath after bath, stitch after stitch, he'd turned into something formless and unidentifiable well before Wyatt's tenth birthday.

"You're too old for a lovey," James had announced that summer, newly eleven and too self-important to play pirates. They'd been tossing rocks into the stream, and the bank was flooded with rainwater, the current running hard and fast. He'd positioned himself atop a boulder, dangling Cubby by a single lumpy leg. Out of reach beneath him, Wyatt bit back tears.

"Give him back," she'd demanded, stomping her foot. *"You're hurting him."*

"He's a lump of fluff," James said. *"He doesn't have feelings. Aren't you tired of being such a crybaby all the time?"*

Nearby, Peter sat propped against a towering birch and watched without intervening. Wyatt had wanted to shout at him, too. For not choosing her side. For not telling James to leave her alone. For his constant, intolerable silences.

Finally, and with the reassurance that he was only doing it for her own good, James launched Cubby into the stream. Wyatt splashed in after him, plunging ankle-deep into the rapids, and watched as the current swept her little bear out of reach. Dropping onto her knees right there in the shallows, she'd wept big fat tears.

James and Peter had left her there alone after that, the former calling her a baby, the latter mute and useless, his hands stuffed deep into his pockets. She didn't move from her place by the stream. Not as the temperature dropped. Not as a bank of heavy clouds rolled in, the skies tearing open. When she finally stumbled home—wet and shivering—she was met with a firm scolding and a hot bath and sent to bed without supper.

By the time she made it back to her room, skin scrubbed pink and hair in braids, it was night. To her surprise, Cubby sat propped atop her bed, nestled into the frilled stack of her pillows. He was soaking wet and dark with mud, his heavy head lolling to one side.

One of his blue button eyes was gone.

Wyatt woke with a start, dragged out of lucid dreaming and into the fusty haze of the sitting room. The ancient wingback creaked beneath her shifting weight, its tufted florals concealed by woven antimacassars. Light slipped sideways through the velvet curtains, sinking the whole of the room in a funny yellow cast. In her open palm sat Cubby's missing button, its middle threaded with shoelace.

She didn't know what had woken her, only that she'd come to with a crick in her neck and pins in her feet, her heart rioting against her ribs. Straining her ears, she listened to the primordial shifting of the house, the too-deep quiet beyond the open cellar door.

And then there it was again—a sound like a specter's wail. A lone, disembodied howl that raised the hairs on her arms, kicking her pulse into overdrive. The cry distended through the whole of the house, rebounding off the pine-paneled walls until she couldn't tell if it was miles away or right in the other room. She launched to her feet as a second howl joined the first. A third, and she was out in the hall, Cubby's button tucked safely into the pocket of her pants.

By the time she made her way down into the basement, the entire house was flooded with the mad baying of hounds. Peter was right where she'd left him, his arms shackled over his head, his stare liquid bright and alert.

"What is that?" she demanded without precursor. "Coyotes?"

"Wolves," said Peter. He was watching the window, tracking a pale cellar spider as it spun a jumbled web along the glass.

"There haven't been wolves at Willow Heath for years."

"Wolves go where the food is," he said. "With no one tending to the orchard, the deer will have found their way back in. And where there's prey, there's predators."

She didn't like the way he'd said it, like he was administering a warning. She was about to say as much when the howling cut short. Off in the distance, there came a final, keening yelp. It wasn't the victory cry of something making a kill. It was, instead, the pitiful yap of something dying. The sound of it raised the hair along the nape of her neck.

"It's too early in the day for wolves," she said. "They shouldn't be out right now."

"That's because they weren't doing the hunting." Peter's gaze rounded on hers, his eyes hard as frost. "They were the hunted."

His answer tiptoed through her on chilly legs. Left her shivering in the gloom. The words from her father's journal played back through her head: *"Only a total offering will appease the eldritch dark."* In the window, a black housefly had straggled into the spider's trap. It tugged and writhed to no avail, tangled in the sticky gossamer webbing.

Uneasy, Wyatt asked, "What hunts and kills an entire pack of wolves?"

Whatever answer Peter might have given, it didn't come. Upstairs, a knock sounded against the front door. Their eyes met through the falling light.

"Don't get that," Peter ordered, but it was too late. Wyatt was already halfway to the stairs.

52

"It could be James."

His voice crawled up the steps after her, dry as leaves. "It isn't."

Another knock sounded, knuckles rapping musically against the wide farmhouse door. She slid into the foyer on lumpy woolen socks, her elbow catching hard against the sideboard. Ahead, the upper half of a man's profile was just visible through the sidelight's macrame curtain. For the first time since she'd returned to Willow Heath, hope unfurled in Wyatt's chest.

A third round of knocking fell silent as she pried open the door. "It's about time you—oh."

It wasn't James Campbell who stood on the porch. It was a stranger. Middle-aged and bowed at the shoulders, he reminded her of a bird—from the sharpness of his features to the way his pale-as-milk hands clutched like talons over the hooked handle of an umbrella.

His head canted to the side at the sight of her. "Am I late?"

His question was punctuated by the scream of a crow on the roof. Its cry fell through the chimney flume, turning the house into an echo chamber. It scraped down the walls. Etched a shiver into her skin. She held fast to the door, the lock bolt biting into her hip.

"I was expecting someone else."

"Ah. I see." His accent was unplaceable, his consonants whistle sharp. "I realize this is somewhat of an unsolicited visit. I'm an old friend of your father's. He was a formidable greenskeeper. All of the Westlocks were. I was deeply sorry to hear of your loss."

"Thank you," said Wyatt. She didn't like the way he looked at her, his beaded eyes bright and birdlike. "Can I help you with something?"

"Can you, indeed? I suppose that remains to be seen. I am looking for someone." His gaze trailed up toward the lintel, where a bit of dried hawthorn had been strung upon a rusted nail. Its brickle twigs were bound in twine, and its once-white petals had yellowed to a sepia stain.

A ward against the dark, she thought. Just like Peter said. Just like the tangle of buttonbush along the front walk. It should have brought her comfort. Instead, unease sparked—sick and fizzling—in her stomach. Here, in front of her, was a stranger swathed in darkness. And she'd opened the door to him.

"Who are you looking for?"

"An immortal," said the stranger, still studying the mayflower. "He'd be a boy. Or, perhaps, a young man. I imagine he's grown over the years."

An immortal. *An immortal.* The words zinged through her without taking root. Surely, he couldn't mean what she thought he meant. Peter wasn't an *immortal*. Immortals were dignified. Cultured. Wise. Peter was the most childish person she'd ever met. He was sullen and messy and maddingly naïve.

She swallowed the brick in her throat. "What else do you know about him?"

A smile caught, tricky and sharp, and she began to wish she hadn't opened the door at all. "Poor dear. I imagine this has all come as quite a shock. I'm told you were very fond of the boy. You must have so many questions. I can tell you anything you might want to know. Where he comes from. What purpose he serves, here at Willow Heath. What sort of beast whispers in his ear whenever the forest draws breath."

The beast again. Just like the men at the gate had mentioned. Another crow screamed. Wyatt peered behind him and saw, in the branches of the sycamore out front, a hundred black birds all clumped

54

together. They preened their feathers and clicked their beaks, watching her with the same acute sharpness as the man on the porch. The feel of their unblinking eyes left her cold.

"Come in," she said on a whim. "Let's talk inside."

The stranger's smile waned. He picked up his umbrella and spun it round, examining the sleek notch of its handle. "Do you think it wise, to invite a stranger into your home?"

"Maybe," she said. "Maybe not."

She glanced again at the clump of hawthorn. A memory swept through her: her father bent over a leaf-thick lattice out in the greenhouse, a glass pipette in his bloodied hand, the liquid within a crimson-laced black. Just a few drops in the soil, and the blossoms had unfurled into bold white clusters. What had Peter called it? Blood tilling?

She thought—though she didn't want to—of the water running under her hands. Her blood on the floor and the widening fans of blue-green blooms. That horrible, drowning voice: *"Wyatt, you bitch. What the hell did you do to me?"*

She stepped aside, letting the door open wide. She hoped her instinct was right.

"Any friend of my father's is welcome here."

The man rapped the tip of his umbrella upon the wood. One, two, three times. When the silver finial jutted up against the threshold, it jerked back with a sizzle. He withdrew, shaking out his hand as if he'd been electrocuted. His smile turned into a wince, bladed sharp.

"The wards won't hold forever." The warning came out on a snarl. "A little bird told me you haven't studied the family trade. With no

55

one here capable of managing the gardens, they'll wither and die. And when they do? We'll be back to claim the boy."

"We?"

As if on cue, the birds fluttered upward, momentarily blacking out the sun in the flurry of wings. Swallowing up the quiet with the eerie sawing of their screams. On the porch, the man burst into a mess of feathers, wings fluttering as he, too, took to the sky with a blood-curdling cry. Wyatt was left alone, staring at the place where he'd been, her heart beating hard.

6

WYATT

There was a time when Wyatt thought she might live at Willow Heath forever.

Lulled by the hazy indolence of summer and still young enough to be uninhibited by logic, she spent her afternoons dreaming up a future full of whimsy. Her plan was this: Horses in the barn. Maybe a unicorn, if she ever managed to find one. Cows in the meadow. A houseful of cats and one wiry little mutt, a hobgoblin in the kitchen to stir up trouble. A half-dozen feral children and Peter in the wood-shop. James visiting at the holidays, his arms piled high with presents.

"We're not playing wedding," she remembered James snapping, his wooden sword halfway out of his scabbard and a scrape across one cheek. *"Peter isn't your groom, he's my best general, and we're right in the middle of a battle."*

Nearby, Peter stood watching the forest, his face bloodless. That particular day, she'd thought maybe he'd been caught up in James's game—imagining the clear ringing of a fife, the steady beat of war drums. Now she knew better.

He'd been listening to something in the woods.

Nothing she'd learned about Peter fit in with the image she had of him—the memories she'd made and the moments she'd treasured. Try as she might, she couldn't bring herself to think of him as

57

something dangerous. She could only picture him as the boy in her window, his face lit silver beneath a thunderhead sky, the feel of a first kiss shredding the air between them.

It had happened their final summer at the farm. She'd arrived home from a year away at St. Adelaide's to find Peter waiting in the wide willow outside her window—barefoot and bored to tears, blowing into a makeshift pan flute he'd knitted out of jute string and straws.

"You're late," he'd said, and nothing more.

James burst through the front door two days later, jet-lagged and already complaining, slapping horseflies from his orbit with the focus of a tennis player. That summer, he hadn't brought home his usual suitcase packed full of stolen trinkets. He only brought a bag of penny candy and a deck of cards.

He'd learned all sorts of games when he was away at school, and he took his time divulging them, doling them out like sweets. Instead of going to battle, they played their hand at war. Instead of pirates, kings. Instead of Vikings, blackjack. They squirreled themselves away in the chapel, hoarding piles of rich milk chocolates and sour Lemonheads. They gambled away their windfalls little by little, squabbling like magpies over their winnings—until the candy was gone and their stomachs were sick and James taught them one final game he'd learned.

"It's called suck and blow." A joker flickered between his fingers, grinning up at them from the seat of a slender red unicycle. *"It's the easiest of them all. You put the card to your lips and suck. Once it's on the next person's mouth, you blow."*

"What if it drops?" Wyatt asked.

58

Amusement glimmered in James's eyes. *"You don't let it drop."*

He'd gone first, balancing on his knuckles as he leaned in close to Wyatt. She'd felt the gush of his breath, the gloss of the card as it stuck to her lips. Quickly, she'd turned to Peter, her stomach caught in a free fall. She'd found him waiting on the other side, reluctance pinching his face. She'd half expected him to refuse—to embarrass her and end the game before it even began. To her surprise, he'd played along, accepting the card and turning quickly to James.

And so, on they'd gone. Round and around, James crowing with delight. On the fourth pass, James let the card fall. Wyatt had time to blink once, surprised, before his mouth collided into hers. She remembered it as a slow, startled something—closed-mouthed and open-eyed, her tongue still burning from the sour scorch of a Lemonhead. A single second lapsed before he broke away, his laughter pluming over her.

"I knew it," he'd said, as though he'd proved something.

On the floor beside Wyatt, Peter had launched onto his feet. His hands were fisted at his sides, and a bright pink flush had swept up his throat. At the sight of James's grin, he'd turned and headed for the door. *"I'm leaving. This game is stupid."*

"Peter, wait." Wyatt scrabbled after him, her stomach sugar sour. *"Wait. Where are you going?"*

But he hadn't answered. He'd only slipped out into the grove, disappearing into the bald snaggle of pine.

"Let him go," James said, dropping into a pew. *"If he wants to be a baby, he can find something else to do."*

She hadn't seen Peter again until later on that same evening, long after her mother had called for lights-out. She remembered the night as hot and windless, the sky outside her open window flickering with pale heat lightning. She'd shot up straight in bed as a figure slid off the branch and landed silently in her windowsill.

"He didn't mean anything by it," she'd said, sure that it was Peter. *"James is always trying to get under your skin. You know how he is."*

Across the room, Peter had been inscrutable beneath the dark. Just a shadow of a boy. Wyatt crawled out of bed and padded her way across the room, climbing into the sill beside him.

"I hate when we fight," she'd said.

Two pale silver moons slid toward her. *"We're not fighting."*

"It feels like we are."

He hadn't answered. Not right away. Instead, he'd plucked a floppy corduroy rabbit from the pile of animals in the sill. The bunny's overlarge head wilted to one side, sateen ears spilling over the white knuckles of his fists.

"What did it feel like," he'd asked. *"When he kissed you?"*

"He tasted like lemon," she'd said, beneath another stroboscopic flash of white.

"Did you like it?"

Her heart thudded dully against her ribs. This was new ground, alien and unsteady. *"Peter,"* she'd said, willing him to look at her. *"It was just a stupid game."*

Buried in the velvet dark, she hadn't seen when he leaned in. She'd only felt the careful whisper of his mouth along the very corner of hers. A single, startled breath stitched out of her. On the other side of the wide-open window, thunderheads piled up along the horizon. At the first low rumble, Peter pulled away, his gaze sliding toward the storm.

"There's a blood moon tomorrow," he'd said, as though nothing out of the ordinary had happened. But something extraordinary had. The air was electric, the night alive. The sky was all storm, and so was Wyatt. Her heart thundered inside her chest. Her pulse was lightning in her veins. Carefully—too carefully—Peter had reached out and deposited the rabbit in her lap.

"I can't do it," he'd whispered, his eyes trained on the far distant trees.

And then he'd gone, back out through the window and into the willow. Leaving her startled and alone, the first fat drops of rain pattering against the glass.

Immortal, the man with the umbrella called Peter. Immortal, as though he was some sort of divinity. A god, and not a boy. That night in the window, he'd seemed more human than anyone she'd ever met.

In the kitchen's predawn dark, the yellow shell of the phone's receiver took on a bluish hue. Several minutes ago, she'd lifted it from the wall and pressed it to her ear. She'd listened to a dead line. No dial tone. No static. Nothing. She'd done the same thing an hour ago. An hour before that. The ritual was beginning to wear on her.

She paced across the tile, skirting around a dozing Slightly as she went. This time, when she lifted the receiver, she didn't bother putting it to her ear—she slammed it against the hook with enough force to knock the entire base out of alignment.

"Useless." Swinging a stockinged kick at the baseboard, she caught her big toe against the corner of a cabinet. The effort left her hopping on one foot, a string of curses slipping between gritted teeth. Slightly

61

took off with a shot just as the phone let out a single, shrill jangle. Startled—still wobbling—she scrabbled for the receiver.

"James?"

Background noise swelled alone the line. She heard the piped crackle of a public address filtering through a loudspeaker. And then, over it, "You're still there."

His disbelief was a tin can echo. He sounded as though he were light-years away. Adrift somewhere in the cosmic tangle of stars, a satellite she'd knocked out of her orbit five long years ago.

"How are you calling me on this phone?" she asked, at the same time as he said, "I thought I told you to get out of there."

She swallowed around the sour taste in her mouth. "Yeah, well, I'm stuck."

"Stuck," James echoed. "Stuck how?"

"For one, my car won't start. For another, there's been people in the woods."

A palpable wariness crept into the line. "What sort of people?"

"No one I recognize. Some creeps in cloaks have been hanging out at the edge of the property. And yesterday a man literally—and I mean *literally*, Jamie—turned into a bird right in front of me."

She fell silent and waited for him to demand more information— to flounder the way she had when first faced with the preternatural truths of Willow Heath. Instead, he blew out a breath and said, "Do me a favor and don't talk to anyone else until I get there."

Another incomprehensible announcement bellowed down the line and James spat out a curse. She tried to picture him as he might look now, but all she could see was a skinny kid in a crowded terminal, black hair curling over his ears and a shiner under one eye.

"Shit luck," he said, and there was nothing left in the careful tenor of his voice to evoke that image. "My flight's been delayed. Mechanical issues. They're looking into securing another plane, but—" He blew out a breath. "Could be hours, I don't know. The gate attendant has gone purple in the face. Doesn't spark much confidence."

"Okay, but—"

"Don't worry about the bone warden," he said, cutting her off. "He's nothing but a charlatan. He didn't *really* turn into a bird, it's just an illusion. It's his only party trick, actually."

Something bitter writhed in her belly. She didn't like how easily he said it—*nothing but a charlatan*—as though he and the funny birdlike visitor were old friends. As though he'd known all Willow Heath's secrets this entire time, while she'd been carrying on without a clue.

She wanted to dig in her heels and demand an apology, but she didn't want to risk starting a fight. Not when he was still so far away. Not when everything already felt so precarious. Peter wasn't talking, and if she wanted answers, she'd need James to fill in the gaps.

With more resentment than she'd intended, she asked, "What does he want with Peter?"

"To collect him, I'd imagine. My father tells me the bone warden keeps all sorts of specimens in his display. He's particularly interested in Peter, for obvious reasons."

It wasn't obvious to her, though she didn't say so aloud. "He said something kind of crazy," she said, feeling ridiculous for even entertaining it. "He thinks Peter's immortal."

The only sign that the call hadn't dropped was the steady beeping of a luggage cart in reverse.

"Jamie? Are you there?"

"You should go out to the chapel," he said, and he sounded distracted. "If you want answers, I mean. Peter kept things there. Keepsakes. I think they're still under his mattress."

She frowned down at the receiver. "His *mattress?*"

"Where did you think he slept? On the floor?"

"I didn't think he slept in the *chapel.*"

A bag zippered shut. "Where else do you house an idol?"

Idol. The word was a cold-water shock. It seeped into her skin in chilly fingers. "Peter's not an idol. He's—he's—" But she didn't know what he was. Not anymore. All her memories of him were going up in smoke, and she no longer knew what was real and what wasn't.

On the phone, James sounded faraway again. "Look, I can't imagine how difficult all this must be for you to accept. I know you've always fancied him."

"*Peter?*" Her throat tightened. "Absolutely not."

"Come off it, Wyatt. Did you think you were subtle? Everyone knew it. Why do you think your parents sent you away?" His voice was choppy, the connection fading in and out. "Listen, I'm later than I'd like, but I'm making progress." She heard the rustle of fabric. The muffle of the loudspeaker. Then, "I've got to go. Listen to me very carefully, okay? If Peter gets out before I'm there—if he comes after you—you kill him. I don't care how. You find a way."

And then he was gone, without even a goodbye. The line went dead with a click.

Wyatt stood frozen in the ensuing silence, feeling as though she'd missed the last step on a staircase. Her stomach was caught in an endless swoop. Carefully—as though it were made of glass—she replaced the receiver on its hook. The cord was a knot in her trembling fist, its coils hopelessly twisted.

Don't cry, she willed herself, blinking furiously. *Don't cry*.

Tugging on a thick cable-knit sweater, she pushed out into the chilly haze of the early morning. The chickens scattered at her sudden appearance in the henyard. Atop his shingled perch, the piebald rooster ogled her through an oily black stare. She ignored his questioning warble, shoving through the birch-woven gate and out into the field, where a morning fog wisped off the meadow in ghostly gray coils.

If Willow Heath had been a bustling hamlet when her father was alive, now it was dead. There was no commotion. No crowds and no noise. There was only Wyatt Westlock and the cold, the morning quiet enough to hear her heartbeat.

She trudged through the waist-high grass—past the guest homes buried in swallowwort—heading for the northernmost acreage of the heath, where the fatwood grove grew dead and dense. Several grazing deer flitted off soundlessly at her approach, the white flag of their departure the only sign they'd been there at all.

By the time she made it to the old wooden chapel, there was a stitch in her side. The nearby tombstones sat like snaggled teeth, faceless and crumbling. Inside, the air hung stagnant. A dry rot had crawled into the pews. She picked her way down the aisle, her wet stockings leaving footprints on the buckled floor. The sound of her own breathing ebbed and flowed around her as she approached the empty altar, stopping just shy of the heavy slab.

An early-morning sun flooded the stained-glass window, casting the great stone table in a kaleidoscope of wan reds and watery blues. The image depicted in the glass was that of a slender pelican, its beak red tipped and saber sharp, its chest gorged open.

"Did you know," James said once as the three of them lay head-to-head on the chilly floor, their skin awash in the jeweled mosaic, *"that people used to think the pelican pierced its own chest to feed its blood to its young?"*

Wyatt crinkled her nose at the thought. *"That's disgusting."*

"Maybe. But it makes a great visual for human sacrifice, doesn't it?"

She'd rolled to face him, horrified. *"That's not what happens here, Jamie."*

He'd tilted his chin up at her, his eyes bright with a secret. *"Are you sure?"*

Later on, as the sun dipped below the trees, they drew shallow lines across their palms with a penknife. They pressed their bloodied hands together: *"It's the three of us. Always. No matter what."*

A pelican-promise. A bond forged in blood. A lie.

She was wasting time. There was nothing here. Nothing but dust and unwanted memories, the cloying taste of rot, and the unwelcome threat of tears. She'd dwindled away entire summers in this chapel, and she'd never seen anything to indicate someone might be living here.

But when she turned to go, she saw it—an open door, tucked just beyond the circle of light. It was only a crack—a sliver of dark against the knotted-pine paneling—but it was enough to give her pause. She tiptoed toward it, moving out of the pelican's dappled gleam and into shadow.

A closer inspection showed that the door normally sat flush with the wall, lacking any sort of architrave to mark its existence. A spate of disquiet ran through her. How many afternoons had she sat propped against this very spot and not known it was hollow?

A set of hidden hinges let out a groan as she pushed the door wide. Beyond was a room. It was narrow and sharply dormered, rusted nails curving out of the ceiling. A distressed bedside table sat in one corner, a camping lantern atop its surface. A twin-sized mattress lay on the floor, yellowed and moldering, its batting chewed loose by mice.

Hardly daring to breathe, she lowered herself onto her knees and drew the mattress up. A wolf spider scuttled out, racing for cover, and she recoiled with an undignified squeak. The mattress flopped wetly onto the floor. Skin crawling, she pried up the bedding a second time, feeling along the floorboards until her fingertips grazed over a small pile of items. Cautiously, she raked them out into the open.

There was the cheap friendship necklace she'd gotten from Gisella Castellanos in grade school, its pink aluminum heart severed in half. Here was the tube of lipstick James had gifted her one summer, the words *Dahlia Red* printed on the bottom. Here was a stainless-steel lighter James had pocketed during his brief tenure at Norrington Prep, dented where he'd dropped it during a scuffle. *"Keepsakes,"* he'd called them on the phone.

Scattered here and there among the items was a series of Polaroids— snapshots from the summer James had briefly taken up photography. Snatching them off the floor, Wyatt fell to sorting through the pile, pausing when she came to a hazy shot of her and Peter in the mill-pond. She sat perched on his shoulders, his fists shackling her ankles. Beneath was a freeze-frame of Peter and James in the barn, the former stifling a rare smile, the latter's head thrown back in an easy laugh. It was followed by a candid capture of Wyatt in the meadow, her back turned and her hair in braids. Hurt swelled in her chest, inflating like a balloon until there was no room left over to draw breath.

The next photo was crinkled at the corners, a sun-faded print of Peter positioned just outside the chapel. He looked small, hardly older than a toddler. Beside him stood her grandfather, grim faced and robed in black, a hand on Peter's shoulder. The pixelated stamp read *07/16/1992*—an entire decade before she was even born.

"Immortal," scurried the bone warden's voice through her head. Impossible, came her own logic, fast on its heels. And yet the proof was here in her hands. It was in the tiny tintype photographs at the bottom of the pile, their colors monochromatic. At the center of one image was Peter, his stare lifeless and his mouth flat. He was dressed in tapered-knee pants and a little white sailor's hat, a stick in one hand. She flipped it over, searching for a date.

And there it was, pencil light and nearly illegible—*July 4, 1910.*

Her hands shook. Her heart beat hard enough to cleave clean out of her chest. *Don't cry,* went the mantra in her head, though she didn't want to cry at all—she wanted to scream. To let out the thing that had been building and building within her since the moment she first returned to Willow Heath and found Peter there waiting.

Outside in the chapel, the main doors slammed shut. She launched to her feet, the photos still clutched in her hands.

"Hello? Who's there?"

No one answered. In the ensuing quiet, she heard the scrape of a shoe. The slow creak of a floorboard. Her breaths tightened as fear crawled down her throat.

"Peter? Is that you?"

Glass shattered, falling to the floor in a shivering rain. She fell back onto the mattress as the sound rebounded all through the tiny scuttle space, its echo cradled in the rafters. Eventually, everything fell silent. She remained frozen in the dark of Peter's little room, hardly daring to make a sound.

She didn't know how much time had passed before she finally garnered the courage to creep out into the chapel. By then, whoever had been there was long gone. She found the meetinghouse empty, a late-afternoon sun cutting sideways across the pews. Above the altar, the stained glass sat dull and dark, a jagged hole through the pelican's gory middle, as though someone had lobbed a rock through its center. Milky-white fragments scattered like teeth across the altar, dazzled here and there with shards of ruby red.

In the center of it all, placed neatly on its mandible, was a skull, picked clean. She didn't need to get close to see that it was something carnivorous, its elongated muzzle set with sharp yellow fangs. Below, someone had transcribed a message in red. It sent a chill through her to see it, though the still-slick words made little sense. *The heart of a wolf is not enough.*

7

PEDYR

Pedyr was awake when Wyatt returned. She blew in at the top of the stairs like a springtime squall—all bluster and torrent, color in her cheeks and her hair windblown. A wide rattan basket sat in the crook of one arm, loaded with items. When she upended a pile of photos at his feet, he didn't look. He didn't need to—he knew at once what she'd brought him. Knew where she'd been, rooting through the hidden dark of his rectory. Prying loose yet another secret from the knot he'd so carefully fastened.

For several seconds, neither of them said a word. Somewhere unseen, a cricket began to chirp. Wyatt drew a single short breath.

"Well?"

He dragged his gaze to hers. "What do you want me to say?"

"Something." The word plunked to the floor between them. *"Anything."*

He shifted in his shackles, his wrists aching. "Here's something— you left the house today. Don't do it again."

He saw the slap coming before it landed, but there was no room to recoil. His head whipped to the side as he absorbed the blow, his cheek heating at the impact. He caught an unwanted eyeful of the scattered photos—a summer's worth of lens-flare captures and hazy candids. Moments he'd carried with him through the crumbling autumns and the colorless winters. Pathetic, how he'd held on to them until spring returned and the world popped into color. Pitiful, how each new year he'd crawled out from his hideaway like a bear from a cave, an internal clock ticking in his chest: *Wyatt. Wyatt. Wyatt.*

Painful, the way his heart beat at a clip when he heard her on the farmhouse stairs, the way his breaths went unsteady, his head electric. He'd blink up at her from the wide old willow outside her window and think she looked just like spring was meant to look, her hair the color of rusted orchids, pink peonies in her cheeks, her smile a bold dahlia red.

She wasn't smiling now. Her mouth was pale as larkspur, her eyes fractured in unshed tears. "Is that really all you can think to say?"

"It's all that matters." He could still feel her open palm emblazoned into his cheek. He relished the sting, let it sink into his skin. "You leave this house, you die. And you're no use to me dead."

Not yet.

For a moment, he thought she might strike him a second time. Instead, she shut her eyes. She took a slow, steadying breath. When she next fixed him in her gaze, the tears were gone. Her stare was bright and cold.

"I hate you," she said, the words chipping out of her like ice.

He flexed his aching jaw and said nothing at all.

"What a weight off your shoulders that must be," she went on. "You won't have to pretend anymore."

On the floor, a summertime of pretending stared up at them. There they were cloud-spotting in the field, Wyatt's head propped on his stomach, her hair spilling over his ribs. Here they were in the barn, their legs thrust over the loft's hay-strewn edge, their knees kissing.

71

His mouth went dry. Out of the corner of his eye, he saw her crouch down and place something on the floor between them. It was a wolf's washed-out skull, its broad muzzle fanged in sharp incisors.

"This was left in the chapel," she said, when he turned to examine it in full. "Along with a note that I'm pretty sure was written in blood. It said, *'The heart of a wolf is not enough.'* What does that mean to you?"

It meant the beast was running out of patience. It meant it was starving—the way he starved, wasting away without ever dying, until the world burned up and the two of them with it. He wouldn't tell her any of that. He wouldn't tell her about the deal he'd struck, when he'd been small and resentful, or the way he came to regret it, in the hours before she left him for good.

Instead, he said, "If something got inside the chapel, it means your father's wards have already begun to fall. Like I said, it's not safe for you to be out there alone."

Heat flashed in her eyes. "Oh, and I'm perfectly safe in here with you?"

"Look at me." He tugged at his shackles. The irons rattled like teeth, sending dust eddying between them in sun-spark glimmers. "I can't hurt you."

The laugh that forced its way out of her was several decibels too loud. Teetering on the knife's edge of hysteria. He knew what came next—knew that, with Wyatt, what went up always came down. Usually in tears and in torrents, the skies cracking open.

"That's funny," she said, her voice thick. "You're funny."

He hadn't meant it to be funny, and both of them knew it. She pushed her fingers through her hair, sending waves of uncombed copper in every direction. Her next laugh came out broken.

"You know what, *screw* you, Peter."

The basket in her arms crashed onto the floor between them. Out flew several wedges of sweet red apple, a brown hunk of bread. His mouth watered instantly at the sight, his stomach snarling, but she was already gone, stalking up the stairs without a backward glance. The crack of the basement door volleying shut sent a violent shudder down his spine. Too violent, as though the slam had a kickback, like a shotgun's recoil. It was followed by the slow groan of wood, a sound like a tree uprooting—the rapid plink-plink-plink of chains uncoupling.

When he fell, he went face-first, his chin cracking concrete hard enough to bloody his lip.

He lay prone on the cellar floor, jaw aching and muscles screaming, the smell of rot sweetening the air. He tried to roll onto his back and found his legs cramped and useless. Upstairs, the house stayed quiet and so did he, sensation slow-creeping back into his joints as he took stock of the impossible.

His shackles had given.

He knew what it took for a Westlock to work their magic—knew the careful compounds required to coax the earth into waking. Wyatt hadn't done a thing. Not intentionally. And yet on the wall, the wide roots of the old willow were warped in angry black cankers, scalloped fungi seeping out through open wounds in the bark. The dank reek of decay bled into everything, as though the tree had begun to rot from the inside out.

He didn't know how long he remained there before he finally found the strength to draw himself upright. By then, it was fully dark, the rectangle of sky visible through the window a deep velvet black. He propped himself against a rusted lally column, pulling at his fingers until he felt the telltale pop of bone—until the needle numbness of palsy began to fade from his limbs.

Around him lay the scattered bits of apple, white flesh oxidizing into brown, little black house ants coalescing into a swarm. He brushed them away and ate every last wedge, his stomach sick and his tongue sour, stretching out his spine until his vertebrae clicked back into alignment.

In all that time, Wyatt never came back downstairs.

When at last he'd regained enough strength to climb onto his feet, he crept upstairs. His legs were paresthesia stiff, and he moved at a crawl, feeding his hands one over the other along the railing. Blood roared between his ears, leaving him dizzy and half-blind, the needle of emaciation stringing through his limbs as his body worked to knit itself back together.

He staggered into the kitchen to find it empty, a cup of tea cooling on the counter. The sitting room was equally abandoned, the piano peeking out from its ghostly slipcover. Rolling out a kink in his shoulder, he hobbled toward the stairs.

He didn't make it far. As he rounded the corner, he was met with a flash of silver, the whistle of something weighted sailing through the air. He threw out his hands just in time to grab hold of a wooden splitting maul. The ax's hefted wedge careened to a stop a mere inch from his temple, bringing him nose to nose with Wyatt in the dark.

He arched a brow at her. "Expecting company?"

Her eyes were all murder, diamond bright and accusatory. "I thought something might have gotten past the wards."

"The wards are intact," he assured her. "It's just me."

"Is that supposed to make me feel better?" She gave the ax a fruit-less tug. "How'd you get out?"

"Let go, and I'll tell you."

"You first."

"I'm not the one who tried splitting your head like firewood." When he gave the ax an experimental heave, she came with it, nearly stumbling clean into him. "Let go, Wyatt."

"No."

Out in the kitchen, the phone rang. The impossible jangle hammered down his spine. In the dark of the hall, Wyatt's eyes flicked to his.

"It's James."

The name was a corkscrew in his chest. "Don't answer it."

"What," she said, "and give you the chance to ax me in the back while I'm on the phone? Please."

"I already told you—I'm not going to hurt you."

The word *yet* hung unspoken between them. A promise and a threat, both. In the kitchen, the phone let out another piercing ring. She let go of the ax without warning, and he staggered back a step, its full weight hefting into his grasp. She was already halfway to the kitchen by the time he set it against the baseboard, tailing after her at a wooden jog.

"Wyatt." His steps were stilted, his bones arthritic. "Wyatt, don't pick up."

"He just wants to know if I'm okay."

"He doesn't care whether or not you're okay." He planted himself in front of the phone just as it let loose a third, haunting ring. "That's not why he's calling."

"You don't think?" She scowled up at him. "Do you know what he told me? He told me I should kill you. That if it comes down to it, I should take your life before you have the chance to take mine. Do you think he would tell me that if he didn't care?"

Pedyr's stomach turned. "Yes," he said, just as the phone cut off midring. The kitchen fell silent. Neither of them moved. "Is that why you had the ax?"

"I told you," Wyatt said, "I thought someone got past the wards. I don't know if you've noticed, but there have been a lot of threats made against my life since I've come back. You, the creeps out in the woods, the bird man, the beast."

His head shot up. "What did you say?"

"The *beast*," she repeated. "From the woods."

Fear coursed along his spine. "How do you know about that?"

"Because the flock of men in capes told me about him, how else? They said if I didn't hand you over, the beast from the forest would come and take you by force."

"How many?"

"How many what?"

"How many men were in the woods, Wyatt?"

"I don't know." Annoyance flashed in her stare. "Five. Maybe six?"

"Seven," he said with sickly certainty. Seven, for the seven guildsmen he'd led to their deaths, after Wyatt and James were gone. Seven, for the seven bodies he'd buried. For seven graves with seven corpses, ripe for resurrection. If they were out there, it meant the beast was taking matters into its own hands.

And that meant they had less time than he thought.

On the wall, the phone began its ringing anew. This time, when Wyatt reached to answer it, he took hold of her wrist.

"Don't."

They were toe to toe in the dark, the phone mocking him without end, her pulse tripping against the pads of his fingers. Westlock blood, jackhammering just beneath her skin. When she wrenched out of his grasp, her pulse stayed behind like an echo.

"Let's call a truce," he rushed to say.

She braceleted her wrist, anger cresting in her stare. "Did you hit your head? Why would I agree to that?"

"Because you don't have another choice."

"There's always another choice." She turned her back on him as the ringing stopped, heading for the hall. Leaving him alone with his haunt, the tattoo of her pulse still inked into his palm. She was nearly gone when he called out after her.

"We were seven years old when you made James and me start sleeping in your room. You were convinced there were monsters under your bed. James told you it was impossible—nothing truly monstrous could fit into such a small space—but you insisted that the darkness got bigger once you were in it."

She hadn't looked at him, but she hadn't left, either. One hand was braced on the doorframe, all but her fingertips swallowed up in the knit cuff of her sweater. Out in the dark, the staccato yip of a coyote sounded and then silenced, snuffed out like a flame beneath a sudden gust of wind. A chill crawled into Pedyr's skin and stayed.

"You weren't wrong," he said. "The beast lives inside those spaces—between the skies, where the dark is so expansive, you can't see an end. And if he gets inside the house, it's over. He'll worm his way inside your head. He'll dash your mind to pieces, until you don't know what's real and what isn't."

She'd turned to face him while he spoke. "Is that what he did to you?"

The question pistoned through him. He thought of that primordial whisper twined around the base of his spine—*She left you. She left you*—the way the glass of her mirror had shattered beneath his fist, the way the bodies of the guildsmen writhed in their gossamer webbing. Lastly, he thought of the way James Campbell looked on his knees, a lightless black swimming into his eyes.

He could still feel the phantom of Wyatt's pulse in the pads of his fingers. He was torn between the desire to scrape it out of him or to stitch it into his skin.

"Only a witch can keep him out," he said, dragging his open palm over his chest.

"I already told you," Wyatt shot back. "I don't practice magic."

"But you can learn." He wouldn't let her back out of this. Not when so much was at stake. "You can learn, and I'm going to teach you."

8

WYATT

Wyatt woke to the scream of the farmhouse rooster. The sound wrenched her clear out of a nightmare, dragging the details with her in fast-fading facsimiles—the chilly rush of water, a dozen little fish, gimlet-eyed and dying. Green fans of algae under her fingertips.

She lurched upright, her vision starry and her lungs aching, taking careful stock of her surroundings as she tried to stanch the hemorrhage of fear.

Don't cry. Don't cry.

It was just a dream.

At her feet slept Slightly, belly up in a patch of sunlight. Her hands were dry. Dry, not wet. Nothing gruesome twisted up and out of her. Nothing rotten corded through her veins. She was strung much too tight along her bones, skin sucked sulfate dry. A headache sparked behind her eyes as, out in the yard, the rooster crowed a second time.

She dressed slowly, pulling on a threadbare top and a pair of rumpled linen overalls. Outside her window, the old willow tree groaned beneath a sudden ruffle of wind. Her heart skipped a beat at the sound and she glanced up, half expecting to find Peter waiting there, his legs dangling and his feet muddied. The thought put a pit in her stomach. Haunted by her ghosts, she turned from the window. *Don't cry. Don't cry.*

On her dresser sat the keepsakes she'd taken from Peter's hidden room—the severed plastic heart on a string. James's dented lighter. The stolen tube of lipstick. She snatched up the lighter first, tucking it into the pocket of her bib alongside Cubby's missing button. As an afterthought, she reached for the lipstick. It twisted out from the tube in a bold dahlia red, the wax gone flat from repeated use. She applied it on a whim, folding her lips together and bending forward to peer in the shattered remnants of her mirror.

It didn't make a difference.

The girl in the glass still looked like a stranger.

By the time she made her way downstairs—wood ax in hand—Peter was already in the kitchen, dressed in a misshapen green sweater and a pair of corduroy slacks. His hair stuck up in short, sloppy spikes, as though he'd given himself a haircut with a pair of garden shears. He worked his way through a heaping plate of scrambled eggs and hashed cauliflower, glancing up only briefly as she propped the ax against the little trifold table.

Swallowing a mouthful, he asked, "Are you going to bring that everywhere you go?"

She sank heavily into the seat across from him. "Depends."

"On what?"

"On several things." Bending over the table, she plucked a fried cauliflower off his plate. He froze, his eyes tracking her movements as she brought it to her mouth and took a bite. She'd meant it as a power play. A display of dominance. Instead, it only felt bone-achingly familiar—a mirror of a thousand other moments just like it. Hastily, she set the cauliflower down, unfinished. "For one, I still haven't decided what to do with you."

"You mean you haven't decided whether or not you're going to try and kill me." He peered at her askance. "Out of curiosity, what's stopping you?"

"This." Reaching into her overfull pockets, she felt around until she found the brittle tintype. Gingerly, she set it on the table between them. The tiny monochromatic version of Peter frowned up at them, his sailor's hat crooked on his crush of white hair. The tines of his fork scraped along the plate. Slowly, his eyes climbed to hers. His throat corded as he swallowed another mouthful of food.

"What about it?"

"If I took a swing at you," she mused, feigning nonchalance, "would it do anything? I mean, this photo is over a hundred years old, Peter. Can you even die?"

A hint of amusement glimmered in his pale blue eyes. *"I,"* he said, reaching for his glass of water, "am excellent at dying."

She scowled over at him. "What's that supposed to mean?"

But he didn't answer. Instead, he took a prolonged sip. She watched him drain his glass, wondering if he'd had anything to eat or drink in the five years since she'd been gone. If he starved the way a normal person starved, or if he felt nothing at all. Setting the glass back on the table, he swiped at a dribble of water on his chin.

"Here's a better question," he said. "Who's Micah?"

The question curdled in her belly. "Where did you hear that name?"

"You were calling out in your sleep last night."

Her nightmare resurfaced in a wave. She blinked and saw the bloody blooms, heard that horrible drowning voice: *"Wyatt, you bitch."*

Across the table, Peter dragged a fingertip along the rim of his empty glass. The sound shivered through the room like a struck tuning fork. Flatly, he asked, "Is he your boyfriend?"

The chair stuttered beneath her as she sprang to her feet. "Excuse me." She grabbed the ax's handle, letting the blunted maul *click-click-click* against the grout behind her as she headed for the door and yanked on a pair of ancient yellow waders.

Peter rose out of his chair. "Where do you think you're going?"

"Anywhere else," she snapped, just as the screen door slammed shut between them.

She was met at once with the scream of the rooster, the wild scattering of chickens. Beneath the shade of a nearby conifer, the goat watched her through flat, funny eyes, gnawing crookedly on a patch of ivy.

She stared back at it and pulled as ugly a face as she could, propping the ax against the peeling siding. Nearby, the ancient willow let out a spectral groan, bones shifting in a sudden buffet of wind. Reaching into her pocket, she pried James's lighter loose, running a thumb over the dent in its side. It struck her as strange, that he'd left it behind. He used to carry it with him wherever he went, snapping it open and shut like it was a tic. He'd practice all day. *Snap. Flip. Spark.*

When she clicked the flywheel, nothing happened. A second attempt sent a single spark sputtering skyward. Scowling, she let the lid fall shut. Maybe it was out of lighter fluid. Or maybe it was user error. Maybe James knew everything, and she knew nothing. A bitter riptide tugged through her and she wound up her arm, prepared to pitch the lighter into the nearby bushes.

A hand caught her wrist in midair just before she could let it fly.

"It's dangerous for you to be out here," Peter said as the door slammed shut at his back. "There's things in the forest that will kill you."

She tugged fruitlessly against his hold. "Oh, like you won't?"

He huffed out a sound that might have been a laugh, had he been anyone else. Working the lighter loose, he released her arm. His gaze dropped to her mouth, and the unwavering blue of his stare pinched her stomach.

"I remember when you first started wearing that stuff," he said, and it took her a beat to realize he meant the lipstick she'd found stuffed under his mattress. "You weren't allowed makeup, but you'd sneak out to the barn and put it on anyway. It made you feel rebellious. Like maybe you had just a little bit of control." His pale eyes flicked to hers. "Do you feel in control now? With your blunt ax and your broken lighter?"

He read her too easily, and she hated it. Hated how he held all her secrets so neatly in the palm of his hand, and all she had of his was a smattering of photographs and a stolen button, enough deception to drown in.

When he took a step toward her, she drew back, groping wildly for the ax's handle. Another step, and her back collided into the door. Startled, a dozen sunning ladybugs took to the air in a red-beetle swarm. Peter paid them no mind, tucking the lighter into his back pocket and ducking down to catch her eye.

"No rebellions," he said. "We called a truce, remember?"

"You called a truce," she shot back. "I didn't agree to anything."

"Hello!"

They both froze, turning toward the direction of the sound. There, beneath the garden's woven trellis, stood an old woman Wyatt recognized. She was dressed in a shapeless floral nap dress, her hair wiry with silver. Her skin was weathered as bark, so that she looked more tree than human, her sunken eyes as dark as the borer holes in an old oak.

"Little miss Wyatt." Her smile was missing several teeth. Her fingers were mottled in pale purpura bruises. "That can't be you. All grown-up. And so pretty, too."

"Don't talk to her," Peter ordered.

Wyatt palmed him hard in the chest, jostling him out of the way. "What's wrong with you? That's Mrs. Germaine."

He blinked down at her.

"From the farm next door? You know, she has all the cats."

"I've never been off the farm," he said sourly. "How would I have met her cats?"

She gawked up at him, certain she'd heard him incorrectly. "What do you mean, you've never—you know what, never mind. Hi, Mrs. Germaine!"

"She shouldn't be here," Peter muttered.

Wyatt ignored him, smiling over at the elderly woman at the gate. "Can I help you with something?"

"I think so." Old Mrs. Germaine blinked, peering over at Wyatt with a funny thousand-yard stare. The hem of her dress was wet with mud. Her feet were bare, her legs discolored in contusions. Something silver sleek glinted in her hand. "I have a message for you."

"Oh." The first spate of unease moved through Wyatt's chest. "Is everything okay?"

"Oh, yes, dear." The treacle-sweet scratch of her voice dropped a register. It became the groan of trees, the bend of old oak beneath a heavy wind. The soft susurration of several hundred voices all at once. "Everything is quite all right, now that you've come back home to us."

Wyatt frowned. "Us?"

"The boy and I," she said. "We have been waiting for you."

"*Wyatt.*" Peter's voice directly in her ear startled her into jumping. Behind them, the door groaned open. "Inside. Now."

With a quickness that didn't match her age, the old woman brought her hand up to her throat. A flash of silver, a drag of red, and gouts of crimson sopped down the pale floral bib of her dress. She gaped, fish-like, gasping for air, blood pouring and pouring out of her.

And then, she began to laugh.

A terrible, keening sound that sent the hens fluttering out of sight.

"Wyatt!"

Peter's arm scooped around her waist and she was half dragged, half carted out of the blinding late-morning sun and into the dark of the kitchen. The door slammed shut. Wyatt stood without moving and felt the hammer of her heart against the anvil of her bones.

"What the hell was that?" She pushed her hands through her tangled hair and asked again—because it bore repeating, "*What the hell was that?*"

Braced against the window sash, Peter didn't look nearly as alarmed as she felt he ought to look. "What do you think it was?"

"The beast?" She thought about the whimpering wolves, the veiled warning from the hooded men out in the street. "How did it look like her? How is that even possible?"

"Things that live in the darkness tend to take on forms beyond human comprehension." Peter stepped back from the window. On the other side of the glass, the yard had gone silent. "If it was wearing her, then she's probably been dead for a while."

Wearing her. Like a skin. Wyatt sank into the nearest chair and bent in half, resting her brow against her knees. She focused on swallowing down one unsteady breath at a time. When Peter spoke again, his voice came from directly overhead.

"What are you doing?"

She didn't lift her head. "Everything you just said makes me want to throw up."

"Well, don't," he said. "It's not productive."

She sat up straight and glowered over at him. "I left my ax outside."

"It won't do you any good." He glanced back at the window. "She's stopped struggling. I'll go out and bury her tomorrow."

The thought of old Mrs. Germaine lying out there all day, at the mercy of vultures, turned her stomach anew. "Why not now?"

"Did you see how close to the house she came? I won't be caught at the edge of the grove when the sun goes down. I'll bury her in the morning."

"And then what?"

"Then we'll get to work." His blue eyes met hers through the kitchen's murky light. "I'm not the worst thing out there, Wyatt. If the last of the wards fall, there are fates worse than death waiting for us beyond the trees."

9

PEDYR

It took Pedyr a little over an hour to dig the grave. Six feet deep and three feet wide, just long enough for a body. The last one he'd dug hadn't managed to reach quite so far down. He'd still been small back then, all arms and anger, and he'd thrown up in the dirt well before he'd finished the job.

He didn't look at the old woman as he lowered her into the earth. He didn't say any last rites as he filled in the mound. Why should he? He hadn't known her. He didn't feel a thing for most of the living. He certainly didn't feel a thing for the dead.

When it was done, he set aside the shovel and waited, listening. The leafless grove at the edge of the wood was silent. No birds sang. Nothing rustled or chattered or scampered through the underbrush. The chapel cast the graveyard in a sundial shadow, the steepled gnomon reaching through the trees like a malevolent arm.

He knew he ought to go back. That to stay would do nothing but tighten the knot in his chest until he couldn't draw breath. He stayed anyway, crossing in and out of pockets of light and coming to stand by a tree sheathed in stacked white oyster mushrooms. Beneath it sat an unmarked grave, five years older and considerably smaller.

For a long time, he stood over it and said nothing at all.

"Wyatt came back," he finally whispered. He sank to the ground, leaning back against the barren pine. Beside him, a carpenter ant picked its way along the flat cap of a toadstool. "You told me she would, and I didn't believe you."

The answering silence felt like a listening ear. It was a needed reprieve. That ceaseless whisper didn't hound him here. The beast didn't like this place—the way the trees grew in close, the way the soil was sucked dry. The way there was nothing left to sustain it but the dead.

He drew James's lighter from his pocket, turning it over until the polished metal caught the light. He'd lain awake the previous night and watched the flint spit feeble sparks, his stomach in tatters.

"I don't think I can lose her again," he whispered. "Does that make me a coward?"

It was an absurd thing, to ask a question of the dead, and he felt immediately ridiculous. He set the lighter on the mound and then sat back, slinging his forearms over bent knees. Eyes shut, he let his chin drop to his chest. He felt dangerously close to crying.

"Fuck." His voice rebounded off the empty trees. "I wish you were here. You'd know what to do."

But it was only dirt. And beneath were only bones.

The phone was ringing when Pedyr came back to the house. For several seconds, he stood in the kitchen, his hands gritty with dirt, and listened to that impossible trill. He let it ring four more times before giving in, lifting the receiver to his ear.

"Wyatt." James Campbell's voice was edged in static. "Thank God. I wasn't sure if you'd answer. I've been calling and calling."

Pedyr said nothing at all. He didn't move. Didn't breathe. Didn't blink. On the other end, James sounded out of breath, as though he'd been running some great distance.

"Wyatt. You there?" Silence followed. Wariness crackled along the line. "Peter."

Quick as a shot, Pedyr hung up. He tore the phone off the wall. He chucked it into the trash and left the wires to hang from the empty jack, his heart beating hard. When it was finished, he went hunting for Wyatt.

He found her in the sitting room, curled on the sofa in front of the old rabbit-ear television. The day was warm, and she'd dressed in one of her mother's old floral sundresses. Braiding and unbraiding her hair, she silently contemplated a wilting crocus in a terra-cotta pot. A splayed-open journal sat cradled in her lap, and two of her fingers bled freely, pinpricks of red mottling the mess of her father's notations.

"I found some instructions in my dad's journals," she said without looking up. "Three parts blood, two parts powder. Add three drops of the compound to the soil. He made it sound easy."

A tiny bottle of ash sat on the table, its contents carbon black and lightless. Nearby, a little glass eyedropper lay tipped against the edge of a white ceramic mortar. A tacky crimson liquid pooled in the bottom. The flower itself looked moments away from death. A wilted petal slipped loose, fluttering to the floor in a withered violet helix.

"The instructions may be simple," he said, bracing his forearms against the back of the couch. "That doesn't mean what you're doing is easy."

She flopped into the cushion, angling her chin until her eyes met his. She'd worn lipstick again today, and her frown was a bold, pretty red.

"What's the difference?"

Face-to-face like this, he could count every last freckle on the bridge of her nose. Could see the ring of gold around her irises. The back of his throat itched. "A knife through the fourth and fifth rib will bleed an opponent dead," he explained. "You go in at a slight angle, you can take out both ventricles in a single strike. It's a clean kill. Simple. It doesn't make the killing easy."

Her eyes went wide. "Have you killed someone like that?"

"No," he said. "But I've suffered it, and dying is the simplest thing in the world. You don't have to do anything but sit there and take it. There are no instructions, no road maps. There's just the bloody end. It's as straightforward as it gets, but there's nothing easy about it."

This close, he could hear her swallow. "I thought you were supposed to be immortal."

"And I thought you didn't practice magic." He cast a sideways glance in her direction. "What happened?"

"We called a cease-fire, remember?"

"We did." He frowned down at her. "But that's not what changed your mind."

She peered into her palm, her bloody fingers curling into a fist. "I just keep wondering if maybe Mrs. Germaine wouldn't have been possessed like that if the wards were all intact."

And there it was. He rounded the couch, dropping onto its unoccupied half. Several more petals pulled loose in his wake, fluttering after him like confetti. "Maybe," he said, snatching a slip before it hit the ground. "Maybe not."

For a while afterward, they sat in weighted silence. He'd nearly ground the petal to dust between his thumb and forefinger before he finally garnered the courage to glance in her direction. When he did, it was to find himself being slowly dissected beneath her gaze.

"Was that James?" she asked. "On the phone?"

His stomach turned over. He focused on brushing remnants of the petal from his fingers, his molars grinding tight enough to crack.

"It was, wasn't it?" She drew onto her knees, her dress pooling around her as she turned to face him. "What did you say to him?"

"Nothing," he said, because that much, at least, was true.

"Okay, fine. What did he say to you?"

His left eye twitched, and he jabbed at it with a finger. He didn't want to talk about James. He didn't want to think about how close Wyatt was, or how many times they'd sat in these very positions, their hands not touching, the old box fan not working, the hot summer air pushing wetly from one side of the room to the other.

"You have to stay awake this time, Peter," James would chastise, pulling battered DVD cases out of his bookbag. *"This is Spielberg at his finest."*

These days, the TV was broken and James was gone and Wyatt was as good as dead.

"Let's work this through," he said, in lieu of answering her question. "Why use the black powder? Why doesn't the journal call for you to add Westlock blood directly to the soil?"

She sniffed, rubbing at the tip of her nose. "I don't know. I only used the ink because the journals told me to."

"Ink?"

"Yeah, powdered ink."

"Is that what you think it is?"

She sliced him a cynical glance. "It's in an *ink vial*. All it needs is a little feathered quill to complete the aesthetic."

"Hmm." He leaned over and plucked the vial off the table. Turning it over in his hands, he watched the hourglass shift of the substance within. "Did you know that bone makes an excellent soil additive? Farmers will often use organic bonemeal from slaughterhouse animals as fertilizer."

"I didn't know that, no," she said cautiously.

"Bonemeal comes in a powder," he went on, fidgeting with the granular stopper. "Sprinkle it on topsoil, add it to compost, and the plants eat it up. It's got everything they need to thrive—potassium, phosphorous, calcium. Add a dash of witches' blood, and suddenly the plants become a ward against evil. Coax them a little, and they'll bloom beneath your thumb."

Her eyes flicked to the vial in his hands. To the lightless matter within. He didn't like to think about it—the contents of the vial. The horrors he'd endured to produce it.

Simple, but never easy.

"This particular bonemeal is made right here on the farm." He did what he could to sound matter-of-fact. To keep her from seeing the way the truth of it tore at his chest.

He could feel her studying him as she asked, "What kind of bone is it?"

The question had claws. They sank into him. "The ingredients are straightforward," he said, tapping a finger to her open journal. "The hard part is collecting blood that's potent. You can tap a tree for its sap, but it doesn't become syrup until it boils. Your grandfather used to say that."

Next to him, Wyatt stiffened. "Why didn't you answer my question?"

"Because it doesn't matter."

"But you could have said chicken bone. You could have said they burned the bones of livestock, and I would have believed you."

It was too difficult to look at her, and so he didn't, sliding forward until his elbows caught against his knees.

"Don't lie to me, Peter," said Wyatt. "We can't have a truce if you're keeping secrets."

Gingerly, he set the vial back on the table. Glass clinked against galvanized wood. The quiet that followed was deep enough to hear a pin drop. "It's mine," he finally admitted.

"Your—"

"Bones. In the ink."

He didn't have to look at her to know that she'd gone perfectly still. That she was turning it over, desperately trying to make sense of it all. He knew, too, that she couldn't *possibly* make sense of any of it. Because he was sitting beside her, whole and hale, and now that she was back, no part of him was missing.

Her question crept out in a whisper. "How can they do that?"

"They burn the body," he said, his delivery flat. "When the fire subsides, they take the charred remains and grind them down to dust."

Mortar and pestle and a thick black paste. Carbon black in a brittle bottle.

That's all there ever was of him, in the end.

Next to him, Wyatt stared without blinking. "But, I mean, how is it *possible*?"

He knew what she was asking, and he didn't want to tell her. He didn't want her to know that he hadn't always been this way, scuttling from the shell of one life to another. That he'd been a real boy once upon a time—gasping for air on the mouth between worlds, blood pooling in his lungs and his father pleading with the hungry dark: *"I'll do anything, just let him live."*

He didn't want to tell her that most curses looked like gifts, at the start.

"The funny thing about immortality," he said instead, "is that death doesn't stick."

A soft mewl sounded, and a furred form leapt onto the back of the couch. His chest swelled at the sight of Slightly, the ancient family cat. She landed in his arms with a flick of her tail—another thing he'd lost the day Wyatt left, and here she was like she'd never gone.

The soft warmth of her little frame brought him a single well of comfort. Burying his hands in the calico mat of her fur, he said, "I've lived and died a hundred times on this farm. Maybe more. You lose track, after so many."

The implication of his confession ballooned between them. He couldn't bring himself to look at Wyatt. In his lap, Slightly butted her head against his knuckles, seeking affection. He rubbed the velvety patch behind her ear and added, "This is the oldest I've ever been."

He snuck a glance in Wyatt's direction and found her eyes wide and unreadable.

"Say something," he ordered.

She stammered, blinking rapidly. "The photos in the chapel—"

"Taken on the days I'd been marked for slaughter. For science."

The blood fled her cheeks, leaving her pale as a wraith. They lapsed back into an uncomfortable silence. Pedyr watched the petals drip from the dying crocus, conscious of Wyatt's stare carving up the side of his face, as though she were scouring him for evidence. He didn't know how to tell her that she wouldn't find a thing—didn't know how to explain that all his hurts were packed inside, festering where no one else could see.

Finally, she spoke, her voice small. "If I bled into the soil without the powder, would anything grow?"

"You could try. It didn't work for any of the Westlocks who came before you."

"That's why they've kept you all this time? To amplify their own abilities?"

"Without a greenskeeper," he said ruefully, "there's no one to hold the wall. It's your legacy."

"But without your bones, there is no Westlock legacy."

"Power has always come by taking. The Westlocks took."

She considered this, watching Slightly purr in his lap, belly up and content. Finally, she said, "No wonder you want me dead."

Maybe once upon a time. Maybe that rainy day beside the forest, resentment hot and sticky in his chest, the beast dangling his freedom before him like a carrot. But now? Now he had no choice.

Coward, crooned that infernal voice inside his head. *Don't put this all on me.*

Pain bit through him and he drew his hand back with a wince. Retracting her claws, Slightly slid onto the floor and trotted disdainfully out of sight, her bushy tail aloft. He sucked a tear of red out of his knuckle and rose to go.

It didn't matter that he'd lost his nerve the last time. It didn't matter

95

that they'd struck a temporary truce, or that he'd lain awake the previous night with guilt souring in his stomach, thoughts of Wyatt hammering in his blood. She was always going to die, before the end. He was always going to kill her. That was the deal he'd made, and there was no way out but through.

"Keep trying," he said, heading for the hall. "You'll get it."

He paused at the door, beckoned by the sound of his name. He didn't turn, but he could feel her stare boring a hole into his back.

"For what it's worth," she said, "I'm sorry for what they did to you."

Her voice liquefied what remained of his courage. He left her there without a reply, his stomach sick and his step unsteady, the beast's ageless whisper hissing down his spine.

10

WYATT

The kitchen table was full of dying plants. Tomato and cilantro, caladiums and touch-me-nots and purple petunias with the petals punched full of holes. Wyatt had gone out into the greenhouse and gathered them up one by one, picking the ones with withered leaves and heavy heads. The dull and the colorless and the dried. *"Nature has always been used as a ward against the dark,"* Peter had told her, and that was what she intended to do.

To bleed, the way the Westlocks who came before her bled—to secure the wards around the house and keep the dark of the forest at bay. Mostly, she wanted to avoid a repeat of what had happened with old Mrs. Germaine.

James would be there soon, and they could figure out the rest together.

He hadn't called again. Not with warnings, and not with advice. Three days had slow-crawled past. Three infuriating afternoons. Three tortured nights. In that time, she'd bled all ten of her fingers dry without success. She'd mixed blood and bone until black swallowed up the red.

She'd done her best not to think about what was in it. Done what she could to ignore the impossible implications of a boy who had lived and died a hundred times over the course of several hundred years.

97

Like Peter was a bud, ripped out of the soil just before he bloomed. Mined for his ashes and then replanted, the way farmers harvested crops and then buried the seeds.

It made her sick to think about it. All those summers smelling blood on his skin, and she'd never dug deeper. All those full moon nights wondering where he'd disappeared off to, and she'd never asked questions. As deep as his betrayal went, her own felt deeper still.

She channeled her agita into focus, following her father's written instruction to the letter. And yet, nothing happened. Simple, Peter told her, not easy, and he was right. Try as she might, the plants continued to slowly decay, until the kitchen smelled sweet and wet and her head began to ache. The crocus sat at the edge of the collection, a white mold blanketing the soil like snow. Like she was hastening its deterioration, just by being near it. Like her blood was a poison.

Now she lay facedown amid the scattered clay pots, music spitting through her mother's old headphones, Peter's shoe-leather cord fastened around her neck. Threading the little blue button along its lace, she let the soft hiss of rain lull her into a trance. For the past several hours, she'd accomplished exactly nothing. She hadn't bled. She hadn't moved. She hadn't had so much as a coherent thought. She'd only watched the silver rain drill sideways against the glass, listening to late-nineties pop on an endless loop.

Across the kitchen, three angry thumps sounded at the door. The current song faded into silence and the track switched over to something new. Dreamy synth chords fizzed through the interior of her skull. Rattled her eyes in their sockets.

Maybe that was it. Maybe inside her was something wrong.

Something warped and strange. Maybe all she knew how to do was make things rot.

Another flurry of knocks thundered through the kitchen. Wyatt flicked at a petunia. She watched its petals swirl to the floor like rotten confetti. She tried to imagine Peter as an immortal. She couldn't do it. Immortals were storybook fodder, stone and stern and prayerful. They were painted icons in a musty old cathedral or a marble bust in a busy museum.

The Peter she remembered always had a streak of dirt on his cheek. He crowed at the birds in the tops of their trees. He crawled after Slightly on all fours. He slept on his belly, one cheek mashed into her pillow. His favorite snacks were Hostess cupcakes. He'd peel the white swirl first, frosting flaking under his nail.

He'd always been the most human person she knew.

Outside, the henyard went far too silent. She stilled, then pried off her headphones, listening to the newly fallen quiet. There was the *drip, drip, drip* of water in the sink. There was the noisy overflow of rainwater in the gutters. There was the rattle of Slightly stalking mice in the pantry. And then, on the far side of the house, there came the shatter of glass. The telltale unfastening of a lock. The front door yanked open with enough force to shatter drywall.

Wyatt was up immediately, tucking the button out of sight beneath the mock neck of her mother's old dress. She veered out of the kitchen and into the hall, drawing up short at the sight of Peter beneath the lintel. He stood vulturine still, his hair dark with rainwater, his T-shirt wrapped around his fist. Frosted glass from the paneled front door twinkled like stardust at his feet.

"Oh," she said as innocently as she knew how. "Were you locked out?"

His lips peeled back from his teeth in a snarl. Silvery rivulets tracked lines down his chest as he stalked toward her on silent boots. She didn't stick around to watch his approach. Instead, she fled, taking the stairs two at a time, her heart climbing into her throat. It felt like a mirror moment from their childhood—Peter and James playing chess in the barn's cobwebbed loft. Wyatt, bored to tears, provoking them until they gave chase.

By the time Peter caught up to her at the landing, a fizzy burble of laughter had built in her chest. His arm crooked around her waist and she spun out, effervescent. She stifled a snort as Peter's hands slammed hard into the wall, bracketing either side of her head. The action brought them nose to nose in the hall.

"Do you think you're funny?"

"A little," she admitted.

One corner of his mouth twitched. "What happened to our cease-fire?"

"I made an executive decision for the good of the team. You're a terrible teacher. You've been looming over me for three days. I can't *focus*."

"So you locked me outside like a dog?"

"There's no reason to be so angry about it, Peter—it's just a little water."

"Is that right?" Something dangerous flitted through his eyes. "Just a little water?"

Before she could protest, he'd scooped her over his shoulder and headed back the way they'd come. Down the stairs and out into the rain, where the air was cold and crisp. She fought him every step, her stomach mashed into his shoulder, her feet swinging and missing. The rain drilled into her back, lashed her hair against her cheeks.

"Put me down," she snapped, punctuating each word with a punch to his vertebrae.

Over the rush of rain, she heard him ask, "Put you down?"

There was a wanton sort of amusement in the question. Her fists froze in midair.

"No, wait," she countered, recognizing too late the wooden slats of the dock, the freshwater cattails bowed low beneath the rain. "Peter, wait—"

Her protests were swallowed up by the stomach-wrench feel of falling, the hard smack of water. With a soundless cry, she sank beneath the murky glass of the millpond. Cold enveloped her entirely, and then she was submerged, kicking her feet free of the hopeless tangle of lily pads. When she surfaced, wet and sputtering, it was to find Peter smothering a smile. She treaded water, the white gauze of her dress fanning around her in lacy ripples.

"Are you *crazy*?"

His smile broadened, going crooked at the corners—the kind of rare Peter grin that used to set off sparklers in her stomach. Cupping a hand to his mouth, he called, "What's the matter, Dahlia? It's just a little water."

"Unbelievable," she muttered, swimming toward him in a half-baked breaststroke. "Such a child." And yet, there was a fizzle in her belly that wouldn't abate. A funny butterfly flutter she remembered all too well. *Dahlia*, he'd called her. The way he used to, back when she still thought they had forever. On the shore, Peter was still grinning ear to ear. She combed through the dense mats of fanwort, flipping him the finger as she went. Whorls of wet coontail clung to her arms.

And then, just when her toes dug into the muddy shelf, she felt it. The creep of fingers closing around her ankle. She met Peter's wide-eyed stare a single heartbeat before she went under. Bubbles erupted around her as she sank into the murky gloom. Lashed in pondweed, she thrashed at her constraints. Her heel connected with something hard as bone and rimed in muck.

She kicked again and again, fireworks popping into airless sparks beneath her chest. White spots danced before her eyes, dazzling the dark in a starry array as slowly, her thrashing stilled. Buoyant, her arms floated out to her sides in a frothy crucifix.

When things went dark, it felt like a mercy.

She woke to the sideways drill of rain, her ribs close to cracking beneath the frantic pump of Peter's palms against her sternum. Flopping onto her side, she expelled mouthfuls of muddied water, her throat burning. When at last she rolled back onto the muddy bank, Peter collapsed with her. They lay in silence among the reeds, both of them breathing hard.

She didn't know how long they remained there, neither of them speaking, before the rain began to slow. Forcing herself upright, she began the tedious task of plucking pondweed from her skin. Peter followed suit, propping himself on bent elbows.

"What the hell was that? Can't you swim?"

"What, you think I drowned on purpose?" She wrung out her hair, stifling the urge to shove him back down into the dirt. "There was something in the water with me."

He sat up straight, his eyes wide and his lashes beaded with rain-water. "What do you mean, *something in the water?*"

"I don't know," she said, untangling a leaf from her wet, knotted hair. "It's not like I could see anything down there. It was probably pondweed, but it was so tightly wrapped around my ankle that I swear it felt like a human hand."

A pause followed. When she peered over at Peter, it was to find him staring out at the surface of the millpond. All traces of familiarity had gone from his face, leaving only the knife-carved countenance of a killer behind. Dully, she wondered if this was what heartbreak felt like—looking into the eyes of someone she'd spent her whole life memorizing and finding nothing recognizable left over in their depths.

She didn't like that thought, and so she refused to sit with it. Twisting water from the hem of her dress, she clambered to her feet. "We should probably head inside."

He mirrored her without argument, going still as they came face-to-face. His temple was streaked in mud, his mouth a thin, angry slant.

"What?" She frowned down at herself. *"What?"*

Soaked in pond water, the lacy ruffle of her collar had turned to a second skin. Through it, the outline of his necklace was plainly visible. A pale blue eye, sheathed in ivory muslin. She didn't have time to be embarrassed—without a word, he'd reached for the stolen pendant. The leather shoelace bit sharply into her throat as he wrenched the cord up and over her head.

"That's mine," she snarled, groping for it.

He raised his arm just out of her reach. "Finders keepers."

"Grow up." Her blood rose to an angry boil, and she resisted the urge to stamp her foot. "You didn't *find it*, Peter, you stole it."

But he didn't answer. His attention had snagged on something just over her shoulder. Following his gaze, she located the source of his distraction. There, on the water's mirror glass surface, the pinched white buds of water lilies had begun to pucker, the flat crowns beneath rapidly yellowing. It looked like a film reel caught in fast-forward, splotches of brown rot punching through the leaves in a preternatural acceleration.

"What is that?" she demanded. "What's happening?"

A groove deepened between Peter's brows. "That's you."

"Me?" The white lilies continued to wither, spiked petals dropping into the water one after the other. "That's impossible. I'm not even doing anything."

His gaze flicked back to hers. Dropped to the little blue button in his fist.

"Impossible," he muttered thoughtfully, as though she hadn't said it first. And then he was off, his shoulders rounded beneath the rain, heading for the house without waiting to see if she'd follow.

By the time she showered and changed, the sun had set. She crept downstairs in a wool sweater and knitted stockings, wringing excess water from her hair. She found Peter in the sitting room, feeding bits of kindling into the fire. His chest was bare, his head bowed, his hair in a still-damp tangle. All of him was burnished in orange, the corded lines of him flickering between light and dark. He didn't look up as she joined him, curling herself like a cat into the battered wingback.

For a while afterward, she chewed on her thumb and watched him work, transfixed by the sight of that little blue button swinging from its cord. Withdrawing the poker from the fire, he sat back and watched the flames. He didn't look up at her.

"You were my first kiss," she said, before her courage could fail her. "Did you know that?"

"Third," he replied without missing a beat. "Emily Rathbone in the girls' locker room at St. Adelaide's. James Campbell in the chapel at Willow Heath."

A bit of bark peeled away from the log, its hide veined in a lit-cinder glow.

"Peter," she said, "in the window in a thunderstorm."

He still hadn't looked at her. Desperation prickled the back of her throat. "You were the first kiss that mattered."

A muscle ticked in his jaw. "Don't do that."

"Do what?"

"What you're doing." He jabbed the log with the poker. Sparks sprayed into the flue in angry red glimmers. "Don't try to appeal to my better nature."

"I'm not," she protested. His eyes met hers, cold and disbelieving. More meekly than she'd have liked, she asked, "Is it working?"

As if in answer, he rose to go. The poker snicked audibly into place against the tool rack, the sound of iron on iron shivering through the quiet as Peter picked his way toward the hall. Frantic, Wyatt launched to her feet after him, cutting him off at the threshold.

"Peter, wait."

He drew up short, inches away from colliding into her. Drained of fire-light, all of him looked marble cold. She swallowed the grit in her throat.

"Why do you wear my button?"

His eyes were as deadly as the millpond dark. "Get out of my way."

"No. Not until you talk to me. Truce, right?"

This made him pause. He regarded her in silence, composing his thoughts. "Do you remember Gaspar Allendale? He used to come every summer for the summit and bring his rifle. In the mornings, he'd take it out back and bag a buck."

"What does he have to do with anything?"

"You couldn't stomach it," he went on without answering. "But James and I would go out into the field and help him dress the stags where they fell. He'd leave the scraps for the coyotes, but he always took a token to celebrate the kill."

"A token." She tried to keep her voice light as a fanged realization bit through her. It didn't work. The words dripped out of her like venom. "A little premature, don't you think? You haven't managed to kill me yet."

His eyes flashed with something treacherous and he pushed past her, heading for the stairs. She didn't let him escape, matching him step for step, slipping in her stockings as she went.

"You know what else? I don't think you ever will. You could have done it my last night here. You had every opportunity." They were halfway up the stairs, her grip tight against the railing. "We were alone in the grove for hours. I know you had a knife. You could have gone through with it. But you didn't. You *didn't*, Peter."

He rounded on her so quickly, she nearly toppled backward.

"And why not?" It didn't feel rhetorical, the way the question ground out of him. The way it pummeled into her at a near shout. "It sounds like you've thought about it. So, tell me why I didn't do it. Tell me what stopped me."

"We were friends." She hated the way her voice shook. "A-and maybe you didn't mean to be. Maybe you didn't plan on it. But we were. I know we were."

His eyes were bright in the dark. The rest of him was all shadow—just the suggestion of a boy, the way he'd been that night in her window, his mouth on hers and the sky electric.

"The thing about Allendale," he said, "is that he wasn't a great hunter. He missed over half of his targets. The deer would hear him coming and take off like a shot. You know what I learned, watching him? It's a lot easier to kill something that doesn't run at the sight of you."

He watched as understanding took hold, the thin rictus of his smile unsteady. "We were never friends, Wyatt," he said. "You were always just the mark."

11

PEDYR

Pedyr had made a great many blunders in his numerous stunted lifetimes, but there were three mistakes that destroyed everything.

The first was befriending Wyatt Westlock. That was weakness—he'd meant to keep her at arm's length. The second mistake was kissing her. That was jealousy—he hadn't wanted James to have something he didn't. The third mistake was telling James what it took to kill an immortal.

That was desperation.

He hadn't planned to do it. It was only that he'd been so tired of dying. It was only that he'd spent so long packed with anger like gunpowder. When they took Wyatt, he hadn't been able to stop himself from detonating. From catching fire to all the things that reminded him how close he'd been to having what he wanted most of all.

The day of his confession, he'd been sitting in the tree outside her window. Her room was a wreck, mirror shattered and drawers askew, her upended jewelry box struggling through a distorted lullaby—things he'd torn apart in a desperate hunt for anything she might have left behind. The sky above the tree was gray. Ash slipped by in flickers of white. The barn had stopped burning hours ago, but the horizon was still dark with soot. He'd swung his feet beneath the branch and poked at the split in his lip, unable to stop fussing with it long enough for the cut to scab over.

He couldn't remember how long he'd sat there before James had joined him. An hour. Ten.

"You're a git," James said, sinking onto the branch beside him. *"You're drawing too much attention. If you don't get a grip, we'll never get out of here unnoticed."*

Pedyr rounded on him, surprised.

"Don't look at me like that." James's left eye had been swollen shut. The angry abrasion of Pedyr's knuckles marred his cheekbone. Though his father had snapped it back into alignment, his nose still looked broken. He flashed Pedyr a blinding grin. *"Obviously we're going to go and get her back."*

Pedyr tongued his lip, tasting blood. *"We can't drive."*

"First of all," James said, knocking into him, *"there's an enormous difference between* can't *and* not allowed. *Example: You're not allowed to set fire to things, and yet you keep on doing it anyway."*

"And second?"

James's smile had hooked at that. *"They can't just take her away from us. I won't let them."*

But it wasn't Wyatt that had been taken from him. It was a home. With her gone, he was trapped. Tethered to Willow Heath and to the ceaseless cycle of death and dying, cursed to live and die and live and die until the rivers dried up and the earth spun out of orbit. Until there was nothing left of men but ash.

He'd seen the dwindling powder stores in the attic. Knew the pressure Wyatt's father was under to return to the old ways, to resume the ceremonial killings and the midnight harvests. So long as he came back to life, he was a renewable resource. Their shield against the forest.

They'd never let him go.

"I can't leave," he'd said, his heart sinking with the weight of what he was about to do. *"But if you help me, I can distract them. You can get to her on your own."*

It was meant to be a secret. Something whispered between coconspirators in the tangled branches of the tree. How could he have known that there was someone listening to every word?

The crack of split wood set a flock of wild turkeys racing for cover. Pedyr stood in the henyard and watched them disappear one by one into the nearby brush, wicking sweat from his brow with the back of his glove. Setting another log atop the stump, he raised the splitting maul over his head and brought it down hard. Two felled halves collapsed onto the chip-strewn dirt. He shook out his hand, the rheumatic ache of his imprisonment still needling his bones. Off in the distance, the forest quivered beneath an unseen breeze.

It was nearly noon, and Wyatt hadn't come downstairs. Not since yesterday, when he'd left her alone in the dark of the stairwell. He set another log on the stump. Felt the snap of wood in his forearms. He was an idiot. He shouldn't have been so openly cruel—not when he was depending on her allegiance to see him through to the blood moon.

But then the way she'd watched him from her chair—her stare liquid gold in the flickering dark—had turned his insides molten. *"You were the first kiss that mattered,"* she'd whispered, and the heat in his blood quickly blistered into panic.

Another log split beneath his ax. Sweat trickled down his spine. He thought about James chasing the car down the drive the morning she left, halfway into his trousers and his father hot on his heels: *"Get back here, lad. You're making a fool of yourself."*

He thought about how he'd railed against his restraints until his wrists were bloody, his throat hoarse. How the voice of the beast was all that was there to console him, in the bitter end. *Sweet, lonely Pedyr. She left you behind. Do you see where weakness gets you?*

He couldn't afford to want Wyatt Westlock.

Not when she was dead already.

"Boy!"

He stilled, the ax frozen over his head, sweat chilling against his skin. A shotgun fired into the air, the reek of nitroglycerin crackling through the ether. The chickens scattered, frantic.

"I warned you, boy," drawled a voice through the nattering frenzy. "I told you what I'd do to you if I caught you sneaking around this house."

Slowly, he lowered the ax to the dirt. He didn't turn around.

"You're wasting your energy," he said to the empty sky. "I'm not afraid of you."

A stick snapped. The smell of spirits pummeled into him. "I'll pump you full of lead, that's what I'll do. Have myself a cold one while you pick shrapnel out of your guts. Is that what you want?"

The next time the gun went off, the bullet glanced off the picketed enclosure. Pedyr ducked down as the gate swung wide, wood exploding like grapeshot.

"You'd better run, boy," came that slow, southern twang. "Or next time, I won't miss."

In life, Billy Deacon had been a red brute of a man. Red cheeks, red nose, red rage. A gun fanatic and a big game hunter, he'd been drawn to the guild by the promise of a mark who didn't stay dead. In death, there'd been nothing red about him. He'd been pale white and wound in webbing, a feast for the forested dark. Tangled in the arachnid shadows where Pedyr had led him, his feet bare and his chest heaving, his ears ringing from a blow.

Now Billy was gaunt and gray. One of his eyes was gone, the hollow wriggling with maggots. Pedyr rose to face him, his hands in fists, his stomach turning over.

"You think you're better than me, boy?" Billy shambled forward in a death-rattle walk. "We're the same. There's not a shred of remorse in you. I saw it. I saw it in your eyes. You watched the widow tear me limb from limb and you felt nothing but rapture. That's what it's all about. The euphoria of a kill."

Pedyr's hands shook. "You're not real."

Billy's smile gaped wide, a skeleton's grin. When he spoke, it was the beast's voice that slipped out. "But the pit in your stomach is. I can smell it. I can taste the bile in your throat, hear the racing in your blood. You want to run, and run fast." A long-legged spider crept out from the black hollow of his nose and crawled along his cheek. "Do you remember how it hurt, digging slugs out of your femur? Do you remember what it felt like to lie awake, listening for the creak of a door, the scrape of a boot? Frightened as a rabbit, and so very alone?"

Pedyr turned away. He headed for the door. He wouldn't stay here and be mocked by his ghosts. The beast was a mind-flayer and a manipulator, not a hunter. It wouldn't hurt him—it only wanted to be fed. Pedyr was all it had. Just like it was all he had.

"You're still all alone," it hissed, both in his head and out of it.

"Even now that she's come home to you. Do you think she cares for your suffering? She left you once. She'll do it again."

"Stop talking." The words scraped out of him.

"As long as she lives," whispered the beast, "you will always be alone."

His fist slammed into the door. The screen rattled in protest, nearly popping loose. He shut his eyes, tipped his forehead to the cool wood paneling. When the beast spoke again, it came from directly behind him—a whiskey-sour reek that soaked into his skin.

"Your mother is waiting, Pedyr. She is trapped in the same eternal loop. Surely you haven't forgotten. Surely you remember where your loyalties lie."

He spun out, fists raised and swinging blind, and found the hen-yard empty. Off in the distance, the forest leered, dark and menacing. He didn't let it see him falter. He pried up the ax and set it to rights, then gathered up the firewood and stacked it in the shed.

He spent the remainder of the afternoon culling weeds in the garden, his knees buried in the fast-drying mud, his stomach sick. When it was done, he dragged a ladder out to the orchard and climbed to the highest branches to pick the last of the Black Oxford apples.

With the magic waning, a rot had crept in, puckering the low-hanging fruit so that it dropped, bug bitten, to the dirt. He carried the mealy helpings back to the house and washed them one by one, polishing them until they shone and setting them in a wide ceramic bowl. He tried not to think. The house around him was deafeningly silent. *Alone. Alone.*

In the garbage, the phone rang.

The sound trilled through the quiet, sizzling impossibly through

113

wires that hung suspended from the wall. Pedyr stood at the sink, apple in hand, and stared without breathing. The phone rang a second time. A third. A fourth.

Ignoring his better instincts, he fished the receiver out of the bin.

"I'm nearly there, Peter," came James Campbell's voice, the moment he'd pressed it to his ear. "Will you tell her what you've done, once we're all together again?"

The line went dead.

What remained of his conviction fractured. When the bowl flew into the wall, it shattered into a thousand shivering pieces. Apples rolled across the floor, collecting bruises, and he felt instantly regretful. His anger deflating, he knelt to collect the fruit, listening for the sound of Wyatt on the stairs.

She never appeared. In the window, a purple twilight had seeped into the sky. Near dark, and she was still in bed. He knew she was angry—knew she was avoiding him after yesterday's altercation—but surely, she would have at least come down to eat. Unease prickling through him, he set the apples on the counter and headed upstairs.

He made it as far as her bedroom before losing his nerve. He'd never gone in this way—through the door. He'd always sidled in beneath the window's open sash, his shins bark scraped and his palms stinging. He'd curl into bed beside her and fall asleep, lulled by the sounds of her breathing.

"I saw a nature documentary in school this year," James whispered once, crooking his arms beneath his head. *"About Komodo dragons. Did you know that they're not even real dragons? They're just giant lizards. They're still pretty ace, though. They have this poisonous anticoagulant in*

their bite. They don't even have to exert themselves. One bite, that's all it takes."

He'd fallen quiet after that, the two of them listening to the distant call of a whip-poor-will. Eventually, Pedyr's curiosity got the better of him. *"What happens afterward?"*

"Nothing, at first." James rolled onto his side. *"They wait. Sometimes for days, stalking their kill from a safe distance until they finally die. And then they feast."*

Pedyr sank back against the unoccupied half of Wyatt's pillow. *"Oh."*

Silence settled again. For a long time afterward, Pedyr thought James must have fallen asleep. But when he'd glanced up from Wyatt's sleeping face, it was to find two bright black eyes peering at him over the curve of her throat.

"You look at Wyatt like that," he'd said.

Pedyr's heart thudded dully in his chest. *"Like I'm waiting for her to die?"*

"No," James said. *"Like you're waiting for the chance to strike."*

The hallway was dark when Pedyr finally talked himself into knocking. He was answered by the muffled creak of the rotting willow. Beneath it came a silence that pitted his stomach. He pushed open the door to find the room empty. The bed had been hastily made, its quilted duvet tugged askew.

Wyatt was gone.

Outside the open window, everything was gray and formless, the wood spilling its shadows onto the meadow. A soft mewl brought his heart crawling into his mouth. He crept back downstairs to find

Slightly perched by the door, meowing to be let out. He opened it just a crack, watching as the old cat streaked out into the newly fallen dark.

And there, just beyond the bull gate, he saw it—a white orb bobbing between the trees. A flashlight, too dim to illuminate more than the white-wool wrist of its bearer. A dozen curses built in his throat as the light came to a sudden stop. It wavered there, chewed to pieces by the stunted arms of the old evergreens.

And then, with a blink, it went out.

Dark descended, and the wood swallowed Wyatt Westlock whole.

12

WYATT

Sometimes, in the dog days of summer—before the seasons changed and Wyatt's parents shipped her back to school—she'd curl up in the porch swing out front and watch the moths cluster around the lit onion lamps. Peter never joined her. So out in the open, it was far too likely that he'd be caught by her mother and shooed off the porch like a stray. But no one ever shooed James, with his dimpled smiles and his private-school manners, and so he was always close by, hands laced behind his head, studying the bats as they swooped through the dark.

"It isn't true that people get bit by bats sitting outside like this," he'd said one night, the swing creaking beneath them. *"Most get bit in their sleep. They don't even know it happened until the symptoms start to show. By then it's too late. They're already as good as dead."*

"Wow." Wyatt prodded at a peppered moth on her sleeve. *"Thanks for the nightmares."*

"It's not a nightmare, it's nature." His eyes had been gilded in lamp-light. His stare glittered with secrets. *"Imagine thinking you're safe, only to find that there's been something rabid trapped in your room with you all that time."*

The path ahead was dark. There was no light to cling to.

Wyatt stood in the pitch black of the front walk and searched the dark for the yellow flash of headlights. Straining her ears, she listened for the telltale crunch of asphalt beneath tires. She did what she could to ignore the way fear crackled like frost through her veins.

She'd spent her morning locked in her bedroom, avoiding Peter. She'd been lying upside down on her bed, dizzy with a head rush and growing hungrier by the minute, when her cell phone rang.

She'd nearly toppled off her bed in her rush to answer it, climbing onto the top of the dresser on all fours in an effort to keep what few bars had managed to find her. On the screen, a heavily saturated photo of her mother smiled up at her.

"Mom?"

"Wyatt, thank God." On the other end, her mother had sounded very far away. *"I've been trying to get ahold of you for days."*

She could have wept; she'd been so relieved. She'd drawn onto her knees, switching the phone from one ear to the other. *"I'm at Willow Heath. There's no service here."*

"Oh, honey, I know."

"You know?"

"Your aunt had a vision. She saw you there. Wyatt, sweetheart, I know what you must be thinking, but there's no need to stay. This was your father's mess. It isn't your burden to bear. Let the Campbells take care of everything—I'm on my way to you right now."

She'd tiptoed around the mention of Peter, the way she always had. Something flagged in Wyatt's chest. Something wordless and hollow. Through her bedroom window, she'd just been able to make out Peter in the henyard, his T-shirt sticking to his spine. She'd watched as he brought the ax sailing through the air. Wood split beneath the blow, and she'd felt the crack of it deep in her belly.

"I can't leave," she'd whispered. *"There's something in the woods."*

"It's okay." Her mother's voice had been just a touch too jagged, the connection choppy. *"You're a Westlock. The beast will let you pass unharmed."*

She'd faltered, going cold. *"You know about the beast?"*

"Do I know about your father's entire reason for existing? Of course." The signal was dying. Only every other syllable came through. *"—home—with me. We—so much—talk—bout."*

"Mom?" She'd risen onto her feet, toes creased and stomach wobbling. Outside, another log snapped in two. *"Mom, are you there?"*

"I'll tell you everything when I see you, okay? Meet me out by the road. I'll be there soon."

That was hours ago. Wyatt had spent the remainder of the afternoon trying and failing to coax Slightly into her carrier. All she had to show for it was a network of claw marks on the back of each hand and several hours of lost time. Still, her mother hadn't arrived.

Salem was just over three hours south. Not a short drive, but not overly long, either. Surely, she should have been here by now. Wyatt cupped her hands together, huffing heat into the space between her palms. She was steadily beginning to regret wandering so far from the house. This deep in the trees, the rancor in the air had a flavor. The quiet had a sound. It was turpentine and rot, the click of talons and the gnash of teeth.

In her pocket sat her father's old penknife, the leather handle engraved with the pelican crest. It was a meager means of protection after the incident with Mrs. Germaine, but she hadn't felt comfortable leaving the house empty-handed, and Peter had her ax.

She leapt as something pale white swooped past overhead. A barred owl, talons extended, its ghostly *who?* staining the silence. Next to her, the goat let out an accusatory bleat.

"I don't want to hear it," she griped. "No one invited you."

The goat bleated a second time, scraping its hoof against a snarl of roots.

"For the record," she added, desperate to keep the quiet at bay, "I'm not bringing you home with me. I don't like you. You don't like me. And even if that weren't the case, my aunt's apartment is definitely not livestock friendly."

Off in the distance, a twig snapped. Something unseen scuttled over the leathery crush of leaves. The sound rustled through her, turning her courage to smoke.

"God." She rubbed at the chill in her skin. "Where *is* she?"

As though she'd summoned her mother just by thinking of her, a pair of headlights rounded through the dark. Silver high beams knifed through the trees, turning the forest skeletal. Blind as a bat, she picked her way carefully forward, an open hand shading her eyes.

Off in the distance, a figure stepped into the light.

"Mom?"

The goat was at her heels, head down and horns at the ready, its bleat turning into alarm. The figure in the high beams came closer, silhouette whittled toothpick thin in the glare. She had just enough time for her relief to wither into fear before the lights clicked off and she was swathed in an impenetrable dark.

She grappled for her cell phone in her pocket, flicking on the flashlight and raising it in front of her. A face lit silver mere inches from her own. It peered at her out of a keenly humanoid stare, its smile split from ear to ear. With a scream, she dropped her phone.

"Disappointing," slithered a voice as she turned to run. "The bone warden said you were a witch, but all I see is an ugly little girl child."

She staggered over rivers of roots, directionless in the moonlight, and felt the bite of something sharp through her belly. Startled, she stared down at her navel. Her father's open penknife protruded from her core; her own bloodied fingers wrapped around the leather hilt. Unseen, the goat let out another shrill *maaa* as Wyatt staggered backward, sucking wind. In front of her, the humanoid creature had devolved into shadow, branch bitten and strange. Its eyes were little more than the fall of moonlight through the trees. There was no one there but her.

The world tipped. Her knees smacked into dirt. She tried to call for help, but all that came out was a wet gurgle. Her hands were tacky with blood. A widening bloom of crimson stained her sweater. There was so much red, and everywhere, pushing out of her in fat, angry ribbons.

Dying was simple, Peter said. But never easy.

"Oi!"

A branch snapped. There came the unmistakable clip of something running at an all-out sprint. And there, barreling into frame, was the knife-sharp version of a boy she used to know. Dark hair, dark eyes, a wide, slanted mouth.

"No." She dragged herself backward as he skidded to a stop, too afraid to trust what she was seeing. "Stay away."

Standing over her this way, James Campbell looked like a dark prince, his head crowned in moonglow. In his hands he clutched a woven wreath of yellow dill.

"Jesus *Christ*, Wyatt." The moonlight leeched out of him as he dropped to his knees. Reaching for her, he stayed her hands. Blood ran and ran in sticky rivers between their fingers. "Leave it. Don't pull it out."

His hands on hers felt real. Human and warm and true.

"Get away from me." She scrambled backward, managing to level a feeble kick to his shin. Stars burst across her vision in a flurry of white. "You're not—you're not Jamie."

He regarded the widening circle of crimson on her sweater. "What the hell did he do to you?"

"This wasn't Peter," she gasped out. "It was—" But she didn't know what it was. The trees. The shadows. That awful, smiling face. Shutting her eyes, she tipped her head back until its crown found purchase against the dirt. Softly, she whispered, "I thought it was my mom."

Her teeth chattered. Her fingertips were slick and sticking. When she finally summoned the energy to peel open her eyelids, it was to find James standing astride her shivering frame, the wreath sagging in his grasp.

"We can't stay out here," he said. "Dill makes a passable shield, but it won't keep the older cryptids away."

"Cryptids," she gasped, feeling a little bit drunk and extremely delirious.

"Yes, cryptids." His dark brows drew together. "I don't even understand what you're doing out this far. This is the mouth of hell, Wyatt, not a state park. Every single thing that crawls out of the dark has been bent by the abyss. If something big sniffs us out, we're buggered. I'll have to move you."

"I can—I can walk."

"Walk? You're hemorrhaging blood."

She shut her eyes again. "Don't be dramatic."

She felt the give of her body as he dragged her, pulling her over the dirt and through the grass, under the metal beams of the bull gate. Out of reach of the violent wood and the watchers in the trees. When at last he drew to a stop, she opened one eye and peered up at him.

"Stay with Mama," he instructed. "I'm going to find Peter."

"James." His name came out on a wet, sputtering hack. She wanted to tell him to stay. She wanted to beg him not to leave her there, dying alone in a dew-slick field. Caught in the crosshairs of hell. All that she managed was, "Who's Mama?"

As if in reply to her question, the goat let out a quiet bleat. It curled up alongside her, the coarse fur of its body warm against the chill in her skin. After that, time came in rushes and in stops. She didn't know how long she lay there, slowly bleeding out.

Her head swam and the stars swam too, wheeling overhead in skeins of brightest white. Eventually she closed her eyes. When she opened them again, it was only for an instant. Only long enough to see that the grass beneath her had been replaced with sheets, the spiral of stars with the sheer gauze of her canopy. Everything hurt. Her eyes were heavy. Somewhere in the room, two shapes converged into one. Duplicated into two. Bodies, formless and pacing.

"What the hell were you doing," snapped Peter, "luring her out there like that?"

"She was looking for her mother," came the reply, and the voice was one she didn't recognize. Soft and sinister, like the slow roll of a stone along gravel. "You forget I don't inhabit the living. There are others out there with a taste for Westlock blood. You should have been watching her."

Dark was rising and rising inside her. Swelling through her in a wet, heavy sleep. She wanted to speak, to cry, to shout, but all she could do was dream.

PART TWO

THE STRANGER

For as well as I have loved thee, mine heart
will not serve me to see thee,
for through thee and me is the flower of kings
and knights destroyed.

Le Morte d'Arthur, Thomas Malory

13

WYATT

Wyatt woke to the groan of the willow outside her window. She opened her eyes, trailed out of dreaming by visions of algae blooms, the memory of skin gone cyanotic beneath an LED glow. Drawing a great, sucking breath, she blinked away the dregs of her nightmare, taking silent stock of her surroundings as she did. There was Cubby, his singular button eye peeking out over the top of the quilt. There was the sagging canopy, bunched at the posts in great gauzy knots.

And there, lounging in a chair by the bed, was James Campbell.

He was fast asleep, his legs propped on the edge of her mattress and his hair a messy flop of black. With a sigh, his chin lolled against his flannel-clad chest.

"Jamie," she whispered.

His head snapped up at once, eyes alert beneath hooded lids. In the bald light of day, it took her a moment to slot his features into place. Everything on him was sharper than she remembered, as though someone had taken a carving knife and whittled the prominent lines of his cheeks, the crooked bridge of his nose. A pale white scar formed a starburst under his left eye. A parting mark from Peter, five long summers past.

"You're awake." He reached for the water on her bedside table, pressing the sweating glass into her hand. "Good. Have a drink."

"Thanks." She tried to sit up and found that she couldn't. Her midsection was stiff with gauze, her belly taut with a stitched-shut ache. "Ow. How long have I been asleep?"

He scrubbed a hand over the length of his face. A dark ring sat on each finger, onyx bands lightless in the gloom. "A day? Maybe more. It's tough to tell. The clocks in this house are all wrong. It's been a while since someone set them."

"Oh." She dragged a bead of water down the glass with a fingertip. "Where's Peter?"

"I'm dealing with him," he said. Then, before she could ask what *dealing with him* meant, he added, "I'm sorry for the position my father put you in. He should never have sent you out here by yourself. I don't know what he was thinking."

She thought of how she'd found Peter, strung up like cattle in a slaughterhouse, the roots of the willow tree slowly devouring him. She thought of the terrible things they'd done to him—the little mattress stuffed with secrets, and the vials and vials of bonemeal in her father's curio cabinet. She shut her eyes. Willed the room to stop spinning.

Quietly, she asked, "Have you always known?"

She heard James shift in his chair. "Have I always known what?"

"About Peter."

He didn't answer. Not right away. The silence felt like a *yes*, and a ripple of anger distended her belly. She opened her eyes, intending to say something scathing. Something in the way James sat—his forearms braced against his knees, his shoulders taut—made her pause.

He spun a black ring slowly around the tip of a finger, a muscle firing in his jaw.

"The first year my father brought me to Willow Heath, I didn't want to be here," he said. "My friends back home got to have real summers. Their parents were jetting them off to Lake Como and Saint-Tropez, and I had to spend my holiday trapped in Maine, playing nice with a weepy little brat and a boy who hardly said a word."

She huffed out a breath. "Don't be an asshole."

"I'm not saying you didn't grow on me," he said, and slid the ring back onto his finger. "I'm only telling you the truth."

"And what's that?"

"I didn't know about Peter. Not at the start. But I'd been threatened with my first expulsion that year. My mother was mortified. My father was furious. He told me that if I wanted him to pull some strings—get the headmaster to look the other way—I shouldn't let either you or Peter out of my sight."

Understanding tilted Wyatt's world on its axis. "You were a buffer."

"I don't think there's a word," James said slowly, "for what the three of us were to one another back then."

She stared at the starburst of white on his cheekbone. Evidence of Peter's true allegiance. Proof that he'd never been theirs at all.

Swallowing the sting in her throat, she asked, "And what are we now?"

"Enemies," he said immediately. "Some of us, anyway." Patting the quilt, he rose to go. "Drink your water. Get some rest. Let me handle Peter."

"Handle him how?"

But James was already gone, the door clicking shut behind him.

She stared at the place where he'd been, fighting back tears. *Don't cry*, went the mantra in her head. *Don't cry.* Though she managed to blink her eyes dry, there was no assuaging the sting of betrayal in her skin. She thought of the chapel's kaleidoscopic haze, the bloodred crush of her hand between Peter's and James's. *It's the three of us. Always.*

In the end, both of them had only been pretending.

All Peter wanted was to escape. All James wanted was to go home. And she, capricious and ridiculous, had found solace in them both. That bitter simmer in her throat rose to a rolling boil. It coalesced into a scream. When she threw the glass, it exploded against her closet door in a thousand crystalline pieces, raining to the floor in sparks and glimmers. She fell back against her pillow and surveyed the damage, sore and unsatisfied.

Minutes passed. An hour. No one came to see what she'd done—to chastise her or otherwise. Downstairs, the house stayed as silent as a grave.

Eventually, she slept—in fevered fits and sweating starts. Tangled in a nightmare, she staggered through the pitch-dark forest, a knife in her belly and blood on her hands, a horrible, terrible rot ribboning out of her skin. And there—*there*—in the shivering abyss, she heard him.

"Wyatt, you bitch. What the hell did you do to me?"

When she woke again, it was morning. The windows were open, and a cool breeze crested through the room, ruffling the gauze of her canopy. Slightly sat in the windowsill, eyes locked on the far-distant trees. Atop her quilt, someone had left behind a tray of food.

It wasn't the stale bread and hard-boiled eggs that drew her eye, though her stomach snarled at the sight. It was the photograph, its now-familiar grayscale peeking out from beneath the chipped floral of a plate. She worked it free to find the much-younger version of Peter peering up at her, his eyes solemn beneath the brim of his sailor's hat. The pang in her chest was an unwelcome one.

She didn't want to feel sorry for him.

She wanted to hate him.

"It was someone's idea of a joke," came a voice from the door. She glanced up, startled, to find Peter hovering in the dimly lit hall. In his hands he held a terra-cotta pot, the blighted stems within gone fuzzy with white. He lifted his chin toward the photo in her hand. "The hat, I mean."

He ducked into the room, his knuckles white against the pot and his boots lipped in mud. His gaze slid to the broken glass on the floor.

"I'm not an easy kill," he admitted quietly. "I can take a lot of hits. The guild took photos as documentation. They wanted a visual record to track which years the ritual worked, and which years it didn't. It changed every summer. The method, I mean. Usually, it was knives. Sometimes swords. They liked the ceremony of it, I think. But there were other approaches. Racks and wheels, bullets and scalpels and slugs. Whatever it took."

Wyatt held her breath. Across the room, Peter still hadn't looked at her. Tucking the pot into the crook of an elbow, he reached for the music box on her dresser. With a butterfly-light touch, he set the ballerina upright on her spring. She sagged instantly, cranking out a single broken note.

"The summer that photo was taken," he said, still fiddling with the box, "a man named George Donnelly had the idea to bind my ankles to bricks. They took me out to the millpond and threw me off the dock."

Wyatt turned the photo over. Her stomach was sick. "Why are you telling me this?"

"Because you asked. The other morning in the kitchen, you asked what it took. I should have told you."

The hand around her ankle. The feel of her heel colliding into bone. Understanding swam into her stomach, vile and wriggling. "It was *you* down there?"

"Your blood," he said wryly. "My bones. That's what it takes to keep the dark at bay. The Westlocks have always felt that the end justifies the means."

"But drowning a little boy? That's unspeakable. It's—it's *monstrous*."

The tendons in his throat worked in a swallow. "Do you remember when you were small, and your mother used to read you the story of the little Dutch boy who saw a trickle of water running from the dike? He plugged it with his finger and sat there all night, freezing and alone, to keep the dam from bursting."

She remembered. She remembered leaving her window open wide, the bit of cornbread wrapped in cheesecloth she'd left on the sill like an offering. The twig snap of Peter's shadow as he climbed into the willow to listen.

"It's not the same thing," she countered. "The boy in that story was a hero. He did something brave. No one bound him with rope and shoved him in there."

Peter's gaze walled off, icing into an impenetrable frost. "The creature you encountered in the woods—it can mimic anything. That's how it hunts."

She wanted to tell him not to change the subject, but all she could think of was that horrible smile—that cold, reptilian stare. She suppressed a shudder. "It sounded just like my mom."

Peter's frown deepened. He looked angry, like maybe she should have known better. "It almost killed you, Wyatt. And it's nothing compared to what else is out there. You think what the guild did to me is *monstrous*? When the wards fall, the dam breaks. What's out there in the dark is beyond your imagination. What's the death of one little boy against the bowels of hell?"

"Are you *defending* what they did to you?"

"Never." Ferocity chipped away at the ice in his eyes. "But I need you to understand what it is we're up against. And I also need you to know what you're capable of." Crossing the room in three hesitant strides, he set the pot on her bedside table. The cloying smell of rot wafted over her. Out of the soil rose a tiny cluster of black trumpet mushrooms, their caps curled like petals. Quietly, Peter said, "Someone once told me that there's a second life in dying things."

Her hands tightened into fists in her lap. "What's that supposed to mean?"

"What do you think?" His eyes slid to the shattered dusting of glass across the floor. "The pots in the kitchen sprouted blewits in the night. Black trumpets typically only grow in calcareous soil, once something living has started to decay."

Something unsteady wormed its way into her chest. Something sick and wriggling. She wanted to ask how it was possible, but it would have been a waste of a question. She knew exactly how. It was innate—the smell of rot, the cloying reek of aquarium water gone sour. The memory of Micah Barclay on his knees, veins popping into purple and his hands clutching his throat, a crowd gathering in the open door.

"What's happening?"

"—shit, he's choking!"

"She did something to him, she's—"

"Someone call 9-1-1!"

She wanted to curl in on herself and disappear. Shutting her eyes, she settled on a lie, cold and flat. "I had nothing to do with that. I've been up here the whole time."

"Dahlia," coaxed Peter softly, and the nickname lit a flame in her chest.

"Don't call me that," she spat. "We're not children anymore."

"Stop acting like a child, then." The floor creaked beneath his boot. "Open your eyes."

She obliged, turning her face toward the window. She didn't want to see the proof, decomposing at her bedside. She didn't want to think about the swirl of ambulance lights against the whitewashed brick of the Barclay house, or the way no one would go near her, after it was over.

"Look at me," ordered Peter.

She fixated on a yellow warbler as it flitted between the weeping cattails. "I don't want to."

"Wyatt." His fingers crooked beneath her chin, guiding her gaze back to his. "You told me you didn't practice magic."

"I don't." Her throat was tight. "Not on purpose."

He withdrew his hand, flexing out his fingers as if it hurt him to touch her. She hoped it did. She hoped it shattered him the way it shattered her.

Sliding his hands into his pockets, he asked, "Do we still have a truce?"

She peered up at him. The leather cord sat knotted at his throat, disappearing out of sight beneath the collar of his shirt. The last time she'd seen him, he'd been a shadow on the stairs, the cruelty of his confession sharp enough to cut bone.

"You were always just the mark."

She wanted to tell him there was never a truce. She wanted to scream in his face, to tell him to get out. To tear into him until he bled the way she did. Instead, her eyes landed on the back of the photo in her lap. The penciled-in date was so faded, it was nearly illegible. A hastily scribbled epitaph for a boy who no one mourned.

Quietly, she asked, "What do you want?"

"Come back out to the millpond with me," he said. "Last time, you rotted the lilies. Let's see if we can find a way to tap into your power before anything more sinister than the mimic slips through the cracks."

14

PEDYR

The walk to the millpond was excruciatingly slow, hindered by Wyatt's abject refusal to accept any help. Collapsing against the drooping bough of a lilac tree, she pressed her hands to her abdomen and stared out at the distant millpond, her eyes glassy and her mouth tight.

"I'm fine," she grumbled, when Pedyr offered her his hand. "Don't touch me."

She'd worn one of her mother's old dresses, the shapeless floral button-down all she'd been able to manage on her own. Her lips were painted in that dark, dahlia red and her uncombed hair fell loose around her shoulders. Framed by the dripping lilac blooms, she looked like something fey—like she'd just stumbled out of a fairy ring after a fortnight of dancing, her shoes in tatters.

It turned his stomach, to think of her alone in the house, the mimic whispering in her ear. He should have known the forest would try to lure her away from him, to swallow her up the moment his back was turned. He hadn't slept a minute since he'd stumbled out into the dark to find her being carried down the walk, her arms limp and her torso bloodied, the light going out of her eyes.

"It's just a few more steps," he coaxed.

"I was stabbed in the *stomach*, Peter," she said, plucking a petal from the collar of her dress. "My eyes are working just fine." She didn't move from her position against the tree. "For what it's worth, I still think we should have let James in on the plan."

"He's not a part of this," he rushed to say, his insides icing over.

Beneath the lilac drips, Wyatt looked unconvinced. "He's going to wonder where we are."

"That's fine."

She fixed him in a hard stare, and he braced himself for an argument. When none came, some of the tension bled out of his bones. She brushed past him without another word, trailing slips of violet as she went, sweat beading on her brow.

The rowboat waited at the water's edge, its hull wedged in mud and the stern bobbing in the reeds. She paused along the muddy bank and regarded the little boat sideways, hugging her arms to her middle as though they were all that held her intact. For several seconds, they stood together in silence and watched a pair of mating dragonflies crest along the pond's glassy surface.

Finally, he cleared his throat. "Let me help you in the boat, at least."

"No, thank you." The blunt force of her delivery transformed the politesse to a profanity. Wobbling slightly, she looped her legs over the hull and sank into the rowboat's weathered helm, wincing as she went. He waded in after her, water ringing the cuffed hem of his trousers as he pushed the boat out of the shallows.

Neither of them said a word as he rowed them out to the middle of the pond. The air was thick with the croak of bullfrogs, the nearby tremolo of a loon. A few yards away, a turtle slid off a log and disappeared under the surface with a soft plop. He watched the ripples distend beneath the puckered water lilies and thought about the little skeleton wedged in the muck below them.

Most days, he tried not to remember drowning. The cold, interminable force of it and the pondweed in his lungs—the way he'd survived just long enough to deteriorate.

At the helm, Wyatt must have been thinking the same thing as she peered over the rowboat's teetering edge. "What if I wake your bones again?"

He froze, the oars halfway out of the water. "What do you mean?"

"The hand I felt around my ankle—was that my doing, too?"

"No," he said, though it came out more brusque than he'd intended. There was a name for that kind of power—a word for the witches who raised the dead, crouching over the graves of their lovers with garments rent and teeth gnashed, their wails piercing the skies.

Banshees, the history books called them. Every last one of them had burned.

"I don't know how to explain the bones," he admitted, dipping the oars back into the pond. The rowboat knifed through the water's glassy dark. "Maybe they were tangled in something else. Like you said, it was dark. You were panicking."

"I felt what I felt," she shot back, a little hotly. "*Something* grabbed me."

"That's impossible."

She huffed and turned her gaze to the shore, where the far distant treetops peeked over the hills like a waiting army. This time, the stretch of silence between them felt unbearable. He wanted to pick at it, like a scab. To pry it up and see what bled out from beneath. He wondered how long they had before their absence was noticed. Before *he* came looking.

"Do you mourn yourself?"

Wyatt's question came out of nowhere, so soft he nearly missed it. When he didn't answer, she fell to picking at the frayed thread of a bandage on her littlest finger.

"I'm only asking because there's all those little graves out by the chapel, and none of the headstones are marked. I used to wonder who was buried there, but now—do all of them belong to you?"

His stomach dropped. "Most of them."

"How do you stand it?" she asked. "I feel like I'm constantly mourning the person I used to be before—" She paused, her thought going unfinished. "It must be surreal, that's all, to stand at your own grave."

"I don't think about it," he said dryly.

"Liar," she said, and sat back on the heels of her hands. "But that's okay. I try not to think about it, either, if I can help it."

Resisting the urge to pry, he pulled the oars out of the water and set them at their feet. Nudged by the wind, the rowboat revolved in a sleepy helix. He did what he could to keep himself from thinking of summers past—of James in the boat with them, sprawled out like a prince on a yacht. Wyatt, her fingers trailing in the water, the gilded figurehead at the prow of their ship—a carved goddess made for guiding men into black seas.

"Do you mourn?" she'd asked. All he knew how to do was mourn.

Across from him, Wyatt watched a swallow wing through the sky over their heads. "Is this the plan? To sit here until dark?"

"No."

"Okay." She fiddled with a button on her dress. "So, what now?"

He didn't know. He didn't know what it took to coax Wyatt's abilities to the surface. Not blood—she hadn't been bleeding the morning she set him free. Not bone—she hadn't used the compound that day in the millpond, or as she lay confined in her bed. She was a Westlock, yes, but she was a Beckett, too. And the Beckett bloodline had a legacy of its own.

"Tell me about the first time you drew on your abilities."

She snapped upright with a wince. "Excuse me?"

"Walk me through it," he said. "Tell me what was happening around you—what was going through your head. Retrace your steps, and maybe it'll help us pinpoint the catalyst."

"It won't."

"It might."

"It won't," she said again, in a voice cold enough to chill the dead. "Try something else."

He slumped back with a groan. Across from him, Wyatt's glower was guillotine sharp.

"Admit it," she said, after a moment's silence.

He pushed at the cuffs of his sleeves, overheating in the itching wool of his sweater. "Admit what?"

"Admit that you have no idea what you're doing."

"I never said I did. And for the record, the only thing wrong with my approach is that you're refusing to cooperate."

"Because it's a stupid idea."

"That's not it." He leaned forward, palms braced against the bench. "You're afraid."

"Afraid?" The laugh that cracked out of her was caustic. "God,

Peter. You're so dense. Look at me. Since I've come back to Willow Heath, I've been threatened, haunted, and nearly killed. *Afraid?* I'm terrified."

He sat back. "So do something about it."

"I can't."

"Why?"

"Because."

"Because why?"

"Just *because*, Peter, okay? Can we please just leave this alone?"

"Is it because of Micah?"

He hadn't meant to say it, but the question flew out of him anyway, bitter and accusatory. Every night since she'd come home, she'd thrashed awake with that same name at her lips. Across from him, all the color had rushed out of Wyatt's face, leaving her bloodless in the boat's bobbing prow.

"Don't," she whispered. "Don't ever say his name to me."

So then, his instinct was correct. It didn't bring him the satisfaction he expected. Instead, a sickly green jealousy swam into his stomach. He was just about to say something more when, out of the corner of his eye, he saw a flicker of movement in the shallows. The smell of decaying leaves rose to meet him just as he caught sight of the thick red algae blooming atop the water's surface.

"Wyatt."

"Don't talk to me," she bit out. "I want to go back."

"Wyatt, *look*."

She followed his gaze. "What—is that *blood*?"

A shout rang out from the opposite shore. There, standing knee-deep in the water, was the very last person he wanted to see. The wind picked up, buffeting the little boat from side to side—carrying with it the unwelcome burr of James Campbell's voice.

"Don't let him see what you can do," Pedyr said to Wyatt, and sank the oars back into the water before she could argue.

By the time they made it to shore, the wind had whipped itself into a frenzy. It batted at the prow, threatening to capsize the little boat entirely. He swung himself into the waist-deep shallows, refusing to meet the storm-dark eyes opposite him as they worked to guide the hull into the mud. When he turned to help Wyatt out, it was to find her ankle-deep in the water, her dress soaked through and her hands on the helm, a wordless challenge in her eyes.

"Here's an interesting little factoid." James's voice pummeled into him, hard and haunting. "The reason King Arthur held his meetings at the round table was so no one person could claim precedence over the other. They all convened as equals. Hard to do, when one of your party isn't alerted to the gathering."

"Told you he'd be mad," muttered Wyatt as Pedyr said, "We were just getting some air."

"There's plenty of air back at the house," came that impossible voice from behind him. "Unless you went out to the pond because you didn't fancy being overheard. In that case, Peter, my feelings are hurt."

He whirled to face his ghost head-on and regretted it at once. They were brought nose to nose, those lightless eyes as unfamiliar to him as a stranger's. The first crack of lightning blistered overhead as that awful smile knifed into a dimpled grin. Too wide to be just right. Too sharp to belong to something human.

"Nothing to say?"

Pedyr bristled. "I have plenty."

"I'll bet you do. But you'll keep it all to yourself until it's much, *much* too late. And then you'll explode, setting fire to everything and everyone in your path. Have I got it right?"

The first drops of rain had begun to fall. "Fuck off."

"Take the compliment, Peter." Thunder rolled along the eastern horizon. "You destroy things so beautifully. I've never seen anything like it."

He surged forward without thinking and careened neatly into Wyatt's outstretched hand. Bristling with visible fury, she wedged herself between them. "What the hell is wrong with you?"

Over her shoulder, that blinding smile was too-perfectly crafted. "Me, or him?"

"Both of you." The wind whipped her hair into her eyes. "I mean, God, if anyone is going to be angry, it's going to be me. I have every right to hate you both, but you don't see me acting like a Neanderthal. We've got bigger problems than some stupid childhood grudge."

"He tried to kill you, Wyatt," came the slick reminder. "And he'll do it again, the moment he has the chance. Is that a *stupid childhood grudge*? Or is it all water under the bridge now that he's finally paying you an ounce of attention?"

She stiffened. "Excuse me?"

"You heard me."

This time, when the thunder rolled through the sky, it was directly overhead. "Wow." Wyatt's laugh was bitter. "I forgot what an asshole you can be when you feel like it."

Withdrawing her hand from Pedyr's chest, she stalked off without a glance back at either of them, swallowed up in the wild undulating of the meadow. The moment she was gone, those brimstone eyes slid to Pedyr. He did what he could to suppress a recoil.

"What the hell are you doing?" he demanded.

"I'm protecting my investments," came the simple reply. "You failed last time. There won't be a second."

Something silver arced through the air, the object lobbed in his direction with perfect precision. Pedyr threw his hands out just in time to catch James's lighter—the one he'd left on the unmarked grave out in the grove. He ran a finger along the dent, fear burrowing into his skin like a tick.

When he looked up, he was alone, the rain falling hard.

Tucking the lighter into his pocket, he veered deeper into the fields, his heart hammering in his throat and lightning lacing through the sky. By the time he crested the hill toward the grove, wielding a rusted shovel from the woodshed, he was soaked through to the bone.

Up ahead was the chapel, lit white beneath an electric sky. From out of the dirt rose the dozens and dozens of crumbling tombstones, his bones left as meager offerings for the beast. He passed them by without a second glance, heading for the solitary mound at the far corner of the graveyard.

He didn't know what he was doing here, only that he had to see it for himself. He had to know the face that haunted him wasn't just a wicked amalgamation, but the real thing—a sock puppet boy with a cryptid grin.

Half-blinded by the torrential fall of rain, he began to dig. And dig. Finally, his hands calloused and his clothes dark with mud, he stood back and wedged the shovel into the dirt. Through the trees, the storm roiled, sick and dark as the sea.

And there, in front of him, James Campbell's grave sat empty of its bones.

15

WYATT

Wyatt was running a fever.

She stood in the upstairs bathroom, barefoot and shivering. Teeth chattering, she scoured the medicine cabinet for something to numb the febrile ache in her skin.

When she was young, her mother used to tell her that she'd catch her death standing outside in the rain. She'd race in from a thunderstorm—her hair sticking to her cheeks in cold, wet coils—and dive into bed, terrified of the chill she'd ferried in behind her. These days, she knew it was only superstition. Something adults liked to say, when there was nothing else worth saying. Like when James's father warned them that drinking coffee would stunt their growth. Or when her aunt Violet told her that if she crossed her eyes for too long, they'd get permanently stuck.

She'd lain awake all night, a flu-like flush creeping up her throat. Unable to exorcise the chill from her bones, she'd piled on blanket after blanket, until the unbearable cold turned to a hellfire heat, and she kicked them all free. In the end, she'd settled for curling in her window seat and listening to the patter of rain on the roof. Afraid to sleep. Terrified to dream.

When her search of the cabinet yielded nothing more than a packet of old plastic razors and some dental floss, she slammed it shut. She was met with her own silver-plated reflection, freckles dark against skin gone sallow.

"Get it together," she snarled.

Toeing across the tile, she drew the curtain shut around the wide clawfoot tub. Everything felt just a touch too loud, sound scraping through her skull like sandpaper. She undressed slowly, steam swirling into the mirror.

Through the bathroom's beveled window, she could just make out Peter in the henyard, the chickens zipping around him in a feathered flurry as he mended the latch on the gate. From this vantage point, he looked gut-achingly human, his hair flopped over his brow and a silver rivet scrunched in his mouth like a toothpick.

He tried to kill you, tiptoed James's voice through her head. *And he'll do it again the moment he has the chance.*

When the water was hot as a kettle boil, she climbed into the tub. The air was thick with steam, and she relished in the scald of heat against her back. Lathering soap into her hands, she did her best not to look at the ugly scarring along her abdomen. She'd seen enough of the wound in the mirror, the line of it pinched and angry, sloppy sutures knotted at the corners.

She was midway through rinsing her hair when, on the other side of the curtain, the bathroom door clicked open.

"Hello?" She rubbed a trail of suds from her eyes, straining her ears. "James?"

No one answered. Not James. Not Peter. Not anyone.

"Slightly?" She shut off the faucet, letting the water slow to a trickle. "Hello?"

The only reply was the ancient rattle of the pipes behind the wall. She groped blindly for a towel, then hastily scrubbed herself dry. Wrapping it tight around her middle, she drew back the curtain and stepped out of the tub, trailing water as she went.

She didn't mean to scream.

A scream forced its way out of her anyway, rending the quiet of the house. She clasped her hands over her mouth, stifling the shriek before it could build into something more.

One of the chickens lay in the sink, its bay feathers bloodied, its neck snapped at a grotesque angle. In the fogged-over mirror, someone had written something in the steam—an echo of the note she'd found dripping down the altar: *It's not enough.*

Downstairs, the door to the kitchen squealed open and then slammed shut. A set of boots pounded up the stairs, and then there was Peter, skidding into the open door, a streak of dirt on one cheek. Upon seeing her there, he froze, his eyes tracking toward the body of the hen.

He didn't have a chance to speak before James appeared. He sidled into the empty space at Peter's side, shirtless and sleep mussed, his chest latticed in a series of pink, puckered scars.

"Where did you come from just now?" Peter demanded.

James's dark brows quirked upward. "The guest room."

"You're lying."

"Oh, come off it, Peter," he said, an edge in his voice. "I just got in two days ago. I'm jet-lagged as hell. I'd still be out cold if Wyatt hadn't started screaming loud enough to wake the dead." His attention fell to the sink. Drifted up toward the letters dripping down the glass. "What's this?"

"A message." Dread fishtailed in Wyatt's stomach, cold and dark as a leviathan. "There's something in the house with us."

"You think so?" James inched toward the sink, taking a closer look at the mess of feathers. "I don't know. I think it's more likely that one of us did it."

Wyatt blinked at him, surprised. "One of *us?*"

"We're the only people here." He slid an implicative gaze toward Peter, still propped against the door. The latter bristled visibly, something lethal icing over in his eyes.

"Don't look at me."

"Why not? You were down in the henyard, weren't you? You've been hammering away at that bloody gate since dawn."

"You think I'd hurt an innocent animal?"

A dour laugh sawed out of James. "Is that meant to be a serious question?"

"Leave him alone," snapped Wyatt.

James whirled on her, astonished. *"Leave him alone?"*

"We're not getting anywhere by fighting like this."

"We're not going to get anywhere by pretending everything's perfectly fine, either." His head whipped back toward Peter. "She thinks you're such a pacifist. Shy, sweet Peter, who never hurt a fly. Did you ever tell her what you did to get locked in the cellar? Did you tell her how angry you were, that the guild had taken her away from you?"

"Jamie, stop," said Wyatt. "This isn't helping."

But James wasn't done. "You led them into the woods, didn't you? Seven of them. My father told me they tracked you out to where the stream becomes a river, where the river becomes a rip, the sky as black as the Styx. Did you kill them yourself? Or did you let something cold and cryptid do your work for you?"

Peter's breathing had gone serrated. His hands shook. "They weren't innocent."

"And what about Wyatt," asked James. "Is she innocent? Or is she just a means to an end? I'm curious to know what lies you'll tell yourself when you're burying her body out in the grove."

Peter stiffened. "I didn't kill the hen."

Wyatt's stomach was leaden. Her throat tight. James was being cruel, yes, but nothing he'd said was untrue. There were three of them in the house, and Peter was the only killer among them. Quietly, she said, "I think you should leave."

Peter's arms fell slack. "Wyatt—"

"Just go."

For a heartbeat, she thought he might refuse. Instead, the fight in his eyes flagged and died. With a last glance toward the sink, he turned to leave. She listened to the fading thud of his boots on the stairs, the muffled slam of the kitchen door.

When he'd gone, she rounded on James. He stood idly by the sink, examining the hen with quiet bemusement, his thumb rubbing absently at the raised ridge of a scar. The wounds on his chest were considerable, tracking from sternum to navel and then splintering outward in a fragmented web.

She wanted to ask him what horrible thing had happened, to carve him up so completely. Instead, she said, "England is five hours ahead."

His thumb stilled against his chest. "What?"

"You said you were jet-lagged, but it's afternoon there. You used to wake up unreasonably early at the start of the summers, not sleep in. I remember, because you'd always force me and Peter to get up with you."

He frowned down at her. "I tell you Peter has the blood of seven guildsmen on his hands, and that's your takeaway?"

"I don't know what to believe," she admitted. "I mean, *God*, Jamie, you were always such an impressive liar. I used to envy it when we were kids. You'd spin some bullshit story and get us all out of trouble. It was like a superpower." She paused, swallowing sharply. "I just never thought you used it on me."

"I'm not lying to you about Peter."

"Maybe not now," she admitted. "But you did for years."

The bathroom felt suddenly too small. Funny, she'd been so desperate for him to arrive—to show up and set everything right again, the way he used to. Now that he was back in Willow Heath, she found she didn't want him here. She didn't like him looming over her this way, with his razor-sharp smiles, his secrets sutured into his chest.

"You can go back to bed," she said, without meeting his eyes. "I'll clean this up on my own."

When it was done, she dressed in a clean pair of overalls and wandered outside in search of Peter. She found him propped against the woodpile, chickens plucking at his bootlaces. In his hand was James's lighter, the lasered crest of Norrington Prep packed with dirt. He flipped it open with clumsy fingers, lacking James's dexterity. The flywheel spat paltry sparks and the lid snapped shut with a click.

"That's Bastard," he said, when Wyatt slumped against the stack beside him.

"Excuse me?"

He inclined his chin toward the poultry-netted pen, where the piebald rooster strutted from one end to the other. "The rooster. And the blue wheaten there—the one nibbling on my laces—that's Mary. The silver girl behind her is Jane, and the pair of silkies fighting over seeds are both called Helen. That cluster of black birchens by the tree are newer. They hatched when I was imprisoned, so they don't have names just yet." He tucked the lighter into his back pocket. "The bay hen in the sink was Scarlett. She hatched seven years ago, while you were away at school. I was hiding in the coop when it happened. I was the first thing she ever saw."

"I never knew you named them."

He shut his eyes. "I didn't kill her, Wyatt."

"I know that," she said. "You're not a killer, Peter. You're—" But the right words wouldn't come to her. She tried to picture him huddled in the coop, lonely and afraid, watching the newborn chicks shove their beaks through fractured bits of eggshell. Imprinting on whatever he could find. "They backed you into a corner," she whispered. "All you're doing is fighting your way out of it."

For a long time afterward, they stood in silence and watched the wild scatter of chickens, the backs of their knuckles kissing between them. The barely-there whisper of his touch made her feel thirteen years old again, reaching for his hand in the bloodred dark.

Only this time, there was nothing left of him to hold on to.

Later—hours after the sun fell back behind the hills—she climbed the stairs to her room to find James already there. He sat in her open window, his eyes on the milky swath of starlight. Wary, she leaned into her bedroom door until it clicked shut behind her. The sound brought his head up like a shot and she was met with the striking black of his stare.

"I forgot how bright the stars are from your window."

"Me too," she admitted. "You can't see the stars in Salem. Not like this, anyway. There's too much light pollution."

"Yeah?" He tipped his head against the wall, shadows carving out the hollows of his cheeks. "I can't remember the last time I saw the sky."

The way he said it, slow and pensive, set her on edge. Against her better instincts, she picked her way across the carpet and joined him in the window. The cool nighttime air was a balm against the fever in her skin. She watched the stars wink awake one by one, and felt unbearably sad.

It was James who broke the silence. "My first summer here, I thought I might die of boredom. My father had repeatedly told me how dangerous Peter could be. *He's trouble, James. He's volatile. You mustn't let him out of your sight.* To a six-year-old boy, it felt like a quest worthy of Camelot. Maybe I had to spend my holiday in Maine, but at least it wouldn't be dull. At least I'd be doing something thrilling."

"Why are you telling me this?"

"Because it's the truth." He crooked a knee, making room. "Isn't that what you wanted?"

When she said nothing, he peered back out at the diamond night. On his middle finger, he spun an onyx ring. Round and round, like a talisman. "I don't think I'd ever been as disappointed as I was that summer. It felt like I'd been promised a mountain lion and then handed a kitten. It was a glorified babysitting gig. Peter wasn't dangerous at all. The opposite, in fact. He'd been perfectly happy to do as you told him. He played the part of your bridegroom, he sat at your tea parties, he hung on to your every word. It was years before I understood what he was doing."

She hadn't realized she'd been holding her breath. "And what was that?"

"Exactly what a kitten does, when it grows into a cat. Toying with his prey."

Hurt spiked in her chest, sharpening quickly into anger. "What are you doing here, Jamie?"

"It's nostalgic," he said without missing a beat.

"I don't mean *here*, in my room," she shot back. "I meant, why did you get on a plane? It's not like we've stayed friends. You never reached out after I left. You never called, never texted. You have no obligation to be here. Willow Heath isn't your responsibility."

"No," he agreed. "But you are."

"What's that supposed to mean?"

"Haven't you been paying attention?" His starless gaze cut to hers. "You're mine. You and Peter. You always have been, ever since that first summer."

"Jamie, that's—" She faltered, uneasy. She'd been about to say *unhinged*. "People don't belong to people."

"Don't they?" The tip of his mouth sharpened into a smile. "I take care of what's mine. I told you I'd handle everything, and I meant it. I already have a plan."

"Are you going to let me in on it?"

Flinted in darkness, he looked less like a boy and more like some malevolent haunt. She felt that same primal flutter as when she'd

153

clicked on the flashlight to find that leering face pressed nose to nose with her in the forest. It was just the dark, she told herself. It was just this house. It was rotting from the outside in. The shadows fell in all the wrong places. It made traps out of empty corners, a monster out of a boy with a switchblade smile.

"Your room looks nice," James said suddenly. "How long did it take you to put it back together?"

She fumbled, caught off guard by the sudden shift. "What?"

"Was it properly ransacked, when you first came back?" He pried a ring loose from his finger and then plopped it back into place. "Peter tore it apart, the day you left. I found him sitting in the willow afterward, picking bits of mirror glass from his knuckles. Your father thought he was acting out, but that's not Peter. He's not explosive without reason. If he upended your room, it's because he was looking for something."

Wyatt frowned. "I didn't leave anything behind."

"Are you sure about that?" When he climbed out of her window seat, the darkness engulfed him. All that remained visible was the sharp slope of his jaw, silvered in a thin bar of moonlight. So buried in darkness, she didn't see when he reached for her. The backs of his knuckles grazed her temple and she jumped at the contact, a flush crawling into her skin.

"Get some rest, Wyatt," he said, and for a moment he didn't sound like James at all. "You look unwell."

16

PEDYR

Pedyr woke to the sound of a piano.

At first, he felt pulled outside himself, as though time had ceased to exist. He was a little boy again, drawn to the sour notes of Wyatt learning to play her arpeggios, mesmerized by the way the music slowly unfolded beneath her fingers.

It wasn't mesmerizing now. It didn't enthrall or enchant him— it flayed him alive. Rolling onto his side, he pressed his pillow over his head. It did nothing to stifle the music. The laborious chords of "Nearer, My God, to Thee" clanged in his chest like a death knell.

When silence finally fell, it felt like a reprieve.

A very short-lived reprieve.

"Do you remember Breakfast?" asked the beast, in a voice so like James, it hurt him to hear it. "That small, ugly shoat Wyatt's father brought home one summer?"

Pedyr lifted the pillow and found James's likeness framed in the open door, its head canted to one side, its fingers restless. "We knew it was only being fattened for slaughter," it went on. "We knew that the guildsmen meant to have a pig roast before the summit's end. But we still loved it like a pet. You more so than the rest of us."

"Don't do that." Pedyr sat up, casting his pillow onto the floor. "Don't talk to me like you're him."

"But I am," countered the beast. "I dug him out of the ground, and now I hold the ripe bulb of his memories in the palm of my hand. When I peel his thoughts apart, do you know what I find? You, weeping while that useless old hog turned on a spit. You, dry-heaving behind the house, when no one but James was there to see."

Pedyr flicked at a lone carpenter ant wandering along the loose binding of his quilt. "If you have a point to make, then make it and go."

The beast smiled a horrible, familiar smile. "Thirteen years ago, I offered you a way out. A witch's heart, in exchange for your own. That offer is withdrawn."

The first beat of panic pulsed through his veins. "We had a deal."

"And you didn't honor it." Its voice carried no echo, as though the house didn't wish to hold on to any part of this malfeasance. "Why should I grant you a second chance? A week out, and I can already smell your failure. The blood moon will arrive, and you won't be able to bring yourself to go through with it."

"And why not?"

"You know why."

Outside in the hall, the music quieted. Pedyr sat as still as he could stomach. Altar steady. Icon quiet. A boy who'd learned how to bleed without flinching.

"You've always been soft." The beast sneered. "This world feeds on itself. It is hard, and it is cruel. It's no wonder you've spent centuries at its mercy. Death is a lesson you cannot seem to learn. Here it is, in simple terms: Your pig was killed because men need to eat, and so do I. I cannot continue to gnaw on the bones of temporal beasts. It is not *enough*."

"If you want me," Pedyr said, "then kill me yourself."

This was met with a laugh, high and thin and thoroughly un-James-like. "You and I both know what sustains me. It has to be her who makes the kill. The way it had to be your father, that first day in the grove. What sweet succor, his sacrifice. I gorged myself on his remains for years. I feasted on his marrow for centuries."

Pedyr was wire pulled too taut. His patience snapped and he launched out of bed, his voice tearing out of him in a snarl. "This conversation is over."

Framed in the narrow doorway, the beast didn't balk. Its smile only grew into something sharp and pleased. "All these years," it marveled, "and still a coward. You've never been able to muster the gall to do what it takes to survive."

Pedyr sucked down an unsteady breath. He thought of burying James in the muddy bottom of a grave. The rain that fell and fell. He'd done what it took that day, and he'd regret it for the rest of his life.

Quietly, he said, "I'll do whatever I need to do. I just want to go home."

"Home." The beast tsked its tongue. "Immortality is wasted on boys like you. A thousand little lives, and you haven't even learned the meaning of the word."

Pedyr averted his gaze and came face-to-face with his own distant reflection in the dresser's wheel-cut mirror. After so many lifetimes of growing into some newer, wilder version of himself, he no longer recognized his own face in the glass. *Coward*, beat the current in his head. *Coward, coward.*

He shut his eyes. "Get *out.*"

Outside his room, the soft tinkle of piano keys started anew. When he opened his eyes, he was alone, his reflection staring out at him from the angled glass.

By the time Pedyr made it to the sitting room, the music had gone silent. The room was dark, the curtains drawn, sunlight spilling through in funny slants of gold. It turned the corners murky and glimmering, motes suspended in midair like gold dust.

He found Wyatt perched on the bench, the sheet pulled off the piano and her fingers moving soundlessly over the keys. On the top sat a wilting tomato plant. Beside it was a vial of powder, black as a little boy's bones scraped from a hearth. The ghost of a melody strung itself in the air between them.

When she didn't look up, he cleared his throat. Her chin lifted at the sound, the slack curtain of her hair falling back to reveal a pale, bloodless face.

"Oh," she said. "Hi."

The feeling that knifed through him was not panic—not yet—though it was something alarmingly close. He took a half step toward her and stopped, his gaze flitting between the slow-dying vegetation and the colorless pall of her skin.

"What are you doing in here?"

"Practicing."

He saw, then, that her littlest finger was newly pricked. Red drips stained the ivory in a scant, bloody dew. He wanted to tell her that there was no point anymore—Willow Heath was compromised. The beast was in the walls, in the floors, in the body of the boy he'd buried five long years ago. They couldn't exorcise it if they tried.

But to tell her that was to confess what he'd done.

"You're not a killer," she'd said, but she was wrong. He was death incarnate, all the way down to his bones. He destroyed everything he touched.

On the bench, Wyatt plunked a single, discordant note. "Did you know that the band on the *Titanic* famously kept performing while the ship sank? I always thought that was kind of ridiculous—where's the survival instinct, you know? But I get it now. What else is there to do while you die?"

"You're not dying, Wyatt."

"Aren't I?" She played another note, and he flinched. She marked it, peering up at him in that soul-carving way of hers. "There's no antibiotics in this house. Just some expired ibuprofen."

That nameless fear twisted deeper still. "You need antibiotics?"

She didn't answer, but he saw the truth plain enough in the furtive gleam of her eyes, the sheen of sweat at her brow. She played another chord, and he recognized it immediately. It was the beginning of an old Irish air—a song she used to sing to him in the summers, when he was too restless for sleep.

"Show me," he said.

"Absolutely not." The melody faded away as quickly as it began. "It's gross."

"I guarantee I've seen worse." Rounding the couch, he ate up the remaining space between them in three long strides. "How bad is it?"

"What do you care?"

"Don't do that. Show me."

She tilted her face to his, sizing him up through the dusky bars of light. Finally, she relented, prying the hem of her sweater over her abdomen to reveal a taped sterile pad, its middle darkened in rust-colored pinpricks. He sank to his knees before the bench, reaching for her without thought—hating the way she stiffened as he peeled back the bandage. Beneath was the gash from the penknife, sloppily stitched with sewing string.

He'd pieced himself back together often enough to know the incision should have stopped bleeding by now, new skin scabbing over the old. Instead, the wound was raw and weeping as the night she'd incurred it, a dark abscess flowering at its center.

"There," Wyatt said hastily, replacing the gauze. "You've seen it."

He was left staring up at her, his touch ghosting along the curve of her hip. For several seconds they remained frozen that way, the air thin as paper between them.

"I'll fix this," he said.

The laugh that exploded out of her was corrosive. She tugged her sweater into place. "Unless you have a secret stash of medicine lying around, it's only going to get worse. In case you've forgotten, we're all trapped here."

He swallowed sharply. "We'll figure something out."

"And then what?" She crossed her arms over her chest, her teeth chattering. "You'll patch me back up, just so you can kill me yourself a week from now? No thanks. I'd rather die of gangrene."

He rose to his feet. "That's not funny."

"It wasn't *meant* to be funny, Peter. *None* of this is funny." She shot up after him, an entire head shorter, even teetering on her toes. Out in the foyer, something battered, *bang! Bang! Bang!* at the front door. They both jumped as a shout boomeranged through the house.

"Police! We received a call about a disturbance at this residence. Open up!"

"Stay where you are," ordered the beast, who had appeared out in the hall, a short stack of Westlock journals tucked under one arm. The image was a study in perfection—exactly what James would have done, if he'd been there with them. Pedyr wondered how long it had been out there, listening to their conversation, finding new ways to bend and break them.

Another series of knocks followed the first, a heavy fist raining against glass.

Wyatt cut a sideways glance toward Pedyr. "What do we do?"

"Nothing," he said. "We wait."

He saw the conflict in her eyes. She was at war with herself—torn asunder by the possibility that help may have arrived. Chewing her bottom lip, she asked, "But what if it's real?"

"It's not," said the beast. "And if you open that door, what's out there will swallow you whole. It already has a taste of your blood, Wyatt. Don't feed it another drop."

"Just wait," said Pedyr again as the hammering began anew. "It'll wear itself out."

By the time the mimic finally tired and moved on, it was near dark. Pedyr lay on his stomach by the hearth, his hands piled under his chin and the glow of a fire warming his skin. On the couch sat Wyatt, her legs tucked under her and Slightly curled in her lap, both of them fast asleep against the faded embroidery of a pillow.

Nearby, the beast occupied the armchair, its knees pushed out and its chin balanced on a fist. It looked disconcertingly imperious this way—a corpse king on a wingback throne, its features pitched half in darkness. It stared at Pedyr, and Pedyr stared back. In the wake of the disturbance, the thickening twilight felt oppressive.

"My aunt lives her life by the lunar cycle," said Wyatt, surprising them both. Pedyr peered over at the couch to find her awake and upright, her skin painted gold in the firelight.

"She cleanses her crystals on a full moon," she went on, picking at a hangnail. "She buys a scratch ticket whenever there's an eclipse. She says it's a *cosmic whirlwind of opportunity*—the best time to try your luck. But a blood moon? If you ask her, she'll tell you a blood moon invites violence. It disturbs the natural order of things."

A log split atop the grate, sending lit kindling crackling into the flue. For an instant, all three of them were cast into stark relief.

"So." Wyatt folded the sleeve of her sweater over her hand. "What's the significance?"

"This doesn't feel like the right time to have this conversation," said the beast, in a perfect imitation of James.

"What else are we going to talk about," she asked hotly, "the weather? If I'm going to die, I deserve to know the reason."

The beast's jaw ticked, every twitch and tell methodical. "You're not going to die."

Wyatt flicked at a yellow tassel on her pillow. "The two of you keep saying that, but neither of you means it."

There was a ferocity in her stare that carved Pedyr's insides out. If there was ever a time to tell her the truth, he supposed it was now—with the beast bearing down upon them both, the brutal end in sight. He rolled onto his back, lacing his fingers behind his head and fixing his gaze on the low, wooden beams along the ceiling.

"I was eleven years old when my father drove an ax into my belly," he said, and he wasn't certain anymore if the memory was real, or if he was only parroting what he'd been told. "He hadn't meant to do it—it was an accident. He'd taken me out to the forest to help him

162

stack wood in the barrow. I don't know exactly how it happened—if he saw the beast peering out between the trees and slipped, or if it was drawn by the smell of blood."

He could feel Wyatt hanging on to his every word, could feel the eyes of the beast on his face, its eonian stare deep as a well and twice as dark. Somewhere outside, a raven let out a rattle call.

"My memories are all secondhand," he continued. "I don't know specifics. Not anymore. I'm told the beast offered my father a gift. In exchange for his sacrifice, our entire bloodline would be granted immortality. As long as I lived, no one else in our family would suffer at the hands of death.

"I woke in the night to find myself alone, a red moon burning in the sky. My father was gone. In the distance, there were lights. They looked like they were dancing. I followed them through the woods, and then through the sky. By the time I realized I'd gone too far, it was too late. The sun had risen. There was no way home."

The pause that followed was airless. A vacuum, swallowing up the sound.

"It's the law of refraction," said the beast, looking every bit engrossed in Pedyr's story. "When the moon passes through the earth's shadow, light from the sun hits the atmosphere and scatters. Only red filters through. That's what gives a blood moon its color. But the scattered light has to go somewhere, has to reflect off something. It catches on the edge of the sky, where the worlds crack open."

On the couch, Wyatt blinked. "Since when did you become an astrophysicist?"

"Since year six at Pepperdine Prep," came the droll reply, "when we learned about the phases of the moon."

Silence settled anew. Pedyr felt restless, near to crawling out of his skin. He'd trained himself to greet death without flinching, but waiting for Wyatt to speak made something inside him scrabble and squirm. When at last she rose from the couch, he rocketed upright.

"It's late," she said, clinging to Slightly. "I'm going to bed."

"Wyatt, wait." Pedyr veered out into the hall after her, careless of how it looked, and found her already doubling back. They collided in the dark of the foyer, slamming one into the other. Slightly leapt from her arms, bolting out of sight in an angry calico streak. In what little light fell through the oriel window, he could just make out the glimmer of unshed tears in Wyatt's eyes.

"Tell me how you'll do it," she ordered.

"What?"

"The forest demands a blood moon and an offering, right? How will it happen? I know you've thought about it. You've had plenty of time—you must have come up with a plan. Will you use a knife? A dagger? Will you drive an ax through my belly?"

His stomach turned over. The words of the beast rattled through his brain: *You've never been able to muster the gall to do what it takes to survive.* He ran his hands over the top of his head, linking them across the nape of his neck. At the sight of his hesitance, Wyatt huffed out a breath.

"Typical."

She turned to go, this time without a backward glance.

"I'll come to your room," he called after her, the words tumbling out of him. "Just after dark." The confession sank to the floor between them, weighted as an anchor. "Is this what you want? A play-by-play?"

Wyatt stood on the bottom step, her eyes shimmering. "Yes."

"You'll be waiting up for me," he said. He'd pictured it so many times, over so many years. The moon in the window, her eyes bright with starlight. A private daydream, too dangerous to share. Quietly, he added, "You always wait up for me."

He heard her suck in a breath. "And after that?"

"I won't be cruel," he whispered. "I won't hurt you. I'll look you in the eye. I've died so many times, and in so many ways. I know how to make it quick."

Out in the dark, another rattle call sounded. A raven, alerting the flock to the presence of a nearby predator. He shut his eyes. His shame threatened to saw him open.

"Sounds simple," said Wyatt at last, and of all the things she could have said, this cut the deepest. He'd have preferred she yelled. Rather she wept, screamed, accused. Instead, the quiet pooled between them like blood. *Simple, but never easy.*

The stairs groaned underfoot, the house marking her departure. He opened his eyes to find himself alone in the dark, his heart outside his body and no way to shove it back in.

17

WYATT

The piano rotted overnight.

Wyatt hovered in the wide mouth of the hall and stared without breathing. There was the pale predawn, pouring through the curtains in dusky shafts of white. There was the tomato plant, its stem furred in white, its fruit puckered and oozing.

And there, beneath it, was the piano—ivory keys flaked in blood gone brown, its body swallowed up as if by the forest. A thick bed of moss, chartreuse green and laced in thin doilies of lichen, covered the whole of the instrument. It looked as though someone had left the piano out in the yard to sit, and the yard had reclaimed it. The room smelled thick and earthy and a little bit damp.

For several minutes, Wyatt stood frozen in the door. The saccharine smack of decay slid into her belly, crawled into her skin. She thought about prying up the thick reams of peat like an old carpet and stuffing it deep in the garbage. Eradicating it, before Pedyr and James could wake and find evidence of her perversion.

In wobbling steps, she crossed to the piano and sat, lowering herself onto the lichen-crusted bench. The wood had warped, leaving the keys snaggled and strange, stained a stippled shade of brown in the places where her blood had flaked to rust. Gingerly, she reached out and splayed her hand in the damp carpet of green.

There, in the moldering quiet, Peter's words crashed into her: *"I won't be cruel."*

A threat, packaged as a promise.

She'd cried herself to sleep, careless of the way the sound carried through the house.

Now her eyes were puffy and her throat raw. The edges of a scream sat caught between her teeth. Maybe her forefathers had been greenskeepers—able to coax Willow Heath to life with a few drops of blood—but that wasn't her. Inside her was rot. All she wrought was death.

Digging her fingers into the springy damp, she peeled it up from the wood. Moss came away in a wet clod, crumbling all to pieces in the palm of her hand. She brushed it off on the leg of her pants, managing to scrape away several more fistfuls before the hammering began.

At first, she thought it was the mimic, back for another afternoon of sneering provocation. It took her a heartbeat to slot the sound into place. By the time she realized it wasn't coming from outside the house at all, the racket had gone quiet. She made her way toward the kitchen, brushing peat from her palms, and nearly tripped directly over a chicken. It gave her a single, scolding warble before fluttering down the hall and out of sight.

She found James and Peter sequestered in the kitchen. The former stood before the door, clad in black flannel and jeans, a nail poking out of the corner of his mouth like a toothpick. A wide, wooden plank was tucked under one arm. Peter sat nearby on the cluttered countertop, a tear in the collar of his T-shirt and a chicken in his lap, his eyes a wary, sunless gray. He didn't look up at her as she entered, and she did her best not to look at him.

At the door, James propped his plank over the frame and set to hammering in a nail.

"What are you doing?" she asked, when the hammering stopped.

"Caging us in," muttered Peter, at the same time as James spat the nail from between his teeth and said, "Keeping the forest out."

The two exchanged a black look, murderous in the gloom. In the open pantry, something heavy slammed to the ground. Dried legumes went sprawling across the tile in an earth-toned spill.

"Another hen was killed this morning," James said, positioning a rusted nail against the board. "They're being picked off one by one. It's been over a month since your father's passing, and the wards are failing by the day. Eventually, the forest will work its way inside, and we'll be screwed. Hand me the hammer?"

Wyatt obliged, sidestepping one of the white silkies as she did. James fell back to hammering just as there came another violent thud from the pantry. Mama poked her wiry head into view, raw fettucine snapping between her teeth. Somewhere upstairs, the rooster crowed.

"Will this help?" she asked, passing James another nail. "The boards?"

"No," came Peter's instant reply.

She didn't look at him. She couldn't. She didn't know if she'd ever be able to again. *"I won't hurt you,"* trickled his voice through her head. *"I'll look you in the eye."* She wondered if he'd slept last night, or if he'd lain awake and listened to her weep. If it satisfied him, to know he'd finally drawn first blood.

"It can't hurt," James said, glancing between them. "Although it would go faster if we had some help."

"It's not what's out there that scares me," said Peter. Hopping down from the counter, he set the hen onto the floor. It fluttered out of sight, tutting wildly as it went. Without so much as a glance in Wyatt's direction, he eased out into the hall. After a moment's hesitation, Wyatt tailed after him.

"Peter, *wait*." She swallowed her pride, the pin-sharp lump of it pricking her throat. "I need to show you something."

Moments later, they stood shoulder to shoulder in the sitting room and stared down at the rotting piano, taking silent stock of the damage. It was Peter who broke the silence first.

"Wyatt, this is—"

"I lied to you," she said, cutting him off. "About never practicing magic."

A pause. "I know."

"It's not that I haven't wanted to help. I'd have strengthened the wards if I could. I'd have helped you, even if—" Her voice broke, the words hanging unsaid between them. *Even if you planned to kill me, before the end.*

At his sides, his hands had clenched into fists. He still hadn't looked directly at her, and she wondered if he'd always hated her this openly. If maybe she'd been so blinded by how she wanted things to be that she'd refused to see them for what they actually were. It hurt to look at him, even askance. It felt too much like poking at a raw nerve. Instead, she fell to studying a bead of sunlight caught in the crackle glass of a potpourri bowl.

"It's just that I'm not like my dad," she said. "I'm not a greenskeeper, or a warden, or whatever he was. My mom used to joke that he could coax anything back to life. A wounded animal, a lemon tree, a meadow flower."

A dying boy, she thought.

"That's not me," she whispered, her throat thick. "I don't make things grow. I make them rot."

There, intrusive as a spider, were the memories she'd worked so hard to keep at bay—the flashing lights of the ambulance. The accusatory stares of her peers. The stink of decay, sulfurous and strange.

"I know," Peter said again. He still hadn't looked at her. The air between them felt thick.

"Maybe I could try," she said, still staring into the bowl's fractured glare. "To strengthen the wards, I mean. Maybe there's something I can do to keep the forest out. I want to help. It's just—I don't know how. It just happens. It's involuntary, like a sneeze."

"It's nothing like a sneeze," he countered. "A sneeze is caused by external triggers. You're drawing power from an internal source."

Something snapped inside her chest. She rounded on him, angry. "And what do you know about it?"

"It doesn't matter," he said. "It's too late. The beast is already here."

Her skin turned to ice. "How is that possible?"

He didn't have a chance to reply. Something heavy clattered to the floor and they whipped around to find James in the hall, a stack of boards askew at his feet. A funny sort of smile carved its way across his face.

"Don't stop on my account," he said, his eyes on Peter. "I'm dying to know what you're planning to say." When Peter only stared, he edged closer. "Are you going to dig up all your skeletons? Will you tell her what's buried out in the grove?"

"What is he talking about?" Wyatt demanded.

Still, Peter was quiet. James crowed out a laugh. "Textbook Peter. The moment things start to slip sideways, he shuts up like a trap."

His eyes flicked to the piano and his smile caught, fading slightly.

"That's new." He picked his way over to the moldering display, shredded moss crumbling under his boots. Digging a thumbnail under blue flakes of lichen, he asked, "Do you remember the summer Wyatt convinced herself a butterflower made an effective lie detector?"

He glanced back at her, the tiniest flicker of light glimmering in his eyes. "You'd pick a buttercup and place it under our chins. If our skin turned yellow, it meant we were lying."

"I remember," she admitted.

"We played all afternoon, out in the eastern meadow. Peter was standing in a shadow, so there was no reflection. But me? I was in the bald sun. You got so mad at me; you were shaking. Do you remember that? Because I do. You bought into every word of your own game, and it infuriated you to think I was being dishonest. By the time it was over, you'd left in a snit, tears streaming down your face. Peter chased after you, like he always did. And I went after Peter."

Next to her, Peter stood as though hewn from stone.

"By the time we reached the barn," James went on, "we'd forgotten all about it. But later—after dinner—my father dragged me out into the fields. He was furious, convinced I was keeping something from him. *You're meant to be my eyes and ears*, he said, but I hadn't the slightest idea what he meant. It wasn't until we came over the top of the hill that I understood. The meadow was gutted. Not a single

171

buttercup left alive. Rings of white caps had pushed up through the dead tangles of grass."

A smile teased at the corner of his mouth. For a moment, a glimmer of the boy she remembered shone through the bladed exterior. "Immediately, I knew it was Wyatt. It was always Wyatt. Every outburst. Every tear. Every unexpected shower. But I lied to my father when he asked what happened. I told him we'd been playing in the barn all day."

Silence rose up to meet them. A cluster of honeycomb-capped mushrooms sprouted out of the moss like potato eyes. James pried one loose, turning the yellow morel over in his hand.

"What was it this time?" he mused. "Was it Peter's little speech? We heard you crying in the dead of night."

"Stop," said Peter.

"Ah, there it is." James rounded on them, a dazzling grin splitting his mouth. "You've found your voice. What have you got to say?"

"Leave her alone."

"I'm only talking," said James, casting aside the mushroom. "It's all a bit ironic, isn't it? You've been so desperate to protect her from finding out what's waiting in the forest, you seem to have forgotten the biggest danger of all is standing right here in this room."

Peter shook his head. "Don't start."

"I'm not starting anything. I'm finishing it. Look at you, Peter. Your guilt is eating you alive. Don't be such a martyr—unburden yourself. Tell her what you're hiding."

For a moment, Wyatt thought Peter might lunge. His knuckles were white as bone, his brows bunched like storm clouds. Silent fury rippled from him as he turned tail and left, heading back out into the hall without another word. James fell in after him, Wyatt at his heels.

"Jamie," she called, rushing to keep up. "Let it go."

He shrugged her off, catching up to Peter beneath the dining room's beamed archway.

"You've backed yourself into a corner," he said as Peter shouldered his way past him and into the sunlit nook. "You can't tell her what you've done without losing her, but you can't keep her safe while she remains in the dark. Do you know what they call that? A catch-22."

Peter braced his palms against the wide trestle table, the sinews in his arms pulling taut. A shallow dough bowl sat in the middle, divots stuffed with apples gone mealy. A black fly hummed around the puckered fruit, irritated by the disturbance. Its ceaseless buzz drilled into Wyatt's ears. Left her reeling.

"What is he talking about?"

"Nothing," snapped Peter, though he didn't look at her. "Don't listen to him."

"Same old Peter," sang James. "You've always been a spineless coward."

Peter's shoulders knotted tight. "Shut up."

"It's selfish, is what it is. You won't tell her what horrible thing you've done, because you know she'll never look at you the same way again, and you can't stomach the thought."

"I said," came Peter's voice, strained through a snarl, "shut *up*."

James's grin stretched wide. "Here's a question—how do you think she'll look at you when your hands are around her throat?"

Wyatt didn't anticipate Peter's lunge. She'd barely managed to throw herself between them before there came the loud crack of his fist exploding across James's jaw. James toppled into the enclosed hutch, the collision knocking mismatched plates from their grooves. Porcelain shattered against citrus glass as he laughed, pawing at his bloodied lip. He looked deranged this way, his smile razor-sharp, red pooling between his teeth.

"Poor Peter. Did I hit a nerve?"

Peter's only response was to charge a second time, tackling James hard into the cabinet. The doors fractured beneath the impact, antique glass raining down around them as James cast Peter off with a shove.

"I'm just calling it like I see it."

Peter shoved him back. The crack of his spine against the hutch jostled the dying cascade of maidenhair atop the cabinet. Loose leaves fluttered around them in yellow-green flurries. "I'll kill you," Peter seethed, jabbing a finger in his face. "I'll fucking end you."

Spitting red, James flung his hands out to the sides. His black eyes were bright with provocation. "There's nothing left of me to kill, sweetheart."

This time, when Peter lunged, it was with a shout. Before Wyatt could fling herself into the middle, his hands had found James's throat. Elbowing her off him, he dug his thumb into the exposed cord of James's jugular.

"Peter!" Wyatt clawed at him, her efforts gouging his bicep. "*Peter.* Get off him!"

But Peter didn't hear her. He was inches from James's face, his grip tight as a vise. "No more games," he ordered as James gasped for air, his hands bracketing Peter's wrists. "From now on, you won't look at her. You won't speak to her."

"Peter, *stop*." Wyatt's panic was a riot of color. It sparked in her chest. It sizzled through her veins. She tore at the tight cord of Peter's forearm. "Let him go."

Peter shook her off, his grip tightening. Pinned against the broken door of the hutch, James eked out single, gagging laugh. Veins bulged from his neck as his heels scrabbled for purchase, blood tracking down his chin in rivers of red.

"You're killing him!" Her voice came out shredded. The beginnings of a scream, swallowed up by the house. She ripped at his T-shirt and felt the cotton tear beneath her, giving way like a sail beneath a storm. The gasp that tore out of James's chest was airless, strange— the sound someone made when they were dying. Fear bled through her like a watercolor.

This time, when the scream built in her throat, she let it fly. *"Peter!"*

There came the instant, immolating crack of earth giving way, the brutal judder of something crashing into the house. She felt it both inside and outside—a great, violent thunder. The feel of the world torn asunder. The three of them were shaken apart, dust raining down from the rafters.

Wyatt was the first to regain her senses. "What the hell was that?"

Across from her stood Peter, breathing hard, his hair spilling into his eyes. James leaned against the cupboard, his bloodied chin tilted toward the ceiling. Already, angry contusions had begun to form along his neck. When he spoke, his voice was gravel.

"Look at that. We've upset Wyatt."

Peter's eyes flitted to Wyatt's and held. Both of them moved at once, heading out of the dining room and into the foyer, where the chickens ran amok, frantic and nattering. They went one after the other up the stairs, stepping wide over smashed family portraits, their frames snapped like bones. At the far end of the hall, light poured out from her open bedroom door in funny swaths of white.

Her room was gone, swallowed up in a weeping bower of branches. Shingles hung down from the ceiling in mossy stalactites. Muddy water trickled from swaying gutters packed with thick leaf litter. The floor had buckled clean in half, gaping fangs of hardwood rising up around a mouthful of bark. Where the window had once been, there was only sky. Uprooted, the willow tree had buried itself into the side of the house. Its rotted innards lay smashed across the window seat.

Where she'd sat. Where she'd dreamed. Where she'd fallen in love with her killer.

Fitting, she thought dully, and laughed right out loud. It was almost poetic. The tree was rotting from the inside out, and so was she.

"Wyatt." Peter stepped in front of her. "Dahlia, look at me."

She didn't. She stared at his chest. At the tear in his shirt. At the little blue button that hung against his sternum. Her button. Her bear. Her bedroom. Her heart. Everything was being smashed into a million little pieces. Somewhere behind her, a boot scuffed over the floor.

"She's in shock," came James's voice, still hoarse. "Can you blame her?"

Peter stiffened. "Get out."

"Me?"

"This is your fault."

"I'd love to hear how you're going to pin this on me."

"Stop talking, both of you." Wyatt's voice sounded alien, even to her. Beneath her chest, her heart beat in heavy palpitations. Her blood was grease-fire hot and impossible to smother. She wanted to shout—to tear them both apart. She wanted to tell them that they were acting like children, that they were destroying everything, but the truth of it was, everything had already been destroyed. She'd just been too careless to see it.

And so, instead of shouting, she pushed out a deflated sigh and said, "Help me get my things."

18

WYATT

Wyatt lay flat as a paper doll on the guest room bed. Sweating out a fever. Staring at the ceiling. Choking on regret. The last time she'd let go of her control so completely, it had been winter. January bleak, the snow melting into soot-dark slush along Salem's cobbled walkways. An EMT had wrapped her in a Mylar blanket for the shock. She'd sat in the back of the ambulance with chattering teeth and bloodied palms, watching them load the body onto the stretcher.

She'd spent every day since that day doing her very best not to remember. Not to feel. To mete out emotion in neat little spoonfuls instead of whole, suffocating swallows. To control herself, instead of unleashing fury vast enough to tear out a tree by the roots.

The air in the room was stale, the window boarded. Between the slats, the sky was dark as ink, though the sun had only set a short time ago. Slightly lay on the adjacent pillow, curled in a ball and brooding, furious at the poultry invasion. In Wyatt's arms sagged Cubby, peering up at her through his doleful Cyclops stare.

On the floor was Peter.

He sat with his back to the door, his forearms slung over his knees. He hadn't moved in hours, but then neither had she. All through the afternoon, James had resumed his hammering, boarding up the downstairs windows in spite of the fact that there was now a great, gaping hole in the side of the house.

"You can go," she said, not for the first time. She didn't mean it. Not really. The idea of being left alone with her thoughts terrified her. But being alone with Peter was torture.

She heard a rustle of movement. From out of the darkness came a gruff, "I'm fine."

"I don't need a warden. There's nowhere for me to run."

A pause followed. Quietly, he said, "You're not a prisoner, Wyatt."

"Yeah? I feel like one."

He had nothing to say to that, and so they lapsed back into silence. Outside, a coyote cackled in the dark, letting loose a hair-raising yip that set her instantly on edge. She rolled onto her side and found Peter staring, the lines of him carved into bars of light and dark beneath the thin slants of moonlight. He didn't look away, and so neither did she. Drawing her knees up to her chest, she tucked her hands beneath her cheek. Eventually, the staccato pitch of the coyote faded back into silence.

"You used to ask me to tell you stories," she said, when it was quiet. "Whenever you couldn't fall asleep. Remember? You'd crawl into bed and pester me until I fed you the details of whatever book I was reading. We'd fall asleep picking apart the plot holes."

He didn't answer, but she could see the rise and fall of his chest— the way his breath caught, quickening. His button reflected the moonlight, winking up at her from the torn white of his T-shirt. Her stomach tightened.

"I wish you'd ask me for a story now."

The quiet part strung between them. *I wish you'd crawl into bed with me.* She knew the danger in wishing. Her memories were lies—he'd never been the boy she thought he was. But she couldn't take another minute of lying there alone, her insides rotting. She wanted to be held. She wanted things to be the way they were five summers ago, before everything went wrong.

For just a few minutes, she wanted to pretend.

Peter's eyes looked black in the moonlight. No trace of blue to be found. He turned his head, the tether between them broken. "Go to sleep, Wyatt."

The pinch in her throat solidified into a lump. She swallowed thickly and rolled away from him, drawing the covers up to her chin. Just outside the window, a bullfrog launched into a rasping soliloquy. She let her eyes drift shut, feeling chipped all to pieces, like wood beneath an ax.

She waited for sleep, but sleep didn't come. She was too aware of Peter's unwavering stare. The feel of it moved through her in a shiver, like a pebble skipped over a lake.

"James said there was nothing left of him to kill," she said. "What did he mean by that?"

Peter didn't respond. She heard the groan of wood as he shifted positions, the whisper of his socks against the floor. Somewhere downstairs, a chicken warbled.

"What happened between the two of you? That last summer, I mean."

"You were there, Wyatt," came the dry-as-leaves reply. "We fought."

It was a lie. He was lying to her. "But you always fought. All the time. Over everything. This is different. It's like—it's like he's not even James anymore."

Immediately, she heard the sound of Peter climbing to his feet. She sat up just in time to see him prying open the door to the hall.

"Peter, don't leave."

His froze, his shoulders tensed. "I have to. I can't breathe, Wyatt."

Something wordless roiled deep inside her chest. "Stay and talk to me, then."

"I can't." His voice caught, cracking slightly. "I've done everything wrong. *Everything*. And I don't know how to undo any of it. And then sitting here with you like this, I—*I can't breathe*."

The door snicked shut behind him. Soft, not a slam.

She was alone.

She eased herself back, wincing at the tug of her stitches. Pressing a pillow over her head, she stifled a scream. She lay that way for a while—listening to the rasping croak of the bullfrog, the stale exhale of her own breath against the pillow—until, eventually, she slept.

She didn't know what woke her. A sound? A feeling? She lay on her side, becoming slowly aware of the steady breaths pluming against the nape of her neck. Soft and slow, like someone was asleep. A dangerous sort of hope swelled beneath her ribs just as a heavy sigh unfolded through the room. The mattress creaked beneath a shifting body.

Softly, she whispered, "Peter?"

The breathing slowed, tightening into a spectral quiet. At the sound, an unfathomable cold crawled into her skin. She knew Peter's silences. She'd grown with them. Raged at them. Fantasized about them. This was something else.

She rolled carefully to her side and came nose to nose with someone wearing her face. A scream tore out of her. She scrabbled backward, taking the sheets with her, her tailbone hitting the floor hard enough to bruise.

On the bed, another Wyatt Westlock sat up and stretched. Her eerie likeness stared down at her through flat, soulless eyes. It wore an ivory dress like a skin, shirred lace steeped in water. Red hair suctioned to its throat in thick, wet whorls, like it had dragged itself here through the mud. Its hands were wet with blood, arms latticed in broad, angry bruises. As though something dead had crept into its veins and turned to rot.

"What are you?" she managed to gasp.

"I am you," it said, in a voice that was so startlingly hers that she thought she might be dreaming. She inched backward toward the door, doing her best not to startle the thing with her face into giving pursuit.

"How did you get into the house?"

"Your wards are all in tatters," said the creature, "and you left such a fragrant path for me to follow. I lapped up the crumbs of your distress all through the willow and into your bed. Sweet, sweet sorrows."

"Why do you look like that?" She was almost at the door, sheets dragging along with her in limp puddles of white. "Like me?"

"I look," the creature said, its mouth quirking into a bloodred smile, "the way you will look at the moment you are most afraid."

The door to her room was yanked open. The knob cracked into the wall hard enough to send drywall clattering to the floor. Peter stood in the hall, yellow light bleeding in from behind him. He didn't spare a glance at Wyatt. He only stared at the thing with her face.

"Leave," he said.

The creature didn't budge. "Do you like what you see? Or does it terrify you?"

Peter's answer slipped out in a curse. He drew James's lighter from his pocket, a spark catching at the wick the moment he flicked open the lid. Without a beat, he tossed it onto the bed. Instantly, the patchwork quilt went up in flames. The creature let out a blood-curdling scream, its red, red mouth contorting into an awful circle, its hands flying over its face.

It scrambled out of bed, its skirt swallowed up in a halo of fire—lurching for the boarded-up window. The patter of racing feet became the skitter of bugs, and Wyatt balked as an entire colony of clicking beetles scaled the wall, scuttling out the barricaded window in an oily, iridescent swarm.

There followed a gulf of silence—the terrible, void-like stillness of oxygen being swallowed up in a vacuum. And then the mattress caught flame. In the middle of the inferno lay Cubby, his blue button eye flashing gold as he burned. Wyatt tilted to her feet, tripping out of her sheets and lurching toward the blaze.

She didn't make it far before Peter caught her around the middle. Her legs swung skyward just as the first bedpost collapsed. A plume of heat blistered her shins and they staggered out into the hall in a mess of limbs. She shoved him off her the moment they were clear of the worst of it.

"Cubby is in there," she said, elbowing her way back into the room. He blocked her advance, catching her by the wrists and walking her back against the opposing wall.

"It's just a bear, Wyatt."

She tried to wrench free, but his grip was tight as a vise. Behind him, the old floral paper began to peel from the wall in yellow curls. The hallway flooded with smoke, black as soot and stung with cinders. She stopped fighting, her eyes pinched with tears. Gently, Peter tipped his forehead to hers.

"Let it go," he whispered.

"Both of you, *move*." James stalked down the hall, shirtless and sleep-addled, the red fire extinguisher from under the kitchen sink clasped in his hand. Shoving past them both, he pulled the pin and unleashed a thick stream of white foam onto the growing flames, suffocating the fire until the bed was reduced to little more than ash. Great charcoal plumes rose off the mattress as if from a chimney stack.

For some time afterward, the three of them stood in silence and stared at the smoking ruins. Wyatt's heart sat neatly in her throat, her world unraveling. She'd come back to Willow Heath because she'd been so certain she wanted to set it aflame—to say her goodbyes in the flick of a match. But this was all she had left of them. It was all she had left of herself.

It was the place where they'd slept, side by side in the slow, sweating summers. The place where they'd dreamed, telling stories beneath the covers, the dark-lit starlight bright beneath the pinprick glow of a tin can lantern. The place where they'd laughed, cried, fought.

The place where they'd grown, even if what they'd grown into were strangers.

Slowly, the smoke slipped out through the cracks between the boards. Wyatt glanced up at Peter, expecting to find him as aloof and unreachable as always. Instead he looked pale as a wraith in the smoky dark, staring without blinking at the remains of the bed, In that moment, she would have given almost anything to know what he was thinking.

In the end, it was James who broke the silence. "What was it?"

"Deathwatch," said Peter.

"It looked like me," Wyatt added, because she didn't want to be the only one with nothing to contribute. "Or a bloody, nightmare version of me."

"Ah." James sniffed and scrubbed a hand over his face. His knuckles were flaked in rust, and a paintbrush stripe of something dark and wet streaked across his clavicle.

She was about to ask what the hell had happened to him when Peter said, "Everyone sees something different in the face of the deathwatch. It didn't appear to me as you."

"Oh." She sank back against the wall, a wobble in her knees. "That's a relief—I looked disgusting." The joke fell flat. No laughter rose to meet it. Desperate to chase away the tender silence, she asked, "What did you see?"

"It doesn't matter." The color hadn't come back into Peter's face.

"It matters to me," she said. "Anyway, the two of you didn't need to come all the way up here and start lighting things on fire. I had it handled."

"Did you?" James said wryly.

"I did. I was seconds away from kicking her right in the spleen."

"This isn't funny, Wyatt," said Peter.

"You're absolutely right. It's horribly unfunny to think that something else might have killed me before you even got the chance."

He pinned her in a withering stare. "It wouldn't have killed you. It doesn't feast on flesh. It draws its sustenance from grief."

185

She suppressed a shudder. "But I wasn't grieving when it found me. I was asleep."

"Not everything operates on the same linear timeline as mortal men," said James, who'd fallen to tinkering with the extinguisher's bracket valve. "You weren't grieving *today*. But you will, before the end."

It sounded like a threat, delivered with the careless ease James Campbell used to announce everything. Shrouded in smoke, he looked dreamlike, his edges opaque. Someone's memory of a boy, instead of a real one. Suspicion slithered, wet and cold, into her belly.

"How would you have any idea how a deathwatch operates? And don't tell me you covered it in primary school, because I know for a fact you didn't."

"I overheard my father talking about it," said James, his shoulder rising in a half shrug.

"Oh yeah? When?"

The first flicker of impatience curled his lip. "I'd have to consult my diary."

"Don't be a dick. We spent every minute of every summer together. We saw all the same things, which means we overheard all the same conversations."

"Same with Peter, but I don't see you shouting at him."

"I'm not shout—" She bit off the end of a yell, swallowing her temper. "Peter's different, and you know it. The James I knew wouldn't have kept something like that from me."

"Are you accusing me of lying, then?"

"I just don't think you're telling me the whole truth."

He didn't deny it. "It's interesting, how you question everything I tell you, but you seem to have no problem trusting Peter."

Wyatt bristled. "I *don't* trust Peter."

"He's right," Peter interjected, just a touch too loudly. "About the deathwatch operating in a space outside of time. That's how it feeds. It peers along your lifeline and mirrors your own face back at you at the exact moment you'll look death in the eye. If it got inside the house, that means the last of the wards are down. A few boarded-up windows won't make a difference—we're not safe here anymore."

"I'm getting better at blood tilling," said Wyatt. "The last plant I practiced on sprouted mushrooms. I mean, it died, but there were little yellow fairy cups in the dirt the next morning. It's better than nothing. Maybe I can try and ward the house."

"If you want to sit around and play Sabrina, go ahead," said James. "Bleed yourself dry for Peter's sake. Let's see where it gets you."

Wyatt's anger snapped into sparks. "I'm not doing it for Peter, I'm doing it for all of us."

"And what's your plan? To survive long enough to die?"

"That's not fair."

"But it's the truth, isn't it?" He eased closer, smoke spilling off him in skeins of gray. "You said you don't trust Peter, and yet you've inexplicably let him talk you into an alliance. What happens when your little partnership comes to an end? Have you given it *any* thought whatsoever? The blood moon is five days from now, Wyatt. We're on borrowed time."

The reminder sat heavily between them, a mirror of the warning she'd received from the hooded stranger that very first day: *"If you're*

as clever as you seem to think, you will offer him up to the beast yourself.
Quickly, before the blood moon rises."

Wyatt glanced toward the boy in question and found him looking back at her, his gaze unreadable. She thought—though she didn't want to—of all those summers in the meadow. Of the airless nights beneath her canopy, Peter's skin smelling of smoke and metal. Of her father's journal, cramped longhand blotted in ink: *It is in my power to end it—to muzzle the mouth of hell and subdue the boy in one bloody stroke.*

As though he knew exactly what she'd been thinking, James said, "We offer Peter up to the beast, and all this goes away."

The air rushed out of her on an exhale. "How can you say that?"

"Because it's the truth." His head canted to the side. "Isn't that what you wanted from me?"

"Enough," said Peter. "Stop pushing her."

Without so much as a glance in her direction, he slipped out into the hall. Wyatt was left staring at the place where he'd been, the taste of ash on her tongue. When she glanced back at James, it was to find him scowling down at her, the hollows of his cheeks turning him gaunt in darkness.

"There's blood on your chest," she said.

James swiped at his clavicle, peering down at the streak of crimson that came away on his thumb. "So there is," he mused as though he hadn't even realized it was there.

A spate of unease moved through her. With Peter gone, she wanted to interrogate him—to demand he tell her where he'd been tonight, and what he'd been doing. More than that, she wanted to ask him what had happened to the boy she grew up with. She didn't recognize this person in front of her, with his too-dark eyes and his leering smiles, his sudden appetite for cruelty. The James she remembered would have done whatever it took to get them out of this mess. All of them. Even Peter.

Instead of all that, she only asked, "Why me?"

The sepulcher dark of his stare skated down her spine. "What do you mean?"

"If you want Peter gone so badly, why don't you just get rid of him yourself?"

He appeared to consider her question, rubbing absently at the blue-green contusions along his throat. Peter's fingerprints, left behind like an echo.

Finally, he said, "Maybe I've already tried."

Before she could parse the meaning of his words, he'd bent down and dropped a kiss onto the tip of her nose. And then he, too, was gone, and Wyatt was alone.

19

PEDYR

The following morning, there was no sun at all. The sky sat gray and bloated atop the hills, blanketing the whole of Willow Heath in a pea-soup shroud. Inside the house, it was dark as night, the windows boarded in every last room.

Pedyr found Wyatt in the dining room, her arm crooked under her cheek, her breathing soft. She'd worn his sweater, and it hung off her like a dress, the twice-cuffed sleeves swallowing up her hands. In her lap sat James's old Polaroid camera, lens winking in the lit twinkle of the chandelier. Several developed photos lay scattered across the table like leaves. Nearby, Mama munched on fallen maidenhair, peering over at him with her usual steely astuteness.

Gingerly, he pulled out a chair and sank into it. At the head of the table, Wyatt didn't stir. For once, she slept soundly—without crying out. The rare sight of her at peace twisted something sharp inside him. For so long, he'd clenched his anger between his teeth like a bit. Chewing on it, until he went lockjawed and raving, driven mad by the aftertaste. Dying in silence. Living in silence. Surviving in silence.

Simple. Simple. Simple.

And then, finally, there was Wyatt. The key to his freedom, with her hazel eyes and her head full of daydreams, her hand sliding into his. There was nothing simple about her. There was nothing easy.

And yet, for years, he'd clung to her as tightly as he could. And now, at the end of all things, he didn't know how to let her go.

The beast was right. He was a coward.

But last night, he'd looked into the face of the deathwatch and saw how it would end. It was the simplest thing of all, to let it come.

Careful not to wake her, he pried up the scattered photographs and flicked through them one by one. The first several snapshots captured the guest room at various angles—the walls charred in black and wallpaper peeling, a pit of ash where the bed had been. The next cluster had been snapped in her bedroom. There was the great, old willow, wedged in the floor like a weeping guillotine. There was her bed, the canopy in tatters. He shuffled through a few more, past the piano swallowed in moss, the cupboard full of shattered plates.

On the last photo, he paused.

It wasn't the kitchen that caught his eye, windows boarded and chickens roosting. It wasn't the blackened grout or the rotting bowl of fruit on the island. Instead, it was the figure in the hall, caught in a candid, his black eyes staring up at Wyatt.

Sweat cropped along Pedyr's skin as unease festered in the pit of his stomach. Because the boy in the photo was a ghost. Where the light fell, he looked every bit like James. Dark hair, dark eyes, the sharp tip of a smile. But in the shadows, he was all corpse. He stood with ribs bared and limbs gone slack, one half of his mouth gorged open in a skeleton's sneer.

Carefully, Pedyr shoved the photo into his pocket and rose to go, cursing as the legs of his chair stuttered over wood. The sound drew Wyatt out of sleep—slowly, at first, and then all at once. She rocketed upright, peering up at him out of fever-glass eyes.

"What are you doing?"

"What are *you* doing?" he asked, redirecting. The photo felt like gunpowder in his pocket. *Coward*, tripped his pulse through his veins. *Coward, coward, coward.*

"This?" She set the camera on the table, sweeping the photos into a pile. "It's for the insurance claim."

"The—*what?*"

"My aunt had to work with insurance adjusters a few years ago, after her shop was broken into. They asked for photos of the damage." She stretched her arms up over her head, his shirtsleeves collapsing around her elbows. The movement resulted in a wince, and she curled back in on herself almost instantly. "I don't think they'll find me at fault for the bedroom, because there's no way to prove I uprooted a whole tree. But the guest room might look like arson. The lighter doesn't help."

He sank slowly back into his chair. "What do you care? I thought you came here to burn this place to the ground."

"I did." She flicked at a stray photograph and watched it pinwheel across the table. "I don't know, maybe James was right. I don't have a plan. I've been sitting around doing nothing for days, just waiting for the end. But we grew up here. The three of us. And maybe I don't recognize what we grew into, and maybe we'll destroy each other before it's over, but it's home."

"It's not my home," he reminded her.

She shut her eyes, but not before he saw the flicker of hurt. "Eventually, this will end," she said. "And when the dust settles, someone will need to see to the house. So I'm taking pictures."

When he was quiet, she glanced up at him. She sat close enough for him to reach out and touch, and yet he'd never felt further from her than in this moment. It was almost laughable. He'd been haunted by the thought of her for the last five years. He saw her when he slept. When he woke. In the black of night and the bitter day. And now she was back, and she was haunting him still.

Both of them were.

The photograph in his pocket weighed ten thousand pounds.

"I didn't think I'd see you today," she said, prodding at a Polaroid. "Not after last night."

He thought of the smoke-laced room, and the way the beast had played with Wyatt's head, cracking the two of them together like little toy dolls: *What happens when your little partnership comes to an end?*

Wordlessly, he lifted the leather cord over his head and set it between them. The little blue eye clinked audibly against the tabletop.

"I wanted to apologize," he said. "About Cubby. I know how important he was to you."

Wyatt didn't take the necklace. She watched the button as though it were a rattlesnake. "I've been thinking all morning," she said. "Turning the same question over and over in my head. What does a boy who has died a hundred times see when he looks a deathwatch in the eye?"

Pedyr thought of the deathwatch's pale face, the things he'd seen written in its sunlit gaze. The knowing way it watched him, its placid smile a mirror of his own. The way he'd suddenly understood, without a shred of doubt, how his days on this stinking side of the sky would crawl to an end.

"Take the necklace, Wyatt," he said.

"I don't want it."

"I'm giving it to you."

"*I don't want it,*" she repeated. "I want you to answer my question."

He launched to his feet, his chair nearly crashing to the floor behind him. His stomach was a rock. His head was all terror. He'd been intimate with death before. He didn't consider it an enemy. Just a temporary, parting gasp.

But this? He couldn't breathe. Not with the deathwatch's reflection in his head. Not with Wyatt's eyes on his face, James's corpse in his pocket. The house was shutting up around him like a sarcophagus. He was being buried alive.

When he turned to go, Wyatt rose up after him. "Peter," she said, "don't walk away."

He edged out into the hall without answering. A chicken went skittering sideways, startled by his sudden appearance.

"James is right," called Wyatt. "You *are* a coward."

The words were a lit match. He exploded, rounding on her in a fury. A half step behind him, she was forced to skid to a stop to avoid a collision.

"Say that again," he ordered, his voice scraping out of him an entire register too low.

Heat flared in her eyes. "You're a coward."

"You think so?" He stalked her back a step and she yielded. "You know, it's funny—I've lived a lot of lives. They were short lives—stunted and empty—but they were mine. And in all that time, no one ever thought to ask me what I want."

Another step, and her hip bumped up against the sideboard, jostling the vase of wilted florals.

"I've been worshipped," he went on. "I've been glorified. I've been anointed in oils and granted every offering. The guild acted like it was such a gift—to be exalted by mortal men. But I never asked for their adoration. I never asked for immortality. I never asked for any of it."

This time, when he stepped into her, she collided into the corner. He braced his arms against the wall, boxing her in. "You want me to give you answers? You want me to bare my soul to you? What about what *I* want?"

She searched his face, her voice slipping between them in a whisper. "What *do* you want?"

And there it was—an impossible question, with impossible answers. He wanted to find out if her mouth still tasted the same after all these years. He wanted to undo every awful thing he'd done. He wanted to go back to last night—to the bullfrog quiet and her eyes dark with implication—and crawl into bed beside her.

But it was too late.

"I want to walk away," he said. "And I don't want you to follow me."

It was late when Pedyr made his way to the primary bedroom. Pawing at the relentless pulse in his temple, he drew up short on the threshold. Wyatt was fast asleep in bed, her chest rising and falling beneath the patchwork quilt. Beside her lounged the beast.

"Get out," Pedyr ordered.

The beast's face cracked open in a grin. "I was asked to be here."

"I don't care. I told you to stay away from her."

In life, James Campbell's smile had been contagious as a yawn. In death, it only looked unsettling. A hollowed-out impression of a boy. "You're showing your cards," it said. "You know I won't hurt her."

"No," Pedyr agreed, "you'll only whisper your poison in her ear."

195

"An offering must be made." The creature leaned back, crooking its languid arms behind its head. "You've seen what's happening out there. The darkest parts of the forest are bleeding out onto the farm. Wyatt's world cannot hold my kind for this long without breaking. It is splitting at the seams."

"So then leave," spat Pedyr. "Slither back into the hole you crawled out from."

That skeleton smile stretched wide. "Not without you, my love."

In the end, Pedyr settled for sitting on the velvet divan by the window, Slightly perched on the adjacent cushion. The cat seemed as tense as he felt, her tail flicking and her eyes keen and cautious. He wouldn't pick a fight—not now, when another scrap might wake Wyatt and rouse suspicion—but he wouldn't leave her here alone, either.

Somehow—impossibly—the minutes choked by. They stacked one on top of the other until they'd built into a silent, suffocating hour. Through it all, the beast watched him fidget, that awful smile on its face. Wyatt snored softly, curled in on herself beneath the quilt.

Eventually—and in spite of his better efforts—Pedyr slept. He fell in and out of dreams, plagued by visions of the deathwatch, its sallow face sun glazed and smiling. Chased by the memory of Wyatt Westlock pressing her mouth to his beneath a thunderstorm sky, by thoughts of peeling back his skin and finding dark blue fans of scaevola laced along his bones.

When he woke, it was to the feel of James shaking him out of sleep. *Not Jamie*, said a voice in his head. *His corpse.* The thought was ice-bucket cold. He launched to his feet, heart hammering, and came face-to-face with his haunt in the early-morning dark.

"She's gone," it said. The collar of its shirt was stiff with blood, a slaver of crimson slipping down its chin. The entire room smelled faintly of decay, as though something had crawled into the walls and died. With a glance at the window, Pedyr saw why. Thick ropes of rotting climber ivy had pushed through the wooden slats in the night.

Fear crowded Pedyr's gut. He shoved past the creature and found the bed empty, the quilt kicked loose. On the rumpled mattress perched Slightly, mewling loudly—a warning caterwaul that raised the hairs on his neck. He rounded on the beast, his fists balling tight.

"I thought you were watching her."

"I had things to tend to."

"Things." He headed for the hall, tripping over his socks as he went. "You mean you were off killing something."

"It's for your own good," came the reply, a half step behind him. "The longer I starve, the more difficult it becomes to retain this form. Unless you want your darkest secret to rot away right before her eyes, I require sustenance. We're in this together, you and I."

He ignored the way the beast's voice slithered through him as he yanked open door after door, tailed from one room to the next by an awful, nagging feeling he couldn't abate. All through the house, the windows were boarded tight. No entrances. No exits. No way in, no way out.

And yet the beast was right. Wyatt was gone.

He was halfway to Wyatt's bedroom when the nagging feeling ossified into understanding. Stuffing a hand into his pocket, he felt for the photo he'd slipped there the day before. His weighted evidence. His eternal damnation.

He shoved into the bedroom, turning his pockets inside out as he went. Above the roof's gaping maw, the sky was a pale, sunless soup. A low-lying mist stretched over the whole of Willow Heath.

His pockets were empty. The photograph was gone.

And there, in the dense wall of fog, Wyatt Westlock was making her way to the forest.

20

WYATT

When Wyatt was young—before she went to live with them for good—she'd spent her spring breaks in Salem with her aunt and cousin. The visits were always long stretches of boredom interspersed here and there with sprinkles of chaos. Her mother and aunt would while away the afternoons cooking poorly and singing badly, day drunk and lost to nostalgia, tasking Mackenzie and Wyatt with the dull-as-dirt job of gathering morning dew off the flower boxes out front.

"I don't see why we can't just color eggs like normal people," Wyatt would say, squeezing out her rag so that the water pooled, pale and cloudy, into a basin.

"Because, turtle," her aunt would answer, sweeping through the room with a stick of slow-burning incense, *"we are honoring the goddess Eostre. The frost has melted. The days are longer. Now is a time of death and rebirth—it's good practice to keep a clear head."*

"I can do that just fine with water from the sink," Wyatt would snipe under her breath, to a snort of laughter from Mackenzie.

Those memories—the ones that came from her mother's side of the family—felt different from those of Willow Heath. The farm had been the loneliest place on earth, for all her father kept it packed with were strangers. Her aunt's messy little apartment was filled to the rafters with laughter, even when it was only the four of them and the cat.

"You have the hands of a gardener," her aunt told her one night, long after the sun had set. She'd talked Wyatt into receiving a palm reading, though Wyatt had initially refused. *"You are of the earth, and the earth is in your blood."*

"Dust to dust," Mackenzie hedged from the couch, scrutinizing a white-gold necklace in the shape of a half-moon. *"We're all made of earth, Mom, that's not exactly groundbreaking news."*

"This is different." Aunt Violet's eyes had gone glassy in the light of the slow-melting candles, her grip on Wyatt's hand sharp as talons. She'd looked up suddenly, her face lit from beneath. *"She's different."*

In the winged armchair in the corner, her mother set down the mug of tea she'd been nursing for the past hour. *"Don't scare her, Vi."*

"I'm only telling her what I see," protested Aunt Violet. Several candles guttered out between them, though neither of them had so much as sighed.

"Cut off your circulation," she'd whispered, *"and the world will rot at your touch. Everything you do thereafter will be mired in death."* There'd been something cavernous about her aunt's voice as she spoke. Something distant and other. A final candle extinguished. They'd been left in darkness, a distant police siren wheeling past unseen. The lamp clicked on over her mother's chair. She'd stared across the room at Wyatt without saying a word, the color gone out of her face.

"She gets too into it," Mackenzie said, from her spot on the couch. *"She can't help it. All Becketts are empaths. We feel way too many feelings. Are you sure you want me to keep this?"*

"It's all yours." Wyatt didn't look at the necklace in Mackenzie's hand. *"I don't want it."*

She'd been about to work her hand free when her aunt bent across the table, her voice childlike in the quiet. *"You can't run from the things you fear. Instead, invite them to your table. Sit with them awhile. Look them in the eye. You will find they are not as big as they seem, and you are not as small as you think."*

Wyatt didn't know where she was going, only that she needed to get away. Away from the house, with its rotting joists and its corrosive air. Away from Peter, with his traitorous mouth and his ice-cold eyes.

Away from James, who wasn't James at all.

She'd woken in the dark to find the bed beside her empty. On the old velour couch lay Peter, his elbow crooked over his eyes and Slightly curled on his chest. Thirsty, Wyatt had slipped out of bed and padded downstairs in search of water.

She'd made it to the landing before she heard it—the telltale snap of bone. Bending over the railing, she'd just been able to spot the feeble trickle of light from the kitchen. She'd crab-walked the rest of the way downstairs, her back pressed flat against the wall and her heart hammering.

There, in the kitchen, she'd found James. He'd stood with his back to her, barefoot and shirtless—scars running down his back in ridges. The last time she'd seen him like this, the marks had been clean and pink. Now angry contusions flowered beneath his skin, the white seam of old sutures gone necrotic. Beneath the low lights of the pendant lamps, he'd looked like he was rotting. The way the house rotted.

She'd watched, frozen, as he braced himself over the farmhouse sink, muscles cording in arms gone violet with bruises. Tipping his head slowly back, he'd let a single trickle of blood spill off his tongue.

Her first thought was that the mimic had gotten inside the house—that it had gutted him, the way it tried to gut her. She'd nearly run to him, desperate to stanch whatever horrible wound he'd incurred, but something in his expression drew her up short. It was the color in his cheeks, rosy pink. It was the flutter of his lashes, his dark eyes hooded. Not panic. Not terror.

But euphoria.

Nearly tripping over herself, she'd raced back upstairs, meaning to wake Peter. He'd rolled onto his stomach in her absence, and his arm hung slack over the edge of the couch. Between his fingers, there'd been a Polaroid, its gloss reflecting the light from the hall. She'd recognized it right away—it was the candid she'd snapped of James. When she'd knelt to pry it loose, her eyes caught on the skeletal gash of a jawline. The hollow socket of an eye.

It wasn't the photo she'd thought she'd taken.

It was the portrait of something dead.

Now she tripped through the field, heralded by the frenzied sawing of crickets. Burrs of brown wooly medic dug into her shins, drawing blood. The stitches in her stomach felt close to popping, the abscess in her skin hot to the touch.

Up ahead was the grove, towering pines mantled in mist. In her hand, she clutched the crumpled Polaroid. Now, in daylight, she could see every detail clearly. There was no questioning what the photo contained. Beneath the lintel stood James, his smile rotted away to bone.

His fingers were skeleton thin. His skin was haphazardly stitched, like he'd been quilted from scraps.

Impossible. It was impossible.

And yet, she knew. Deep down, she knew it was true. She'd seen the evidence in the well of his eyes. In his smiles, too sharp, too tricky. In the way he spoke, always just a touch too cold. Fighting back tears, she staggered onward, tripping over crumbling fieldstone as she went.

He'd known. All this time, Peter had known the truth.

And he'd kept it from her.

The grove was shrouded in a chilly mist, the trees girdled in pale webworm silk. The moment she crossed beneath its branches, the crickets fell silent. A terrible hush came over her. Up ahead was the chapel, its door hanging open, darkness spilling out from within. And beyond—beyond were the graves. Dozens of them, all for Peter. She made her way through the graveyard, stepping over the little mounds one after the other.

At the far end of the dense necropolis was a shovel, discarded. It rose like Excalibur from a bank of overturned soil. She tiptoed toward it, terrified of what she'd discover.

She found herself standing over an empty grave. Thin white tubers poked out through the dirt, reaching for her like mangled fingers. Somewhere nearby, a twig snapped. Her head shot up just in time to catch sight of Peter stepping out of the fog. She wrenched the shovel out of the dirt, brandishing it before her like a weapon.

"Stay back."

He continued his advance, taking one careful step at a time, like he were treading through an active minefield. "What are you doing out here, Wyatt?"

"You told me the beast was wearing Mrs. Germaine." It took considerable effort to force the words out. Her throat was thick, her stomach in knots. "You said it was like wearing a skin suit."

Peter's eyes were the color of the sky. Cold and gray. They hid so much. He glanced at the photo, crumpled against the shovel's wooden handle. Softly, he said, "I can explain."

Her laughter sounded wild, even to her. "It's a little too late for that, don't you think?"

"I'll tell you everything, but back at the house."

She didn't budge. "Is this where you buried him?"

"Wyatt—"

"It's a yes or no question, Peter. *Is this where you buried him?*"

He staggered to a stop. "Yes."

He wasn't even giving her the courtesy of looking at her. Instead, he stared up at the empty treetops, the unseasonal cold pinking his cheeks.

Nearby, something dark and formless broke away from the shadows. She watched the vast shape grow steadily smaller as it approached. It folded in on itself like paper, crumpling into the familiar silhouette of a boy.

From between the trees stepped a picture-perfect rendering of James Campbell. The beast walked carefully, edging its way forward with the same level of caution as Peter. As though one misstep would blow them all sky-high. Its hands were tacky with blood, red flaking to rust in the crooks of its fingers.

"Wyatt, pet," it said, in a voice like smoke, "you've gotten us into a mess."

Peter bristled. "We need to leave."

"I'm not going anywhere," said Wyatt, holding her ground.

"It isn't safe out here."

"Better here than trapped in that rotting house, letting the two of you screw with my head."

Peter's mouth opened, a retort at the ready, and then clamped shut. "This isn't the time to be stubborn."

"I'm not being *stubborn*. I'm making it easy. The last time the three of us came out here together, you planned to kill me. So do it. Finish it. Put me in the ground with James, if that's what you want so badly."

Silence rose to meet them, deep and absolute. Funny, how she didn't notice the ambient trill of bugs until they were gone. Her father used to tell her that crickets went quiet in the presence of a predator. Here, in front of her, were two. When the beast stepped forward, she drew back instinctively, jabbing the shovel toward it like a pitchfork.

"You shouldn't fault Pedyr. He has been marked by me for centuries." Its voice had gone old and cold, no trace of the posh elocution left over. Even Peter's name sounded different. *Pettier*, he'd called him. Pettier, not Peter.

"We don't have time for this," Peter said, still studying the trees.

"We don't want to be rash." The beast smiled, its teeth sharp. "I'll tell you the truth. All of it. And then you'll agree to leave here with us. You'll go back to the house without a struggle. You won't look over your shoulder."

Tension knit her muscles tight. "What's over my shoulder?"

But the beast didn't answer. It only tilted its head, peering at her through that black unseelie stare. "Pedyr was never meant to come through the sky. He was meant to grow old at home. To fall in love. To have a house full of children. And then, one day, when he'd outlived most mortal men, he was meant to pass down his gift and give himself over to me. I am very patient, you see. And immortality tastes so sweet on the tongue."

A sudden noise came from directly behind her—a terrible skittering sound that made her hair stand on end. She pulled the shovel toward her like a shield.

"Wyatt." Peter's eyes were trained on hers. "Don't look back."

"I never intended for him to stumble into the hands of the Westlocks," continued the beast. "That was a mistake. Mortals are always hungry for power, but your bloodline was greedier than most. They cut him down before he could take root. They fed him to me in unripe slivers. Each time, I replanted him. He was never theirs to kill. He has always been mine.

"And then came you. You and the boy, both. With the two of you at his side, Pedyr didn't just take root. He blossomed, though he'd never admit it. Finally, he had something worth dying for. That's what makes the sacrifice so succulent—the love that flavors it. Mortal life is so fleeting, but love is as enduring as death. An equal trade."

Understanding iced through her like a frost. "You've been pushing me to kill him since the very first day. It was you on the phone."

The beast's incisors glinted ivory in the light. "Yes."

"Why not do it yourself, if you're so desperate?"

"I cannot. It has to be you."

"Why?"

"Because you love him, Wyatt Westlock." The truth catapulted through the silence of the grove. It sank bone-deep. "You have loved him all your life. And that is everything to me."

The shovel fell slack in her grip. Without meaning to, she met the chilly gray of Peter's stare. His face was unreadable in the gloom, his jaw wired tight.

"When you bury him," said the beast, "it will be everlasting. I will drink from far deeper and sweeter a well than ever before."

Over their heads, something scuttled through the treetops. She suppressed the urge to glance skyward. "And after that?" she asked. "Once you've had your fill?"

"I'll sleep," said the beast. "I have been waiting for Pedyr a long time, and I am so very tired. When I am gone, the wound between worlds will heal. There will be no more need for Willow Heath, or for a Westlock to play the part of greenskeeper. You will be free."

A branch snapped overhead. Pine rained down around them in sticky orange needles. Peter's chin kicked up, his eyes silvering with urgency.

"We need to go."

But Wyatt didn't move. "What about James? What happened to Jamie?"

"You should listen to Peter," the beast said, brushing pine from its shoulder. "We need to leave while we still can."

"I'm not going anywhere until you tell me what you did to him." She swung the head of the shovel, gripping it like a lance. "You want me to leave? Tell me what happened."

Peter started toward her, but the beast threw out a hand to stop him. "It's okay. She wants the truth. It's time we gave it."

She noticed, then, that his hands had begun to deteriorate. In place of skin, there was sinew and bone. "Several years ago," it said, "a wealthy man came by the farm. His wife was dying, and he was searching the world over for a way to stop death in its tracks. He'd heard of

Pedyr, and he wanted to glimpse his immortality firsthand—to see if there was anything more to harvest than ashes. He left disappointed, but his visit planted the seed of an idea in Joseph Campbell's mind. If Pedyr's gift had been given, then surely it could be taken away. In the end, he thought that perhaps James might be the one to take it. But he was wrong, and his miscalculation cost your friend his life."

Between them, Peter had gone as still as stone. A marble boy, mired in his own personal mausoleum. Her starved god. Her secret saint. Her killer. His hands were balled in trembling fists. A single tear tracked down the side of his face. He let it fall.

"Is there anything left?" she asked. "Is there anything left of James inside of you?"

At that, the beast smiled. It was a small, close-lipped sneer, a bit of incisor bared, and in that moment, she didn't know how she'd ever mistaken it for the boy she'd grown up with. "We are out of time," it said. "The widow is here. And it appears that she's nesting."

21

PEDYR

Pedyr could feel it everywhere he turned. An imprint of wrongness, thin as film and sour as mildew. It was in the trees, scaled in yellow chanterelle where the light didn't touch. It was in the shadows, thickened with milky jumbles of silk. His tongue was dry, his mouth chalky—as though he'd swallowed down a mouthful of ash.

It wasn't the widow that left him frozen in place, though he'd seen firsthand that there was no outrunning her once she began to give chase. It wasn't the countless silken sacs, sewn into the trees and full to bursting.

It was Wyatt.

All around them, the grove was slowly waking under her thumb. Not in moldering sheaths of rot, but in full, bold blooms. Over the mounds of his graves, pale yellow dogbane unfurled, velvet buds shaking dirt loose from their petals. Sleeping alyssum exploded into dainty white blossoms.

And there—just three feet in front of him—was Wyatt, her grief cracked open. She was as awake as he'd ever seen her, a living flame against the colorless grove, the lines of her rendered all in Technicolor. Her mouth was dahlia red, her cheeks a shining, fever pink. Beneath her feet, the flowers burst open and open.

A cosmic shadow moved overhead, scurrying between branches. Pedyr didn't look up. He didn't need to—he knew what it was, knew precisely what sort of nest they'd stumbled into.

"Pedyr Criafol," came the voice of the widow, siren sweet and old as time. "It has been a long time since you brought me a meal."

Wyatt blinked, peering around as though shaken free of a trance. "What was that?"

"That was me." The sound came from everywhere and nowhere. From inside and out. At Wyatt's back, a shape lowered itself to the ground—a vast, eldritch being from the cracks between worlds. Double-jointed and arachnid, it peered up at Wyatt through myriad eyes bright with anticipation.

"What's this? A girl?"

"You will not have her," spat the beast. "She belongs to me."

It was becoming increasingly apparent that the beast couldn't hold on to Jamie here, so close to the mouth of hell. Already, it had begun to slake apart, the neat pink of old scar tissue puckering open at the base of its throat.

"You have no dominion here," said the widow. "You are too young, and too hungry. You live in the dark, but I *am* the dark. And I will swallow up whatever I please."

Pine cones popped, dropping their seeds. The air was thick with turpentine, the camphoraceous reek of balsam. Wyatt gripped her shovel tighter, turning to look at the primordial thing looming just over her shoulder.

"Stop," Pedyr ordered, and she did. "Don't look."

Her grip didn't waver. "Why not?"

"Because once you do," crooned the widow, "I will unravel your spirit. I will spin your nightmares into reality, weave your darkest fears into my web. Once I have you, little mayfly, there is no escaping."

A shudder of movement caught Pedyr's eye. On the nearest grave, a bit of dirt fell away in pebbled clods. The earth turned, roiling beneath the thick cords of Wyatt's power. The beast marked it as well. They met eyes, a wordless understanding passing between them.

Another shudder ran through the ground, and the beast listed to the side, catching itself on the wide trunk of a tree. Everything about it was wrong—a wretched permutation of the way James Campbell looked now and the way Pedyr had seen him last. Its nose was cracked and swollen, its fingers a dark, cyanotic blue.

"Get her out of here," it ordered, in a voice like an iceberg. "Now."

At the command, the widow's head turned on its axis, her wide thorax humming in agitation. "You owe him nothing, Pedyr. He has kept you tethered to him all these years, luring you in with false promises. But he is nothing more than a liar and a trickster. It is not in his power to extend immortality beyond its bearer."

Pedyr floundered, confused. "What do you mean?"

"Poor, sweet Pedyr," she murmured, spinnerets thrumming. "There is no mother waiting for you on the other side of the sky. Catrin Criafol died two hundred years ago, grief-stricken and alone. And he has kept it hidden from you, wretched as he is."

Pedyr swallowed the sharp bite of grief in his throat. *Catrin.* Memory came rushing in, clear and cold. He saw his mother bending in to drop a kiss on his brow. He saw her seated at her loom, a melody caught on the tip of her tongue and her voice soft as a stream: *"Your father is taking you out to the wood today, my heart. Be sure you stay close and mind what he says."*

He could feel Wyatt's eyes on his face. Beneath a nearby birch, another grave began to crumble. He banished the onslaught of memories, willing himself numb.

"Why are you telling me this?"

"Because I like you," said the widow. "And because you are like me. We are solitary beings, you and I, and we are not moved to aggression unless threatened." At Pedyr's feet, a skeletal hand worked its way through the ground, dirt wedged between slender metacarpals. The widow watched the bleach-white wriggle of fingertips. "I like her, too—this witch you have brought me. I have not witnessed power like hers in an age."

High up in the trees, the first cocoon split open. Spiderlings poured out by the hundreds, skittering down the rotting pines in a surge of black. Wyatt let out a strangled yelp just as another sac rent open. The grove was flooded with the ceaseless scuttle of legs, the starveling keening of newborns looking to feed. Under the branches of a balsam, the beast fought to cling to James's form. It didn't look up at the scurrying mass. It only stared down at its hands, its fingertips necrotizing to bone.

"Wyatt," Pedyr barked. "When I tell you to run, you run."

At her feet, the earth had begun to envelop the toes of her boots. Mold grew in dark follicles along the yellow rubber. The air around them was snowy with spores, stinging with power.

For once in her life, she didn't argue. "Where?"

"Anywhere but here."

With a curse, the beast scraped at its arm. A single black spiderling picked its way over the dry white of its ulna, squeezed itself between sinews raw and bundled as nerves. Another dropped down from the branches, silk dripping in its wake. More followed, silvering the tree in pale, lustrous tinsel. The beast slapped them away one after the other, staggering backward into the tree. Half-bone, half-boy, it watched in horror as webbing built like spun sugar along its calves.

"You will do as a meal," hummed the widow, "though I don't relish the taste of sulfur."

Wyatt watched in mounting horror as eight furred legs pushed past her, moving through the trees in a crush of branches. Obscured by the silver fall of silk, the beast let out an inhuman roar.

"Run," Pedyr commanded.

Wyatt took off at once, casting her shovel aside and disappearing into the mist. Pedyr lingered long enough to risk a final glance back at the beast. A venomous rigor had crept into its decomposing form. All that remained visible was a single gaunt sliver of its face, eyes gone wide with terror.

It was so reminiscent of the way James had looked up at him in those final, bloody heartbeats that Pedyr froze. But then—in a blink—the moment was gone. There was nothing left of the beast but a milky-white sarcophagus. He didn't stick around to see what happened next. He took off after Wyatt, tearing through the grove, branches ripping at his skin as he went.

Outside in the meadow, the air tasted like wet wool, the sky primed for a storm. His courage veered sideways as he oscillated on the top of a hill, turning this way and that, lost beneath the endless slate of gray.

There was no sign of Wyatt anywhere. Cupping his hands to his mouth, he bellowed her name. His shout was snatched up by the wind, his echo shredded to pieces. When there was no answer, he headed back in the direction of the house.

213

She'd left him something of a trail, and he didn't know whether it awed him or terrified him. In the farm's eastern valley, the low-lying meadow had exploded into a broad array of color. The air was powdered with sweet-smelling pollen, the towering grasses woven with wild quinine and pale white foxglove, purple-petaled aster and spiked bee balm. He pushed onward, driven by urgency, his blood pounding between his ears.

When the towering meadow finally spat him out, he was on the easternmost acreage. Ahead was a shivering paper birch, its trunk girdled in red Virginia creeper. Beneath the tree's pendulous blooms stood Wyatt. She watched his approach, her expression remote.

"Are you all right?" he asked, the moment he'd reached her. It was the wrong thing to say. Her head jerked up and she stared at him in disbelief. In the electric sizzle of the oncoming storm, her eyes looked green all the way through.

"You killed him."

His grief was a wound, raw and unhealing. "It's not what you think."

"What am I supposed to think?" The words spat between them like poison. "You buried him in an unmarked grave. And then you let me believe that *thing* was him. You let it into our house."

A defensive prickle started up his spine. "You have no idea what happened."

"Explain it to me, then."

"It's not that simple."

He saw the shove coming a half second before it happened. Furious, she cuffed him hard in the chest. He fell back a step, absorbing the blow. "I thought death was always simple," she spat out, and shoved him again, this time into the birch. "Isn't that what you told me? Or were you lying about that, too?"

When the third shove came, he caught her by the wrists, hauling her into him just as the first roll of thunder sounded overhead. The earth shook, sending a swarm of brittle mourning cloaks fluttering skyward. They were momentarily caught up in a flurry of yellow-tipped wings.

"I'm sorry." Pedyr lowered his brow to hers. "You have no idea how sorry I am."

Slowly, some of the fight went out of her. She sagged against him, her body racked with sobs, her hands unfurling against his chest. The fever in her skin scalded him through the thin cotton of his shirt.

"I thought I could carry it," she whispered.

He pulled back just far enough to see her face. "Carry what?"

The wind whistled over the hilltop, knifing sharply between them. She drew out of his reach, her cheeks flush with color, creeping thyme popping into pale purple spikes at her feet.

"I've had a really bad year," she said, dashing a tear from her cheek. "Really, truly bad. When I got here, I was barely keeping my head above water. And then I found you, and all of these horrible secrets were dragged out into the open. And I get it, Peter. I do. You have every right to be as angry as you are. As—as broken and as cruel."

He saw where this was going. Panic jabbed at him like a cattle prod. "Don't."

"I don't know how you've carried your heart for so long," she went on, crying freely. To the east, the sky darkened, clouds piling one on top of the other. "I thought maybe I could take some of the weight for you. I thought that, in spite of everything, we could kick our way out of this together. But it's too heavy, Peter. You're too heavy. You're drowning me."

"You're leaving," he said. It wasn't a question.

"I'm going home. To Salem."

"You can't. The woods aren't passable."

"Peter, look at me."

But he was already looking, transfixed by the way the world quivered at her fingertips. Her every move tugged at the seams of the sky, dragging the building thunderhead behind her like a mantle. She was a live wire, crackling with energy.

If anyone could walk through the woods unscathed, it was her.

He would never see her again. He'd spent five years in the dark, slung up and starving, counting each miserable day. Clinging to his sanity by a thread. At least then he'd been tethered by the possibility of escape, comforted by the thought that something better waited for him on the other side of the sky.

A home. A life. A mother.

All he had now were ghosts. Ghosts, and a girl who could rattle the dead. If Wyatt left, there was no one else. Dark would descend, bearing hell upon its back, and he'd be forced to carry the weight of an eternity alone.

"You can't go," he said desperately. "Not now."

"I have to. This place will bury us. I won't stay here and rot with you."

"I'll follow you. If you leave, I'll come after you."

"And then what?" Her cheeks were damp with tears. "You'll kill me? Keep me?"

He felt like he was being cracked open. Ribs split, his chest scooped hollow. He'd been pulled apart in so many ways, snapped and broken at the whims of men.

None of it felt like this.

"God." A watery laugh stuttered out of her. "You don't know what you want. You're stuck, you're—you're haunting this place. You're a ghost, Peter. Just like Jamie."

Somewhere behind him, he heard the sapling pop of scattered seed, the near-silent creak of earth stretched to the quick. Wyatt took a step toward him, power crackling in the air between them.

"I didn't understand it at first," she said. "I didn't know how to tap into my veins without bleeding them dry. How to draw on a well without spilling a drop. But I can feel it now. There's a thread inside me, tight as a snare. All I have to do is pull it, and look."

Stalks of silver-leafed lupine exploded into thin blue spikes. Sensing danger, Pedyr took his first step backward.

"Wyatt—"

He was cut off by the feel of something furred creeping over his ankle. He glanced down, surprised, and found a vine girdling his calves. Wide red leaves unfurled as the canes thickened, cordoning along his thighs. He was being slowly grafted to the birch's slender trunk—consumed, the way the beast had been woven into the widow's web.

Only, instead of silk spinnerets, Wyatt was weaving the world through sheer force of will. It was beyond anything Pedyr had ever seen. All the Westlocks knew how to do was bleed and borrow. Her father had shackled him in chains of iron, spent the next five years pruning the roots of the willow like an arborist—patient and persistent—until they grew where he wanted them to grow. There

217

was nothing patient about Wyatt. She was all fury, all fervor—studying the rapid progression of the vines with a preternatural focus.

"Wyatt," he said again, firmer this time than before. "Wyatt, stop."

The vines continued their climb, new shoots forming and then braiding with an unearthly quickness. Power singed the air as Wyatt's rage went unfettered. He struggled against his restraints, refusing to beg, even as his arms were pulled cruciform taut.

He felt the instant it stopped. The vines cinched just tight enough to slow his circulation, leaving him strung up like a strawman. Wyatt drew beneath him, regarding her work with quiet wonder, her rage evaporating beneath the miracle of what she'd done.

There were a thousand things he wanted to say, but there was no time to say it. She was going. She was going, and he would be left behind to suffer an eternity alone. He wanted to tell her what he'd seen, staring back at him out of the deathwatch's sun-soaked face. He wanted to beg her to stay. But it was too late.

He was always too late.

"You were right," he told her instead, "when you said I'm broken. I've scattered my own ashes so many times, sometimes it feels like there's nothing left of me to piece back together. And, yes, that has made me cruel. And it made me angry. So angry that sometimes I can't even look at you. The thing about anger, though? It makes an excellent accelerant, but it burns out fast."

Her eyes searched his. "What are you saying?"

Overhead, the skies were turning black. The clouds churned into a bilious sea of dark. "You're angry at me," he said. "That's good. Anger is propulsive. Hold on to it. Cup it tight in your chest, and move quickly. And maybe you'll make it out of here alive."

"You're not going to beg me to let you go?"

"Is that what you want? You want me to beg?"

A tear slipped down her cheek. Another. Another. She let them fall, white woodruff bursting open at her feet. "I wanted you to love me," she admitted. "But I don't think you know what that is."

Her words pummeled his gut. The grasses bent around her in a feathered array. He would never forget the look in her eyes, even when all that was left was darkness.

Even when the world burned.

Heart thundering, he watched as she turned her back to him. The last time she left, she'd gone kicking and screaming. This time, she held her head high. She didn't look back.

He didn't know which was worse.

22

WYATT

The trees at the end of the driveway stood silent. They rose from the earth in thin, branchless stalks, like ancient sentinels watching over the gate. Wyatt stood in the knee-deep grass and stared down the dark tunnel of road. Her stomach felt gorged open, festering and raw. The fever gripped her hard enough to rattle her teeth.

The last time she'd come out this way, she'd been attacked by the mimic. Gutted and left for dead. It wouldn't happen again. She wouldn't let it.

"Anger is propulsive," Peter told her. *"Hold on to it."*

And so, she did. She clenched her fists around her wrath until it bottlenecked at her pulse points, coagulating into hard clots of power that left her seeing stars. She let it flood her. The betrayal. The lies. The years and years of deception. James Campbell's open grave, Peter's gaze as cold and as desolate as ice. It filled her up and up, until she was close to spilling over.

Her plan was simple: She'd follow the narrow packed-dirt lane until she came to the first intersection. From there, it was a hard right onto a paved road. There were houses there. Neighbors. Telephone wires and transformers and knotted bundles of Wi-Fi cables. She'd find service. She'd call her mother.

From where she stood, the canopy looked curiously dark. Spurred by the whipping winds, the topmost branches clicked together like talons. There was something malevolent about it. She braced herself, listening to the roll of thunder at her back.

Move quickly.

The moment she stepped out onto the path, the winds died. It was as if she'd stepped clean out of time, the world cranking to a stop. No birds sang. No bugs trilled. Nothing rustled, skittered, or snapped.

She made her way down the road, watching green buds poke their heads through the matted carpet of last autumn's leaves. The sight of pale yellow cowslips unfurling at her feet melted her anger into marvel. Until now, everything she'd manage to coax into life was borne of rot. Germinated by death. But this? This was new. This was lovely. She idled on the path, transfixed, and watched as a cluster of white bloodroots yawned open against a nearby log.

"Wyatt!" The sound of her name was gunshot loud. She froze up, her heart missing a beat. Somewhere overhead, wings fluttered past. Footsteps followed, hard and fast, and then the voice was directly behind her. "I know you heard me. Don't pretend like you didn't."

She headed down the lane at a clip, clutching the white-hot locus of pain in her belly.

"Look at me when I'm talking to you, Westlock!"

The shout barreled into her. She tripped over a root, catching herself, and pushed onward. Quick. Quick. Quick. Directly behind her, Micah Barclay's voice came out wet and strangled.

"What's the matter? Afraid to look me in the eye?"

"Stop it." She clapped her hands over her ears. *"Stop."*

"You did this to me," garbled that impossible, drowning voice. *"You did this,* so turn around and face me."

"You're not real." She walked faster, crashing through a wilting carpet of bluebells, petals papering themselves to her boots. "You're not here."

A cold breath plumed along the back of her neck. She tripped again, her foot catching on a rock, and broke into a run. Far above the trees, the skies burst open. Rain fell around her in a silvery hiss.

This was her doing, she realized, with an awareness that nearly bowled her over. Her terror twisted, sick and angry, under her skin and the world responded in kind, a steady push-pull between the beat of her heart and the beat of the earth.

As suddenly as the shouting began, it stopped. She didn't slow her pace. She kept on running, her lungs burning, the rain plastering her hair to her cheeks. Rounding a bend in the path, she slammed neatly into a body. She reared back at once, recognizing too late the bone warden's neat suit and feathered lapels.

This time, he wore a mask. It was a wolf's snout—bleached to white and handsomely fanged. Tipping back his open umbrella, he flashed her a gentleman's smile. A pair of humanoid eyes peered out at her from the mask's hollow orbital sockets.

"Was it bothering you? The mimic? It does so love to play."

"I'm fine." Wyatt tried to push past him, but he turned with her, swallowing up her exit in a wall of dark. Rain flew off his umbrella in silver sparks as he gave it a jaunty twirl.

"I like to collect skulls," he said. "Did the boy tell you that?"

"He didn't. But I could have guessed."

His smile widened. "I have all sorts. Man and beast, things that roam the earth today and those that have long been extinct. Creatures of this world, and creatures of others. It's a painstaking hobby. I've spent quite a long time refining my collection. But there's a gap, you see. I do not yet possess the skull of an immortal. I'd very much like one."

"Can't help you, sorry." Wyatt ducked around him, attempting another failed side step. A crow shrieked, flitting past in a blue-black flutter of wings.

From the meadow, she'd thought the trees looked dark. Now, trapped beneath them, she could see that the branches were full of birds. They sat preternaturally still, wings blue black and eyes oiled dark. Not preening. Not chattering. Only staring.

"The boy and I have had centuries to play cat and mouse," said the bone warden, cutting off her escape. "We have centuries yet. Today, I have my eyes on quite another prize. You see, what is precious to him is precious to me."

Nearby, a single broad root tugged loose from the earth and shook itself free of mud. Wyatt stifled a gasp, watching as it stretched, waking. The bone warden didn't appear to notice. Reaching out a taloned hand, he raised her chin. She was forced to meet his face, blinking away the rain that streamed into her eyes.

"My birds have sung me the song of Willow Heath," he said, inspecting her. "A witch who can weep a storm into the sky is no small trophy."

To her left, another root plucked itself out of the dirt. It crawled across the muddied lane in severed fingers of bark. Power crackled in her chest, building like an electrical storm.

"I should like you for my collection, I think," mused the warden. "I'll pluck out the little aviary of your ribs. I'll watch your heart rot upon my mantel. And when he comes looking, I'll take him alive."

The roots stretched nearer. A crow let out a warning rattle. The call pinged off the trees, its echo dying. Alerted, the bone warden glanced toward the wood.

"I prefer my bones inside my body," said Wyatt, recalling his attention.

"You can't run from the things you fear," her aunt told her, that solstice afternoon in Salem. *"Sit with them awhile. Look them in the eye."* And so, she did. She let memory engulf her, swallowing down the dregs of her anger and the crush of hurt, letting in the demons she'd tried so hard to keep at bay.

Micah Barclay's outstretched hand engulfed in rot. The ambulance sirens and her staring classmates. The shower water running red, red, red. The missed prom and the skipped graduation, the endless months of voluntary solitude. The long drive to Maine, gasoline rattling in the back of the truck. *Don't think. Don't think. Don't think.*

The electricity in her chest popped into sparks. Skated along her bones. Bark cracked, branches splintering. The woods silvered as—high above the trees—lightning streaked through the sky. It severed the thunderous dark in a thousand lit fragments at the exact moment she let loose a single, blood-curdling scream.

Everything that came after appeared before her in flashes—the whites of the bone warden's eyes, the round gape of horror at his mouth. The claw of roots stretching wide, like a bear trap about to clamp shut. Thunder snarled through the wood just as the crows echoed her shriek, crying out in a chorus of strident screams.

She saw the very instant the bone warden snapped, pried in half by the strong arms of the trees. Bones popped from sockets. Flesh tore. She staggered backward, the spray of blood hot on her face. Dizzy, she shut her eyes.

When she finally garnered the courage to open them, the trees were still, as if nothing at all had happened. She swayed where she stood, her face tacky with blood, her hair suctioned to her throat. The woods were filled with a great and terrible quiet.

And then, over it all, came the call of a thousand crows.

Wyatt broke into a run just as they descended. Beaks tore at her hair, talons ripped at her skin. She drove deeper into the woods, running as fast as her feet could carry her. Reaching for the threads of power, she found them in tatters.

Depleted, she caught herself on the wide trunk of an oak, sagging to her knees in the dirt. Her fingers closed around a rock and she worked it free, then flung it blindly into the mass of feathers. It didn't stop the attack. Talons gouged her arm, drawing blood. She pried up another stone. Another, doing what she could to shield her face from the onslaught.

And then, all at once, the screaming fell silent. The birds abandoned her with a flutter, taking to the skies in a cloud of dark. Their sudden departure should have brought a wave of relief. Instead, she only felt a bone-deep dread. She wasn't naïve enough to think it was her poorly aimed rocks that sent them fleeing.

There was something else nearby.

She drew herself onto her knees, heart hammering and stomach sick, searching for the path. It was nowhere to be seen. She was waist-deep in a glade of ferns, buried in thick fans of jade-green fronds. Slowly, unsteadily, she rose to her feet, conscious of a shape looming just out of her periphery.

Lightning streaked overhead, illuminating a reassuringly familiar face. Peter's hair was rainwater dark and matted to his brow, his jaw wired tight. She should have been furious to see him there. Instead, all she felt was relief.

"I ripped a man in half," she said, speaking over the rain.

"I saw."

"Oh."

With a sickening swoop, her adrenaline crashed. Magic stuttered in her veins, the very last of it guttering out like a candle. Her knees gave a violent wobble and she dropped to all fours, the contents of her stomach swimming into her throat. Her hair was pulled back from the nape of her neck just in time for her to be sick.

By the time there was nothing left inside her but air, the rain had trickled to a stop. Sunlight fell through the trees in pinpricks of gold. Slowly, the feel of Peter's touch felt less like a comfort and more like an alarm. She scrabbled upright, scooting out of reach.

"How do I know it's you?" she demanded. "How—how do I know you're not going to unhinge your jaw and swallow me whole the second my guard is down?"

His frown deepened. For a moment, she thought he might say something scathing. Instead, he reached under his shirt and pried the suede necklace loose. Cubby's button winked up at her as he tugged it over his head and held it out in offering.

"This is the only one."

Hesitantly, she accepted it. It was more proof than she needed. The placid gray of his eyes was gut-achingly familiar. There was nothing malevolent in their depths. Nothing strange or other. This was Peter, just the way she'd memorized him. Solemn, silent, steady. Hands shaking, she drew the cord over her head. The button slipped out of sight beneath her shirt.

Peter exhaled. "You believe me?"

"Maybe," she said. Then, softer, "Yes."

"Good. Come here." Cuffing her collar, Peter drew her into his chest. They fell together against the broad trunk of a pine. Cradled into the warmth of him, she listened to the steady cadence of his breathing. His heartbeat radiated through her, allaying the live-wire crackle in her veins.

The first sound that came out of her was a hiccup. A sharp, breathy spasm that was halfway to a giggle. It wasn't funny. None of this was funny. And yet, the very next sound that ruptured out of her was an unmistakable snicker. Beneath her, Peter went perfectly still. His alarm struck her as hysterical. She doubled over in a spasm of laughter and regretted it immediately, the festering knit of her stitches snapping her back upright. The crown of her head smacked Peter's chin, and then he was laughing, too.

"Ow." She rubbed at her scalp, collapsing against him. His arm crooked around her middle, steadying her. For a moment, they were thirteen years old again, the summers stretching out as long as an eternity.

Eventually, the laughter resolved into a breathless quiet. Tears slipped steadily down her cheeks. She hadn't even noticed she'd begun to cry. She swept them away, watching sleepy blue-eyed grass wink open at the base of the tree. She didn't know how long they sat like that—flowers blooming, Peter's thumb tracing circles into her back— before her phone rang. It rattled through the quiet, setting her heart racing. She sat bolt upright, wrenching her phone free of her pocket.

"Hello?"

Her cousin's voice on the other end was little more than a crackle.

227

"We're ten minutes away," Mackenzie said, and Wyatt's stomach churned. She should have been ecstatic, but all she could think of was the mimic with her mother's voice, the feel of the dark closing in. She shut her eyes.

"Say something only you would know."

"Uh, okay? Oh, here's something—our fifth year at St. Adelaide's, I found your diary shoved under your mattress, and it was full of love letters you'd written to that boy from your dad's farm."

Peter's thumb stilled against the base of her spine. Mortification laced through her. "Mackenzie."

"It's true, I remember." Her cousin snapped her fingers. "What was his name?"

"Mackenzie."

"No, wait, it was Peter," said her cousin, triumphant. "Hah! I knew it would come to me. Did I pass your test?"

"Yes, that's great." Her voice wobbled. "Thank you."

"Stay right where you are," Mackenzie instructed, broken up by the poor connection. "We'll be right there. And Wyatt?"

"Yeah?"

"You're not going to believe what we have to tell you."

PART THREE

THE SOLSTICE

Two bodies hast thou slain and one heart,
and two hearts in one body, and two souls
thou hast lost.

Le Morte d'Arthur, Thomas Malory

23

PEDYR

They'd gone nearly an hour before anyone said anything.

"He's not here." The girl in the front passenger seat had an unplaceable accent, the lilt in her voice like falling rain. She fiddled with the radio controls, visibly restless, her white hair falling around her chin in a blunt slash. "I can't feel him."

In the driver's seat, Mackenzie Beckett only readjusted her rearview mirror. It brought the Beckett hazel of her eyes into clear view, her gaze bright with suspicion behind the cat-eye lenses of her sunglasses.

Pedyr had met Wyatt's cousin once before. They'd been nine years old when Wyatt's mother reluctantly consented to a weekend sleepover. Mackenzie and James had proved to be oil and water— disastrously so—and so her first visit to Willow Heath had also been her last. All these years later, she looked just as Pedyr remembered her—her curls red as a flame and her nose patterned in freckles. As if she sensed him staring, her eyes flicked to his. It was a warning glower, quick as a blink.

He knew what it meant. Furthermore, he knew how this looked. Next to Pedyr, Wyatt sat with her temple resting on the window, her face streaked in grime. She watched the guardrail run past in a rusted sliver, a spot of the bone warden's blood drying on the glass beneath her. In her lap, she'd picked her cuticles nearly to the quick.

She hadn't said a word since getting into the car. Not to him, and not to anyone.

"It's just that it doesn't make any sense," said the girl in the front. The radio skipped over stations, static sizzling through the car. "How can he have been there one minute and then gone the next?"

Mackenzie accelerated through a bend in the road. "I feel like we have more pressing issues than your newest ghost buddy."

The girl peered around the headrest, scrutinizing both Pedyr and Wyatt through a hooded green stare. "He should be here." She sank back into her seat, seat belt snapping. "He said he'd be waiting."

Mackenzie threw on her blinker, changing lanes. "That's a weird thing to say to people with zero context, Lane."

"She's covered in blood," muttered the girl. "I think it's safe to say they were already having a weird day before we arrived."

The crackle of the radio continued anew. Rock. Pop. Instrumental. Static. Static. Static.

Pedyr glanced sidelong at Wyatt. She peered out at the distant mountains with a thousand-yard stare, blood drying to the side of her face, his sweater going cracked and stiff with mud. One of her fingers had begun to bleed. She kept picking at it, oblivious to the beads of crimson that dripped into her lap. Reaching for her, he folded her fingers in his. She tensed up immediately, stiffening like a hare. She didn't pull away.

Looking out at the road ahead, Pedyr found Mackenzie assessing him again. "What did you do to her?"

"Nothing," he said.

Mackenzie's gaze drifted briefly to Wyatt, and then back to the road. "Whose blood is that on her face?"

"Not hers."

"Where's the other one? The insufferable one. James, right?"

"Don't talk to him," said Wyatt, surprising everyone. A strained silence followed, during which the only sound in the car was the faint pulse of electronic dance music. Flatly, Wyatt asked, "Can you take us to your mom's?"

The deepening pool of Mackenzie's suspicion was palpable. "Auntie Dora will murder both of us if we show up at the shop with you looking like this."

"We can stop by Colton's," said Lane. "It won't bother him."

"Uninvited guests always bother Price," Mackenzie fired back, taking a sharp turn.

Wyatt glanced down at the bloodied crust of her sweater. "How are you going to explain all of this?"

"Oh, this is nothing." Mackenzie waved her hand in a dismissal. "You think a little blood will upset any of us? Lane is dating her sleep paralysis demon. We don't ask questions."

"Maybe we should," said Lane, stopping the radio on a channel full of static. She turned up the volume, white noise flooding the car. "There's no doors meant to be open anymore. If what he told me is true—" She tapered off into silence, turning to a new station. She seemed to be listening for something, but Pedyr didn't know what.

"So," hedged Mackenzie as the sting of an electric guitar solo flooded the quiet, "your mom has been freaking out. I mean, it's not like no one knew where you were—we all assumed you went to the farm. She thought you might want to clear your head after—well, you know. At first, she thought you might have turned your phone off on purpose. But she started to panic when a few days went by and she still couldn't get in touch with you."

"Bad service," said Wyatt.

"Right." Mackenzie and Lane shared a glance. "Was there anyone else there with you? I mean, other than you and Peter?"

Beneath Pedyr's hand, Wyatt had begun to pick again. He tightened his grip, stopping her.

"No," she said. "We were alone."

It was a lie, bald and apparent. Pedyr knew she was thinking of James, his body emptied, his bones home to something parasitic. A beast from the blackest hell. Something cold strung itself along Pedyr's bones. "Why do you ask?"

Lane peered around at him. "Well, because—"

"Because the two of you never went anywhere without that British spawn of Satan," said Mackenzie, cutting her off. "Although I still can't understand why."

The car lapsed back into an uneasy silence. Eventually—and with Wyatt's fingers curled in his—Pedyr fell to watching out the window. He'd been in a car before—Wyatt's father used to drive an old blue Ford from point to point along the property, a bag of salted sunflower seeds in the cupholder, the bed stuffed with newly warded plants from the greenhouse.

Sometimes—when Wyatt and James were away at school and the farm was quiet—he'd let Pedyr take the drive with him. They'd ride in silence, listening to classic rock and spitting seeds out the open windows, the truck's loose struts rattling like old bones.

This was nothing like that.

Funny, how Willow Heath had always felt as big as a kingdom. Now that he was outside it, he realized just how small his world had been. The road unspooled endlessly ahead of them, curving out of sight into the distant blue-peaked mountains. There was nothing green. Nothing in bloom. The world was zapped of color, cold and concrete.

It looked like James's movies, Spielberg shots and Kubrick angles. On the other side of his window were things he'd only ever seen on a screen—towering roadside ads and rusted gas stations, bold green highway signs and dented guardrails. An overlarge semi screamed into the lane directly in front of them, expelling smoke, and Pedyr groped for his seat belt, his heart hammering.

Slowly, he felt Wyatt's hand turn over. Her fingers laced through his. He cut a glance in her direction and found her watching him, the whites of her eyes bright against the bloodied palette of her face.

"I'm fine," he said through gritted teeth.

She didn't answer, but she didn't let go of him, either. Pedyr tipped his head back and watched the world blow past, feeling as if he'd just been wrenched awake after a centuries-long slumber.

Eventually, the highway gave way to a stacked, urban landscape. Mackenzie slammed to a stop at a blinking red light, rolling down her window to cuss out the driver in the car next to her. The light turned green. Lane switched over from one static-eaten station to another.

In the front seat, Mackenzie began rattling off a to-do list. "You can shower at Price's. I'm sure Lane has some clean clothes you can borrow. And a brush. We'll need a brush. Comb some of the pine needles out of your hair, maybe."

Wyatt stayed silent through it all, the static crackling through the car's cramped interior, her fingers threaded through Pedyr's.

It was nearly four long hours before they reached their destination. By then, he felt close to crawling out of his skin. The car turned down a long, thin road and drew to a stop outside a row of sharply steepled homes. Several overly manicured trees rose out of the concrete, clawing at the stifled stretch of sky.

Pedyr climbed out of the car, his stomach unsteady. He thought maybe something inside him had been pieced back together incorrectly. He'd spent so many lifetimes searching for a way out, and now here he was. The beast was gone—he'd seen it destroyed. For the first time in a long time, the voice in his head had gone quiet. Willow Heath was miles from here, tucked away in the mountains of Maine.

He should have been happy. And yet everything felt wrong.

"I think we should say something," he heard Lane whisper.

"Later," Mackenzie said. Then, coaxing Wyatt up the stairs of the nearest house, she beckoned Pedyr like a dog. "Let's go, blue eyes. Inside."

But Pedyr didn't want to go in. Now that they were here, the front door falling open, he could see that the inside of the house was dark. Shadows, cool and corporeal, slid into places where they shouldn't. A car whipped past, windows down and music blaring. He followed Wyatt up the stairs, reluctant to let her out of his sight.

In the foyer, the darkness deepened. There was something heavy in it. Something cold. It reminded him of staring down the beast, caught in the lightless crosshairs of that brimstone stare. Without meaning to, he edged in close to Wyatt, folding her into his side. Lane was gone, swallowed up in the house's murky dark. Only Mackenzie remained, propped against the coat closet and surveying them both over the top of her sunglasses.

"She's barely said two words."

Pedyr met her glower through the gloom. "She's in shock."

"That's painfully obvious. Are you going to tell me why?"

"No," said Wyatt, before Pedyr could cobble together a response.

Lane reappeared, hovering beneath the sunlit prisms of a chandelier. "Colton's down in the gym," she said. "He probably won't come up. You know how he gets."

"Unfortunately, I do." Mackenzie pushed her sunglasses onto her head and peered round at the empty foyer. "Where's the bathroom?"

"Second floor," said Lane. "At the far end of the hall. The water tends to run cold, so give it a minute to warm up."

Pedyr bumped into Wyatt's shoulder. "Do you need help?"

"She *has* help," said Mackenzie, with no small amount of venom. Ushering Wyatt toward the staircase, she coaxed her up the steps and out of sight before she could answer Pedyr one way or another. Lane fell in behind them, flicking on lights as she went.

"I'll just stand here, then," Pedyr said wryly, scuffing his boot on the mat. Lane paused midstep, peering down at him as though she'd only just remembered he was there.

"Your friend that Mackenzie mentioned," she began, hesitance lacing her every word, "does he wear five black bands on his fingers?"

Pedyr's stomach hooked. "Yes. Why do you ask?"

But Lane had already resumed her ascent, her voice trickling down the steps behind her. "We might be a while. You can head into the living room if you'd like. Or help yourself to anything in the kitchen."

"I'm fine," Pedyr said, but she was gone.

He didn't know how long he stood there after, a clock ticking heavily somewhere out of sight, the dark crawling over and through him. He didn't like it here, with the shadows thick as a film and the smack of brimstone in the air. It felt too much like standing on the open mouth of hell. Upstairs, he heard the rattle of old pipes, the rush of water. Female voices trickled down in a wordless murmur.

Eventually, he became aware of a presence at the far end of the foyer. He turned and found a man standing in the quiet of the hall. He was tall and shadowed, his T-shirt dark with sweat and his face partially obscured beneath a ball cap. An angry scar extended the unsmiling line of his mouth into a disquieting grin. Price, he assumed.

"Who are you?" Price asked, in a voice that was neither friendly nor otherwise.

His suspicion rankled Pedyr beyond measure. He met it with equal wariness. "I'm a guest."

"Hmm." Price lifted his hat, pawing at a trickle of sweat on his brow. "Lane brings home all kinds of guests. Usually, they're a little less corporeal."

"You mean, she talks to ghosts."

"A medium talks to ghosts," Price corrected him. "Lane errs a little more on the side of necromancy. You need a drink? You look like you've seen some real shit."

"I'm set."

"You don't like me," Price noted. His chin lifted, and there at last were his eyes, blown black beneath the ball cap. "But you're the one in my house."

"Colton?" Lane appeared at the top of the stairs, her arms laden with crisply folded towels. "Is everything okay?"

Price's smile softened at once. The effect lent him a boyish, earnest air that made Pedyr doubt what he'd seen. "Everything's fine. Just being a good host."

"I don't believe you."

His cheek dimpled, all traces of darkness gone from his eyes. "Would I lie to you, Wednesday?"

"Yes," she said, but there was nothing accusatory in it. To Pedyr, she said, "She's nearly done."

"Thank you."

"Are you sure you don't want something to eat while you wait?"

"I'm fine."

"Okay. Hang tight." Lane disappeared back up the stairs, towels balanced in her arms. When Pedyr glanced back to the place where Price had stood, he was gone. Only shadows remained. Shadows, and the soft snick of a door at the far end of the hall.

Alone at last, he slumped boneless against the wall. For the first time in a long time, he allowed himself to think of what might come next. He was free. The beast was gone, a feast for the widow and her spiderlings. There was nothing left to hunt him, hound him, play his head like a fiddle. There was only the solitude of his thoughts, the possibility of a life with Wyatt.

A real life, not a pretend one. Something built on honesty and not deception. It seemed impossible, to entertain the idea of a future. He'd never had one before. Every life he'd ever lived was cut short before he even knew to dream of more.

Even as he thought it, the face of the deathwatch swam back into the forefront of his mind. Awash with the light of a rising sun, his likeness had stared out at him from a resigned, bloodless face. He knew what it meant.

There was death in his future.

And it was imminent.

It was another twenty minutes before Wyatt finally returned. By then, his legs were stiff, his belly hungry. She crept down the stairs one at a time, her knuckles white against the railing and her face scrubbed clean. Her right cheek was marred in three shallow gashes. She was in a patterned skirt and borrowed sweater, and it reminded him of the changing seasons, the year's end—Wyatt coming home from St. Adelaide's in her pressed uniform and leather clogs.

Something about the memory made him ache. They would never have that again. Not the carefree summer days or the sleepless summer nights. Not the stories in the dark or the games out in the field. He'd spent all that time, all those years, desperate for someplace else.

Wishing for a place that had only ever been a dream.

And now all of it was gone—the dream and the reality, both—and he'd never gotten the chance to savor either. He'd been given an eternity, and he'd squandered every minute.

He'd make up for it now.

He'd find a way.

He shuffled his feet, conscious of Mackenzie sizing him up as Wyatt tried on a pair of shoes at Lane's prompting. Finally, after several precarious seconds passed them by, Mackenzie's curiosity won out.

"Okay, I've been patient for long enough. I think it's time—"

Wyatt picked her head up, alarmed. "Mackenzie, don't."

"—you explain what the hell happened to my cousin."

"Leave him alone," Wyatt bit out. "He didn't do anything."

Mackenzie scoffed. "I didn't say he did. But now I'm suspicious."

"Well, don't be. Everything's fine." Wyatt bent down to lace her shoe, the color draining out of her face as she did. Cubby's button swung loose like a scrying crystal, blue pendant spinning out as she gritted her teeth through obvious pain.

"Everything's fine," Mackenzie parroted. "Yeah, okay. You expect me to buy that? Wyatt, honey, you can't even tie your shoes."

"The shoe is tied." Wyatt toppled back, sweat beading on her brow. Kicking out a foot, she intoned a flat, "See?"

"He told me you were stabbed," said Lane, glancing up from where she sorted shoes out of the hallway closet. "He said he found you in the forest, but he couldn't get to you."

Wyatt froze, halfway through jamming her left foot into a second shoe. Nettled by the quiet, Pedyr pushed off the wall. "Your boyfriend says you can talk to the dead."

"They visit me from time to time," Lane admitted. "Sometimes, people can't cross over. Sometimes, something horrible is tethering them to this plane. When that happens, they find me."

"Laney," warned Mackenzie.

"You asked me to wait until she was safe, and she's safe," said Lane. "I can't keep this from them. They need to know."

"Know what?" asked Wyatt. In the dim light of the foyer, her eyes had gone funny.

"It's James," said Pedyr as understanding turned him cold. "It's Jamie you've been talking about this whole time, isn't it?"

He felt, more than saw, Wyatt's eyes cut to his. He couldn't bring himself to look back at her. Not with the terrible truth etched into Lane's face.

"I hear him in the static," she admitted. "In white noise and in silence. I've seen him, too, but it's hard for him to hold on to any sort of form for very long. That happens sometimes, when there's no final resting place for a body."

Wyatt rose shakily to her feet. Her face had gone bloodless. "He's here?"

241

"Not right now," Lane said. She looked faintly apologetic. "I would have told Mackenzie sooner, but I didn't know who he was. Not at first. I had no idea there was a connection. He told me things about himself in bits and pieces. They always do. It wasn't until the last visitation that I even thought to mention it."

Pedyr thought he might be ill. "What happened?"

"It was awful," Lane admitted with a shudder. "He showed up in the dead of night. His energy was so strong, it shook me awake. I have what Colton calls hypnopompic hallucinations. Sometimes, I'll wake up paralyzed and be absolutely convinced spiders are crawling up my arms. But this time, they were. I could *feel* them. And your friend was there, standing over me. He was in this unimaginable pain. I've never heard a person make a sound like that before, dead or alive. But he managed to get out a message, just before he went quiet."

Pedyr was going to be sick all over the floor. He palmed his jaw, hand shaking. Swallowing around the prickle in his throat, he managed to grit out, "What was the message?"

"Find Beckett," said Mackenzie.

Pedyr wasn't given the chance to say anything more. There came a thud, the sound of a body hitting the ground. In the shuttered dark of the foyer, Wyatt had fainted dead away.

24

WYATT

Wyatt woke to the steady beeping of a monitor. Prying open sticky eyes, she found herself staring up at unlit fluorescent troffers, the curved rod of a privacy curtain. She blinked the room into focus, taking in the menthol green and sterile white, laminated posters of surgical safety standards plastered to the walls. A hospital. She was in a hospital. Her skin crawled. After the boarded-up dark of Willow Heath, everything here felt too bright. Too quiet. Too big. A gurney pushed past in the hall outside, marking its journey with a steady *click, click, click*. A distant PA sounded, a garbled code filtering through the speakers.

She tried and failed to sit up, falling back against the thin sheaf of her pillow with a grunt. She was in a paper gown, floral and flimsy, a hospital-grade blanket folded just beneath her arms. Every part of her felt like a bruise, from the butterfly-taped gouges on her cheek to her torso bound tightly in bandages.

A swollen IV bag hung from a metal pole at her bedside, releasing a steady *drip-drop-drip* of fluids into a tube. On a tiny wheeled cart, someone had left a garish vase of gift shop roses. A folded note sat open on the tray, the typeset within just barely visible:

> *Don't do that again.*
> *—Mackenzie*

The sun poked in through white vertical blinds, falling over the green flop sofa beneath the window. Sprawled across the cushions was Peter, fast asleep on his stomach, his right arm crooked under his cheek. Something unidentifiable swam through her at the sight of him. He'd come after her. He'd followed her. She'd left him to rot, and here he was.

"He's been there all night."

Wyatt glanced toward the door, surprised, and found her mother hovering there. Theodora Beckett looked the way she always did, fair skinned and whimsical, her iron-gray curls pulled into a frizzing bun and a velvet floral kimono draped to her ankles. In her silver-ringed fingers, she clutched a lidded cafeteria cup. The smell of weak coffee wafted into the room.

Wyatt didn't know how to feel. She didn't know what to say, where to begin. She'd spent the last few weeks digging up bones, and she wasn't stupid enough to think her mother hadn't buried at least a few of them. Fidgeting with a curl of tape around her central catheter, she said, "I'm surprised you didn't send him away."

"I tried," said her mother. "But Peter is Peter."

"Did you know what he was?"

"I did."

Another admission, heavier than the first. It stagnated between them. "And you let them hurt him? You let them use him like a science experiment?"

Her mother sank into the green polyurethane seat by the door. She looked tired. Older, as though the last several weeks had aged her. "I think you overestimate my standing at Willow Heath. The guild is centuries old, its members stuck in their ways. My opinions were neither asked for nor welcome. Why do you think we left?"

"I always thought it was because you didn't want me spending time with Peter," said Wyatt, unable to keep an edge from creeping into her voice. "You never liked him."

Something softened in her mother's eyes. Bending down, she set the coffee on the floor between her feet. "Is that what you've thought all these years? That we left because of Peter?"

"Isn't it?"

"Wyatt, *no*. Not at all. I took you away because it wasn't safe."

"Because of Peter."

"Because of the guild." Her mother sighed, tugging loose the wedding ring on her finger. Raw diamond winked in its tension setting. "Your father was a good man. His heart was always in the right place. But he was tangled in a centuries-old practice, with no idea how to unravel it. And the nature of the guild—well, something as old and as ritual driven as that tends to draw in men with dark aspirations."

"What do you mean?"

"You're an anomaly, Wyatt," her mother said. "I know you've felt it. The things you can do—I did what I could to protect you. I sent you away to school. I taught you how to manage your emotions. But the more you grew, the more unpredictable your power became. You'd burst into tears, and the skies would open. You'd cry out in your sleep, and my azaleas would bloom in the dead of the night. It was erratic, and it was noticeable. And that made it dangerous.

"Your last night at Willow Heath, you were so upset, you nearly brought the chapel down around your ears. It wasn't safe for you there. Not anymore. I couldn't stay and let you be used. Men like that—the disciples, the fanatics, the zealots—they're insatiable. They find a light, and they cling to it until they snuff it out. So, I left. And I took you with me."

Wyatt shut her eyes. Tilted her head back into the pillow. In the machinery hum, she was dragged into a rip-current memory—James and Peter in the chapel, the world rattling awake, someone shouting out for her to run. The vision slipped. It became a beast with James's face, snared like a fly in sticky white webbing.

"Unimaginable pain." That's what Mackenzie's friend said, just before Wyatt lost consciousness. *"I've never heard a person make a sound like that before,"* she'd whispered, and Wyatt's world tunneled into black.

He'd been there with them. He'd been *there*, and they left him.

A tear squeezed out of the corner of her eye. Slid down onto the pillow. Her voice mangled, she managed to ask, "What about Jamie? Did you know he was dead?"

Her monitor beeped. Outside in the hall, something metal clattered to the floor. She opened her eyes and found her mother staring, aghast. "He's—*no*. My God, Wyatt. I'm so sorry. I had no idea. I would *never* keep something like that from you."

"Are you sure?" She couldn't stop the anger from building inside her. "You had no problem keeping everything else from me."

"Your father and I made choices—deliberate choices—to wait until we both felt you were ready to learn the truth."

"Oh, so now you're on the same team?"

Her mother's mouth thinned. "I didn't come here to fight with you."

A knock sounded at the door and a doctor appeared. Black and petite, she was dressed in mint-green scrubs and a sterile lab coat, her locs tucked into a low bun.

"Welcome back," she said, pulling an electronic chart onto her tablet. "I'm Dr. Delva, the chief physician on today's shift. I was just starting rounds—I'm glad I caught you awake. I see here that you're eighteen. Is it okay that Mom is in the room?"

"That's fine," Wyatt said, though she still felt wired tight, primed for attack.

"Wonderful." Dr. Delva flashed her an amiable smile, and Wyatt couldn't help but wonder how much of the argument she'd overheard. "How are we feeling?"

"I've been better."

"I'll bet." Dr. Delva slipped her stethoscope from her neck. "Mind if I check your vitals?"

"Sure."

She winced at the chilly kiss of metal through the sheer paper of her gown.

"Your patient chart mentions you lost consciousness. Your vitals showed evidence of vasovagal syncope." The doctor straightened, slipping her stethoscope back into place beneath the white lapels of her coat. "Do you have a history of fainting?"

"Uh, no." Wyatt glanced at Peter, still asleep on the couch. "Should I be worried?"

"I wouldn't panic. It's not uncommon. Triggers can be anything from extreme stress to the sight of blood."

Wyatt nearly laughed right out loud, though there was nothing funny. She thought of the farmhouse closing in around her, the staccato snap of ribs pried open, the way the shower drain at Price's town house had run red, red, red.

"I haven't been feeling very well," she admitted.

"I'd say that's an understatement." Dr. Delva slid her hands into her pockets. "You were admitted with an abdominal wound dehiscence. Do you know what that means?"

"No," said Wyatt, "but I can guess."

"Whoever did the stitches in your stomach didn't properly sterilize their equipment. That, plus sloppy suturing, led to a reopening of the wound edges, and a fairly nasty infection to boot. Fortunately, the damage was superficial—no need for surgery. We've got you on an intravenous antibiotic, but quite frankly, you're lucky you got here when you did. Delaying treatment like that can be fatal."

On her chair, Wyatt's mother sat rigid, her face losing color by the minute. Wyatt squirmed, feeling like an ant beneath a microscope. How did she tell them she'd been trapped on the farm, the woods full of teeth? How did she explain the things that she'd witnessed, felt, done without sounding insane?

"When can I go home?"

Dr. Delva gave the IV bag a squeeze, eyeballing the fluids within. "I'd like to keep you another night, just for observation. But as long as your vitals stay where they are, I see no reason why we can't get you on an oral antibiotic and send you on your way."

The rest of the visit went quickly, and soon Wyatt was left alone with her mother, eighteen years of secrets bricked between them like a buttress.

"Clearly, you and I have a lot to talk about," Theodora said, staring down into the dregs of her coffee. "But not right now. You should get some sleep."

Eventually—and after several back-to-back episodes of bad reality TV—Wyatt dozed, lured under by the white-noise hum of machinery.

She woke from an oft-interrupted sleep to find the room dark. Her mother was gone. A muted infomercial flashed across the mounted television, a 1-800 number blinking in a bold *buy-now!* yellow. At the edge of her bed was Peter, dead asleep and breathing deeply, his head cradled in the crook of his arms.

"Peter." She reached out a tentative hand, pushing the messy flop of white out of his eyes. "Peter? Wake up."

His lids fluttered open. For a heartbeat, he stared up at her, distant and dreamlike.

"Hi," she whispered.

He shot upright, digging the heel of his palm into his left eye. "Dahlia." His voice was rough with sleep. The lines of her blanket were imprinted on the side of his face. "You're up."

She didn't waste a second. "We have to go back."

He froze, his arms in midstretch, and gaped over at her as though she'd just sprouted a second head. "To Willow Heath?"

"We can't just abandon him."

She didn't need to clarify. They both knew she was talking about James.

"We're not abandoning him," said Peter. "He was never really there in the first place."

"You don't know that for sure."

"But I do," he insisted. "I know it's hard for you to hear, but it's the truth. James Campbell died five years ago. I was with him. I buried him. The beast dug up whatever scraps were left and used it to mess with our heads."

"Then how did Mackenzie's friend hear him?"

"I'm not sure." He scrubbed a hand over his face. "Maybe it was some sort of death echo. She said some people can't cross over. If that's the case for James, it's because the beast was tethering his spirit to the waking world. But you and I watched the widow destroy the beast out in the grove. It's gone, and so is Jamie."

"And what if what we saw was wrong?"

The question was a cup placed over a flame. Some of the fight extinguished in Peter's eyes. On the television, a man with blindingly white teeth demonstrated how to cut through shoe leather with a steak knife. Queasy, Wyatt watched as the pelt peeled back like a skin.

"I won't take you back there," said Peter with a ferocity that sent a shiver down her spine.

"And what about you?"

"What do you mean?"

"Will you go back? The blood moon is tomorrow night. If everything I've been told is true, the opening in the forest will be visible to the naked eye."

"Maybe," Peter said. "Now that the beast is gone, the gap might have sealed itself closed."

"And if it's still open? There's nothing tying you to this side of the sky anymore."

The look he gave her was strange. "Is that really what you think?"

Twin spots of heat swam into her cheeks. She thought of her tearful confession in the meadow: *"I wanted you to love me."* She'd been out of her mind when she'd said it—angry and grieving and half-mad with power. She thought she'd never see him again. She wouldn't have laid her heart so bare otherwise.

"I just mean that you can finally get what you want," she said quietly. "You can go home."

A shadow passed over his face. "There's nothing left for me to go home to."

Silence lapsed between them, broken only by the muffled noise of the television.

"So, what," she said, just as the quiet began to grow unbearable, "that's it? We just let him go? We move on with our lives?"

"I've had five years to make my peace with it."

"Well, I haven't," she snapped. "There's a reason Jamie told Lane to find Mackenzie. He was trying to communicate with us, Peter. We can't just ignore a message like that. What if he's stuck? What if he needs our help crossing over? We owe him that, at least."

Peter sat back, kicking out his legs. For a long time, he regarded her without speaking. She was just about to lash out at him—to chastise him for shutting up like a trap, the way he always did—when he finally spoke.

"There's this necklace. It's an old Westlock family heirloom. Maybe you've seen it. It's a white-gold pendant in the shape of a—"

"Half-moon," Wyatt finished. "I know it. Is that what you were looking for when you ransacked my room?"

He didn't deny it. "Do you have it?"

"Not anymore. I gave it to Mackenzie."

"Can you get it back?"

"Why?"

"If you're right, and James hasn't crossed over, it means the beast

251

survived the widow's attack. It's still inside him, feeding on his soul. The only way to cut Jamie loose would be to send the beast back through the gap."

Wyatt narrowed her eyes at him. "I'm not seeing how some cheap gold ties into this."

"The necklace was your father's scorched-earth policy." At the look on her face, he went on, "It's a military strategy—destroy anything that might be useful to the enemy, so they can't use it against you. It was a fail-safe, in case things went wrong. The necklace is infused with old alchemical properties. Destroy it, and theoretically, it will snap the beast's tether to this side of the sky."

"Theoretically?"

"It's not like he ever tested it." He stared down into his hands, avoiding her gaze. "There's no undoing magic like that. Once a tether is broken, that's it. It can't be remade."

Some of the blood had drained out of his face. There was something he wasn't telling her. Something he was leaving out.

"Peter—"

"Call Mackenzie," he said, before she could say what she was thinking. "Get the necklace. And then I'll go back."

"With me."

"No, Wyatt." That flat, chilly stare met hers. "Alone."

By the time Wyatt's mother arrived, the day was in full swing, and neither Wyatt nor Peter had reached an accord. He stood vigil over her bedside, arms crossed and scowl menacing, evidence of their argument strewn about the room in a flurry of rotting rosehip. Bristling with irritation, Wyatt nearly pushed the nib of her pen clean through her discharge paperwork.

"Just need one more autograph from you," sang the nurse. "Perfect. You're free to go."

"I'll pull the car around," said Wyatt's mother, when he'd shut the door behind him. Her gaze cut toward Peter. "Can you help her down to the lobby?"

The question came out flinted, and so did his answer. "Sure."

Wyatt took her time changing back into Lane's borrowed clothes, examining the limp mess of her hair in the bathroom mirror. When she finally emerged, her waves forced into a semblance of a topknot, it was to find Peter waiting just outside, a storm brewing beneath the dark pinch of his brows. Their wordless stalemate persisted as they made their silent way to the elevator bank.

Rounding a corner, she nearly collided clean into a figure wielding a Styrofoam coffee tray. Peter tugged her out of the way just in time for an iced beverage to smash against the checkered tile. Cold brew pooled in a muddy puddle.

"Sorry," chirped a too-familiar voice. "That's on me for texting and—*Wyatt*?"

Wyatt reared up, panicked, boxed in by the wall of Peter's chest. In front of her stood Natalie Rivers, fair skinned beneath a dark curtain fringe, her cell phone clutched in a prettily manicured hand. Wyatt forced a watery smile on her face as Natalie slid her phone onto the tray.

"Oh my God. It *is* you. It's like seeing a ghost."

Wyatt's smile wavered. Coffee seeped beneath her boots.

"I honestly can't believe it." Natalie glanced around, lowering her voice to a hush. "I mean, *God*, Wyatt. No one's seen you in months. People are saying you killed yourself."

"Oh?" The corners of her mouth hurt from smiling. Her head ached. She tried to remember what Dr. Deval had told her about fainting triggers just that morning. *Avoid them* was definitely a big one. Doing her best to imbue her tone with a lightness she didn't feel, she said, "Surprise."

"It's kind of ballsy of you," Natalie said, leaning in closer. There was something conspiratorial in her posture. As though they were still friends, swapping gel-pen notes in trigonometry. Sneaking out after dark to hang out down by Pickering Wharf. "Coming back here, after what you did. If it were me, I'd never show my face again."

The air scooped clear out of her, leaving her hollow as a husk. She was saved from having to conjure up a response by the feel of Peter's hand sliding into the small of her back.

"We should get going," he said. "Your mom will wonder where we are."

"Who's this?" Natalie demanded as they pushed past her without another word. She remained rooted to the spot, openly staring as Wyatt jabbed an unsteady finger at the elevator button. She watched the numbers illuminate in a bright green display as the winch climbed between floors. When the doors finally ground open, she all but threw herself inside, desperate to escape.

"I'll tell Micah you stopped by," Natalie called after her, just as the doors trundled shut.

It felt like the closing of a tomb.

They made it to the front of the emergency department before Wyatt's knees gave out. She sank onto an unoccupied bench, breathing hard. Shutting her eyes, she banged the crown of her head against the tinted plexiglass. Beneath her skin, thin threads of panic began to knit into something sharp and corrosive.

"Hey." The bench creaked as Peter sank into the open space next to her. "Talk to me."

She squeezed her eyes tighter. "I can't."

Somewhere out of sight, an ambulance turned into the lot, sirens wailing. Funny, how all it took was a specific sound, and she was back there again, the January cold sinking into her like teeth.

An arm snaked around her shoulder. Gently, Peter drew her into his side. His mouth landed, featherlight, upon her temple. To anyone passing by, they might have looked like a couple—folded one into the other.

"You're rotting the planters," he warned.

She opened her eyes, peering toward the poured-concrete urns just outside the doors. The florals were a mixed array of white gladioli and red geraniums, concentric leaves curling to black. A thin man in a beanie stood by the nearest pot, side-eyeing the dying planter through a screen of cigarette smoke.

"Breathe," coaxed Peter.

And she did. Slowly, the knots in her veins began to unravel. Power turned to smoke, pale and ashy. She glanced down into her lap to find their hands laced together, his thumb tracing the hills and valleys of her knuckles.

"You did so good." She could feel Peter smiling into her skin. "You made it look easy."

A honk from her mother's Prius brought both their heads to the direction of the roundabout. Peter helped her off the bench, steadying her all the way to the car. They slid one after the other into the back seat, hands clasped between them.

In the rearview mirror, her mother's eyes were obscured behind dark sunglasses. Still, Wyatt could feel her watching them. Assessing. The moment they were both buckled in, she bent over the console and popped open the glove box. She fished through its depths, then held up an envelope, sealed with the waxy insignia of a bloodred pelican.

Wariness swam into Wyatt's stomach. "What's that?"

"Something I should have given you a long time ago," said her mother. She passed it to Wyatt and put the car in drive. "Let's get to your aunt Violet's. And then I think you should see what your father has to tell you."

25

PEDYR

If Pedyr had ever dreamed of a life away from Willow Heath, he couldn't remember. In this current lifetime, all he'd cared about was finding his way home. Back through the sky. Back to his mother. He never thought about what lay on the other side of the little dirt road. He never imagined how the rest of the world might have grown around the farm, the way the ebb and flow of rivers corroded the earth around an unmovable stone.

So far, he didn't like it here. He didn't like the food. He didn't like the smell. He didn't like the sounds and the speed and the way all of it seemed so hastily thrown together, stacked bit on top of ugly bit in a palimpsest of sleek glass and crumbling brick.

By the time they reached Salem, he was motion sick, his equilibrium reeling. The roads slipped from sprawling, four-lane arteries to thin, cobbled stones. He rolled down his window, breathing in the gasoline reek of traffic and the salted smack of brine.

"I've never seen the sea," he said, when Wyatt explained the smell.

Outside his window, people congregated in droves, swallowing up the sidewalks in thick pedestrian throngs. The car turned down a narrow side road, streaking past a patchwork quilt of old brick buildings and parking in a little lot behind what appeared to be a washed-out fire station.

From there, it was a short walk to the shop. Wyatt clung tightly to his hand, drawing him after her through the colorful crowds. Everything was movie-screen loud and Hollywood fast, and he kept tripping over his own feet. He felt like a fish who had suddenly and unexpectedly sprouted legs—like he'd only ever glimpsed the outside world through a glass bowl.

On one corner stood a woman wearing a bold yellow sign that read *Repent! The end is nigh!* On another, a bowed man with graying hair spooned kielbasa onto sausage rolls. A few more blocks, and they came upon a boy beneath a strangled yew, drumming wildly against a cluster of overturned buckets. A crowd had gathered to watch, and a few passersby dropped coins into a cap.

"Come on," said Wyatt, tugging at his hand. "It's just a busker."

He didn't budge. "I don't have any money."

"It's okay. You don't have to leave anything."

"Everyone else is." He tugged his hand free of hers, fishing in his pockets. He came up mostly empty, save for a melted candy bar in a bright orange sleeve. Dropping it into the hat, he relented to Wyatt's continued prodding.

"He didn't want that," Wyatt assured him as he reached for her, threading their fingers together. "Where did you get candy, anyway?"

"They had machines full of snacks at the hospital."

By the time they reached the Beckett storefront, Wyatt had fallen back to leaning on him for support. A bell jingled overhead as they stepped over the threshold. The inside of the shop was cluttered with oddities, shelves stacked with scrying glasses and healing crystals, sticks of incense and sleek tarot decks. In the back were entire round racks of shirts bearing various slogans. Pedyr picked up a pink T-shirt and let it unfurl in front of him like a flag. *We're the daughters of the witches you didn't burn* seared across the cotton in thick black ink.

"Put that back." Wyatt snatched it from his hands and shoved it back on the shelf without folding it. "Don't touch anything."

"Not unless you plan to buy it," said Theodora, sounding distracted. She stood by an open curio cabinet, rooting through a series of garish pendant necklaces slung on hooks. She hadn't looked Pedyr in the eye—not since she'd first shown up at the hospital and found him pacing the halls, angry and afraid and close to crawling out of his skin. Now, agitated, she snapped the cabinet closed. "I need to go upstairs and grab something. Your aunt is doing a reading. You know how she gets about noise in the apartment when she's with a client. Will the two of you stay put?"

"Sure," said Wyatt, though she looked suspicious.

"Don't get into trouble."

"We never do."

Theodora raised her brow, but held her tongue. Grabbing a few items from behind the register, she slipped out of sight through a door at the back of the shop. Somewhere unseen, a cat mewled.

Pedyr picked up a candle and sniffed at it. "Have you called your cousin?"

"Not yet." Wyatt pried the candle from his grasp and set it back on the shelf. "First, I want you to promise me we'll go back to Willow Heath together."

He ground his teeth and didn't answer. The deathwatch's smile flickered again through his mind.

The bell jangled, signaling the arrival of a customer. Wyatt caught sight of the newcomer a beat before Pedyr. She froze, going still as a doe, all the blood rushing out of her face at once. Glancing round, Pedyr found a boy on the entrance mat. Broad-shouldered and red-faced, he stood framed between two tower racks of kiln-fired mugs and glossy paper calendars. He was dressed in shorts and a ball cap, his shirt dark with sweat—as though he'd just come in from a jog.

"Hey, Westlock," he said, his delivery frostbitten. "Nat said you were back in town."

Next to Pedyr, Wyatt said nothing at all. In her silence, he felt it—a slight stirring in the air. Magic, raw and unrefined, seeped out of her like air from a punctured balloon. With a yowl, a black cat sprang out from beneath a shelf and darted out of sight. The boy didn't appear to notice the sudden crackle of energy in the air.

"Heard you were in the hospital. Did you stop in and see Micah while you were there?"

"No." Wyatt's answer came out on a wobble.

"Yeah, I didn't think so." He drew closer, flipping the bill of his cap. "He's still on a vent, you know that? They've got him intubated. Lucky break for you, I bet."

Wyatt's response was nearly too soft to hear. "I wouldn't call it lucky."

"Doctors told his parents there were spores and shit growing in his lungs." The boy gestured to his throat, sunlight eking in through the tempered glass at his back. "They've never seen anything like it. They're saying he must have drowned."

"That's terrible," Wyatt said, though her delivery came out flat.

The boy let out a laugh, hard and bitter. "Say it like you mean it, at least."

"I do mean it." Wyatt's eyes fractured with tears, and she quickly blinked them away. "It's horrible, what happened to him."

"You say it like it was an accident," the boy spat. "But what's Micah gonna tell the cops when he wakes up, Westlock? Huh?"

"That's enough."

Both Wyatt and the boy blinked up at Pedyr, the former as though she'd only just remembered he was there, the latter as though he hadn't been aware they had an audience at all. He huffed out another laugh, thumbing his nose.

"Did you tell your boyfriend what you did to the last one? Did you tell him you're a freak?"

Pedyr stepped between them. "Wyatt, go upstairs."

She peered up at him, wide-eyed and circumspect. Veins popped, fat and dark, along the backs of her hands. "I don't think I should."

"Yeah, stay out of this, man," said the boy. "Westlock and I are handling a little bit of personal business."

Pedyr ignored him, wary of the current that built and built beneath Wyatt's skin. Pressure with nowhere to go but out.

"Go," he told her. "Now."

He found her several minutes later—not upstairs, but huddled on the tiled floor of the storeroom out back, hemmed in between shelves upon shelves of merchandise. A yellow mop bucket sat nearby, its matching wet-floor sign knocked onto its side. Wyatt sat hugging her middle, her legs pushed out. On the floor beneath her, wild-flowers exploded from scattered paper seed bags in a vast array of colors, burying her in a makeshift meadow.

He shook out the ache in his hand as he sank to the floor opposite her, his knees bent and particleboard shelving biting into his back.

"I hope you didn't hurt him," Wyatt said to the floor. "You can't just kill people you don't like. This isn't Willow Heath."

Pedyr only sniffed in reply, lifting a scrying crystal down off the shelf nearest his head and peering into it. He'd expected to find his own reflection peering back at him—the deathwatch's likeness, flipped upside down by the curve of glass. Instead, all he saw was a pair of fractured hazel eyes. He glanced up to find Wyatt watching him, the coppery nest of her hair tipping to one side.

"What did you do to Braden?"

"I was extremely polite," he assured her, and set the glass orb back on its stand. "I told him the store was closed."

Wyatt didn't look convinced. "Your hand is bleeding."

"Is it?" He examined the broken skin along the pale peaks of his knuckles. "I've never been great with words."

To his surprise, a laugh cracked out of her. Bright as a flare, it faded just as quickly as it ignited.

"If Micah dies," she said, "it'll be me that killed him."

Pedyr didn't say anything. Instead, he watched as she worked a bluebell free and began plucking the petals one by one by one. Thin blue slips fluttered around her like rain. He was hit with a flashback of them as children— James tracking a spider through a patch of clover and Wyatt pulling petals from a yellow-white daisy: *Do you love me? Do you love me not? Do you love me?*

"I bet you feel pretty ridiculous," she went on. "All this time, you've been treating me like I'm this helpless basket case who has no idea what she's doing. In the end, it turns out I've been capable of striking you dead all along." The last of the petals fell. "Doesn't that terrify you?"

"Yes," he said, and he meant it.

"You could have lied," she said with a huff.

"What would you like me to tell you? That I don't lie awake at night in fear of the end? That I've never met anyone who can do the things you do?"

"Terrible things."

"Horrible," he agreed. "Beautiful. Perfect."

She plucked an entire fistful of flowers, folding her fingers over the pale blue florets, stem to stamen. Crushing them in the tight tremor of her fist. When her fingers unfurled, the flora was ash in her palm. His pulse kicked into a gallop at the sight of it—power, raw and real. No tricks, no compounds, no ground-up bones. Just Wyatt.

"We had a plan," he said. "James and me. He was going to come after you. I couldn't leave without being noticed—there were always too many eyes on me. But we thought if one of us could get to you, it would be okay. We'd made a pact, remember? The three of us, always."

She brushed the ash from her hands, watching him out of the corner of her eye.

"We were supposed to meet out by the chapel at sunset. James got there first." It felt strange to trot the naked truth before her, when he'd guarded it so carefully and for so long. "By the time I found him, he was already dying. He'd ingested some sort of poison. I don't know what it was, but his lips were discolored. The tips of his fingers had gone blue."

Her mouth twisted into a grimace. "Who would do something like that?"

"Someone who knew us well enough to think my immortality would transfer to James." The memory was like a rebroken bone. He wasn't sure it would ever properly heal. "He'd been given a knife and sent to carve out my heart."

Wyatt looked aghast. "James would never do that."

"He didn't."

He died instead, he thought, his throat pinching shut. It didn't matter that he hadn't said it aloud—Wyatt understood perfectly well what he meant.

"Whoever poisoned James would have been killing two birds with one stone," she said. "If he'd been successful, the beast would have been satisfied by the offering, and James would be immortal. That night by the fire, you said the way your gift worked was that no one else in your family would be touched by death as long as you lived."

"That was a lie," Pedyr reminded her, thinking of his mother, "as we discovered in the grove."

"But Joseph Campbell wouldn't have known that."

The truth sank between them, heavy as a stone. Pedyr's father had carved out his own heart rather than let his son die an early death. He'd bargained with the devil himself, and at the cost of his life. It seemed impossible that the inverse could be true—that a father would feed his only son to the wolves in an empty bid for power.

Across from him, Wyatt was having quite another revelation entirely.

"That's why the beast wanted me to kill you," she said. "That's what he was talking about that day in the grove. James couldn't go through with it, and if it wasn't him, it had to be—"

She fell silent, and in the quiet he heard what she was too afraid to say. *It had to be me.* Wyatt Westlock, who had loved him all her life, even when he hadn't asked her to. Wyatt, who would put him in the ground before this was done.

In a voice that was all scrape, no mettle, he said, "I may not have killed Jamie, but his blood is on my hands."

Wyatt blinked. "No, it isn't."

She pushed herself upright, slipping toward him. The storage space was cramped and claustrophobic, and she was forced to wedge herself between his knees to get close. Fingertips ghosting the hard knots in his jaw, she coaxed his gaze to hers.

"It's not your fault, Peter."

"Isn't it? I could have saved him. I knew what it took. Instead, I held him as he died. I buried him in the grove. And then I retaliated. They found me at his grave—seven of them, coming to the chapel to pray—and I ran like a coward. I led them into the darkest parts of the forest, where the widow sleeps. They wanted an eternity, and I gave it to them."

Her breath hitched. "Good."

"Don't." He captured her by the wrists, easing her down onto her haunches. A cyclone of regret spun inside his chest. He thought of the years of cellar silence, the beast whispering in his head: *You stayed behind for her, you spared her life, and how does she thank you? She leaves you here to rot.*

"Don't try to absolve me, Wyatt. I'm not a martyr. I spent the next five years in chains, thinking of all the terrible things I'd do to you once I saw you again. You left both of us behind, and you never looked back. I wanted you dead."

"And now?"

Bracketed between his knees, Wyatt looked very small. The cyclone began to slow, sinking deep into his solar plexus. Before he could think better of it, he'd reached out and tucked a loose copper strand out of her eyes. Her breath caught, shallowing. Emboldened, he dragged a bloody knuckle across her pulse. Something primitive sharpened inside him as she raised her chin to grant him access.

"There was an aquarium at Micah's house," she blurted as his touch traveled lower. His finger froze along the notch of her throat. "That's what I see first, whenever I dream. They kept it in the bonus room, on the top of a wide black credenza. There were all kinds of fish in there. Clownfish and little minnows and this one tiny scuttle crab they called Lou. The whole thing was decorated in massive aquatic plants."

"You don't have to tell me this," he said.

"No, I want to." Her insistence came out quiet but firm. He hooked a finger in the shoe-cord necklace and paused, waiting for her to go on. "In my nightmares, it happens just like it did that night. There's glass raining down on my head, and I'm on the floor. I see Lou, scuttling over my hand. A fish stares up at me, its gills flapping open like little mouths as it dies. There's blood under my nails. Some sort of root crawling up my wrist. Micah is shouting, and there's something wrong with his voice. He's saying the most awful, angry things."

"I'll kill him," Pedyr said without missing a beat.

"And what if everything he said about me is true?"

"What if it is?"

"Then it's me who's a killer," she whispered. "Not you."

The door creaked open, a bar of light widening across the dark. Theodora stood in the opening, peering down the freckled slope of her nose. Pedyr half expected Wyatt to spring away from him, but instead she stayed planted where she was, her hands tangled in his shirt. Tethering them one to the other.

If Theodora had an opinion, she kept it to herself. "Do either of you want to tell me why there's an entire shelf of smashed snow globes out in the storefront?"

Wyatt's eyes cut to his. "Not really."

"I didn't think so." Her mother pinched the bridge of her nose. "Your aunt's session is over. Why don't you come on upstairs? I have something I think you both should see."

26

WYATT

Wyatt sat on the yellow chaise in her aunt's cluttered living room and stared down at the necklace in her lap. The chain was white gold, the pendant a chilly half-moon.

Scorched earth, Peter had called it. It didn't look like anything special.

"Where did you get this?" she asked, speaking over the clatter of pots and pans that sounded from the kitchen. "I gave it to Mackenzie."

"She gave it back." Aunt Violet appeared in the alcove, her apron splattered in sauce, a dripping ladle in hand. "I raised Mackenzie to never look a gift horse in the mouth, but extenuating circumstances called for a bit of reevaluation."

Wyatt felt uneasy. "What sort of circumstances?"

"Your necklace was poisoning her." Aunt Violet's silver curls bobbed as she spoke. "And not in the way cheap costume jewelry turns your skin green. In a nosebleed and black tar sort of way. It's got dark energy." An alarm let out a series of warning beeps. Aunt Violet sniffed. "What is that?"

"The fire alarm," said Wyatt's mother, from her perch on the velvet hassock.

Aunt Violet let out a gasp. "My lentils!"

Wyatt watched her disappear. On the coffee table was her father's letter, the seal unbroken. Nearby sat Peter, much too large for the tiny old wingback he occupied. He sat with his knees pushed out, his elbows notched against the plum-colored armrest, and she'd known him long enough to know that he was seconds away from clawing clean out of his skin.

Surrounded by the mismatched odds and ends of her aunt's cluttered home, he looked woefully out of place. Like she'd taken a pair of scissors to a Renaissance painting and then superglued the scraps to an abstract watercolor. Or maybe it was just that she'd never imagined him here, far from the insular bubble of Willow Heath.

"I imagine you've been searching high and low for that pendant," said her mother, and it took Wyatt a beat to realize she was talking to Peter, and not to her.

Wedged into the chair, he looked unusually grim. "Yes."

Her mother's eyes thinned. "And I expect you don't want my advice, either."

When Peter was quiet, she sighed. "I'm not your mother. I've never tried to be. And I don't apologize—not for any of it. Wyatt was always my objective. I did what I had to do to keep my daughter out of harm's way, and I know you don't like me very much because of that. But I do hope you'll accept this one piece of guidance."

Again, Peter was quiet, his blue eyes shimmering with intensity.

"Wyatt's father passed without naming a successor," said Theodora. "As far as anyone knows, Wyatt inherited none of his ability. As the first Westlock daughter in a long line of sons, they believe she marks the end of a legacy."

"Misogynist bullshit," chimed in Aunt Violet from the kitchen.

Theodora fluttered a hand over her eyes, bangled bracelets jangling.

"The guild has been scrambling to rebuild for some time now. Without an alchemist on-site, there's no one left to muzzle the forest."

"We noticed," said Wyatt dryly.

Her mother's eyes touched briefly on hers before sliding back toward Peter. "You think just because I wasn't warm to you, that I didn't see you. But I did. I saw everything. The way you followed her. The way you watched her. You saw in her the same things I saw. You know, too, that without a keeper, the dark of the forest will bleed and bleed. Eventually, the guild *will* come looking for someone to stanch it."

"I won't let them hurt her," said Peter.

"I know you won't." Something unidentifiable flickered in her mother's eyes, there and gone before Wyatt could decipher it. "Take the necklace. Go back to Willow Heath. Finish it."

"The skies can't be left open," added Aunt Violet, who had reappeared in the door with flour on her cheek. "I can feel it, you know—the hunger in the dark. The longer a mouth goes unfed, the wider it stretches. Left untended, the entire fabric of our world will tear clear down the middle. If that were to happen, it would be chaos—akin to the ancient Greeks throwing open the gates of Tartarus and letting the Titans wander free."

"It won't come to that," Peter assured her.

"I hope not." Wyatt's mother rose from the hassock, smoothing out the front of her shirt as she went. Her next words slipped out like an afterthought. "I may not apologize for how I chose to protect my family, but I am sorry that you never had anyone to care for you. I'm sorry you were alone."

"I wasn't alone," said Peter. "I had Wyatt and James."

· · ·

An hour later, Wyatt sat on the edge of the bed in the guest room, freshly showered and dressed in her very own pajamas. Finger-combed, her hair waterfalled around her in still-damp waves. In her arms, she clutched the pale ivory linen of a dress. She felt strange— stretched out like taffy, her nerves pulling, spreading, folding.

Across from her was a refurbished dresser papered all in holograph stickers. The top was cluttered with items, her father's letter unfolding in their midst. She'd read it the moment she'd gotten back to her room, ripping into the seal with shaking fingers. She hadn't known what she'd find. Apologies? Excuses?

My dearest Wyatt, it began.

> *Your mother is taking you away today, but I doubt you'll read this letter until you are older. There is so much I would like to say, but time is short. Instead, I will tell you this: The day you were born, flowers bloomed in the dead of winter. Summer daisies, pushing up through the ice. In all my studies, I've never seen anything like it. I have spent my entire life mastering my craft. Scraping up dregs of magic wherever I could find it. And then came you, and you were a breath of hope. An oasis in the desert.*
>
> *Your mother says I have not been a father to you. I will admit that I am driven to distraction by the things I chase. It is easy for me to forget what's there in front*

271

of me, in my pursuit of deeper understanding. For that,
I am sorry. I'm sorry I didn't see you. I'm sorry that
you're gone.

Most of all, I'm sorry that the terrible burden of
Willow Heath will one day fall on your shoulders. But
I know this—if anyone can bear the weight of it, it's
you. The last Westlock.

I've sent something into your keeping. A half-moon
pendant. Keep it close. Peter will know what to do, at
the end of it all. He knows its power innately. Just as I
suspect he has always known yours.

And when our legacy is done, let it be forgotten.

Your father,
Wyatt Westlock II

She'd read it three times through, her eyes burning. She didn't know what she'd expected. A letter wouldn't undo five years of silence. It wouldn't rewrite eighteen years of invisibility. It wasn't a cure-all, or a magic fix, or a voice from beyond the grave. It was just a piece of paper.

She sat without moving and stared into the wide, petal-framed mirror that hung over her dresser. Her reflection was a wraith, backlit by the twinkling wall of string lights over her bed. She looked flame haired and haggard. A scream, trapped inside a girl.

A knock nearly rattled her clean out of her skin. Peter stood in the open door, his wet hair scrubbed into spikes. He'd dressed in a dark blue novelty T-shirt and pair of gray House Stark joggers—things her aunt had rummaged from the shop. *If the broom fits, ride it* was scrawled across his chest in fat gold lettering.

"You look ridiculous," she said.

"Mm-hmm." He angled his head to the side, studying the spill of lace in her lap. "What's that?"

"It was supposed to be my graduation dress," she admitted, fingering the scalloped hem. "I didn't walk though, so. Now it's just something I take out and stare at when I'm feeling tragic."

He let the door fall shut at his back. Through the string-light twinkle, she could just make out the icy assessment in his gaze. "Are you feeling tragic right now?"

"I'm a regular Ophelia." His unwavering stare was making her lose her nerve. Casting her eyes toward her lap, she fell to fiddling with a loose thread. "What did my mom mean, when she told you to finish it? Finish what?"

A floorboard creaked under his advance. "What are you doing with the dress?"

"I asked you first."

"Don't dodge my question."

"You're the one dodging," she fired back, and felt immediately childish. With a groan, she cast the heap of fabric onto the mattress beside her. There was no point in keeping secrets. "This is the dress the deathwatch was wearing, the night it visited. I wasn't totally sure at first, but now that I have it here in front of me, there's no doubt."

Peter froze midstep, his eyes flickering between the crumpled ivory heap and her. He looked more on edge than she'd ever seen him, like live ammunition, primed to explode at the slightest touch. The sudden intensity made her want to draw her knees to her chest—to curl in on herself and disappear.

"Burn it," he said, in a voice like flint against stone.

"And what good will that do?" The question came out armed with a bite, though she hadn't meant for it to. "If I've learned anything from growing up with clairvoyants, it's that you can't escape fate. Aunt Violet said she can still feel the tear in the sky. You know what that means, right? It means the beast survived the widow. It means it's still there, waiting for us. It'll always be waiting for us. We have the necklace. We can send the beast back through the sky and put James's soul to rest. It's what he deserves."

Peter's swallow was audible in the quiet. "Wyatt, there's something you—"

She didn't give him space to talk her out of it. "We're going back to Willow Heath. Both of us, together. Whatever happens will happen."

Peter's eyes, normally ice cold, burned propane blue in the dark. She stared back, bracing herself for a fight. When none came, she flopped stiffly onto her back. Her stitches were pulled tight, her nerves tighter. Overhead, the ceiling fan spun in a lazy rotation. A pot clattered out in the kitchen.

Still, Peter said nothing. A moment later, the mattress creaked, groaning beneath additional weight. Prying open her eyes, she tipped her chin up and up until she spotted Peter at the head of the bed. He sat propped against the headboard, quietly examining the small army of plushies on her pillow.

"Come here," he said, the moment he caught her staring.

She wanted to say something clever, but the look in his eyes robbed her of wit. Obedient, she climbed up toward the headboard, sinking onto the pillow beside him. The moment she'd settled into place, he rolled onto his side to face her—his head propped in the bent crook of his elbow, a plushie spooned against his stomach.

So close, she smelled the clean notes of his borrowed soap. And beneath it, an earthy, familiar head she'd come to associate with mornings on the farm. Meadow grass and bluebells and grass slick with dew. Home, she realized. He smelled like home.

"Tell me a story," he said suddenly. "Like you used to."

She rolled to face him, tucking her hands under her cheek. "What do you want to hear?"

"Anything." He reached for her, threading a damp ribbon of her hair through his fingers. "Something happy."

She thought it over, hyperaware of the way his touch slipped lower, tracing her clavicle through the thin cotton of her pajamas. "Once upon a time," she whispered, "there was a girl who lived on a farm beside a forest. And there were two boys who lived there with her."

"And were they friends?"

"No. They hated her. One of them more so than the other. He thought she was loud and angry and ridiculous."

His hand slipped under her shirt, fingertips skimming the soft curve of her hip. "You're telling it all wrong, Dahlia."

"Am I?"

"You are. He didn't hate her. He loved her so much that it was like holding his heart outside of his body."

All the breath rushed out of her in an audible hiccup. "Don't say things you don't mean."

"I never do." He fisted a hand in the hem of her shirt, coaxing her closer. "Keep going."

"There's nothing else to tell. That's the whole story. All three of them lived very dull, very normal lives. They died very dull, very normal deaths."

He smiled ruefully. "Side by side?"

"Old and gray."

It felt cruel to say, to a boy who'd never lived past eighteen. But she'd never been able to keep herself from dreaming. Peter didn't seem to mind. His fingers skated down her spine, leaving a trail of gooseflesh in their wake.

"Happily ever after?"

She pulled a face, her stomach tightening. "That's very corny of you."

"It's how every good story ends." He touched the tip of his nose to hers. His eyes were a deep-ocean dark. She saw everything and nothing in their crushing depths. "Ask me what I want."

She felt singed like paper, her skin burning wherever he touched. "What do you want?"

"I want to kiss you, Wyatt."

His admission sank into the quiet. She lay perfectly still, her pulse thrumming in her ears. "What have you been waiting for?"

She didn't know who moved first. She only knew that one instant they were nose to nose, both of them breathing hard and fast, and the next his mouth was crashing over hers. It was nothing like that night in the windowsill, chaste and nervous. This was tongues and teeth. It was desperate and grasping. It was hungry, open-mouthed kisses in the string-light dark.

All those years wondering what a real kiss from Peter might taste like, and now she knew. He tasted like a tragedy. An end, before they'd even begun. They rolled together so that she was bracketed beneath him, his mouth at her pulse and her fingers threading through his hair. Magic braided through her blood, popping into sparks of color, until the feel of it ruptured out of her in a gasp. He pulled back and she chased him, propping herself on her elbows to kiss the hard column of his throat.

"Is this okay?" His eyes dropped to the substantial layer of medical tape around her abdomen. "Am I hurting you?"

She answered him with another kiss, slower and deeper than the first. He folded himself into it, the room around them sinking into a nebulous haze. They moved together, molding one into the other, summer after summer of wanting ribboning between them. His careful touch crystallized the molten glass of her veins. Shattered her into a thousand glimmering pieces.

A pebble at the window brought both of their heads rearing up. Peter scowled, tossing a glance toward the blackout curtains. "Did you hear that?"

"Ignore it," she said, and kissed the corner of his mouth.

Another pebble followed the first. A few seconds later, a third. A fourth splintered the glass. Wyatt nearly leapt out of her skin as Peter shoved off the bed. Heading for the window, he tore back the curtains with a muttered curse. Three shadowed figures huddled in the street below, two of them still as stone, the third gesticulating in a distinctly Beckett way.

Peter undid the latch and swung open the window. A flurry of voices rose up to meet them.

"—absolutely unnecessary," sniped Mackenzie. "Haven't you seen *Romeo and Juliet*, Price? You don't *lob* the rock through the window like a brute."

"No one was answering," came the voice of a boy, flat and cold.

"Go away," called Wyatt. At the sound, three faces angled toward the window.

"Oh good." Mackenzie's smile was ivory in the lamplight. "You're still awake. I wasn't sure—you weren't answering your phone. Come down. We have something to show you."

By the time they managed to slip into the lamplit shadows of the street out front, the blue pops of morning glory in Aunt Violet's flower boxes had just begun to pucker closed—a last gasp of whatever magic they'd woven between them in the breathless hush of Wyatt's bedroom. A boy in a ball cap stood over the nearest flower box, the thin slash of his mouth turned down in a quizzical frown. Lane peeked out from behind him, her arms locked around his middle in an easy embrace, her fingers pale as opals in the gloom. Next to them, Mackenzie was breathless with impatience.

"You live here," Wyatt said, shrugging off her cousin's embrace. "You could have just come inside."

Mackenzie looked aghast at the suggestion. "And bring a demon in the apartment? My mom will be cleansing the place for *days* to get rid of the stink. Sorry, Price."

Wyatt glanced toward the boy. He didn't give any indication of having heard Mackenzie at all as he glanced down at the silver face of his watch.

Peter didn't share the same indifference. "That wasn't a joke, back in the car? He's *actually* a demon?"

The boy's eyes flicked up. "Do you have a problem with that?"

"He doesn't have a problem with you, Colton," Lane assured him. She drew away from him, shivering in a fall-flannel jacket, though the

278

night was warm. The first kiss of summer clung to the air. "Actually, that's why we're here. It's your friend. James? I saw him."

Wyatt's chest caved in. "You did?"

"I tried to ask him some more direct questions this time. He seemed agitated, so I didn't get a whole lot out of him. He kept saying things that didn't make sense. But he mentioned you, Wyatt."

"Me?"

"He, um, told me to tell you he saw the stars."

"I forgot how bright the stars are from your window." Wyatt's stomach spun. Understanding fermented in her chest, sour and vinous. "I knew it. He was there that night. It was him. He—he's been trying to communicate with us this whole time."

"That's not possible." This from Peter, his voice strained. "He's dead."

"Death gets a little fickle," said Colton, "once you start to mess around with it."

Out in the street, a car went past. Headlights chased away the shadows in fleeting spotlights of yellow. Wyatt watched the flurry of moths in the light, her nerves haywire. "James is trapped inside of that *thing*, and we left him strung up alone in the widow's web."

A palpable silence followed. "The what?" asked Lane.

"Widow's web," repeated Colton, prying his hands out of his pockets to form a corresponding sign. "You heard her right."

Wyatt's heart was giving one shock paddle start after the other. She thought of the way James would surface sometimes—the way the sunlight would skitter over him in slips of silver, and there, in the spaces between shadow and dark, she'd see the boy she remembered staring out of that stark, starveling face.

Rounding on Peter, she said, "It's not some death echo, or

whatever you called it. It's him. It's Jamie. He's in there."

Peter laced his fingers over the crown of his head and peered up at the starless strip of sky between buildings. He looked unsteady on his feet, like a firm wind might bowl him clean over. He didn't say a word.

"We have something that might help," said Mackenzie. "It's why we're here."

"Colton is like your friend," explained Lane. "He died, and he came back Other. There are parts of him that have been twisted by his time in the afterlife. Mackenzie has been messing around with developing an elixir to try and see if there was anything that might help him feel a little more—"

She paused, searching for the right word, and Colton chimed in with a flat, "Human."

"I wasn't going to say that," Lane said softly.

"It's kind of like a suppressant," Mackenzie hedged. "It helps him control his urges."

Colton's scarred mouth turned down at the corners. "I told you to stop calling it that."

Mackenzie ignored him, her bright eyes exultant. "It's a mixture of my own making. I had to work out a few bugs at the start, but Price makes an exceptional guinea pig."

"And that," muttered Colton darkly.

"I can't get him out of my head." Lane's green eyes glittered in the lamplight. "He's fighting so hard to work himself loose, but he can't do it on his own."

Next to Wyatt, Peter had gone white as a sheet.

"So we could get him back," Wyatt whispered. "We can save him?"

"His body is functioning as a host," Colton said. "Think of it this way—have you ever seen a parasitoid wasp suck a spider dry?"

"Literally no one has seen that," Mackenzie replied in a clipped voice. "Don't be disgusting."

Colton's shoulder lifted in a shrug. "That's what's happening here. Only, instead of internal fluids, there's an ancient entity feeding on your friend's soul. Making him behave in erratic ways. If he can take back control, there's no reason he can't stay on this plane. Legally dead or otherwise."

"It's not a permanent fix," added Mackenzie, when everyone was quiet. "It's administered in a metered dosage. I've been borrowing ingredients from my mom's surplus stock, so I can only make a little bit at a time, but if you ration, it should be enough to keep him contained until I can get you more. Anyway, here it is." She held out her hand. In her open palm sat a tube of green, a recycled canister crammed into the top of the plastic actuator. Triumphant, she sang, "Ta-*da*."

"An inhaler," remarked Wyatt flatly. "Wow."

"That was my reaction, too," said Colton, glancing once more at his watch.

"People!" Mackenzie snapped her fingers at each of them in shutter-quick succession. "Can we stop criticizing the presentation and instead marvel at my *utter* Wiccan prowess?"

"It looks rudimentary," admitted Lane with another glance at Colton. "But it works."

"It does," he agreed, "but you'll have to convince him to take it. And from what Lane has told me, it sounds like you have your work cut out for you."

281

27

WYATT

The house was dark when Wyatt and Peter finally returned to the farm. The day had settled slowly into dusk, and set against the azure sky, Willow Heath looked like something alive, braided into the earth. Only the roof was visible over the thick cling of ivy, its shingles coming loose and the chimney cap knocked askew by a fat tuft of pigweed.

And there, snared in the branches of the far-off trees, was the blood moon, rosy and rising.

They moved side by side through the meadow, picking their way past the millpond rimed in red algae, the little rowboat moored in the reeds where they'd left it. Everything felt frozen in motion, time slowing to a crawl. It was as though the whole of the farm had been caught midyawn. She wasn't sure if Willow Heath had always felt this way, or if it was only just now falling asleep, the enchantment seeping out of it. Awareness sparked between them, bright as a June bug— somewhere out there was the beast, lying in wait.

Before the night was over, they would send it back into the bowels of hell.

Or they would die trying.

They found the front door gaping open, boards ripped free as though by some great goliath. They entered one after the other, broken glass crunching underfoot. Inside, the lights didn't turn on. Wyatt stood in the foyer and clicked the switch on and then off and then on again. The hall stayed dim as a tomb, a chicken fussing somewhere unseen, the rafters milky with cobwebs. It looked as though the widow's spiderlings had found their way into the house, coating every corner in their thick, gossamer tatting.

Peter pulled the door shut and leaned against it, watching as she flicked the switch once more into the on position. Off. On. Off. Giving up, she flopped against the door beside him.

"The power's off."

"Oh, is it?" He plucked a bit of stray webbing off the lacy eyelet of her sleeve. The blood had drained from his face when she'd come downstairs wearing the dress that morning, but she hadn't given him space to argue. *"It has pockets,"* she'd said. *"It'll be perfect."*

Now, brushing cobwebs from his hand, he cut her a sideways glance. "If this goes south, promise me you'll get out."

"And leave you here alone? Not a chance. That's a direct violation of our truce."

He didn't laugh. "You have the necklace. If your cousin's contraption doesn't work—"

"It's going to work."

"Maybe. You have to admit, it's a half-baked plan at best. At worst, it's a suicide mission. I don't like the thought of you getting that close to the beast. We don't even know for sure if binding it will give us access to James. We don't know how much of him is left in there."

"All of him," she said, though she had no way of knowing for sure. "It'll work."

"But if it doesn't—"

"It will."

"—you know what to do."

"Smash the necklace," she said, reaching instinctively for the half-moon pendant at her throat. "You've only told me a hundred times."

"Make sure you use something heavy. A rock. A hammer."

"The instructions are self-explanatory, Peter."

His mouth turned down at one corner. Tilted as it was, it looked dangerously close to slipping off his face altogether. She thought he might be about to berate her further, but he only caught her to him, ducking his head to capture her mouth in his. She made a noise of surprise, a shiver running through her as his breath skated across her tongue. Rising up onto her toes, she kissed him back, her hands braced against his chest.

Loving Peter had always felt a little bit like poking at a bruise. Impossible to stop, even when it hurt. But nothing had ever hurt quite as badly as this—kissing him at the world's end, surrounded by a living monument to all their wasted time. It felt like a goodbye, and that, more than anything else, set her entirely off-center.

When at last they came up for air, they were both breathless. A dahlia-red smudge darkened the corner of his frown. Her trademark color. She wiped it away and he chased her touch, pressing a kiss to the pad of her thumb.

"What was that for?"

"Nothing." He touched his brow to hers. "You look beautiful, that's all."

He was lying. She could feel it.

She didn't have the chance to interrogate him. A mewl sounded, drawing them apart. Slightly trotted out of the shadows, her eyes big and green, her tail twitching. Wyatt bent down and scooped the old cat into her arms, nuzzling her cheek into the furry top of her head.

"There you are. I knew you were indestructible."

"It's too quiet." Peter squinted up the empty staircase. "I thought the beast would be waiting here for us."

Wyatt clung tighter to Slightly. "Maybe it's still in the grove."

"I don't think so." He moved deeper into the hall, peering down at the dense forest of maidenhair that spilled out from the dining room. "It might be an ambush. Stay here. I'll check out the rest of the house."

Her heart gave a violent squeeze. "I want to come with you."

"Bad idea." He prodded at a stray bit of webbing, brushing the sticky remnants from his fingers with a backward glance. "Slightly isn't the only one here who's indestructible, remember? Stay put. Wait for my signal."

He left her there before she could argue, disappearing into the ghostly funnel of the hall. She watched him go, fear spearing her in the gut. He was right. It *was* too quiet. She waited, listening. A minute crawled past, slow as an eon. On the wall, a spider skittered out of a crack in the plaster and disappeared behind the sideboard.

Somewhere across the house, there came the resounding smack of something heavy hitting the floor. Glass shattered. Slightly yowled, leaping from her arms and bolting off into the dark. Wyatt fell in after her, her breath rattling in her lungs.

She found Peter in the greenhouse.

And he wasn't alone.

Moonlight poured in through the steepled panes, washing him and a half-dozen robed occupants in pools of limpid pink. Peter knelt before them, forced to his knees in a crush of broken glass. Nearby, a potted plant lay shattered on the floor, soil leaking out around the colorless claw of a root.

And there, just behind him, stood James Campbell's chiseled likeness, the lightless depths of his eyes as alien to her as anything. Broken blood vessels mottled his throat, veining over his jaw in thinning violet splinters. He looked pumped full of venom, his eyelids as swollen and shining as plums.

She felt for the inhaler in her pocket just as Peter's eyes found hers. "Do it," he mouthed.

She knew what he wanted—for her to forget about the inhaler and smash the necklace instead. To snap the tether and send the beast back into the waiting dark. But what would happen to James if she did? *"I can't remember the last time I saw the sky,"* he'd said, that night in her bedroom. He'd spent five years rotting in a grave. Five years at the mercy of something old and insidious.

She wouldn't banish him to an eternity in the dark. Not without doing everything she could to stop it first. It was the three of them, always.

On his knees, Peter gave the slightest shake of his head. She pretended not to see it.

"You know," mused the beast, and it sounded nothing at all like Jamie, "I used to think that this side of the sky sucked the magic out of men. It's ugly here—cruel and cannibalistic. But three days ago, I watched Willow Heath experience a rebirth under your thumb."

Her fingers tightened around the inhaler. "So?"

"So, imagine what a witch like you could do if you lived forever."

"I'm not interested in immortality."

"That is a lie," crooned the beast. "Humans are born with a natural instinct to survive, at whatever cost. You should be grateful. I am offering you an eternity on a silver platter."

As if on cue, a cloaked figure set a dagger on the nearest table. Needle sharp, the ceremonial blade gleamed pink between the rows of cracked terra-cotta pottery. A pelican sigil was etched into the quillon, the bird's stigmata encrusted with a bloodred ruby that throbbed in the moonlight.

"Allow me to make this simple," said the beast as the figure retreated back into the shadows. "Much like you, I am only doing what is in my nature. I need to feed. You need to live. Neither of those things can happen so long as Pedyr draws breath."

Wyatt didn't rise to his bait. She was too busy conducting a head count. There were six hooded figures altogether, staggered like statues in a shadowed semicircle. She and Peter had expected to find the beast alone—weakened by its brush with the widow. But this? They were outnumbered.

They'd never be able to fight their way out of here on their own.

Standing over Peter, the beast watched her wrestle with her dwindling options. "It needn't be brutal, if that worries you. I can show you how to make it so he doesn't feel a thing."

She glanced again at the dagger, a very bad idea taking shape. If she was going to use the inhaler, she'd need to get closer.

A lot closer.

And Peter was kneeling right at the creature's feet.

She did her best to school her features into uncertainty. "I'm not a killer."

At the wobble in her voice, the beast's smile stretched wide. "Ah, but Pedyr is. The Westlocks made sure of that. Your family whittled

287

him away bit by bit, until he became sharp and unfeeling as a weapon. If the situation were reversed, he would drive that blade into your heart without a second thought."

"You're lying." She blinked tears into her eyes, reaching for the threads of her power as she did. It wasn't difficult to grab hold of them. She was knotted tight, the snarl of panic in her stomach in desperate need of release. To her left, a row of potted purslane withered to black.

"Careful, little witch," said the beast, though it looked triumphant. "We wouldn't want your emotions to get the better of you at a time like this."

There was a sudden flicker of movement, and Wyatt caught sight of several cloaked guildsmen drawing in close. Unlike the first guildsman, their hoods were tipped back, their features awash with moonlight. She found herself peering up at a pair of living corpses, their grins wide and lipless, their empty orbital sockets dark.

The sight sucked the breath from her lungs. "What is this?"

"The other victims were a little more difficult to rouse than your James," admitted the beast with a dismissive wave of its hand. "They didn't piece themselves back together quite so neatly. No matter. They did the trick. That first day back at Willow Heath, you stood at the gate and never once suspected you were talking to a corpse."

"What do you mean by victims?"

"These are Pedyr's kills," said the beast. "That's what I've been trying to tell you all along. Every last body in this room has been slain by the boy in front of you. And if you don't do anything about it, you'll be next."

"Peter would never hurt me," Wyatt whispered, letting doubt creep into her voice. Brown russet spotting darkened the nearby heads of winter lettuce.

"Are you truly that dense?" The beast tsked its tongue. "Look at you, in a ceremonial gown, all trussed up and ready. You've made it easy for him. What was it he told you, that night on the stairs? I was watching you both, even then. I remember every word. And so do you."

"I do." She hoped Peter knew this was all for show. "He told me it's easier to kill something that doesn't run at the sight of you."

On his knees, Peter recoiled as though she'd struck him.

Above him, the creature looked jubilant. "You saw the end in the deathwatch's face. I know you did. You were dressed all in white, the lace gone red with blood. You've always been Pedyr's final sacrifice. Do you think his plan has changed? Do you think a few empty promises undid lifetimes of careful scheming? The blood moon will rise, and he will gut you stem to stern."

"He's lying to you." Peter's voice was gravel. "Wyatt, look at me. It's a lie, and you know it."

She ignored him, reaching for the dagger. It dragged off the table with a scrape, steel singing. The hilt felt heavy in her grasp. Her heart thundered against her ribs. She closed the space between them in an unsteady stride, plants rotting in her wake.

And there, directly behind the beast, the first of the touch-me-nots began to bloom.

"I don't know what to believe," she said, soft and meek.

The beast flashed her a look that, on anyone else, might have been mistaken for sympathy. "You've always been a dreamer. It's your fatal flaw—you find the fantasy so much easier to swallow than the truth."

At the creature's back, the touch-me-nots flowered, sparking into jewel-bright corollas.

"Did you like the way he kissed you, out in the hall?" asked the beast, taunting her still. "Was it everything you'd ever hoped?"

Her eyes snapped to its horrible face. Its smile stretched carnivore wide. "Go ahead, Dahlia. Keep playing make-believe as the world withers around you. You'll be dead by morning. Or kill him now, and be done with it."

She'd drawn directly before them both, the dagger gripped tightly in her fist. All around her, the plants wilted on their stems, leaves desiccating to ash. Only the touch-me-nots thrived, their seed pods hanging ripe and green, flesh pulling taut over capsules filled to bursting.

Pleased by her compliance, the beast grabbed a fistful of Peter's hair. His head was wrenched back, the bare column of his throat exposed. Standing over him like this, she could see the hard flutter of his pulse. The uncertainty in his eyes.

"This is what you want." Overeager, the beast traced a ringed finger along the raised artery of Peter's carotid. "It'll make things quick and easy. You can worry about the heart later, once the struggle has gone out of him."

With a trembling hand, she pressed the dagger to the underside of Peter's throat. He didn't flinch. He didn't even blink. She wondered how many times he'd endured this same fate. How many times he'd looked into the eyes of a Westlock as he died.

It felt like a replay of the last blood moon—only she was the one with the knife. The color red was in everything. In the dormered panes. In the midnight blooms. In the round face of the moon, the blood in James's sneer. They'd come full circle, as if all of Willow Heath was cursed to endure the same forsaken story in an endless, bloody loop.

This time, she wouldn't let it end in death.

"We were banned from the greenhouse," she said, a touch too quickly. "Eight summers ago. Middle of August. Do you remember?"

Peter searched her face, his skin dimpled beneath her blade.

"James had learned a new word in Latin while he was away at school. *Dissilīre*, 'to fly apart.' He said he wanted to do a demonstration. You almost lost an eye."

"That's enough," snarled the beast, spittle flying. "Finish him."

But Peter understood. He took his shot, rearing up and cracking the back of his skull into the beast's face. Crimson spurting from its nose, the creature staggered back against the table bearing the row of overly ripe touch-me-nots. With a pop, the first of the pods exploded. Seeds scattered like buckshot. The beast threw up its hands as the shucks detonated one after the other, a chain reaction moving down the row.

If Wyatt was going to make her move, she needed to do it now, while the beast was distracted. Her fingers closed around the inhaler, full of smoke. James's voice swam, unbidden, into the forefront of her mind. It was the voice of a ghost, five summers old and clear as yesterday.

"It's called suck and blow."

28

PEDYR

Everything was red. The moon in the sky. The light in the greenhouse. The blood that gushed, crimson and angry, from the swollen crack of James Campbell's nose. Pedyr lurched forward, seeing stars, his head ringing from the impact.

Moments ago, and as though they'd been waiting for a cue, the beast's arsenal of corpses had leapt to life. One moment they'd stood like undead sentries, all gristle and skeleton, and the next they were moving, closing in on the trio at the greenhouse's crux. He took a quick mental stock of the figures in the room. There'd been seven when he arrived.

Seven, for the seven guildsmen he'd led to their deaths. He'd put down one when he first entered the conservatory, his stomach turning at the snap of bone between his hands, the limp fall of a bodily weight against the floor.

Six remained.

Six, in a room where he could only see five.

He scanned the shadows and saw nothing but spots. Beneath the firecracker pop of split husks and the shattering of clay, he heard the single scrape of a footfall.

He didn't even have the space to turn before cold steel bit into his side. A wordless bellow twisted from his lips as the knife slid out of him and then in again, plunging home with a wet squelch. Somewhere in the seed-strung dark, he heard Wyatt shouting his name.

He saw red.

He tasted red.

He thought of the deathwatch, smiling up at him—the sun-kissed serenity on its face.

Do you like what you see? Or does it terrify you?

The wild scatter of seeds began to slow, and the room fell eerily quiet. Wyatt had stopped shouting. The realization sent a zing of terror through him. He whirled, half-blind and all dizzy, knocking the dagger free of his cloaked assailant's hand just before a third blow was able to land.

A flash of limbs, a brief scuffle, and a second neck snapped between his hands. The body fell, and so did he. His knees slammed hard into the floor. He threw out his hands, bracing himself against the spills of soil. Pain needled, white-hot, through his veins.

Over the ringing in his head, he became aware of a deep and preternatural silence. All around him, the remaining corpse-guard stood at perfect attention, as though they'd never moved at all. He lifted his head, dazed and losing blood, and saw at once the source of the shift.

Wyatt and the beast stood at the center of the greenhouse, locked in a kiss. She'd caught it by surprise—its arms were crooked to the side, its open palms bloodied. She kissed the creature like it was a resuscitation, never once coming up for air.

Slowly, the tension went out of it, its arms folding around her in an embrace. The sprinklers burst on overhead, spitting water. It fell around them in a mist, plugging the conservatory into a chilly haze. In a flash, Pedyr was fourteen years old again, the stones of the sanctuary baked hot beneath his feet, a strange gooseberry ache blistering through him as James leaned in and kissed Wyatt on the mouth.

At Wyatt's feet lay the inhaler, its polymer green casing bright against the stone. Understanding settled in Pedyr's gut as they broke apart, high color swimming into Wyatt's cheeks. James Campbell stared down at her, breathless and bewildered, blood streaking his face like paint.

"Wyatt?"

"Jamie. It's you." Crying freely, she drew him into an embrace. On a nearby vine, the tomatoes swelled into a tight, glassy red. Her relief, ripening in the air. "I did it. I can't believe it. It worked. It *worked.*"

James folded her into his arms, meeting Pedyr's gaze over the top of her head. There was nothing hard and cold in the depths of his stare. Nothing eldritch. Nothing strange. Only a warm, liquid brown, ashy with starlight, as though he were just now coming out of a dream.

"Peter?" he said.

At the sound of his name, Pedyr's chest crumpled. He tried to rise to his feet and failed, slamming hard onto his knees. Inky spots swam in front of his vision, and he clutched at the wounds in his side, feeling ribbons of red seep through and through his fingers.

"Jesus," James said, letting go of Wyatt. *"Peter."*

This is nothing, he thought, though he'd meant to say it aloud. He wanted to tell them that he knew what dying felt like, and this wasn't it. Not yet, anyway. But he couldn't find his voice. Wyatt dropped to the floor in front of him, her dress soaked through, her eyes big and round and afraid.

"Peter." She took his face in her hands. "Look at me. Look."

He did. Her lips were their usual shade of bold, dahlia red, lipstick smudged. "You did good," he said. "Very innovative."

Her smile broke on a hiccup. "I improvised."

James drew in behind her, breathing hard—as though he'd forgotten what it was to suck down a lungful of air. His mouth was rouge stained, his cheeks ruddy, and Pedyr couldn't summon the energy to feel anything but relief. Here was Wyatt and here was James, both of them full of color. Vibrant as a photograph.

The three of them, always.

He would take whatever came next.

"Hey." Wyatt shook him and he opened his eyes, peering up at her. He hadn't even realized he'd closed them. "Can you walk?"

"Sure," he said, though he remained firmly planted, air whistling past his lips. She rocked back on her heels, frowning up at him.

"Why isn't he getting up?"

"Wyatt," said Pedyr, but she didn't appear to hear him.

"This shouldn't have hurt him." Worry edged into her voice. "He's supposed to be immortal."

"Wyatt," he tried again, a little louder than before.

"He still has to heal," said James, scrubbing a hand through the wet flop of his hair. "I'm pretty sure it takes time."

"Pretty sure?" spat Wyatt, her nerves turning her irritable.

"Well, yes," said James drolly. "I'm not a doctor."

"Wyatt!" barked Pedyr, in a voice that cracked through the arboretum quiet. "Look at me."

She did. She looked lovely in the moonlight, everything on her colored red. Like she'd been bathed in ichor. Baptized in blood. He was such an idiot. He'd never needed to go home. Home had been right here in front of him. *A thousand little lives,* the beast had mocked him, *and you haven't even learned the meaning of the word.*

He was always learning his lessons just a moment too late.

"This isn't over," he said. "We bought ourselves some time, but the skies still need to be sealed shut. That means you'll need to break the pendant."

A crinkle formed along the bridge of her nose. "I don't know if I like that plan."

"It doesn't matter whether you like it or not. It has to be done."

"What if it doesn't snap the tether between the beast and James? What if it destroys them both? I mean, we don't even know for sure what smashing the necklace will do."

But Pedyr did. He knew perfectly well. And there was nothing left to do but wait for the moment of reckoning to come.

"There's no other choice. You remember what your aunt said—an open mouth needs to be fed, or it will swallow everything whole. We didn't send the beast back into hell, we trapped it in a cage. The task is unfinished."

"I can't take that chance," she said, dropping her voice to a whisper. "We *just* got him back."

A tear slipped down her face. He reached out and caught it before it could fall. "We came to Willow Heath to put him to rest," he reminded her as gently as he could. "You knew that. It was your idea."

"But if there's a way we can—"

"There's not." He cut her off before she could find false hope and cling to it. "Death is death. You can't cheat it forever."

"You did," she snapped.

"No," he disagreed, "I didn't. I've been bound to it, one half-life after another. I died three hundred years ago, with an ax in my stomach. The rest has been lived in scraps and pieces."

Tears glimmered, unshed, in her eyes. "How can you say that?"

"Because it's true." He blinked away visions of the deathwatch, reaching out to touch a bloodied finger to the half-moon at her throat. "This is a goodbye, Wyatt. Not a reunion."

They both peered up at the object of their disagreement. James Campbell, the third member of their strange, summertime triumvirate—an undead boy, on borrowed time. He stood several feet away, slowly flexing his fingers open and then shut.

"What the hell did you give me?"

"I don't know," Wyatt admitted, sniffling. "Some sort of elixir. It won't last forever."

"Oh." James's jaw ticked as he swallowed. "How long do I have?"

"There's enough puffs in the inhaler for eight hours," she said. "One puff, every two hours. Longer, if you can stand it. Mackenzie will bring more when she can."

"Wyatt," warned Pedyr. "Don't make promises you can't keep."

Outside the greenhouse, a bestial snarl carved through the dark. Wyatt launched to her feet alongside James, staring out at their watery likeness in the reflective glass.

"What was that?" she demanded.

"Nothing good," said Pedyr as he tried and failed to wedge himself off the floor.

"Let's clear one hurdle at a time." James cracked his knuckles, eyeballing the bodies that stood staggered throughout the greenhouse. Puppets, rendered motionless without their puppeteer. A sickly tinge crept into his face. "That's creepy as hell. Wyatt, help me get Peter on his feet. Let's bring him inside before these tossers decide to wake up."

29

WYATT

It took considerable effort to get Peter back into the house, even with James's help. Through sheer determination, they managed to prop him in a kitchen chair.

"Are the wards down?" James asked, flicking the light without success.

Wyatt dropped to her knees at Peter's feet, the muddied lace of her dress mushrooming around her. "They've been failing little by little." She reached for the tacky hem of Peter's shirt, swatting at his hands. "Don't touch. Let me look."

At the counter, James crushed a spider beneath his palm. He inspected it silently for a moment before scraping the sticky remnants onto the leg of his pants. Outside in the henyard, something chittered.

"This feels extremely *Night of the Living Dead*," said James. "I assume there's a plan?"

Wyatt swallowed thickly. She didn't want to tell him about the necklace, or the widening tear out in the woods. She didn't want to tell him that the only way to seal it shut was to send the beast back through the sky, or that they very well might condemn him to an eternity in hell along with it. Not yet.

Instead, she said, "That's not my focus right now."

"James is right." Peter shifted in his chair with a grimace. "We should talk about how the rest of the night is going to play out."

Wyatt shot him as deadly a look as she could muster. "I said, *That's not my focus right now.*"

Peter ignored her, peering over her head at James. "We've solved one problem, bringing you back, but we've created another. There's a tear in the sky, and it's widening. Anything can get through. Those noises you're hearing outside? That's only the first wave. There are older and bigger things still waiting to wriggle free."

"I'm very familiar," said James blandly, "with what sort of creatures make their home in the dark."

"Then you know how critical it is that we shut the door before they get free."

"Sounds straightforward enough," said James. "What's the catch?"

"As long as the beast remains here on this plane, the skies stay open."

James leaned back against the countertop. "I see. And it's trapped inside of me."

"That's our current problem, yes."

"Brilliant." His smile didn't touch his eyes. "I take it a crucifix and a dash of holy water won't fix the issue."

Wyatt whipped around to face him. "That's not helpful."

"It's just a little gallows humor," he said. "The mood in here is abysmal."

On the chair, Peter let out another groan. Hooking a finger in his shirt, he drew it up to inspect the damage beneath. At the sight of his mangled torso, Wyatt's stomach bottomed out. He tugged it quickly back into place, his eyes finding hers across the dark of the kitchen.

"I'm not dying," he said.

"Who says you're dying?"

"You're looking at me like you're standing at my grave."

"He's fine," James said. "It's barely a graze."

"A papercut is *barely a graze*, Jamie," she bit out, the remnants of her patience going up in a puff of smoke. "Peter, you're bleeding everywhere. I couldn't even see where the gash was."

"Two," he said, a little feebly. "One in my side, one in my lower abdomen." He tipped his head back, his eyes drifting shut. "I'm not worried. They didn't hit anything vital."

"All of you is vital."

To her surprise, Peter laughed.

"Stop that." A hard lump of panic lodged in her throat. "Peter, *stop*. You're making the bleeding worse."

His only response was to laugh harder still, his shoulders shaking, his shirt red, red, red with blood. She glowered up at him until the laughter finally subsided into a breathless waver.

"Ouch."

"Why isn't it healing?" Wyatt demanded, batting his hands out of the way and folding his shirt up over his navel.

"It looks deep," James said, bending in to take a closer look. "He'll need stitches."

"I don't know how to do stitches."

"I can do it." Peter sucked in a breath, pinching the shred of flesh just under his third rib. "I'll need one of you to get the sewing kit."

"On it." She scrambled to her feet, her own injury screaming in protest. "Don't move."

Another laugh followed her out.

"*Now* she listens," she heard Peter say.

She ran upstairs, tripping over carpets of creeping Charlie as she went. The sewing kit was shoved inside her mother's old wardrobe, stuffed between battered boxes of paperback books. She snatched it and ran, dropping several thimbles in the process.

When she skidded back into the kitchen, it was to find Peter on his feet, swaying in the yellow flicker of a kerosene lamp. The door to the pantry was open, and in it stood Mama, her eyes big and black, a hen running wildly around her cloven hooves.

"I told you not to move," grumbled Wyatt, shuffling Peter back into his chair. He lowered himself uneasily into the seat, air escaping between his teeth in a hiss.

"Can't do stitches in the dark."

"James could have lit it for you. Where is he, anyway?"

As if he'd been summoned, James reappeared in the doorway, holding aloft two dark bottles of liquor. "I've located the wine."

"Is this really the time?" Wyatt asked darkly as he set to loosening the cork.

"I've been dead for five years." The cork came loose with a pop and he sniffed at the contents. "I was in hell for considerably longer than that. I can't think of a better time to have a drink. You should have one, too. You're wound too tight. It's making Peter anxious."

When he poured her a glass, she didn't turn it down. The smell of caramel filled her nose as she took a cautious sip. Whiskey hit the back of her throat and she came up coughing, slamming the glass hard onto the countertop.

"That's not wine."

"No?" James peered mildly into his glass. "Huh."

Peter paid them no mind, hyperfocused on his task, the color draining from his face. The sight of the open wound made her knees wobble. She clutched the edge of the counter, steadying herself.

"Peter?"

"Almost there," he said, and the words came out strained.

James stayed quiet through it all, nursing his drink and watching Bastard peck at his trailing laces. Eventually, Wyatt fell to pacing, tailed by Mama, a gaggle of hens underfoot. Slightly slunk into the fray not long after, her shadow making her appear large as a lioness in the lantern's throw. The old cat took a seat atop the table and set to cleaning her paws, the green of her eyes luminescent in the dark.

Finally, Peter slumped back into his chair. His arms fell slack, the needle dropping to the floor with a click. Lifting his chin, he sought out Wyatt across the dim miasma of the cluttered kitchen.

"I'm all stitched up," he said. "Happy?"

"No."

"Can we talk?"

"Not yet."

"Wyatt."

"Bathroom," she blurted, her panic turning her evasive. "Let's get you cleaned up."

Whatever effort it had taken to get him inside, it took considerably more for the two of them to get him up the stairs. All three of them were a wreck—Wyatt adrenaline high and wobbling, and James more than a little bit drunk. Peter slung between the two of them, gritting his way up the steps one at a time. Slightly circled the trio in irritation, taking the occasional swipe at their ankles.

Eventually they made it onto the landing. James pushed into the tiled dark of the bathroom, setting the kerosene lamp atop the vanity.

"We're wasting time," he said, peering out the window.

Wyatt ignored him and turned on the faucet, sending up a silent prayer that the pipes still worked. She heard the rattle of copper, the rush of water, and the spigot spit a clear, cold stream into the tub. She let it heat and then fill, turning to find Peter propped against the door, his souvenir T-shirt bloodied, his eyes closed. James stood beside him, silently assessing.

"You're wearing a ridiculous fucking shirt."

Peter's smile was faint. "I think it's nice."

"Peter," Wyatt snapped, "you're supposed to be undressing."

He pried open a single eye. "Hmm?"

With a groan, she shut off the faucet and climbed to her feet. He moved like a drunk, listing to the side when she worked his shirt over his head. Fumbling into James as she shimmied the sweatpants free from his hips. Finally, and clad only in briefs, he consented to let James help him into the tub. They entered with calves submerged, steam rising off the water.

Wyatt hovered nearby, caught by the quiet sight of them together—a boy pieced together with salvaged parts, and a boy who'd become equals with death. And then there was Wyatt, packed to the teeth with something she didn't entirely understand. Something that popped out of her in sparks and in shimmers. In fragrant blossoms and in mildewed sprawls.

Maybe the deathwatch was wrong. Maybe the dawn would arrive, and they'd get the happy-ever-after they'd only dared to dream about in the dark. Maybe they'd find a way to dispel the beast and keep Jamie here with them. Maybe they'd nurse Willow Heath back to life and stay here forever, tucked away in their private pocket of the world.

The three of them, always.

Thoughts spinning out, she climbed in after them and set to locating a washcloth and a bar of soap. As she did, she found James studying her, Peter's head lolling back against his chest. They sank deeper into the suds, James staring up at her in that too-calculating way.

"Your necklace," he noted.

She wrung water out of the cloth, doing her best to appear nonchalant. "What about it?"

"Nothing," he said, after too long of a pause. "It's pretty."

"Thanks."

Her stomach felt like lead. Her heart beat rabbit quick. She'd learned, in her summers at Willow Heath, that there was nothing more dangerous than James Campbell with too much space to think. She should have taken the necklace off, back in the kitchen. She should have stashed it somewhere hidden.

She didn't want to think about the rest of the night.

She didn't want to tell him that she was wasting time because there was no way to save him. This was it. It was all that was left.

Gingerly, she began to scrub the blood from Peter's skin. She started with the tacky ridge of his knuckles, her hands shaking. For a while, the only sound was the intermittent splash of water, the spatter of runoff along the tiled floor. Outside in the fathomless dark, something let out a series of high-pitched clicks. A leathery shape glided past the boarded-up window.

"Bats," muttered James. "Just what we needed."

Desperate to quell the knot of panic in her chest, Wyatt began to hum. Softly at first, the melody of an old Irish aria rising into the air between them. Beneath her ministrations, Peter's chest went impossibly still. She wrung out the washcloth and wet it anew, the hum turning to a song, half-remembered.

Peter let her worry at him, listening to her sing as she scrubbed the rust from his skin. The task brought them impossibly close, the ivory of her dress wreathing her waist in the water. She wavered, her voice cracking as she tripped over the refrain. In front of her, Peter drew his first breath in what felt like minutes.

"Don't stop."

Her heart hammered in her throat. "I can't remember the rest."

"She's lying," said James, swirling an idle finger through an eddy of suds. "She knows every word. You just make her nervous."

"Jamie."

"What? Are we going to keep pretending like we don't know what this is? We could all be dead by morning." He paused and added, "Some of us already are."

"Don't say that."

"What?" His shoulder lifted in a shrug. "It's true."

When she stayed quiet, Peter reached out and took hold of her wrist. The washcloth plunked heavily into the tub as he guided her in between his knees, careless of the way James sat just behind him, steadying him at the water's edge.

"Stop worrying," Peter said, easing the pinch in her brow with a kiss. "Haven't you been paying attention? I'm notoriously difficult to kill."

"This is a bad time to develop a sense of humor."

"If you ask me," said James, "I think it's the perfect time."

Wyatt dashed her hand through the water, splashing him. "No one asked you."

"Eat me," he shot back, his mouth splitting into a grin.

Over his head, a sliver of moonlight bled through the boards. Peter followed her gaze, and then James. Silently, they watched the nacreous rock flood the gaps in shades of pink.

"There's a Welsh word I learned in school," said James. "*Hiraeth.* There's no direct translation for it in the English language, but it means a deep longing for a home you can never return to."

His words crowded in Wyatt's gut, recognition slinking through her veins. There it was: a word for this feeling. For the way she'd spent the long, lonely year grieving who she'd been. Missing a Wyatt she could never go back to.

"None of us will ever be who we were again," said James, pulling her thoughts clean out of her head. "And Willow Heath will never be to us what it was."

"Stop," said Wyatt. "Stop talking like this is the end."

But it was. She knew it, and so did he. She couldn't keep the truth from him if she tried. In the bath, the water had begun to go cold. Her fingers were slowly pruning. This time, when James's gaze dropped to the necklace, she covered it with her fingers.

"What's the play?" asked James. "I doubt a few old planks and rusted nails will hold the house for long."

"We have a plan," said Peter. "And Wyatt is going to stick to it."

The white gold of the pendant felt chilly against her hand. "All three of us make it until dawn," she said. "That's the objective."

James's eyes sparked kerosene gold in the dark. "Is it?"

At that, Peter rose unsteadily to his feet. Water ran off him in rivers as James and Wyatt lurched up after him, each of them taking an arm. He shrugged them off, swinging a leg out of the tub and reaching for a towel.

"I'm fine." He draped the towel around his neck and scrubbed at his hair until it stood up in all directions. "Stop fussing over me. Jamie, take another hit of the elixir. I don't like the thought that the beast might creep back in and we won't even know it."

"I feel fine," countered James.

Peter reached for his sweatpants with a wince, digging into the pocket and prying loose the inhaler. Tossing it to James, he began to slip on his pants. "Take a hit," he said. "Do it now."

James frowned, but obeyed. Nebulized incense released into the room in a perfunctory hiss. Wyatt climbed out after them, fighting the urge to go to Peter. To help him dress, and damn his pride. To make him promise: *We all make it out of this alive.*

The slipshod stitching on Peter's abdomen was raw and angry. It matched her own, the scarring on her belly gone pink with scabs. It matched James, too, his torso pieced together like patchwork. They were the same, inside and out.

If anyone could find a way to circumnavigate death, it was the three of them.

"Dry off," said Peter, and tossed them both a towel. "We're leaving."

Wyatt stilled. "Where are we going?"

"The grove." He tugged a clean shirt over his head. "That's where everything started, and that's where we'll finish it."

30

PEDYR

It was a short walk to the grove, to its graveyard tucked away in the labyrinthine twist of conifers. Once, before the beast burrowed in its roots, the trees must have flourished. Evergreen and turpentine, their branches full of animals and their trunks sticky with pinesap.

Now they were dead.

Nothing grew there, not even Pedyr.

They moved quick and quiet through the meadows, staying close together—keeping their eyes trained on the sky. Ducking low whenever something fluttered past. Up ahead, the chapel rose up out of the pines, the pitch of its roof spindle sharp in darkness, its foundation engulfed in pale white florets. The surrounding trees were strung with sagging webs, evidence of the widow's presence everywhere he turned.

He wished he didn't feel quite so unnerved by it all. They'd come this way a thousand times before. Summer after summer. In rain and in shine, with the sun beating down on their backs and under a glittering spread of stars.

There was something right about it, that the three of them were here again now.

In spite of death, and because of it. Driven back together at the end of it all.

Overhead, the moon was nearing its zenith. Too soon, it would be midnight. The eclipse would come and go. Dawn would bleed into the sky, the world igniting in starbursts of gold. He knew how it went. He'd seen so many sunrises, they'd all begun to look the same.

He'd seen this one, too, in the eyes of the deathwatch.

He knew what was coming. There was no way around it.

Wyatt drew to a stop a few feet shy of the chapel's rotting steps, staring up at the opening. Since their encounter with the widow, the first bit of regrowth had begun to take root. The wide planks of the wooden structure were engulfed in vines, as though all that held it together were thick cords of ivy, the lacy girdle of sweet-scented honeysuckle. Reaching out a finger, Wyatt touched the opaline head of a flower, pale enough to appear to glow beneath the moonlight.

Softly, she said, "I've never seen anything like this before."

"Hell-flowers," Pedyr noted. "That's not great."

James tugged a flower free and tucked the stem behind his ear. "They're also known as asphodels, if you're a fan of Homer."

Pedyr ran the velvet curl of a petal between his thumb and forefinger. "Leave the mouth to hell open long enough, elysian blossoms tend to creep in through the cracks."

"Hmm." Wyatt plucked a petal loose and let it flutter to the ground, picking her way up the stairs and into the chapel. The moment she was out of sight, Pedyr's resolve crumbled. He wobbled, unsteady. James was there in an instant, propping himself under Pedyr's shoulder in a makeshift human brace.

"You absolute git," he said. "You know what that necklace is."

"Yes." Pedyr shut his eyes.

"And you're letting her wear it anyway?"

"I'm letting her destroy it."

James loosed a quiet scoff. The sound ballooned between them in the dark. "She's never going to forgive you."

"I know."

They found Wyatt in the chapel's slow-decaying crux. The roof had caved in during the rain, the rotting joists finally giving way. The great gape in the ceiling boasted a waterfall of dripping ivy, a splash of pale moonglow that left the floor awash in watery shades of pink. Wyatt stood in the fall of light, staring up at the moon. She looked ethereal this way—glazed in moonlight, the wet ivory of her gown clinging to her like gauze—and for a moment he was met with a sharp pang of doubt. Maybe she was right. Maybe he should wait.

Maybe they'd watch the dawn together.

James whistled the old Irish lullaby at half speed, and the sound broke Wyatt from her trance. She turned, scrutinizing him and James as they made their way between the pews.

"What's wrong?"

"He's just a little tired," James answered, lowering Pedyr into a pew.

"I knew it." Her complexion paled. "I knew we shouldn't have made you leave the house."

"It was my idea," Pedyr reminded her as James sidled in next to him, elbows braced on the back of the pew. Eventually, Wyatt joined them. For a while afterward, the three of them sat in silence, staring up at his empty tabernacle.

Strange, that he'd sat there lifetime after lifetime, small and afraid, and watched the guildsmen bend low before his dais. Strange, that he'd been exsanguinated and dissected, his blood spilled in chalices, his body tossed into the dirt. Strange, how pain disappeared, fading away until you couldn't remember what it felt like, only that you felt it in the first place. He tried to stretch his thoughts back, to remember dying, and found that he couldn't.

He could only remember this lifetime. This maddeningly slow grind of the earth on its axis. He could only remember James. The way he laughed, lit from beneath by a winking firefly glow. He could only remember Wyatt, and the way the skies thundered when he'd kissed her that first impossible time.

He didn't know when sleep claimed him. He only knew what woke him.

It was the click, scrape of onyx over wood. He opened his eyes, rolling out a kink in his shoulder, and found James Campbell slipping away under cover of dark.

"Stay," Pedyr said, careful not to wake Wyatt. She lay curled on the bench, her head in his lap, her hair unbound and drying into waves. At the sound of his voice, James fell to a halt. He crooked his neck, cracking bone, and peered slowly back at Pedyr. His gaze had slipped back into that uncanny, lusterless black. He looked stitched tight, the hell-flower wilting behind his ear and the widow's kiss gridding his throat.

"What, you want an audience?"

His question reverberated through the cavernous quiet. Wyatt shifted, and they both fell silent, watching as she settled.

"I want you close," Pedyr said, once her breathing deepened. "In case the plan goes sideways."

"Are you mad? If anything goes to shit, it'll be *because* of me."

"You can't know that for sure."

"I can feel it, Peter." He tapped two fingers to his sternum, his mouth contorting into a grimace. "It's inside, picking away at me. Tugging me apart in little slivers. Whatever brilliant concoction you cooked up, it's not stable. We can't trust it."

"So take another hit."

James's throat corded in a swallow. "I've already taken two."

Pedyr scrubbed a hand over his face, feeling as though he were slowly deflating. He was assuaged by a bone-deep exhaustion, a stagnating sort of weariness that left him seeing double. "Can you hold on just a little while longer?"

"What for?"

When Pedyr didn't answer, James swore, pacing away from the bench. The fall of his boots carved all through the quiet, even as he was swallowed up in the chapel's rosy dark. When he came back, it was at a clip, his cheeks flush with color and his hair a mess, as though he'd been tugging at it. He pushed into the bench in front of them, bracing his hands on the cap rail and bending in close.

"You did a lot of stupid shit when we were kids," he said. "I never held it against you. And why would I? Your world is so small, it's a speck. You didn't know any better. But this? I'm meant to just stand by while you let her destroy everything?"

"You'll wake Wyatt" was all Pedyr said.

"Oh, I'll wake Wyatt, will I?" His laugh came out strangled. "If she wasn't asleep, I'd deck you in the face."

"It wouldn't change my mind."

"No," agreed James, "but it would make me feel better." Cuffing his sleeves, he leaned back against the wooden lip and looked out at the bald expanse of sky. White starlight blistered across the midnight dark. It was a long time before he spoke again. "There were no stars, where I was. Did you know that? It ate at me—the complete darkness. There was nothing to do but scrape at it until my fingers bled. Until it came away in pieces. Space has a way of making you feel finite, but down there—" He peered down at the black rings on his fingers. The bands were crude, hammered by hand. Five rings, for five mortal years in the depths of hell. For a moment, he looked far away, thrust back in the lightless depths where Pedyr had buried him.

"You never had any sort of formal schooling," he said at last. "Do you know what happens when a star collapses?"

"No," Pedyr admitted.

"It swallows itself up. Nothing escapes, not even light." His eyes met Pedyr's. "If that necklace does what it's meant to do, that's precisely what you'll be setting into motion."

Pedyr swallowed. "I'm not afraid of the dark."

"And what if I am?" James's mouth kicked up in a wry smile. "What if I don't want to go back?"

"You're already dead, Jamie," Pedyr whispered. "I can't save you. But I can still save her."

A clatter from outside brought their heads up. Wyatt rocketed upright, sleep falling away from her at once. "What was that?"

James touched a finger to his lips. "Quiet."

"Wyatt," called a voice from out in the grove. Cold prickled through Pedyr as he recognized Mackenzie Beckett. "Wyatt, are you in there? God. I just stepped in something wet. Hello? Anyone? The lights are off at the farm. Please don't tell me we drove all this way for nothing." There was a scrape. The creak of a rotting step. The voice dropped a register, going low and garroted. "Wyatt?"

"It's not her," Pedyr said, only to find Wyatt twisted round on the bench beside him, her legs crossed under her and her palms upturned in her lap.

"Wyatt," sang the mimic. Talons scraped along the chapel's wooden siding, the sound like nails on a chalkboard. "Come out and play."

Wyatt's head twitched to the side, tracking the sound. Her eyes rolled to white, until her stare was all sclera. James reached for her, but Pedyr threw out an arm to stop him.

"Leave her."

They watched, transfixed, as veins raised into her arms in thick, discolored ridges. For a moment, there was silence, consummate and catholic. And then, without warning, her head flung back in a violent kick. Eyes open, she stared unblinkingly up at the moon.

"I don't love this," James muttered darkly, just as she let out an unholy scream.

31

WYATT

Wyatt's throat was raw, her voice shredded. She gasped into the dark, a starry array bursting inside her chest in red supernova sparks. Power ribboned through her veins, satin sleek and unspooling. And there, woven into the fabric of her mind, she felt it—a sucking pop like a boot pried loose from mud. The earth churned. The skies turned over. Somewhere outside the chapel, buried in the deep, velvet dark, the woods reared back from what she wrought.

A quirk of her head, a mental tug, and there came the answering weave of climber ivy pulled through bowed intercostal spaces. Cords of ivalace wrapped membrane tight around a spiked ladder of verte-brae. Funny, how she'd spent so long grasping at nothing—feeling untethered and intractable—only to find the threads she needed had been lying dormant inside her all along. It was the simplest thing in the world to pluck at them.

Another twitch, another tug. Something rose up from the earth with a bodily shudder. Simple, simple, simple. She could see it all laid out so clearly, like she was seated before a loom—her heart a heddle, her pulse shuttling wefts of power through the batten of her veins. Slowly, a picture began to take shape, a leafed tapestry of bone and blossom both. Wyatt opened her eyes just in time to see the chapel's main door lace shut in a thick trellis of ivy.

James bent forward over the pew, his eyes narrowing. "Holy shit."

It took Wyatt a moment to understand what he was seeing. The instant she did, her stomach went leaden. An unearthed skeleton hung in the doorway, intricately woven into the wall of green.

Wyatt slumped, staring. "I was trying to ward the chapel."

"And instead, you reanimated Peter. Well done, you." James swung himself over the back of the pew, heading down the aisle to prod at her creation.

"It's not like I meant to do it," Wyatt bit out. "Peter, I'm so sorry."

But Peter was gone. She spun out, searching the collapsed shadows for any sight of him, and found the little door to his rectory pushed wide. Tailing after him, she poked her head inside. The old camping lantern was lit, its bulb sputtering meekly. Peter stood over his rumpled mattress, his head bowed beneath the sharp slant of the ceiling. Scattered across the floor were the items she'd pulled loose the day she raided his room—yo-yos and Matchbox cars and little plastic action figures, their paint chipped away. He bent down and picked up a kneeling army man, examining it from all angles.

Wyatt rapped lightly on the wall, announcing her presence. He didn't look up at her. His attention was pinned on the broad green bazooka balanced on the soldier's shoulder. *Scorched earth*, she thought idly.

"What are you doing in here?"

He set the toy on the table and watched it topple onto its side. "Saying goodbye."

Something in the way he said it put a great swell of sadness in her chest. She felt for the silver moon around her throat and found her fingers closing over Cubby's button instead.

"We don't have to," she whispered. The snag in her voice drew his eyes. In the flickering LED, they looked slate gray. A stream in April, its ice slowly thawing. "We don't have to say goodbye, I mean. When this is over. What if we stayed?"

If no one else would say it, then she would. In front of her, Peter looked hewn from stone. The current of his stare was enough to bowl her over. "How exactly do you see this ending, Wyatt?"

"Easy. I get the wards back up." She refrained from mentioning that she'd plucked his skeleton clean out of its grave, skirting around the terrible truth of her ability. She felt no better than the beast, puppeteering something dead for her purposes. Fighting to keep a waver out of her voice, she said, "I can do it."

"I know you can. You always could." His shoulder lifted in a shrug. "And then what?"

"What do you mean?"

"The wards will wane. Everything living always does." He drew closer, a slight list in his walk. "Will you stay here for the rest of your life? Day after day? Tending to the wards until you're old and bent and at death's door?"

She swallowed, her nerves trilling. She didn't like the way he was looking at her, his eyes wide with intent. "I'm just trying to survive the night, Peter. I'm not thinking that far ahead."

"Why not? Dream with me for a minute—you love to do that." He was hovering over her, shoulders bent, boxing her in. "What if you have children?"

"Children?" She sputtered, startled. "We're eighteen."

We, she said, not *I*. Mortification sank through her, wet and cold. He took no notice of the way she balked at her own words, color in her cheeks. "We won't always be," he said quietly. "What if they can't do what you do? What then? Will you teach them to bleed for the forest? Will you show them how to carve me up and grind my bones to dust?"

"What?" Horror bled through her. "No. Never."

His mouth thinned. His eyes were snow-melt blue and as familiar to her as anything. "I won't do it, Wyatt. I won't bind you to this place just to keep you. And that's what it will take to keep the dark confined to the forest. This place will swallow you up more than it already has."

A breath shuddered out of her, halfway to a sob. "*None* of us will be bound to this place. We're sending the beast back through the sky tonight."

"That's right. We are." He reached out and traced the round curve of the pendant. "When the eclipse is full, you break this. Before anything else gets into the chapel."

Another knock sounded at the door and James appeared, looking subdued. His dark eyes lingered too long on the necklace. "It's nearly time."

The three of them headed back out into the nave, where the moon sat red and round in the ivy-throttled skylight. The sky was a funny dark, the chapel spilled with a dim, rosy coloring. The last time they'd all been out this way, they'd been lying head-to-head in the grove, watching the moon pass into the shadow of the earth.

Wyatt remembered that night as if it had happened yesterday. With the memory of Peter's kiss still looping through her head, she'd given in to impulse and reached for his hand under cover of dark. She'd been terrified by the thought of rejection, dizzy beneath the feel of James tracking her every move. But then Peter only held fast, anchoring them together in the bottomless black. She'd lain perfectly still, hardly daring to breathe. Beneath her chest, her heart thrummed like a bird.

James was the first of them to hear the guild approaching. He'd knifed upright, searching the press of trees. *"Someone's coming."*

They'd scrambled to their feet after him to find him staring down at the ground. Blooms of white night phlox had poked their heads up through the dirt, petals yawning pink and pretty beneath the moon.

"Shit," he'd breathed. Off in the woods, someone bellowed their names. The light of a flashlight split the dark, knifing sideways through the trees. For an instant, the fear was illuminated on James's face. *"Peter, do you have it?"*

Peter had only stared off into the wood. The way he always did, listening to the slow breathing of the forest. Stepping into his line of sight, James had taken him by the shoulders and shaken him, hard. *"Peter! Look at me. The knife. Did you bring it?"*

"Yes." His reply had been laconic. Careful. He hadn't looked at Wyatt. *"It's in my boot."*

"You absolute wanker." James shoved him hard in the chest. Peter yielded beneath him, the heel of his boot dragging up flowers by the root. *"They'll gut you if they find it on you. What were you planning to do with it, huh?"*

"Nothing."

"Nothing," James mocked, shoving him a second time. Peter's spine slammed into the wide body of an elm. *"You just like to think about it? You just want to pretend that you might?"*

Without warning, Peter's fist flew, cracking James across the nose. He'd staggered back, blood spouting from his face, spitting red. Wyatt wedged herself between them, doing what she could to keep Peter from taking a second swing. There'd been an entire array of flash-lights by then, light sweeping through the rows and rows of trees, the grove spliced all in silver.

Swiping blood from his chin, James kicked dirt onto the phlox. He rounded on her, fury gleaming in his eyes. *"Get out of here, Wyatt. Don't let them see you."*

Now they were alone. Sewn into the crumbling chapel with threads of ivy, buttons of bone. There was no one coming for them. There were no more secrets. And there was no more time. The blood moon was in full array, red and dull. Her aunt had once called it the most violent moon. She didn't doubt it was true.

At her side, James gave the inhaler a shake. It rattled emptily in the quiet. "I guess that's that."

"What?" She glanced over at him, startled. "You're all out? Already?"

"Turns out there's no exact dosage for my condition. Pretty clever witch, though, your cousin. Don't tell her I said so."

Her heart gave an awful wrench. "So, what? That's it? We're just supposed to let you go?"

James flashed her a wry smile. "That's typically what you do with the dead."

"There's nothing typical about this, and you know it. We have to do *something*."

"We *are* doing something," Peter reminded her, and she knew he meant the necklace.

"Not *that*. Something else."

"Like what?"

"I don't know!" Her shout cast out through the dark. "Anything!"

Peter rubbed at the nape of his neck, looking wearier than she'd ever seen him. "There's no point in fighting. The decision has already been made. James is leaving."

Propped against a nearby pew, James didn't deny it.

"Jamie, you *can't*." She felt like she'd been punched in the gut. "It's not safe out there."

"It's not safe in here, either," he said. "Not as long as I'm with you. I don't fancy being on the wrong side of the wards when the worst happens."

She couldn't think of anything worse than him not being here with them, to face the uncertain end together. She was about to say as much when he spoke again.

"I recognize that necklace, you know."

She drew an unsteady breath. "You do?"

"Sure. My father was fixated on it for years. He knew yours was tinkering away at something secret in his attic, and he drove himself half mad trying to suss out what it could be. Some days, it was all he talked about."

"So, then, you know what it does?"

His eyes met Peter's over the top of her head, something wordless passing between them. "Yes," he said at last, resigned. "I know what it does."

"You don't have to do this," she rushed to say. "You don't have to go. Mackenzie can make more. She knows how."

"Mackenzie isn't here."

Out in the woods, something howled. It was long and low, the cry of something hunting. Her throat was sand. Her body was an hourglass. Time was running out and running out.

"We just got you back," whispered Wyatt. "You can't go. Peter, tell him."

But Peter stayed silent at her side, staring up at the moon through a shuttered gaze. His shirt stuck to his side, blood pinpricking the cotton in crimson spots.

"He knows I'm right," said James, pocketing the inhaler. "And he'll let me leave, because he doesn't want me here alone with you when the time comes."

"What are you," she snapped, "his *translator?*"

James bit off the end of a laugh and pulled her to him, enveloping her in a great bear hug. She tried to shove him off, but he held fast, dropping a kiss on the top of her head. "I love you, Wyatt Westlock. You know that?"

She wormed out of his grasp, tears streaking down her face. At her feet, pale red fallopian buds poked through gaps in the buckled wood. Slowly, they unfurled into bleeding hearts. She wanted to rip them up, one by one. To tuck herself back away where no one could see. She'd spent so long trying not to let anything slip out of her, and now she was bursting at the seams. Raw and obvious, every part of her heart exposed. It was too much. All of this was too much.

"Say it back," he said. "'I love you, Jamie.'"

"No."

The ghost of a smile played across his lips. "You'll regret it."

All along the skeleton-strung door, the hell-flowers had unfurled into papery heads of white. Midnight florets, the blacks of their stamens lending them the hollow gape of skulls. In the gloom, James's eyes looked a touch too black. He was fading already, the beast stealing

him back from them bit by bit. He cracked his knuckles, bone popping audibly into alignment.

"Well, this should be fun."

"A riot," said Peter dryly.

James's grin turned blinding. "Are we not going to have a goodbye?"

"We already had one," Peter said, clutching at the wound in his
side. "When I buried you, remember?"

James tsked. "Touchy as ever."

He crossed the remaining steps between them, grabbing hold
of Peter's neck so that they bumped heads. Pushing out a tattered
breath, Peter shut his eyes. They stayed like that for a beat—for
two—neither of them speaking. Out in the woods, something let out
a warble, high and clear.

Finally, James said, "I think you're bleeding out."

"A little bit."

They broke apart, the pinpricks in Peter's side widening to a bloody
gash. James glanced between them both. "Summers in Lake Como
would have been quieter."

Peter and Wyatt stood together and watched him go—through
the hellebore blooms and out into the bald press of trees. Away from the
sanctuary where they'd fought and grown and played.

When he was gone, and the night was quiet, Wyatt turned to Peter.
"What now?"

"I need to sit," he admitted. "Before I keel over."

"Oh God. I'm sorry." She braced herself against him, helping him
to the base of the altar. He slid down against it, dragging her with
him, both of them hitting the ground just a little too hard. With a

groan, he kicked out his feet. He looked ghostly pale, the wound in his side bleeding freely.

"I thought you said you knew how to do stitches," said Wyatt.

"I didn't say I was any good at them. Who do you think did yours?" He didn't wait for an answer. Instead, he bent in and kissed her, slow and sweet.

"You know what to do," he said, when they broke apart.

"Right now?"

"We can't put it off any longer," he said. "It isn't fair to Jamie. You came here to put him to rest, not to let that monster tear him apart."

Outside in the woods, something heavy crashed through the trees. A Titan, crawling out from the depths of Tartarus.

"Now, Wyatt," Peter said, an edge in his voice.

She reached for the pendant and tugged it loose hard enough to pop the clasp. The chain spiraled into her palm in a silvery helix. Fingers fumbling, she ran her touch along the edge until her finger notched against a hinge, hidden in the peak of the silver.

"I don't even think I need to smash this," she murmured. "There's a little hinge. It looks almost like a locket."

She frowned down at the pendant, fiddling with it until something clicked. She thought she heard Peter draw a breath as the hinge came loose, the pendant opening in the shape of two half-moons. Blood dribbled out, black and wet, trickling down into her palm.

"Gross."

"Blood of the beast," Peter explained as she shook out her hand. "Tapped from the dead trees in the grove. It's an old alchemical ritual. Exposed to air, the compound ingredients will eventually separate, severing the beast's tether to this side of the sky. Both parties will be sucked back into the abyss."

"But that makes no sense," said Wyatt, still inspecting the pendant. "Jamie only died five years ago. The beast has been here for centuries."

"That's true," said Peter slowly.

Her head spun. "Also, Price said the beast was feeding on Jamie's soul. That's a parasitic relationship, not a bonded one."

"It is."

The air in the sanctuary hung stale and still. A terrible cold crept into her skin. "You said it was a compound inside the locket. Blood of the beast, and what else?"

"Wyatt—"

"What else?"

"Bone ash," said Peter softly.

All the air guttered out of her. The locket slid out of her hands, dropping to the floor between them with a clatter. "The beast was never tethered to James. It was tethered to you."

She looked up at Peter and found him staring back at her, the twin pools of his eyes as pale and cold as ice. A thin line of blood slid from his nose. Black as tar. Slick as sap.

"No."

His mouth kicked into an almost-smile. "I love you."

"No." Her voice ground out of her like stone. "This isn't happening."

"Wyatt," he said, calm as ever, "did you hear me?"

"I heard you, you liar. I heard you, and *I hate you.*"

A smile tugged at his mouth. "You don't mean it."

"You tricked me."

His eyes were rosy bright. "You wouldn't have gone through with it if I hadn't."

"This is why he left," she gasped out. "James, he—*God*, he knew? He knew, and he walked off into the woods to let me kill you?"

"We had a difference of opinion," said Peter, though the words came out winded. He was losing air. He was dying in front of her. And it was her fault. As though she'd said it right out loud, Peter said, "I chose this, Wyatt."

"Like hell, you did," she cried. "Tell me how I stop it."

"You can't. It's already done."

"I don't want it to be done. I told you what I wanted. I want to stay here with you. I—I want everything we talked about." The words rushed out of her in a ceaseless babble. She couldn't stanch them. "We can fight. We can hate each other. We can tend to this place until we're old and bent. I don't care. I don't care what we do. Just stay here with me."

He shook his head. "I told you—I've cheated death long enough. I wasn't ever meant to live like this."

She wanted to hit him. She wanted to scream. To let it tear the earth asunder. She scrambled to her feet, searching, wild and frantic. There was nothing to help them. There was nothing but the dark, the first fingers of dawn bleeding into the stained clerestory window.

It occurred to her that James was nearby—possibly still within earshot. James Campbell, their schemer and their planner. He'd understood the workings of the guild far more than she ever had. He'd know what to do.

"James," she called, her voice vaulting into a shout. *"James Gavin Campbell!"*

326

"It's no use," Peter said. "He's gone."

"No." She sank back to her knees, collapsing in front of him, taking his face in her hands. "You've ruined everything. *Everything.*"

His eyes fluttered shut. She felt the stutter in his breath and she groped for his chest, feeling the slowing beat of his heart under his shirt.

"This was always going to end," he told her.

"Not like this," she eked out. "You were supposed to go home."

"It's okay." He pressed his lips to her eyelids, one after the other. His kisses were wet with her tears. "Wyatt, it's okay. I was already home."

She wanted to say something scathing, but then a groan cracked out of him and he fell back against the stone bulwark at his back. The altar where he'd died, over and over, at the hands of her family. Blood slipped from his right ear in a river of red. Wyatt wiped it away with a thumb, tears sliding unchecked down her cheeks.

"Please," she whispered. "Please don't leave me alone."

"The skies will seal shut. You'll be safe."

"I don't care about the skies!" It came out of her in a near scream. The stones shivered beneath them, earth turned seismic by her grief. "You can't leave me here without you."

"It's okay." His eyes clouded over, the color in them dulling. "Dahlia, you'll be okay."

There came a funny clatter, like dice rolled over wood. A set of footfalls brought her wheeling around to face the door. A pair of cloaked guildsmen stood framed in the opening, staring down at a pile of ivy-clad bones. At first, she thought her wards had failed. She thought the reanimated acolytes in the greenhouse had finally come after them, springing back to life as the beast broke free of James's tenuous hold.

But the wards were only meant to hold back the darkness, not mortal men. A second glance toward the newcomers told her they were very much alive. She recognized some of them—her father's ilk, stern and unsmiling. They took her in through shuttered stares, watching Peter die beneath her.

"What is this?" Wyatt demanded. "What's going on?"

"Campbell sent us out here to wait," the taller of the guildsmen said. "We were given clear instructions. Stay out of sight and let the boy see his plan through to the end." With a laugh, he said, "This looks pretty final to me."

32

WYATT

"Campbell?" Wyatt staggered to her feet, not understanding. Beneath her, the floor severed as thick wefts of lamb's-quarter pushed through the stone. "James isn't here."

The guildsman peered down at her with bemusement on his face. "James Campbell has been dead five years," he said as though she were terrifically ignorant. "We're here at his father's orders."

Another figure appeared—Joseph Campbell, tall and formidable in a three-piece suit. The man who had set this all into motion, back in Salem, when he'd first handed her the deed to Willow Heath. Now he studied Wyatt with a dark, assessing gaze that made him look remarkably like his son.

"You've played your part quite well," he said. "I'm ecstatic."

"Help him," she gasped out. *"Please."*

But Joseph didn't move. "The boy is beyond help. He's been marked for death since the day his father drove an ax through his stomach."

"No." She shook her head. "I don't accept that."

The look on Joseph's face turned contemplative as he regarded her through a keen sideways stare. "In the hands of the Westlocks, the mission of the guild has always been a passive one. Your father, like his forefathers, sought to muzzle the forest. They saw themselves as gatekeepers, shielding the mortal world from whatever ancient horrors might crawl out from the mouth of the wood."

Reaching out a hand, he plucked an asphodel from the doorway. It spun, paper white, between his fingers. "I've never been one for sitting idly by. I prefer an actionable plan. There was a time, early on, when I thought that maybe one day you and James would marry. It seemed a smart match. Peter would be cared for, you'd be managed, and Willow Heath would fall to the Campbell name. In our hands, the vast powers of hell wouldn't be muzzled. They'd be harnessed. Bridled like a stallion and used as a mount of war."

Wyatt barely heard him. All she could feel was the slowing thump of Peter's heart beneath her chest. All she could hear was this horrible whine between her ears. Fallen petals crushed under the tip of Joseph's boot as he came closer, eyeing her like she was something wild and fanged, ready to lunge.

"Imagine, the gift of immortality in the hands of someone who knows how to wield it. A man, and not a boy. Only Peter's gift is not, as I discovered, so easily shared."

Wyatt found her voice. "*Discovered?* You poisoned your own son."

"The end justifies the means," Joseph said, brushing off the mention of his only child as though it were little more than a hiccup. "Niccolò Machiavelli said that. It's all consequentialism, you see. Whether something is good or bad depends on the outcome. And look at this payoff—what a beautiful solution to a centuries-long dilemma. Wyatt's father thought banishing the beast would set his daughter free. Instead, he's only handed her reins over to me."

"You won't touch her," Peter snarled, trying and failing to rise to his feet. Blood bloomed at his lips in a wine-dark spill as he slammed to his knees, Wyatt's grip on his shoulders all that kept him upright. "I'll kill you."

"Empty threats." Joseph sniffed. "You don't remember, but I was ten years old the first time I watched them kill you. It's something of an honor, to be welcomed into the chapel before a formal initiation. My father thought it would be good for me, to see history being made. Instead of wonder, all I felt was disgust. All that power, and nobody got to use it but you."

He turned toward Wyatt, examining her with a strange fervor gleaming in his eyes.

"Now you," Joseph breathed, and there was wonder in his voice. "Wyatt Westlock. Good God, who would have thought? We were privy to your earlier performance, you know. We stood out in the grove and watched as you tore Peter's bones clean out of the ground. You brought up the wards without spilling a single drop of blood. No tinctures, no powders, no visible wounds. Only power, pure and raw. This world hasn't seen magic like yours in centuries. Imagine the things I could do with a girl who can sever the earth beneath her feet. I could topple cities. I could wage wars."

"You won't touch her," spat Peter again, but the sound came out broken. He drew a single, gurgling breath. Wyatt reached for him, frantic, but an arm hooked around her middle. She was pried off the ground, feet flinging skyward, a feral scream lashing out of her throat.

"Take her," ordered Joseph. "Burn this place to the ground."

"What do we do with him?" came a voice from somewhere behind her.

"Leave him," Joseph said. "He's already dead."

"No." The word scraped out of her in a cry. Her eyes met Peter's, wide and afraid. He tried to rise and fell, one time after another, his hands braced on the pews for support, his knees cracking over and over against the wooden parquet. She struggled in equal measure, snarling and clawing like an alley cat, drawing blood more than once. Overhead, the very first bars of dawn bled into the broad pelican clerestory. Light refracted along the floor in sparks of reds and yellows and blues.

"Let go of me," she cried. *"Let go!"*

"Bind her hands," Joseph called, somewhere out of sight. "Don't let her conjure anything."

She kicked out her feet, swinging them in a wild fury. Satisfaction lit in her chest when her heel found a mark. She fell, her captor dropping to his knees with a groan. Momentarily free, she hit the ground hard, the air knocked clean from her lungs. And then she was crawling—back up the steps, moving on all fours like an animal.

"Peter," she wept, pulling herself onto her feet. "Peter!"

"Grab her, damn it!" Joseph's shout was swallowed up in the rising wind. Along the sun-splintered horizon, the trees whipped into a frenzy. "Someone grab her at once!"

"Peter," she called again, staggering into the open door.

Peter lay unmoving on the floor, slumped lifelessly onto his side. His eyes were open, two unseeing pools of blue. One arm lay outstretched, his fingers furled as though he'd been reaching for her.

Her heart stuttered, tithing several beats, and then started anew. *Fast, fast, fast.* It pulsed through her at a tick, her dress dark with mud, her hands slick with red. She was a mirror reflection of the deathwatch, grief knitting itself into something warped and wefted along her bones.

She swallowed a single lungful of air. The dawn was cool and crisp and clear.

She screamed.

It was a scream that fractured the skies. She pushed it out of her and out of her, until she felt the fabric of her mind tear beneath the sound. The world slipped off its axis, severing open, wood buckling under her feet.

Over her head, the glass exploded, raining down on her in a rosy kaleidoscope. It nicked her skin and dazzled her hair, shuddering against the floor in a broken rain. She screamed and she screamed, until there was nothing but dust left in her lungs, and then still beyond that. Her voice became wretched and *Other*, pulling from a well that was deep and dark. All around her, the chapel sank into a fuzz, formless and gray, as though she'd stepped clear out of the fabric of time.

And then, with a sob, she fell quiet. All the rage coiled out of her on a breath, leaving her hollowed out and gasping. The chapel careened back into focus. She found herself standing in a sea of shimmering glass, daylight swimming into the fractures. The only sound was her breathing, harsh in the quiet. The distant trill of a lark.

Knees wobbling, she searched the chapel for the slow bloom of her power. She listened for the angry snap of trees, the rumble of an approaching storm. A hurricane. A tempest. The end of the fucking world.

Instead, there was quiet.

The winds fell. The leaves fluttered to a standstill.

Nothing moved. Nothing breathed. The world around her sat stagnant, the echo of her scream swallowed up in a sudden vacuum. She heard the patter of shoes on stone, felt the rustle of cloaks as the guildsmen crept closer. Sinking low, she braced herself for what was to come.

But nothing happened.

Their footfalls fell silent, their approach halted as—in the severed crux of the little wooden chapel—Peter sat up.

33

JAMES

James Campbell was seven years old when his father first introduced him to Peter and Wyatt. He remembered that day in pops of color. The couch in the sitting room was orange. The old hardwood was cherry. The sky in the wide, trifurcated window was blue.

James Campbell was a well-bred boy, with well-bred manners. He knew how he was expected to behave. He left his shoes on the mat by the door. He said *yes, please*, and *no, thank you*. He took a seat where he was bidden and waited without fidgeting, taking in the scrubby-looking boy who sat swallowed up in the wingback across from him. Nearby stood a woman, her features tight and unsmiling, an owl-eyed girl peeking out from behind her legs.

Here were more colors: The boy had white hair and blue eyes. The girl was red all over. Red face. Red hair. A hideous red dress.

He didn't remember the conversation that followed, but he did remember this: The woman ushering the girl out of the room. The men whispering out in the hall. The little white-haired boy, small and unrepentant, his bare feet caked in mud.

In the end, James was given an assignment.

"*You'll stay here in the summers,*" his father said. "*You are to go where Peter goes. Do what Peter does. If he gets into anything that seems like trouble, you'll tell me immediately. Understand?*"

But James hadn't understood at all. He'd wanted to go on holiday. He wanted to swim in the sea, and eat gelato until his stomach was sick. He didn't like it here, in this funny house with its miles and miles of meadow and its tiny, dusty television. His friends would be playing football and lawn tennis and he would be here, bored to tears.

But being a well-bred boy meant being an amenable boy. And so, he agreed.

The three of them grew together after that. It was impossible not to. They sprouted up much in the way trees did—first alongside one another, and then twined all together, their branches entangled. He'd learned about such a naturally occurring phenomenon in year seven. Inosculation, where the trunks of multiple trees grew so close together that they grafted into one. That was them, he'd thought, only half listening to the lecture.

He, Peter, and Wyatt, their roots so intricately knotted that none of them could tell where one of them ended and the other began.

The months in England were long and dull, full of stuffy lectures and endless family functions. Tooled brogues and salad forks and smiling until his cheeks hurt. He developed, in those days, a penchant for mild acts of larceny. Every time his parents dragged him to another too-large house in the too-lonely country, he took it upon himself to find one thing that reminded him of Willow Heath.

A lighter for Peter, who was fascinated by fire. A tube of lipstick for Wyatt, who never went without. There was a specific thrill in it—doing something so simple as slipping a fountain pen into his pocket when he knew he wasn't allowed. Taking what he wanted instead of waiting for it to be given. He went from house to house to house,

well-bred and well-spoken and perfectly docile, pocketing his souve-
nirs and counting the days until June.

The summers were for dreaming. For lolling by the stream and
streaking through the meadows, fighting and playing and growing
one into the other. It didn't take him long to discover that he found
the same sort of thrill in stuffing away Peter and Wyatt as he did in
stealing trinkets back home.

It was exhilarating, having a secret—slipping the two of them
into his pocket. He watched them grow steadily closer, and he didn't
breathe a word to his father. He fell asleep curled beneath Wyatt's
canopy and didn't tell a soul that Peter had been there, too, his arm
curved around her in the dark. He stood guard at the barn's crumbling loft while Peter tore the blue button eye off of Wyatt's favorite
bear, and felt a little zing of rapture in his belly.

Back home, perfection was demanded of him. The quality of his
grades. The caliber of his sportsmanship. The knot of his tie. He dis-
mantled it little by little, hitting back at his father where he could.
Turning detentions into suspensions, suspensions into expulsions. All
the while, he hoarded his stolen moments and his pilfered treasure
like a greedy dragon. He didn't tell his father a thing.

He should have known Joseph Campbell would catch on.

He remembered his final day in pinches of disquiet. Wyatt had
gone kicking and screaming the day before, packed into the family car with the family cat and taken to her aunt's apartment in
Massachusetts. Peter, apoplectic with his usual amount of silent fury,
had sought immediate retribution with a lit match. For hours, the old
barn collapsed in on itself, soot staining the sky.

It had taken James nearly an hour to talk Peter off his ledge. They'd go after her, he'd assured him. Of course they would. They were inosculated. And furthermore, they were his.

And he didn't like people taking his things.

He'd just returned to the summer cottage from the main house, planning to pack his bags, when his father happened upon him.

"There you are," boomed Joseph, herding him into the low-beamed kitchenette the second he'd ducked inside. *"I've been looking all over for you."*

"I was with Peter."

His father's smile had been unusually cold. Looking back, he should have seen the danger in it. *"Sit with me awhile,"* he said. *"We haven't had a real conversation all summer."*

The table was set in a wide assortment of foods. The sort the staff made back home, whenever it was a holiday. Or whenever his mother caught his father with a mistress. But that day, there was no holiday. There was only the oppressive summer heat, the skies outside still charred with smoke. His mother was back home in England, hosting callers of her own.

James hung back in the door, suspicious. *"What is this?"*

"I thought we'd eat," his father said, ushering him into a chair at the head of the table. *"I'm worried about you. What father wouldn't be? You were attacked."*

"Peter hardly attacked me."

He'd spat the words out, razor-sharp, even knowing how it looked. They'd cracked his nose back into place, but it was still too tender to touch. His left eye was swollen shut. Still, he'd known better than to defy his father. Sinking into a chair, he'd picked up a fork and stabbed at a red glob of cranberry sauce without taking a bite.

At the head of the little cottage table, his father undid the button of his jacket. Without a word, he reached for a sleek crystal of red wine and set it in front of James's plate. James halted the four-pronged assault on his food.

"I'm not allowed," he'd said, because he was a good boy, and he knew what was expected.

"You're not allowed," his father agreed. *"But that doesn't mean you can't."*

James stared at his father without reacting, a bit of Yorkshire pudding stuck to the end of his fork. His father's smile broadened.

"Did I get it wrong? That's the code your headmaster assures me you live by."

Again, James said nothing. Between them, the glass sat full of wine, red and dark as blood.

"You think I don't see you," said his father, leaning back in his chair. *"You think I don't know your luggage is full of stolen goods, or that you and Peter sneak into Wyatt Westlock's room each night after dark. You think I don't know all the secrets you keep. But I see you, James. I see everything."*

He'd wanted to lash out, to shout, to storm off in a rage, but he was far too well-mannered to do anything but continue to sit there, white-knuckling his fork in a furious silence.

"Drink," ordered his father, and raised his own glass in a toast. *"Your mother raised you with better manners than this."*

James did as he was bidden, wishing he were anywhere other than here, caught in the unremitting crosshairs of his father's stare. The wine burned on its way down. It ate a hole in his stomach, put blisters in his head. He'd dropped his fork, falling back into his seat with a wet, wordless gurgle.

"What is this," he'd managed to gasp out. *"What was in that?"*

"Water hemlock," said his father, as though it were a garnish. He glanced down at his watch. *"I'd say you have ninety minutes, at best."*

James staggered to his feet then, and the tablecloth came with him. He hadn't realized he was clutching it in his fists. Several plates went toppling to the ground, porcelain smashing into pieces. His father hadn't flinched. He'd only laced his hands across his stomach and smiled, watching his only son clutch at his throat.

"Do you know how to kill Peter?" he'd asked.

James said nothing, groping blindly for an antidote, the world turning to a Milky Way eddy as his vision tunneled.

"I think you do," said his father. *"I think he told you exactly how to do it. And it can't be one of us, can it? Because we don't care for him. Not like you do. You and that rotten ginger whelp."*

With that, his father had risen from his chair. Setting down his napkin, he'd taken one last look at his son.

"Kill Peter," he'd said, *"and live forever. Or die, and I'll find a way to get Wyatt Westlock back here myself. Even if I have to kill her father to do it."*

And then he was gone.

And James never saw him again.

He was looking at him now. There, flanked by a five hooded guildsmen, stood his father—older and grayer and thicker around the middle. He didn't see James, waiting in the shadows. He didn't know

340

his son was lurking just out of sight, pieced together with residuum from hell, a beast thrashing against his bones.

From where James stood, he could just make out the impatience etched into his father's face. He cursed himself for his shortsightedness. He should have never left Peter and Wyatt alone. He'd thought he was protecting them, removing himself from reach. He thought he could keep the demon at bay long enough for Wyatt to do what needed to be done.

He should have anticipated that his father would be three steps ahead.

The way he'd always been ahead.

He paced the line of trees, restless and uneasy, wicking sweat from his brow with the back of his hand. He didn't know what to do—double back and intervene, or run far in the opposite direction. He was a ticking bomb, his time running out. Behind the welded cage of his ribs, he felt the slow unfurling of a waking entity. A barbed wire prickle of something insidious, the scrape of talons along his spine. His stomach growled, hunger pangs gripping his body.

He groped at his pocket, wrenching loose the inhaler. An empty whoosh of air gusted into his lungs. When he chucked it into the forested dark, a bellow that was not entirely his ripped from his throat. *Not now*, he thought, tearing his hands through his hair. *Not right fucking now.*

A scream cut through the detritus of his thoughts. A banshee howl, high and clear and broken. It rattled through him, stopping the air in his throat. Robbing him of breath.

It was Wyatt, her shriek scraping the predawn sky.

The world cracked open beneath his feet, a fissure splitting the earth into deep tributaries of dark. He sidestepped a widening chasm, nearly toppling clean into it, and stumbled hard into a tree. He didn't know if this was Wyatt's doing, or if the locket had done its job. If the world was responding to the inhuman pitch of her scream, or if it was preparing to swallow him up.

On and on the screaming went, the trees bending overhead, the grove uprooting itself like an imploding star. James clung fast to a branch and waited for the end to come—for the bottomless dark, the endless night.

Nothing happened. Everything fell quiet. Too quiet. Too still. Deep within him, something purred. Something old and sated and more familiar than it had any right to be. He salivated, stumbling— caught between an eonian hunger and a terrible horror.

She has stopped time, crooned the beast. *She is either a very clever witch, or a very thoughtless one. The worlds cannot hold their breath like this. They will break apart. Someone must go and get the clock ticking anew.*

"Get out of my head," he snapped, clutching at his temples.

Is that what you want? seethed that horrible voice. *You want me gone? You want to live a half-life, like Pedyr did?*

That terrible stillness persisted all around him, as wrong as a river freezing solid in summer.

I can show you how to exorcise me, James Campbell, crooned his parasite. *But you must be quick. Run back to your witch, and I will show what it will take for you to keep from losing sight of the stars.*

His head full of whispers, his mouth full of teeth, he broke into a run.

34

WYATT

There were hands at Wyatt's arms, but they fell away at the sight of the boy in the chapel. Or maybe she writhed free. She couldn't be certain. The hush of the earth tugged at her like mud, so that she moved as if through a dream. Legs leaden. Steps blocky. Her pace slowed to a crawl.

By the time she reached the place where Peter had fallen, he was on his feet. A soundless half laugh, half cry hiccuped out of her as she collided into him, rising up onto her toes to try and catch his eyes. The placid blue of his gaze was gone. Instead, there was only black, deep and cold.

"Peter." Her hair was strung all with static, and ribbons of copper stirred the air between them. "Peter, look at me."

Her hands found his chest, sliding over the place where—just minutes ago—she'd felt his heart. There was nothing there. Only a horrible stillness.

"No," she whispered. *"No."*

A loose stone skittered down the aisle. The sound of boots drew nearer, and she knew the guildsmen stood just behind her, waiting to move in. She didn't care. She'd let them come.

"There is a name for what you've wrought," Joseph Campbell said, stepping into her periphery. "It is connected to an old and deeply for-bidden magic. I must admit, I never thought you capable."

That terrible hush swallowed up any echo his voice might have car-ried. It was as though a great and unholy void had yawned open in the middle of the room, sound sucking into it like starlight into a vacuum. Everything felt magnified, twisting into too-sharp focus.

"There's a reason the banshees burned," spat a guildsman. "Look what you've done. This is the devil's work. You'll never see heaven now."

At the disgust in his voice, Peter's head quirked to the side. He looked all wrong, his movements animal quick. An awful smile caught at the corner of his mouth. Wyatt saw the cold flash of fury in the deep well of his stare and her stomach dropped. Too late, she real-ized where the wrath in her scream had come home to roost.

"This wasn't what I meant to do," she gasped out.

Sunlight sparked through the shattered window, yawning across the floor in shifting prisms of gold. Peter was suddenly shrouded in light, looking every bit the exalted saint they'd imagined him to be. All that was left of him now was a body, filled to the brim with the rage of the girl who'd loved him.

"This is an abomination," whispered a guildsman.

Joseph Campbell's order cracked out sharp as a whip. "Don't let him leave."

The terrible stillness exploded as everyone moved all at once. A pair of guildsmen shoved past Wyatt, closing in on Peter with ceremo-nial daggers drawn. Instinctively, Wyatt reached deep within her core and pulled at a thread. It felt leather thick in her grasp, hardy as reins. Peter feinted a step, his lips peeled back in a bridled snarl.

Horrified, Wyatt staggered backward. A terrible understanding welled within her. She'd done that. She'd tugged at Peter's will the same way she'd pried his bones loose from the dirt.

Hesitant, the guildsmen advanced. Sunlight swam into the tip of a dagger and Wyatt splayed her hand wide, the movement reactive. Shuttle, weft, pull. Peter lunged. Bone snapped beneath his hands, the body crumpling to the floor. A second followed the first. Peter moved as though bidden, the thread between them taut.

Scrabbling backward, a third guildsman turned and fled, heading for the door. Wyatt took a single treadle step and Peter responded, cutting off the cloaked figure's escape. His hand closed around the disciple's throat. He stared down at his victim through flat, lifeless eyes, watching as the wriggling stopped.

"Peter, look out!"

His head jerked up just as a fourth guildsman sprang from a pew and plunged a dagger into the base of his spine. Peter pitched forward at the impact, casting aside the body in his grasp and turning to face his attacker. The dagger's hilt protruded from his back, plugging the wound as blood spread outward in a widening circle. If he felt pain, none registered on his face. He looked stark and cold and unkillable as a god.

Weaponless, the guildsman dropped to his knees. "Please." He lifted his hands in benefaction. A disciple, praying to his saint. "Please, have mercy."

There was nothing curious in Peter's expression as he watched the man on his knees. Nothing angry or vengeful. There was only that horrible indifference. Slowly, he reached out and laid a gore-flecked hand atop the kneeling man's head. A sigh wobbled out of the acolyte, snarled up in equal parts relief and fear.

Bone snapped.

The body fell to the ground.

Behind him, the final guildsman stared without moving.

"What are you doing?" Joseph Campbell's voice cracked through the quiet. "Finish him!"

The trembling guildsman readied his knife, approaching Peter in slow, reluctant steps. Peter watched him draw nearer. Nearer. Wyatt's pulse stitched through her veins just as the guildsman broke into a run. Peter threw out his hand. With an ugly crack, the man's head pinged off the edge of a pew. A starburst of red bloomed across his temple as he sank lifeless to the floor.

When at last Peter turned back toward Wyatt, only Joseph Campbell remained. James's father stood sweating in his suit, his face the color of milk gone sour.

"Now, Peter," he said, in the voice he'd reserved for them when they'd been up to no good, "think this through. You know my son. You grew up together. Do you remember the summer I taught the three of you to play cricket? The gifts I brought you, year after year?" Glass crunched under his dress shoes as Peter continued his advance, shoulders taut and eyes unblinking. Cuffing Joseph by the lapels, Peter dragged him effortlessly onto the balls of his feet. They crushed nose to nose in the circle of sunlight, ivy cascading around them in an emerald waterfall.

"Call him off," Joseph begged, his voice shaking. "Please, call him off. You're a good girl, Wyatt. You're not a killer. This life was never meant for you. Your father said that about you, just before he died."

"My father?" repeated Wyatt. It was the first sound with an echo in several minutes. It shivered through the vine-choked pillars of the little chapel. Grief sparked fresh and angry in her chest. "Did you kill him, too? Like you killed James?"

She didn't need confirmation. She could see the truth of it written plain upon his face. She'd thought it was strange, how she and her mother had never heard of any official diagnosis. Strange, how they'd never gotten a call from the hospital. Even during their estrangement, Wyatt was listed as next of kin.

She should have known better. She should have seen the trick for what it was. A lure, to get her back to Willow Heath. A trap, meant to set into motion the sorts of things that couldn't be undone.

At the altar, Joseph clawed at Peter's wrist to no avail. "Please. I don't want to die."

"Peter," said Wyatt. "Look at me."

Too quick, his head snapped to face her. Lifeblood leaked from his ear like water, painting the side of his face. There was no familiarity in his gaze. No comfort. No recognition. All she saw reflected in the glass of his stare was a mirror of herself. The empty well of her rage. The slow decay of her courage.

She thought of him out in the henyard, naming all the chickens. The way the goat followed him from room to room, chewing at his sleeves. The way he'd sharpened himself into something cruel, to hide the fact that all he wanted was someplace soft to land. He'd never wanted this for himself—to be a killer. He hadn't wanted it, and yet she'd made him into one anyway.

It wasn't fair.

He stood extraordinarily still, a soldier waiting for an order—emblazoned in all the colors of the sunrise. Somewhere outside the chapel, daylight unfolded over the fields, the forest, the farmhouse. All the world, waking.

"I love you," she told him. Too late. Too late. The wind picked up, the world drawing a breath at last. Her whisper ferried forward in a brace of skull-white petals, tugged loose from their blossoms. "But no more. Let it be over. Let him go."

Peter's grip loosened and Joseph staggered backward, toppling into the altar. He clutched at his chest, patting himself down in a mindless panic as he struggled to catch his breath.

A few feet away, Peter stood slack and staring, his eyes full of sunlight. Watching without seeing. With a thunderous shout, Joseph withdrew a pocketknife from inside his jacket and launched himself at Peter.

Wyatt hardly had time to react before a figure stepped out of the shadows, planting himself between the unmoving Peter and the lurching Joseph. With a squelch, Joseph's blade buried itself into James Campbell's ribs. His father fell back, white as a sheet.

"Impossible," he gasped out. "It's impossible."

"Ow," said James, poking at the hilt.

Mouth agape, Joseph collapsed to his knees. "This is a trick. I-it's a trick. What sort of demon are you?"

"Your son," James grunted, prying the knife loose. "Christ, that went in deep." Blood bloomed crimson against his shirt. He turned the weapon over in his hands, cutting a sideways glance toward Wyatt. "Ready?"

"For what?"

"You knocked the worlds out of alignment." His cheeks dimpled in a smile. "I've come to set them back to rights."

348

She braced herself, readying for his retribution—for the inevitable plunge of the knife into Joseph's heart. Instead, James turned to face Peter. For a moment, all was quiet. James's smile flickered, fading.

"You absolute arse," he breathed, and drove the blade into Peter's chest.

Through the ribs. Through the heart. Her heart, though it no longer beat. A terrible shudder went through the earth, its aftershock rippling through the ether. Wyatt was thrown back, her head cracking against the wooden pew. Her vision doubled, going starry, and she blinked it away just in time to see the ground sever in a black, angry maw. With a crack, the buckled flooring widened into a chasm.

There was a scream as Joseph Campbell toppled headlong into it, the earth swallowing him up in one bottomless gulp. Overhead, the ceiling began to cave in, as though the earth itself was preparing to swallow the chapel whole. Wyatt scrambled to her feet and found James struggling to bear the weight of a lifeless Peter, half dragging, half carrying his body down the crumbling aisle.

Wyatt rushed to his side, dodging falling shingles. Together, they pulled Peter out into the bald light of the grove. They were met with pandemonium. Trees uprooted by the dozens, toppling one into the other like a house of cards.

"Go," barked James. "Go, go, go."

They broke free of the line of trees just as the world behind them crumbled. It fell with a violent shudder, heavy as the tectonic grind of plates.

And then, as soon as it had started, everything fell still.

They lay on the lip of a cavity, deep and wide. It stretched the length of the grove, a massive sinkhole where the grove used to be.

It looked as though the mouth of hell itself had swallowed it down, chapel and all.

They were granted a beat of quiet. A moment of immaculate stillness. Wyatt lay without moving, afraid to look around, Peter's fingers cold in hers. Tears fell and fell without end, and she let them come. Far off in the distance, a songbird let out a warble.

And then the silence was severed. Next to her, James let out an agonizing bellow. Wyatt shot up quick, her heart pounding, just in time to see him scrabble backward, clawing at his stomach. His back arched off the ground, bending upward in a locus of pain.

"Jamie!" She crawled after him, but he gave no sign of having heard her. *"Jamie!"*

He continued to writhe, raking at his skin until she thought he might rip himself clean down the middle. She finally managed to grab hold of him just as he lurched partway over the sinkhole's edge. Darkness yawned away beneath them, falling and falling without discernible end.

He caught his hands on the shelf, gagging horribly. She held tight to his waist as his body convulsed, seized by some unseen tremor. Veins popped in his forehead and he loosed another scream, higher and keener than the first. Something ink dark slithered off his tongue, slick and slippery as an eel. It swam into shadow, its elongated body careening into the depths below. Gasping, James fell still, consenting at last to be dragged back from the edge. He collapsed facedown into the dirt, and Wyatt fell with him, the hard beat of his heart through his back slamming into her own.

Eventually, they rolled over onto their backs. A heavy sense of finality hung over Wyatt, the feeling as weighted as a blanket. It was done. It was over. She lay in a patch of clover, watching the clouds blow in. Not storm clouds, but fluffy white cumulus. The sky was pale cerulean. A summertime color.

The exact shade of blue that always drew her home.

35

WYATT

They buried Peter in the garden, beneath a teetering cairn of loosely stacked stone. A pauper's grave, unmarked. When it was done, they stood side by side and stared down at the dirt, watching the slow unfurling of blue forget-me-nots in the freshly dug soil.

"Should we write his name somewhere?"

James frowned down at the pile of rock. "I'm not sure how to spell it."

"You—" She scowled up at him, shading her eyes against the sun. "It's not a difficult name to spell, Jamie."

"The beast called him something different," he said, bending down to pluck a flower from the dirt. "I heard it, when I was trapped inside my head."

"Pettier," she said, remembering.

James nodded. "Pedyr Criafol."

A bevy of emotions roiled through her. Surprise. Sadness. And then, beneath it, acceptance. It made sense, in the end, that she'd never really known Peter at all. That he'd been like a dream to them both, something neither of them knew how to lay a claim to.

But he'd loved her. He'd loved them both. And she loved him, too—whatever pieces of him he'd seen fit to give her. That counted for something. Unlooping the leather cord from around her neck,

Wyatt set Cubby's button on the topmost stone. James watched her do it, his hands in his pockets.

"He'd want you to keep that."

She sniffled. "It was never mine in the first place."

They stood there awhile longer, watching honeybees buzz between spikes of wild indigo.

"I keep going over last night in my head," she said, when the silence grew too heavy. "I can't stop wondering what I could have done differently."

"That's a waste of time," said James. "It's over. We can't undo it."

A bolt of anger rippled through her. "We undid your death, didn't we?"

He had no answer for that. Glancing over at him, she found his eyes narrowed against the sun, his expression grim. She wondered what he was seeing, in the dark of his head. What sorts of memories he'd carried with him from the bowels of hell.

Hesitantly, she asked, "How's your injury?"

"Better." He smiled, but it did little to dispel the air of worry between them. "See?"

He lifted the hem of his shirt, offering her a glimpse of his torso. The angry crisscross of scars had begun to fade. Already, the puncture mark from his father's knife had puckered closed.

"Are you—" She paused, unsure what to say, and landed on "back for good?"

"I don't know," he admitted, watching the sky. "But whatever was inside of me is gone, and I haven't crumbled to a pillar of salt. Feels promising."

"Do you think you're immortal? Like Peter was immortal?"

He quirked a brow. "It's not a theory I'm keen to test."

As they spoke, Slightly crept in at their feet, her eyes wide and cloudy. She looked tired, slow, her fur patchy and her movements arthritic. Circling atop the grave, she sought out a sunny spot in the flowering scorpion grass. When it was done, she glared up at Wyatt with a steadfastness that told her she wouldn't be moved.

"It's okay," Wyatt whispered. "You can go, too."

Slightly let out a mewl and closed her eyes, nestling deeper into the blue crush of petals. Wyatt swiped at a tear before it could fall.

"She was always Peter's cat."

"Everything here is Peter's," James said. "It always has been. And you know what he would do if he were here with us, don't you?"

He held up the silver lighter, significantly more dented than the last time she'd seen it. The wind picked up, tugging at her hair, and she found herself smiling up at him.

"He'd set it alight."

36

WYATT

In the end, everything burned much faster than she thought it would.

The house, with its pitched gables swallowed in peat, decorative tracery gone green with moss. What remained of the roof was crusted in lacy rings of lichen, the widow's watch buried in wisteria blooms. There was something lovely about it—the way it curled in on itself, wood popping, smoke pouring out of the windows in great charcoal columns.

Wyatt Westlock stood at the edge of the flagstone walk, James Campbell at her side and the rooster tucked under one arm. Next to them, the goat munched on a bit of clover, unbothered by the budding conflagration. A cluster of chickens darted in and out of sight, plucking up beetles from the grass.

Overhead, the sky was full of clouds. They sagged open, rainwater falling in sheets on the place where she'd grown. Slowly, the thick wall of smoke dissipated as the early-summer shower doused the inferno. The flames diminished to a smolder, and then—eventually—a last, smoky hiss.

She stood there another hour.

Two.

She watched the fire gutter out until all that remained of the house was a charbroiled husk, sunken and strange. She took a big swallow of air. She felt a thousand things at once.

"Let's go," she said to Mama, clicking her tongue. "Mackenzie is going to hate you."

"And what about me?" asked James, tailing after her.

"Mackenzie already hates you," she reminded him. "But I think her friends might find you tolerable."

Together, they turned their backs on the burning house.

On her legacy.

They loaded the animals in the car, chickens fluttering in their poultry crates. The ignition kicked over, the engine starting up with a grumble. In the rearview mirror, a last line of smoke rose into the sky. Wyatt said a silent goodbye to the boy who'd lived there. To the girl who'd dreamed there. To her heart, left in the garden to grow into something new.

And then she went home.

ACKNOWLEDGMENTS

When I was young, I used to pretend I was Wendy Darling. I'd sit in my bedroom window and wish for the kinds of adventures that came with having a friend like Peter Pan. When summer arrived, I'd organize the neighborhood into a cache of lost boys. We'd burn up daylight streaking through the woods with Popsicle fingers, leaping from stone to stone until we began to think ourselves truly capable of flight.

As an adult looking back, those endless summers hold a sort of magic of their own. They seem to exist outside time, back in the insular bubble of childhood. Though they are largely happy memories, they carry with them a particular sort of melancholy. They're moments you'll never have again, experienced by a you that is gone.

I wrote this book as a love letter to those days, and to that feeling.

As with anything you pour a lot of love into, it takes a team of people to make it all come together. It's another act of magic, really. The fact of the matter is, I could not have written Wyatt Westlock's story alone. The list of people I could thank from here on out is endless, but I'll try my best to keep it brief.

To my husband—thank you for spending night after night, month after month, listening to me unravel this story. Thank you for entertaining the girls during deadlines and for bringing me coffee whenever I stayed up too late. You are truly the best partner a girl could ask for.

To my agent, Josh—thank you for always championing these strange little books I write, and for having confidence in me when I don't have any in myself. Your advice has never been anything short of invaluable, and I'm so thankful to have you a phone call away when I need to talk things through.

To my editor, Mallory—thank you for your endless patience and your brilliant insight, and for giving me the space to write the story wrong as many times as I needed to in order to get it right. You always manage to see the vision, even when the words on the page are just vibes and mess.

To Lucy and the wonderful team at Gollancz—thank you for giving me the chance to tell not one, but two stories. You've worked so hard to get my books into as many hands as possible, and I'm blown away by your constant creativity in finding new ways to reach readers.

To my publicist, Daniela—thank you for working so tirelessly to help me get this story out there, and for helping me navigate the world of publishing with grace.

To Maeve and Sasha—thank you for putting together another breathtaking cover. I am truly in love with that gorgeous design, and I couldn't have ever imagined something so perfect back in the early days of drafting and daydreaming.

To David and the rest of the creative team at Scholastic—thank you for welcoming me back with open arms and for being as excited as I've been to share this story with readers. I know this can be an exhausting job, and I'm so thankful to have you all in my corner.

To Jackie and Janell—thank you for your painstaking work in copy edits and for graciously accepting that I will likely never learn the difference between gray and grey.

To Shannon—thank you for always being willing to drive over at the drop of a hat, coffees in hand. I could not have finished this book without you there, quilting away at my kitchen table and wrangling our four small children between stitches. Words are not enough to say how much your company meant to me throughout this process.

To my parents and my brother—thank you for entertaining my family when I was locked in the office on a deadline. It means more than you know that you've invested so much time in the girls, and I know they are making magical childhood memories of their own in all those sleepy afternoons by the lake.

To Jen and Meryn—thank you for the late-night writing chats in an iced-over ski cabin in Vermont. I unraveled a lot of my plot snaggles over those endless mugs of cocoa, and I'm immeasurably thankful for your genius (and that your weird matches my weird).

To De—thank you for the hours of rambling voice notes and unedited scene snippets and for never balking when I send you a new and unhinged subplot at five in the morning.

To the rest of my writing community—you all know who you are, and your company, humor, and wisdom help make the creative process feel a little less lonely.

To my readers—thank you for picking up this book. If you're here, I assume you made it to the end, and I truly hope you enjoyed the ride.

And last but far from least, to the kids of a wooded cul-de-sac in New England—thank you for those endless summer days of dreaming. For street hockey tournaments and forts by the stream and the scary stories we terrified ourselves with out in the meadow. For rooftop heart-to-hearts and wiffle ball in the rain and the intense, weeklong *Lord of the Rings* reenactment we inexplicably committed to in summer '04.

That was *real* magic, and I will forever be grateful for it.

ABOUT THE AUTHOR

Kelly Andrew lost her hearing when she was four years old. She's been dreaming up stories in silence ever since. Kelly lives in New England with her husband, two daughters, and a persnickety Boston terrier. You can find her online at @KayAyDrew.